Penguin Books

THE
LA...

...MIT

Penguin Books

THE LAND OF LOST GODS

AHMET ÜMIT

Translated by
RAKESH JOBANPUTRA

PENGUIN BOOKS
An imprint of Penguin Random House

PENGUIN BOOKS

Penguin Books is an imprint of the Penguin Random House group of
companies whose addresses can be found at
global.penguinrandomhouse.com

Published by Penguin Random House India Pvt. Ltd
4th Floor, Capital Tower 1, MG Road,
Gurugram 122 002, Haryana, India

Penguin
Random House
India

First published in Penguin Books by Penguin Random House India 2024

Copyright © Ahmet Ümit, 2021
Translation copyright © Rakesh Jobanputra, 2023

All rights reserved

10 9 8 7 6 5 4 3 2 1

This is a work of fiction. Names, characters, places and incidents are
either the product of the author's imagination or are used fictitiously
and any resemblance to any actual person, living or dead,
events or locales is entirely coincidental.
The opinions expressed in this book reflect the views of the author.

ISBN 9780143472933

Typeset in Adobe Garamond Pro by Digiultrabooks Pvt. Ltd.
Printed at Thomson Press India Ltd, New Delhi

This book is sold subject to the condition that it shall not, by way of trade or
otherwise, be lent, resold, hired out, or otherwise circulated without the publisher's
prior consent in any form of binding or cover other than that in which it is published
and without a similar condition including this condition being imposed on the
subsequent purchaser.

www.penguin.co.in

MIX
Paper | Supporting
responsible forestry
FSC® C010615

Ahmet Ümit

Ahmet Ümit is Turkey's most popular and best-selling author especially known for his mastery of crime fiction, as reflected in many of his bestselling novels. Drawing on the unique political and historical background of his home country, Ümit delves into the psyches of his well-wrought characters as he weaves enthralling tales of murder and political intrigue.

Ahmet Ümit was born in 1960 in the city of Gaziantep in southern Turkey. He moved to Istanbul in 1978 to attend university. In 1983 he both graduated from the Public Administration Faculty of Marmara University and wrote his very first story. An active member of the Turkish Communist Party from 1974 until 1989 Ümit took part in the underground movement for democracy while Turkey was under the rule of a military dictatorship between 1980-1990. In 1985-86 he illegally attended the Academy for Social Sciences in Moscow. Ümit worked in the advertising sector from 1989-1998 and is currently employed as cultural advisor at the Goethe Foundation in Istanbul.

Rakesh Jobanputra

Rakesh Jobanputra was born in London and studied at the University of Birmingham and at SOAS, University of London. He previously taught at Qatar University in Doha, Istanbul Technical University and Istanbul Şehir University, and currently teaches English at Boğaziçi University. He has translated numerous works of literature and collections of poetry from Turkish into English.

*Dedicated to the memory of
Khaled el-Asaad, who was tortured and beheaded for protecting the artefacts of the ancient city of Palmyra…*

Contents

1. Those that forget shall pay the price for forgetting!   1
2. What you did to me shall be brought upon you   35
3. This is I, Zeus, King of the Gods, overlord of all creatures of the earth and sky   75
4. Twilight of the Gods   119
5. Do not underestimate Man, Mighty Zeus   169
6. Those that fail as fathers shall also fail as Gods   216
7. Dionysus has always been closer to the heart than to the mind   265
8. Whether you are a father, a king or a God, never stray from the path of justice   307
9. The one that will destroy you is the one that created you   359
10. Zeus, father to all creatures!   411
11. Heracles has atoned for the killing of your sons   459
12. They are coming, Zeus, Mother Earth's wild children are coming for you   528

They were walking in the dim light of evening. The music that was shattering the silence of the early night was clawing at their ears. A red light was flashing through the open door. The stench of blood struck her nostrils. She grimaced, knowing what was in store for her, but she did not stop and carried on behind her assistant Tobias, who was shuffling forward in his hooded coveralls towards the crime scene. As they neared the scene, the noise from the flat became almost unbearable. It felt like an earthquake. The entire building was shaking, and the smell was becoming even more powerful. She noticed that Tobias, who was now at the door, had stopped. She could not see his face but she could sense his horror. Chief Inspector Yıldız was not scared; she was just curious as to the scene that had so horrified her assistant. She hurried forward and tapped him on the shoulder. Tobias jumped, and stared at Yıldız as though seeing her for the first time.

'Oh my God… Chief. It's… It's like an abattoir in here. The whole place is drenched in blood…'

Yıldız did not even hear Tobias. Her eyes were fixed on a huge picture dominated by yellows, oranges and browns that had been painted on the wall opposite. Under a flashing red light was a painting of a regal figure, a long-haired, bearded king wearing a crown and sitting with great solemnity upon a throne. Although his golden hair and beard gave him a wizened, elderly look, he also had a body that would have made any athlete jealous. A winged nymph of some kind was perched on his right hand and in his left hand he held a staff, the head of which featured the head of an eagle staring menacingly at them. Near the bottom of the painting, by the base of the throne, were some red stains. That was when she saw the body on the ground. He was lying naked face-up on the ground, his hands tied at the wrists and palms facing up. She held her breath, took a few steps forward and saw it. A bloody piece of meat in the man's hands. It couldn't be… Surely not? She took a couple more steps forward… Yes, she was right. In the dead man's hands was a heart, still dripping with blood. The left side of the victim's chest had also been carved open.

'How the hell did…' said Tobias, switching on the room's lights. 'How…. You mean he sacrificed his own heart to the king?'

Yıldız did not answer but instead turned to face the source of the red lights, less foreboding now that the room's lights were on. A music video was booming out of a computer on a nearby desk, making the entire room shake. On the band at the bottom of the clip on the screen was the title of the song:

'*Altar of Zeus.*'

'Not to a king, Toby. To Zeus. The victim offered his heart to the King of the Gods.'

1
Those that forget shall pay the price for forgetting!

I shall start where you have forgotten. In the last city where my name was erased, in the last temple where my last statue was destroyed, from the last words of my last prophet's final prophecy, in the smoking flesh of the last animal sacrificed on my Altar, from my last subject's last pleading invocation, uttering my name with love, veneration and terror.

The ruthlessness of time, the treachery of man, the impotence of speech, the inadequacy of prayer, the disintegrating stones, the crumbling marble nor the rotting wood shall prevent my imminent rule. Once again, I shall cleave the skies open with lightning and rain thunderbolts down upon your gleaming cities; once again, I shall submerge your lands under water and curse you with sickness and disease; once again I shall deceive your foolish kings and drive you to war; once again I shall fill your seas with fat fish and adorn your branches and vines with sweet fruits; once again I shall enrich your soil with golden ears of grain; once again I shall fill your barns with fertile livestock; and once again you shall fall to your knees before me in supplication and file into my temples in reverence, your bodies and your tongues trembling as you utter my name.

Once again, you shall remember how I detest you, how I love you, how I doubt you and how I trust in you. You shall remember, one by one, that which your ancestors, grandfathers and fathers forgot. You shall remember how merciless I can be, as well as how merciful. You shall know once more my unbridled fury, as well as my infinite compassion. You shall know once again how I protected you from woe and from ruin, how I dispelled the adversity and pestilence that sought to coil themselves around you and how I brought ruin and calamity upon you.

You! People of weak memory, of weak mind and of low morals. I shall commence on the day you forgot me. I shall once more sit upon my golden throne in Olympus so that I may witness all of your sins. I shall reinstate my kingdom so that your plunder of the skies and the earth shall come to an end. I shall once again bring abundance to the soil, sanctify the seas and purify the air. I shall become more powerful than before, more despotic and more ruthless, and all that you have forgotten about me I shall write and record, word by word, line by line in your blood...

Once more I shall recount tales of eternal darkness, of chaos, of Gaia, our Mother Earth, of my grandfather Uranus, of my father Kronos and of I, Zeus. I shall recount the tales of my bloody and terrible battles with the Titans and the Giants and of my glorious victory over them so that you may read and remember and never forget. If you do not read my words, then I shall carve them into your wretched bodies.

Tyranny shall become your wisest teacher. Oppression shall open to you the gates of virtue and keep you cowed. You shall beg for forgiveness. You shall build temples in my name more spectacular than those built before, you shall fashion even more wondrous statues of me and you shall sacrifice your own flesh to me on ever vaster Altars to beg for my mercy. Mercy, however, shall not be easily gained. And this is because you are traitors, hypocrites and liars. You love comfort, whilst you flee from that which is arduous. God, however, is reached via the path of toil and struggle. Because God is the truth: unchanging, irrefutable, unforgettable.

Yet you have forgotten. You act as though Zeus never existed, as though you never worshipped him, as though you never begged for his mercy, as though you never died and killed for him. You thought that time would overthrow Zeus' rule. That my rule, like those of my grandfather Uranus and my father Kronos, would come to an end. You thought new Gods would replace me and that these new Gods would be more powerful, wiser, more ruthless and more merciful than I. You thought that I would turn to dust were my temples to be brought to ruin and that my Immortal body would be scattered to the winds were my statues to be destroyed. It was your belief that I would cease to breathe were you to cease reciting your prayers to me. That were you to stop bringing me sacrifices, my soul would not be nourished and would be lost in the depths of darkness like a fading star.

Do not deny it. This is what you thought, and that is why you were so eager to forget me. Kings, heroes, noblemen, slaves, women, the elderly, children; all of you. This is what you did, and as you did so, you laughed, drank wine and made merry. You danced and shamelessly satisfied your lust. You wished to eradicate from your miserable lives the God you had worshipped for more than a thousand years. Like an accursed being that no longer wished to be remembered, you entombed Zeus, for whom you were once willing to lay down your lives, in your marble sarcophagi and in your sealed underground vaults. You mocked my loves, you made light of my triumphs, you scorned my miracles and my name became the subject of your hilarity and your cheap mirth. You wished to erase my name, my form and my word from your weak memories, remove them from your cowardly hearts and banish them from your sinful souls. And such was your foolishness, you looked at your eras without me and thought you had succeeded in this. However, the time of the Gods is not the same as the time of man. The years that make up one of your lifetimes is for us Gods but a moment, a single breath. And now that fleeting moment is over. Now, the most terrible era of your fate is about to begin.

That is why I shall begin in the place you thought you had forgotten. Those that forget shall pay the price for forgetting. Those that did not show due respect shall be rewarded with the severest of punishments: those that tore me from their hearts shall have their hearts torn out, those that turned their faces away from me shall have the skin flayed from their faces, those that denied me shall have their mouths filled with dirt, those that did not enter my temples shall have their legs cut away at the knee, and the arms of those that did not bring me sacrifices shall have be severed from their roots. None whatsoever shall be spared my wrath.

I, Zeus, Lord of the Earth and the Sky, Supreme God, Lord of the Titans, of the Giants, of man and of all creatures, have this to say to you:

Let this be my pledge to Gaia, our Mother of the Earth, to my grandfather Uranus, to my mother Rhea, to my father Kronos, to the Titans, to all the other Gods and to all the creatures of the World; those that betrayed me shall suffer the most terrible vengeance, and those that defied me shall remain accursed and be cast into the flames to writhe in agony.

Chapter One

'Those that betrayed me shall suffer the most terrible vengeance, and those that defied me shall remain accursed and be cast into the flames to writhe in agony.'

Tobias read aloud the words in the bottom right-hand corner of the painting of Zeus, words that had been written almost in the style of an artist's signature.

'We might be wrong, Chief. This guy hasn't been sacrificed. He's been punished for not heeding Zeus' words. Killed by the King of the Gods, no less.'

'What a load of nonsense. Who believes in Zeus in this day and age?' Yıldız answered while going through the pockets of a light-green summer jacket in the wardrobe. Tobias went back to the words in the painting.

'I wouldn't know about that but that's the only meaning that can be derived from what's written here.'

Yıldız did not answer. She had found an ID in one of the jacket pockets: Cemal Ölmez, born in Berlin.

'Looks like the victim was Turkish,' she muttered. 'Odd…'

Her assistant did not seem to think the victim's background was that important but Yıldız could not dismiss it so easily. When Turks were involved in murder cases, usually it did not involve such elaborate arrangements. Rather, the perpetrator and victim usually knew each another and the killings were usually over a debt, a woman or an inheritance. No, this was very strange. She shut the wardrobe and walked over to the desk with the computer. The music was still booming, but they had grown used to it, just as the stench of blood no longer bothered them. Next to the keyboard on the desk were some sheets of paper with sketches of human faces. The victim must have drawn the sketches, but the faces looked as though they were from another era.

'It says here, *The most terrible of vengeances shall be visited upon those that betrayed me,* Chief,' Tobias said insouciantly. 'I'll tell you what, this King of the Gods certainly has good handwriting. Just look at this lettering. It's beautiful.'

Still holding the sheets of paper, Yıldız turned to her assistant. 'Handwritten, you say?'

Tobias' face was so close to the writing, his nose was almost touching the wall.

'Looks like it.' Then, suddenly struck by doubt, he added, 'Or isn't it?'

Yıldız put the sheets of paper back on the desk and walked over to the painting. Although her coveralls made it tricky, she bent over and began examining the letters lodged between the two front legs of Zeus' throne.

'No, Toby. I'm afraid Zeus did not write this. It is a computer printout. The killer cut it to size and carefully stuck it to the painting.'

As she stood up, she looked over at the body again. He looked to be in his thirties, and had a handsome face; death had yet to ruin his fine features. Instead, the large black eyes just stared blankly at the ceiling. 'Far too calm,' Yıldız said to herself. 'No expression of fear or terror. It's possible he was under heavy sedation when his heart was being removed. He didn't notice a thing.' While she was relieved for the victim, she could not help feel a growing consternation as she looked at him. It truly was a grim sight. The heart in the young man's large hands was growing darker by the moment, like a red flower losing its brilliance, and the drops of blood seeping through his fingers and falling onto his chest were growing heavier. The body was rapidly turning cold.

Yıldız leant over and examined the gap between the body and the wall and checked around the feet and the head. When she did not find what she was looking for, she turned to her assistant.

'Any sign of a tool or weapon? Because a serious surgical procedure has been performed here.'

Tobias was still fixed on the writing on the wall.

'Sorry, what was that, boss? Erm, no. Nothing.' He was now looking at the victim's gaping chest. 'It must have been a knife, right?'

'A knife, yes, but also perhaps a scalpel or something more professional,' Yıldız replied, scanning the room. 'You cannot remove a man's heart with just any old cutting instrument. You need to get through the ribcage. He was given an anaesthetic, or at least an extremely powerful sedative. Do you see anything like that around?'

Her assistant scanned the room but he did not see any blade sharp or strong enough to slice a human chest open all the way down, nor did he see any bottles of medicine or serum equipment. As he looked around, he noticed a little bookcase by the desk. He walked over to have a better look. The books were all about art and artists, with names like Picasso, Dali and Van Gogh standing out.

'Looks like the deceased was an artist, boss. He must have been the one that painted Zeus.'

'Looks like it, Toby.' Yıldız turned to look at the Chief Deity. 'I can't say I know much about art but he hasn't done a bad job.'

Her assistant's eyes opened in amazement.

'Hasn't done a bad job? Boss, the picture is stunning. I can't even draw stickmen.'

Yıldız gave a distracted laugh before walking over to the books on the shelves.

'Otto Dix, Rivera, Chagall, Monet, Gauguin, Cezanne,' she muttered. 'All the important artists of the twentieth century are here. Yes, Toby, our victim was most definitely an artist.' Scanning the titles on the spines of the books on the lower shelf, she noticed books on another subject. 'And here there are books about computing. These are all technical books. Nothing to do with art.' She looked over at the body again. 'Seems the deceased had a wide set of interests.'

They heard a bell ring. At first, they thought it was the doorbell but then they realized it was a telephone. However, neither Yıldız nor Tobias had that particular tone on their phones. They exchanged glances and began looking for the ringing phone. There was no phone on the desk so Tobias opened the top drawer. There it was. A mobile phone ringing amongst all the other odds and ends. The name 'Rafael' lit up the screen. Tobias picked up the phone and pressed the answer button.

'Hello? Yes?'

'Hello? Cemo?' a male voice at the other end asked. 'Cemo? Is that you?'

'No, this isn't Cemal,' Tobias replied sternly. 'Who is this?'

'Where's Cemal?' The man's tone had changed.

'This is Inspector Tobias Becker. Who is this? Answer me now!'

After a pause, the voice answered, 'Inspector? Why is there an Inspector there? What's happened?'

Tobias raised his voice. 'Tell me who you are first and what your connection to Cemal is.'

'My name is Rafael Moreno,' came the anxious reply. 'I'm a friend of Cemal's.'

'And why are you calling him?'

'We are working on a project together. A mural on the walls of one of the squatter houses on Köpeniker Street. We were supposed to be working on it together this evening but he hasn't turned up. Everything is okay, isn't it? Has something happened to Cemal?'

'Why are you worried? Is something supposed to have happened to him?'

'Of course not, no. That's not what I meant. It's just that Cemal is very punctual. He's the type to let you know if he can't make it and so when I didn't hear from him, I started to worry. That's why I'm asking if something has happened to him. He is okay, isn't he? Everything is in order, isn't it?'

Tobias ignored the man's growing unease.

'When did you last see Cemal?'

After a few moment's silence, Rafael answered.

'Two nights ago. He came to our place for dinner.' There was another pause before he went on, imploringly. 'What's happened to Cemal? Why aren't you telling me?'

'I'm very sorry, Mister Moreno,' Tobias eventually said, 'but Cemal is dead. He was killed this evening. The perpetrator has yet to be identified.'

'What?' the voice cried out in horror. 'How? What do you mean he's dead?'

He could not say any more and began weeping. Tobias stood there holding the mobile phone and listening to the man's sobs and wails. Tobias waited but Rafael would not calm down. It was all too much.

'Now listen to me, Mister Moreno. I have to hang up now but I will need to speak to you again, face to face. We will need your help so we shall be calling you in the near future. My condolences. I am sorry for your loss.'

With that, he hung up and turned to Yıldız.

'The guy sounded pretty distraught. They must have been good friends. He sounded like a foreigner, one of the new arrivals. You can tell he wasn't born here by his terrible German.'

Yıldız was looking at the mobile phone.

'Does that phone have a password?'

Tobias pressed the screen with a gloved finger.

'No.'

'Well, have a look and find out who the last person to call was.'

Her assistant tapped the screen on the device a few times.

'Here we are... The owner of the phone called someone by the name of Alex.' He held the phone up to his boss. 'No surname. Just Alex. Called him at 21.47. Around five hours before that, someone by the name of Peter also rang. They talked for quite some time too. Apart from that, no other callers.'

Yıldız nodded her head.

'We'll have to look into both of them,' she said and headed back to the bookcase. However, this time it was not the books but a framed picture on the wall that grabbed her attention. Taken at an excavation site, it was a black and white photo of fourteen workers holding digging tools and posing next to a man in a suit and tie and a colonial hat. Marble statues, broken columns and giant rocks could be seen in the background. Yıldız could not figure out where it was. Troy, perhaps, or the site of another ancient settlement.

'Looks like the deceased also had an interest in archaeology.'

'Hardly surprising, boss,' Tobias replied. 'The guy painted a picture of Zeus. He's bound to have been into archaeology.'

Yıldız shot him a disparaging glance.

'That's not what I mean, Tobias. The guy wasn't just into Zeus. He was into archaeological digs too. Look. This photo is from an excavation site. See? No statue of Zeus or any other God but he still put the photo up on his wall. The photo must mean something to him. perhaps he was close to someone in the photo.'

Tobias was looking at the man in the colonial hat.

'This guy? His grandfather perhaps?'

His boss shook her head dismissively.

'I doubt it, Toby. The victim here is Turkish.' She pointed to the men in turbans and wide shalwar trousers holding the shovels and digging equipment. 'If Cemal was close to anyone in this photo, it was one of these guys.'

'And who the hell are they?' They both turned their heads to see who had asked the question. Inspector Kurt from the Crime Scene Investigation Unit was standing in the doorway, his eyes gleaming like those of the King of the Gods in the picture on the wall. However, his plain white coveralls, gloves and galoshes made him somewhat less intimidating to the two officers present. Kurt knew this and so raised his voice in an attempt to create an impression of authority but his voice was too high-pitched to impress.

'You've made a complete mess of my crime scene,' he shouted. 'I'm going to tell Markus about this.'

Yıldız grinned.

'Don't be silly, Kurt. We've taken all the necessary precautions and kept ourselves completely covered. See? Gloves and galoshes, so we won't have messed up any clues or compromised any potential evidence.'

Kurt walked up to them, bag in hand.

'And a bloody good thing too. Compromising evidence! That would not look good at all now, would it, Yıldız?' He noticed the body on the ground and jumped back. 'Fuck me, what the hell is this?'

'Welcome to the abode of the King of the Gods, Kurti,' Yıldız said, heading for the door. 'We are leaving you now so you can be alone with the AlMighty Zeus. All the best.'

Yıldız had only taken a few steps when she realized the music's volume had been turned down. Kurt, never known for his patience, had clearly been unable to take any more of that Godawful racket. As Yıldız made her way through the dim corridor, she noticed another painting on the wall, this one stretching from floor to ceiling. Actually, it was not a painting. It was a huge collage of dozens of black and white squares featuring reliefs and statues, but they were all missing arms, heads, legs or trunks. The reliefs depicted a brutal and mighty battle. Yıldız stood there, pondering the scene in front of her. Had she seen these engravings before?

'More statues of Zeus?' Tobias asked as Yıldız pondered the images. 'This is more like an archaeology museum than a crime scene.'

Instead of answering, Yıldız carried on walking down the hall. A murder in the middle of Berlin and allusions to an ancient God. The body of a young man who had had an interest in art, archaeology and computer programming, and a Turk to boot. It was all very strange. Her mind awash with unanswered questions and possible scenarios, she reached the end of the hall. A gentle nudge and the wooden door swung open, revealing a large room. A weak light was streaming in through the large windows to the left, going some way to dispelling the dimness of the interior. There was a vast bookcase in front of her next to another door. The wall to the right was covered with one immense painting but it was hard to make out the details in the dim light. Tobias walked in behind her and switched the lights on.

A familiar site appeared before Yıldız. She had been stunned when she saw the original for the first time in a museum decades earlier. It was the Pergamon Altar, one of the most remarkable monuments of the classical world. She suddenly realized. The statues in the pictures she had just seen in the hall used to line the walls of the Altar. A Turkish murder victim, archaeology, the Pergamon Altar... A whole new flood of thoughts and hypotheses came rushing back but once again, she could make neither head nor tail of them. She took a few steps forward but then stopped, worried she would not be able to see the whole picture if she got closer. The Altar was reminiscent of a vast marble monument. In the centre were the staircases, which the people of old used to climb to reach the sacred fire at the top of the structure. On the walls around the staircases were fabulous carvings and engravings, and along the walls were rows of columns whose capitals were made up of smaller carved figures. She was standing in front of a magnificent Altar, one without peer or equal in the world.

'Is this painting connected to Zeus too?' her assistant asked. 'What is this? Some kind of temple?'

'You could say that, yes,' Yıldız answered, eyes still on the picture. 'It's an Altar. A place where offerings were made to the Gods. People would come here to offer the best cuts of their best fed animals to the Gods and those cuts would then be burnt on the second level of the Altar. So yes, Tobias, this does have a connection to Zeus. This is an Altar that was constructed solely for the King of the Gods. In fact, its other name is the Altar of Zeus.'

Her assistant stared at the picture on the wall but he did not seem as captivated by it as his boss. Yıldız went on with her explanation.

'It was brought here from Anatolia, from a place called Bergama. It's been here for around a hundred years. The Altar is on display in Berlin.'

'In the Pergamon Museum?' Tobias asked, a little excitement finally beginning to flutter in his voice.

'Yes. In fact, the museum takes its name from this Altar. It's a priceless artefact. The original is much bigger, of course, and far more impressive. Dozens of people used to be able to wander in and around it at the same time. I've been there so many times and every time I go, I am blown away. I have been to Bergama too and seen the original site. All that is left of the original is the plinth. It made for quite a melancholy sight, to be honest. The replica on display in the museum in Berlin looks fantastic though. The last time I was there must have been around fifteen years ago.' She pointed to the twelfth step in the picture. 'I sat here on this step.'

'How do you remember which step you sat on, boss?' Tobias asked, his grey eyes widening in amazement. Yıldız gave him a playful wink.

'Because the twelfth step made me think of the twelve Gods living on Mount Olympus. Twelve steps, twelve Gods. Easy to remember. If I remember correctly, this Altar used to be known as Zeus' residence on earth. In other words, it was an earthly version of the Gods' palace on Olympus. Have you visited the museum? It used to be in the old East, before reunification. Surely your school arranged trips to the museum for you?'

'They did,' her assistant admitted sheepishly. 'Our school principal was mad about mythology and stuff and so he arranged a school trip to the museum. I was really keen on going too but as luck would have it, I caught a terrible fever at the time and so wasn't able to go. My classmates went on about it for days afterwards. I never got around to going in the end.'

Yıldız was still staring at the painting.

'It really is an incredible structure. The people of Pergamon used to revere the King of the Gods. If they could build an

Altar of such grandeur like this in his name, who knows what offerings they must have made to him.'

While she said this, Tobias cast his mind back to the corpse with the chest split open.

'Then that guy back there really was sacrificed to Zeus,' he said solemnly. 'The poor guy's heart was ripped out and offered to the King of the Gods.'

'I wouldn't know, Toby,' Yıldız said, unfazed. 'If an offering was to be made to Zeus, then don't you think the sacrifice should have been performed here, in front of his Altar?'

'Actually, both scenarios are daft,' her assistant muttered. 'This is just a house, after all, not a temple, and the paintings on the walls are just that — paintings. Paint a picture of a God on the wall and then cut a man up in front of it? Some sacrificial ceremony! If you're going to do it properly, you need to make a sacrifice on an Altar. And judging by what you said, even that isn't enough because you have to burn the sacrifice afterwards.' He stopped and grimaced, disturbed by his own thoughts, before going on. 'Isn't that so, boss? That guy's heart would have had to be thrown onto a fire.'

'Absolutely,' Yıldız said, casting a quick glance at her assistant. 'But this savagery could hardly have been carried out at the museum so whoever it was that did this just created their own temple. And it also looks like the victim's drawings helped feed his imagination. One way or another, what we have here is a lunatic with a vivid imagination, someone who thinks what we think is just a picture is an Altar on which humans can be sacrificed. And worse than that, he or she is a monster who will not hesitate to cut a man up. A highly skilled one too, who is meticulous enough to be able to carry out a grisly crime like this and not let it get too messy. We're up against a serious adversary here, Toby.'

'I'm also at a loss too, boss, as to how organized everything is. And I find it baffling that the victim did not put up a fight. Maybe this Cemal was willing to be sacrificed. Maybe they were both into ancient Greek mythology, him and the killer. Maybe this Cemal thought his life would have some meaning if he were sacrificed to the King of the Gods and then he found someone who thought like him and managed to convince him to sacrifice him. What say you, boss? There isn't a trace of fear on his face. No fight, no resistance, all the furniture in order.... Even the chair in front of the desk is still in its place. It wasn't turned over or anything. Aren't you surprised by how neat and tidy it was in there? Who's to say that the victim and the killer did not arrange this sacrifice themselves? Humanity in general has gone off the rails as it is, so perhaps these two wanted to carry out this deranged fantasy rather than live dull, ordinary lives and die dull ordinary deaths.'

It was possible, of course. Didn't some pervert a few years back somewhere around Rotenburg find a willing respondent when he put up an ad looking for a human being to eat? Didn't the victim knowingly and willingly meet his own killer and then happily, even enthusiastically, offer him his own flesh? Didn't the killer cut and eat parts of his victim before killing him and sticking a fork in him? Yıldız knew all too well from experience that when it comes to performing acts of evil, the creature known as mankind possessed an almost infinite creativity.

'It's not out of the question. An assumption, yes, but still just an assumption. Let's wait for the results of the autopsy, read the deceased's correspondences on his computer and check out the people in his phone's contacts. Let's also find out who this Peter and Alex are. Maybe we'll encounter something along the lines of what you've just described. But right now, we need to assume the victim was killed against his will. Let's not unfairly judge a man who has been brutally murdered unless we have some hard evidence, or at least something to go on.' Tobias did not object. Yıldız's eyes slid over to the bookcase. 'I'll take a look at this room. You go through the books. We may pick up a few leads.' She took a few steps forward. 'Maybe we'll find some other areas the deceased was interested in beyond archaeology, art and computing.'

Tobias smiled wearily.

'It wouldn't surprise me at all. That poor sod inside looks like he was quite a multi-talented guy.'

When Yıldız opened the door, she was struck by an overpowering smell of paint and glue. It was harsh but it was still more tolerable than the stench from the other room. In fact, had it been not so intense, Yıldız would have liked it. She groped around for the switch, eventually managed to find it and turned the lights on. She found herself looking at a studio of some sort, most probably the area in which Cemal used to work. The studio was like the twin of the earlier large room. Thick, black curtains hung in front of windows that looked out onto a garden, a huge table stood in the middle of the room and an easel leaned against the wall, with rows of cardboard packets, tins of paint, bottles of glue and brushes lined up on the floor against the wall. He was also struck by a sketched drawing of three faces pinned in a neat row on the facing wall. Three bearded men… She did not recognize them so she moved closer and narrowed her eyes to get a better look. She managed to identify the one on the right as Zeus. Cemal had expertly replicated the face of the God sitting on his throne in the other picture. As for the other two, they had long hair and beards, strong jawlines, broad foreheads and haughty demeanours. They were probably Gods too, possibly Poseidon and Hades, Zeus' powerful brothers, but she couldn't be sure. She went over to the next wall. That too was also covered in sketches. She moved closer to the wall and began inspecting the etchings. They were drawings based on the photograph in the hall. Yes, they were sketches of the statues and sculptures that had once adorned the walls of the Altar of Zeus. They pictures had not been completed but they were still incredibly beautiful. There was also a story behind the engravings in these sketches. Yıldız tried to remember. They described a war of some sort but which war? Probably a war between the Gods. She was not sure. Or was it the war between the Gods and the Titans? While standing there lost in thought, she saw the photographs on the table. They were larger prints of the photos she had seen in the hall and like the originals of the Altar, the statues were missing heads, arms and feet. She turned back to look at the pictures on the wall. Yes, in his mural, the artist had included the missing parts. Yıldız felt a strange sense of satisfaction. Even if they were only statues, the bodies with missing parts disturbed her. It was the same when she had wandered around museums too. Instead of all those statues, mosaics and frescoes with missing parts, she would have preferred to see those works of art complete. That is why she was eager to examine the pictures that depicted the completed engravings of the Altar. It felt like reading a novel.

What she saw in the pictures were Gods, Goddesses and bizarre, semi-human creatures in the midst of an almighty battle, using a multitude of weapons — spears, swords, clubs, bows and arrows, as well as claws, teeth and nails. Creatures with human upper bodies and reptilian lower bodies, winged Gods and Goddesses, eagles, snakes, dogs, horses and lions were all in the midst of a ferocious engagement. Captivated by the drama in front of her, for a few moments Yıldız forgot she was in the middle of a murder investigation. She managed to identify Zeus in the thick of the battle in the painting, and with a complete body too, but that was as far as she could go. The rest of the picture was a mystery. Who were the other figures in the battle? Why were they at war? What were the people of Pergamon trying to say when they built this fabulous temple two thousand years ago? She must have heard or read about it somewhere but she could not remember.

'Boss? Can you have a look at this for a minute please?'

Tobias was calling her from the other room. Had he found some important evidence? Yıldız momentarily pushed aside the images of Zeus and the Gods at war and headed for the other room.

'What have you got, Tobias?'

Her assistant had not found any evidence but standing next to him was a gaunt, deathly pale woman. She was pregnant and trembling with fright.

'This lady is a friend of the deceased. She lives upstairs. She says she has something to say.'

The small lounge in the flat on the second floor was lit up by the amber light coming out of a handmade wooden chandelier. The pregnant lady was huddled up in a cheap armchair which Yıldız had asked her to sit in. Her tiny frame was still shaking and she had given up trying to wipe away her tears, which were now flowing freely down her cheeks and chin and onto her neck.

'I thought they were having a party,' she finally managed to say with a heavy accent. 'Cemo was a fun guy… He used to invite everyone in the apartment… He was so friendly. So when I heard the music, I thought it was just another party. But it was the same song over and over again… And so loud too… Cemo would never be so inconsiderate.'

She told them her name was Pilar. She was young, very young, and was wearing a brightly coloured maternity dressed decorated with wild flowers and had her curly hair gathered at the back of her head in a ponytail. When Yıdlız saw her, she wondered how her tiny body could even bear the child. Pilar, it turned out, was the neighbour that had called the police.

'I knew something was wrong,' she went on. 'So I went up to the door... All I could hear inside was the music. No talking, no shouting, nobody singing along to the music. I knocked on the door but no one answered... The door was already open, though, so I gave it a push and when I did....' She could not go on. She covered her face with her hands and began to cry.

Tobias sighed impatiently, while Yıldız got up and opened the balcony window. The scent of linden filled the room and she breathed in the fresh fragrant air. That is when she heard the sound of wings. It was not a bat or an owl, but a bird with much stronger wings. A cry pierced the night sky, the cry of a wild animal. She looked at the trees in the garden but it was too dark to pick anything out. It must have been a hawk or some such bird that had ended up in the city from the forest. She turned around and, not bothering to ask permission, headed for the kitchen and filled a glass with water from a jug with a smiling Pinocchio face. She took another glass, filled it up and took it back inside. It looked like the clean air had helped calm Pilar down a little. She handed her the glass.

'Here, drink. You'll feel better.'

Pilar took a sip.

'Thank you,' she mumbled and put the glass down on a coffee table. 'Please excuse me. It's just come as such a shock.'

Fidgeting impatiently, Tobias, still wearing his coveralls, like Yıldız, took over the questioning.

'Not to worry. Now, Cemo — is that what you called the deceased?'

Pilar blinked.

'Actually, his name was Cemal. Cemal Ölmez.... We called him Cemo because it was easier to pronounce.'

Yıldız's hazel eyes were fixed on the pregnant woman. It was hard to say whether she was genuinely sad for her or just trying to understand her.

'Drink some more, Pilar,' she said, pointing to the glass on the coffee table. 'Or would you prefer a hot drink?'

She blushed.

'Oh no, thank you. Actually, I'm the one who should be offering you something to drink but Cemo's death has come as such a shock. He was so full of life… Who could have done something so ghastly?'

Yıldız looked at her sympathetically.

'We'll find them, Pilar. Trust me, we will. And you'll make it easier for us if you answer our questions.'

She forced herself and took another sip of water.

'So, was Cemal an artist?' Yıldız asked, settling down into a chair. 'We saw lots of paintings in those rooms, as well as a workshop.'

'The paintings with mythological themes? Yes, Cemal painted all of them.'

She didn't say anything else. Tobias repeated his boss' question.

'So was the deceased an artist?'

'Huh? Oh. No, he was a software engineer…. He worked for a company. An energy company.'

The Inspector frowned.

'So why did he draw all those pictures? Why was he so interested in mythology and in the statues around the Altar of Zeus?'

Pilar shrugged her petite shoulders.

'His whole family are into it. They live in a place like that in Turkey. In Pergamon.'

'You mean Bergama,' Yıldız said, correcting her. 'It's called Bergama over there.'

'I know but its old name was Pergamon.... Like the museum... His grandfather used to work there. A long time ago... In Pergamon, that is... It was part of the family tradition. His grandfather's crew were the ones that found those reliefs.'

'You mean the ones on the Altar?'

There was a note of scorn in Yıldız's voice. Seeing the inspector's disbelieving expression, Pilar changed tack.

'Well, that's what Cemo told me.'

Realizing the subject was leading nowhere, Tobias decided to steer the conversation elsewhere.

'How did you know Cemal? It looks like the two of you were quite close.'

Pilar eyes filled up.

'We were. He was our friend.' She looked around the room tearfully. 'He found this place for us. We were in a squat last year. Cemo and Rafael used to paint murals for the squatters.'

She must have been talking about the guy they had just spoken to on the phone but Yıldız still asked to make sure.

'Who's Rafael?'

The pregnant woman's face softened into a smile.

'My husband. He and Cemal were like brothers. I haven't even called him yet. I don't know what I'm going to say. They were so close. We all were... We met Cemo in the squat. We had a great time there but six months ago, Cemo said, "You can't have your baby here so I'm going to find you a more suitable place to live." Within a week, he'd found this place. He was a good man. A really good man.'

'And was he a good artist, this Cemal?' Yıldız asked.

Pilar pointed to a picture above the bookcase of a youth with a beautiful face filling a floral cup with liquid from a golden decanter.

'See that painting? He did that. That handsome youth is Ganymedes.'

'Who's Ganymedes?' Tobias asked.

'Ganymedes was the cupbearer and lover of the King of the Gods… Zeus assumed the form of an eagle, abducted him from Mount Ida and took him to Mount Olympus. As for your question, yes. Cemo was a good artist. He always said he was an amateur but he was extremely talented.' She pointed to the painting again. 'He painted that a year ago. Look at how superbly executed it is. When it came to art, even my Rafael, who is an exceptional artist, used to insist upon them having a joint exhibition.'

Tobias couldn't care less about the details. He only wanted to know if this woman and her husband were telling the truth.

'Where is Rafael now?'

His tone was unnecessarily harsh, frightening Pilar.

'At the squat… Why? What's happened?'

Tobias shrugged.

'Nothing. Where is the squat?'

The young woman swallowed several times.

'Over on Köpeniker Street… Rafael is painting a mural there.'

Tobias was not convinced.

'At midnight? Why doesn't he do it during the day?'

Although she was in her own home, Pilar shrunk back into her chair.

'He works whenever he gets the chance. When circumstances allow.'

Again, the conversation was at risk of veering off-topic.

'So, did Cemal live alone?' Yıldız asked. 'Didn't he have a wife or a girlfriend?'

Pilar paused but she did not keep them waiting too long.

'He had a lover. A guy called Alex. He is a drummer in a heavy metal band. They're not very successful commercially but that's not Alex's fault. He just plays wherever he can find work. They've been on tour many times in many countries.'

So… Alex, who was the last person to speak to the deceased on the mobile phone, was his lover. Yıldız needed to find out if the number saved as Alex on the phone was the right one or not.

'Do you know his number?'

Pilar reached for the address book under the coffee table.

'His home number is here but he doesn't use a mobile. Alex is a weird guy.' She opened the address book. 'Here, this is his number. Could you write it down? I can't read very well without my glasses.' While Tobias saved the number on his mobile, Pilar went on. 'But they're playing at The Tartarus tonight, in a musical called *The Gorgons' Grin*.'

Yıldız knew the place but she still wanted to be sure.

'You mean the theatre on Oranien Street? It's also a concert venue.'

'Yes, that one, on that street. Actually, Alex is a really talented musician but…'

She screwed up her face when she said it.

'He's a bad person?' Yıldız offered matter-of-factly.

'He's not a good person… Cemo really loved him but Alex… How can I say it? He is a selfish, surly guy. Sometimes he was quite rough with Cemo.'

The two police officers were now listening attentively. Yıldız asked the next question.

'When you say rough, what do you mean? He beat him up?'

Pilar bit her lower lip and nodded her head.

'He couldn't beat him up because Cemo was younger and fitter than him and he knew how to fight. But Alex was constantly causing probleMs They had another fight two nights ago. They turned the flat upside down. Then Alex stormed out and slammed the door shut.'

There was a gleam in Tobias' dark grey eyes.

'Do you know why they were fighting?'

Pilar looked hesitant. Yıldız spoke up to encourage her.

'If you do not tell us, we may not be able to find your friend's killer. We need to know everything.'

She took a deep breath, looked at Tobias and then at Yıldız, and then began.

'The same as always. Alex was jealous of Cemo.' Her eyes wandered to the door before carrying on in a pained voice. 'I don't know what state he is in now but Cemo was a really handsome kid. Alex was ugly and he was also older than him. He made Cemo's life hell.' She suddenly stopped and her eyes grew wide with shock. 'You don't mean to say that bastard killed Cemo, do you?'

'We don't know,' Yıldız said uneasily. 'What do you think? Do you think Alex could have done it?'

Her black eyes blinked a few times.

'I wouldn't rule it out. He once threatened to kill Cemo, right in front of me. Two days ago, right here, in this very room, at this very table. We'd invited them to dinner. Alex had been drinking heavily and he started getting rowdy, again. At one point, he lost his cool and flew into a rage. He turned to Cemo and said, "If you ever leave me or if you ever do this or that, I won't let you live." That's what he said.'

Finally, they were getting somewhere. Tobias leaned forward.

'Why did Cemal put up with all this guy's nastiness? It's not even nastiness. It's just plain old violence. Why didn't he leave him?'

She smiled a faint smile.

'Like I said, he loved Alex... adored him.'

'Maybe he liked it when Alex was rough with him,' Tobias said, repeating his earlier conjecture. 'Perhaps that is why he loved him so much. Maybe he was even willing to lay down his own life to make the man he loved happy.'

Pilar looked shocked.

'No, Cemo was not that kind of guy. He was a proud man. He never let anyone insult him. He hit back just as hard in his fights with Alex. Like I said, he knew how to fight.'

'I think you've misunderstood,' Tobias said. 'This has nothing to do with pride or honour. There are people out there who have no boundaries when it comes to love. People who will even incorporate death into their relationships. We've come across such cases before.'

Pilar did not like what she was hearing.

'No, Cemal was no psycho,' she said in a broken voice. 'Yes, he was a bit odd compared to other people but he loved life. He wanted to live. He was not the sort to want to die. He did not want to kill anybody, nor would he have let anybody dare harm him.'

The flame from the lighter glowing in the dark lit up Tobias' brooding face. He took two deep drags on his cigarette, as though it was the last cigarette on earth. The bitterness of the tobacco overpowered the scent of linden that was infusing the night with a sweet drowsiness.

'You couldn't wait, could you?' Yıldız said, needling her assistant, as she began taking off her coveralls by the boot of their grey Passat, parked next to the Crime Scene Investigation crew's van. 'You're not even changed and you've gone and lit one up! It's a filthy habit and it only leads to disaster. I'm telling you. Don't say I haven't warned you. Your family already has a history of cancer. What you're doing doesn't make any sense.'

Tobias grinned impishly.

'You don't really think we're going to just peacefully grow old and die, do you, boss? Come off it! We both know that at the end of the day, some nutter is going to come along and stick a knife in our guts or put a bullet in our brains during a shootout so I doubt I'll even have the chance to get cancer. So why not just enjoy it while I can, eh?'

Yıldız tried not to laugh.

'Fair enough. Well, hurry up and smoke that thing then. You're going to stink the car out, I just know it.'

Her assistant didn't seem bothered by it and instead took two more deep hearty drags.

'Seriously though, boss, when did you quit again?' he asked, smoke billowing out of his mouth and nose. 'It's been, what, fifteen years?'

Standing there in her white coverall, she looked like a polar bear that had come down to Berlin in the dead of the night.

'Fifteen years, three months and seventeen days,' she answered, shaking her head in surprise at her own answer, before stepping out of her protective gear and throwing it in the trunk of the car. 'But I'll tell you one thing, I count each passing day. I don't even miss my first boyfriend as much.' She closed the boot of the trunk. 'But it's done now. No turning back.'

Yıldız looked much younger, standing there in a leather jacket and a pair of black jeans that accentuated her long legs. With her slightly upturned eyebrows, her petite nose, full lips and the deep dimple that formed on her right cheek whenever she smiled, she was, even in the dim light, an incredibly alluring woman. Of course, Tobias had noticed this but he did not feel the need to mention it.

'Even if you did want to rekindle it, I don't know if Franz Abi would be up for it,' Tobias said, using the Turkish word *older brother*. 'You threw him out of your house.'

'Your pronunciation of *abi* is very good. I see your Turkish is coming along. But I wasn't talking about Franz, I was talking about the cigarettes. And when I said my first lover, I meant Volker. We used to be in the same class in secondary school. He was a sweet guy and all that, but no one marries their first crush.

Franz was a mistake, though. A youthful mistake. Every woman has these foolish periods in her life when they let people like that into their lives and Franz was one of them for me.'

She stood on tiptoe and faced Tobias, who was a good head taller than her. She took the cigarette out of his mouth, flung it to the ground and stubbed it out.

'What did you do that for?' he cried out. 'What did I do to deserve that?'

Yıldız was about to jokingly scold her lovable young assistant when an old man suddenly appeared before them, his steely blue eyes, even in the darkness, clearly seething with anger.

'What's going on here? Why are there so many police here? Has there been a murder?'

Tobias immediately stepped up to him and blocked his path.

'Can't you see the security tape here? You're not allowed past this point.'

With an angry, trembling hand, the man pointed to a single-storey building in a garden to the right.

'I'm going home. Or is going for a walk at night not allowed now either? You're blocking my path so how am I supposed to get home?'

Two uniformed officers up ahead heard the raised voices and were about to walk over but Yıldız gestured for them to stay put and smiled at the old man.

'We're sorry, sir. Please. Come through.'

However, the old man did not budge but rather turned to look at the building in which the murder had taken place.

'They've been at each other's throats again, have they?'

Tobias was becoming irate.

'That's none of your concern. Off you go now. You should have been in bed hours ago anyway.'

The hostility in the man's eyes deepened.

'You watch your mouth, lad. I'll decide when I go home and what time I go to bed.'

Tobias growled a warning in response and was getting ready for a verbal altercation but Yıldız stepped in.

'That's enough, Tobias. Why don't you go and get out of your coveralls?' She turned to the old man, smiled coolly and gestured to the building with the garden. 'And sir, you are free to go home.'

Tobias complied with his boss' wishes but the grumpy neighbour was having none of it. He stayed where he was, his frail body hunched over and his eyes still flashing with rancour. He stared at the woman in front of him disparagingly.

'Who was it this time — Turks? Arabs? Or was it those junkies who wear those stupid hippy outfits? Well? Out with it. Who killed whom?'

Yıldız remained courteous.

'Why are you bothering yourself with these unpleasant incidents, sir? Please. Just go home and leave this to the police.'

As she spoke, she touched the man gently on the arm but he angrily jerked his arm back.

'Don't touch me! This is harassment!'

Yıldız took a step back.

'I'm sorry, sir, I apologize. I didn't mean anything by it. I meant you no harm. Please believe me when I tell you that there is nothing of interest here.'

The man grew incandescent with rage.

'What the hell do you mean "nothing of interest"? Do you know this place? This is Neukölln! It used to be a quiet, lovely neighbourhood before these bloody foreigners turned up. My wife and I thought we would settle down here. Retire in comfort and spend the last few years of our lives in peace here before giving up the ghost. So what did we do? We saved up and bought ourselves a house here, didn't we? And then what happens? First the Turks, then the Arabs and then the bloody Iranians come swarming in. And if that isn't enough, those punks who think they're bloody artists turn up too and start occupying houses left, right and centre. Every day there's a new incident. Some fight or commotion or bickering. "Nothing of interest" she says! Bullshit!'

Tobias had been listening all along on the other side of the car and could take no more. He got out of his coverall, threw it away and began walking angrily back towards them. Luckily, Yıldız saw him and raised her hand.

'You may be right, sir, but we cannot do anything about the things you have just mentioned. Now, would you please just return home?'

The old man had noticed Tobias walking towards them. He turned to confront Tobias.

'And now you're attacking me, eh? Instead of protecting me, you protect this bloody foreigner. You should be bloody ashamed of yourself. It's because of traitors like you that we're losing.'

'You're the one that should be ashamed!' Tobias erupted. 'Foreigners, eh? What foreigners? The person you are insulting happens to be a German police officer. A police officer who risks life and limb every day so you can sleep safely at night. An officer whom you are also, incidentally, obstructing in the course of her duties. And anyway, how do you know there's been a murder? Or are you involved in it as well? Eh?'

The man's expression changed instantly into one of astonishment.

'What the hell are you on about? How the hell could I commit a murder? In my state, at my age? I overheard the guys at the buffet stand on the corner talking, that's all.'

Tobias pretended not to believe him and looked him up and down.

'So you're not a part of it then, eh? Is that what you're saying?'

For the first time that evening, there was trepidation in the man's eyes.

'I told you, I was on my way home.'

'Then go home,' Tobias said, pointing in exasperation at the old man's house. 'We have things to do. Stop wasting our time. Unless you want me to file charges against you for obstructing police work?'

The old man hesitated before angrily pulling back.

'Alright, alright, I'm going. But I'm going to complain about this. You're blocking the entrance to my house.'

He then turned and began trudging away, but he was still moaning.

'And even if I do complain, what will happen? Nothing. They've even infiltrated the police. Taken over the whole bloody country, they have... They're the ones killing each other and then they're also the ones leading the investigations. Police and thieves, all one and the same nowadays. If I go ahead complain, they'll only go and chuck me in prison too...'

Tobias stared angrily at the man as he walked off.

'Senile old fool. Like I forced him to buy a house in Neukölln.'

Yıldız playfully punched Tobias on the shoulder.

'Come on, Toby, take it easy. Don't let it get to you. He's just a grumpy old man. And he's right too, in his own way. He has his reasons. This place has been going downhill of late.'

Although she was doing her best to calm him down, she was also uneasy at what had just transpired. It was not her first experience of such bigotry. As a child, she used to encounter the same xenophobic attitudes when playing on the streets with the other kids and it used to upset her terribly.

At school, her classmates would often ignore her and she had also been subject to subtle taunts by some of the teachers too. She couldn't understand why they did it and she used to cry for hours and sometimes even refuse to go to school. One day, however, she decided to do something about it. She began to fight back. She started to speak up, she complained and then, one day, she lost control and punched one of the girls in her class in the face. Naturally, she was punished for it and her father gave her a sound telling-off but nothing changed, not on the streets nor in school. That is how she learnt that the answer to bigotry was not violence, even though she knew that xenophobia was like a virus that could not be eradicated. As soon as it had the chance, it took over a person's soul. That is why she was delighted when her son Deniz had blond hair and dark blue eyes just like his father when he was born because at least having those features meant he would not stick out as an outsider and so there was less chance of him being bullied. That is also why she named him Deniz; so that the Germans would call him Deniz and have no problem pronouncing his name.

The name Deniz remained but around three months after he was born, his blue eyes turned a dark shade of brown and a year later, his hair also turned dark brown. He was a handsome lad, though, with pale skin like his maternal grandmother's that contrasted beautifully with his dark eyes and dark hair. She was actually pleased that her son looked like his grandmother but there was no getting away from the fact that he was going to have to deal with racism his whole life the way his mother had. She had wanted to believe that this particular evil would be eliminated from the world by the time he became an adult but reality was something else. Indeed, it seemed now that the xenophobes in the country were becoming more and more outspoken and more and more emboldened by the day. It was astounding that a country that had produced so many brilliant philosophers, statesmen and scientists and which had suffered perhaps more than any other from racism could not defend itself from this poison. Like an unstoppable virus, fascism continued to pose a threat to society. She suddenly had an urge to smoke. To do what Toby had done a few minutes ago and light one up and suck that smoke deep into her lungs. Of course, she was not going to do it but... She turned to look at Cemal Ölmez's flat. There were shadows flickering in the window of the room in which the body had been found.

'The Crime Scene Unit have their work cut out for them,' she murmured. 'The killer set the place up wonderfully. He or she is clearly the meticulous type. He probably hasn't left a single clue behind.'

Tobias grinned.

'Kurt says the same. He says they're set for an all-nighter in there.'

Yıldız smiled in appreciation.

'I trust Kurt. I know he'll do his best up there. So, come on. We should go and do our best too.'

As Yıldız made her way to the driver's seat, her assistant stared at her in bewilderment before complying. While she was still getting in, Tobias, with an agility unexpected for someone of his size, was already seated and ready.

'So,' he laughed. 'Where are we going? Rafael's?'

Yıldız crinkled up her nose.

'You're stinking the car up, Toby. Seriously. I'm not even joking. I'm warning you. Either you quit or you at least refrain from smoking when you're with me...' She then turned around and started the engine. Her assistant was silent. 'And no, we'll talk to Rafael tomorrow. I reckon we should go to The Tartarus theatre first and have a little chat with the deceased's lover. This drummer fellow called Alex. Let's hear what he has to say.'

'Sounds good,' said Tobias gleefully, unfazed by the stern dressing-down he'd just received. 'Let's go. I haven't been to the theatre in ages.'

2
What you did to me shall be brought upon you.

I shall begin where you have forgotten. I shall begin writing from the very beginning. So that you shall never forget again. So that it shall forever be in your minds. So that my presence shall be felt in your bodies like a second heart. I shall tell of the times when neither the Titans, the Giants, the Gods, you humans nor the other creatures of the world existed. When the earth was not yet ready for life. When the light had yet to descend upon us. Yes, I shall tell of that profound darkness, of that vast infinity, of that grand void.

Yes, in the beginning was darkness. A darkness without frontier, without beginning or end, an endless darkness that crashed onto no coast or shore, which surrounded and enveloped everything, all of us. It was in this darkness that life first began to stir. It was this infinite darkness that was the first and the originator. Clouds the size of suns roamed within it, clouds of yellow, blue, red and green. Worlds collided, and beautiful Gods were born of these collisions. There were explosions the size of suns, such that a scream of rage lay hanging in the heart of the darkness. When I speak of darkness, do not think of an emptiness, for I speak of a living creature, a vast creature with long and deep breaths that lives in the uncharted and unknown depths of the underworld, the scales along its back glistening as its glides and moves and shuffles.

It is from this darkness that Gaia, the mother of my mother, was born and it was she that gave birth to us all. It was she that created the life that trembled in the infinite darkness. She was the embodiment of fire cooled to rock, of rock crushed into stone, and of stone crumbling into fertile soil. Gaia was fertile, warm and moist. She was ready. To procreate was her inescapable destiny, and so she created the mighty Uranus so that he may impregnate her. Uranus, father of my despotic father, lord of the radiant skies, the seed of seeds. Gaia then transformed the entire earth into a bridal chamber. Because for the female, the act of love is not merely to come into union; it is also an act of beauty, elegance and tenderness. That is why she created snow-topped mountains with purple skirts, wild grains to colour and adorn the fertile plains, deep valleys decorated with pine trees, long rivers with banks bejewelled by flowers, and sweet, blue seas… When the largest, the most beautiful, the most colourful, the purest and most fragrant bed was ready in the centre of that infinity, she beckoned to Uranus, who had been awaiting her call. The vast sky approached her. He held her and he lustfully sunk his teeth into the neck of the most fertile female of them all. Suddenly, light erupted in the darkness, the wind became a pleasant whisper, the mountains, plains and valleys were caressed by the softest of touches, touches that soon increased in force. A dance of beauty that had never been seen before began and a wild scent that had never before been sensed emanated forth in all directions. My grandfather Uranus gathered unto himself all his strength and took Gaia as his and thus were born the twelve Titans, one of whom was to become my father. Thus, also, were born the single-eyed, one hundred-armed, fifty-headed creatures that made the mountains tremble.

And yet, whilst the creatures begat of the Gods were to live in bliss in this paradise, Uranus was displeased with those that fell from his seed unto the earth. Instead of taking his children in his strong arms and lifting them up in glory to the sun, he buried them deep in the earth. Gaia, mother of our mother, was distraught by this act. How could her husband be ashamed of his own wondrous progeny? For a female, if there is any being more important than her husband, it is her children. Regardless of whether they are foul of appearance or character, the mother distinguishes not. And if she has to choose between her spouse and her children, she shall, without hesitation, choose those that have issued forth from her body, even more so when the father of her children is in the wrong. And this is what Gaia did. The spouse she created for herself she cursed, but there were none willing to enact the curse so she became the one to fulfil it, with the help of her own issue.

Gaia had decided upon her course of action, but none of her children wished to join her in her bloody scheme. They shrunk before their father's awesome power. From the void into which they had been buried, they watched what was to be. Fortune favours the brave, and the one that would dethrone their father and put an end to his tyranny would be the bravest of the twelve Titans. Most loving and most beloved of their mother, and, like the father that he would depose in a bloody ambush, one that was merciless towards his own progeny. Kronos, my own, dear father.

For Kronos, Mother Earth fashioned a scythe of steel that burnt like the fire of the Sun and which cleaved in two any object it touched. She handed it to her son and said:

'Take this. Take this and depose him. Children that live in their father's shadow are doomed to remain children. Those that are bound to their father can never be free. Sons that shelter under their father's mercy do not possess the right to live.' She thrust the scythe into Kronos' hands. 'Hide it,' she said firmly. 'And every morning and every evening, hone it with hatred, fury and conviction. Sharpen it such that it shall slash the despot that is your father without needing your touch. Show no mercy to that brute Uranus. Let this weapon render the tyrant that has brought us such misery impotent.'

My father Kronos took the scythe and, with a solemnity worthy of the Titans, replied:

'Rest assured, beloved Mother, I shall bring righteousness to bear upon the tyrant. I shall end the rule of this father that could not be a father. No more shall he sit upon a throne he has not deserved. With your permission and support, I shall become ruler of all the creatures of the worlds, and I shall rule all with love, justice and care. None shall be unhappy under my rule.'

Patiently, he waited for the opportune moment, and that moment would be when Uranus' mind was warped by lust, when he was drowning in the rivers of ecstasy, when he was holding Gaia in his arms. He did not have to wait long. When the sun warmed the blue orb and the blood flowed in the veins of the lustful sky, he felt the need to embrace Gaia. He sent forth his mating cry and the sky rumbled and lightning flashed and the mountains were struck by thunderbolts. He opened his arms in desire for Gaia the way he always did and the sky, suspecting nothing, descended unto the earth, ready for the act of copulation. As he was about to enclose his wife in his arms, Kronos leapt out from behind a huge rock and, with one fell swoop, he severed his father's essence, the source of the seed that had given Kronos life. A terrifying scream pierced eternity, a cry of pain that was heard even amongst distant stars. It was done. Uranus had lost his manhood, and the drops of blood that fell from his severed member gave birth to new species on the soil of Mother Earth; monstrosities of unimaginable appearance, freaks and ogres with legs like serpents and the bodies of strange Giants. And this act of terrible revenge passed from lip to lip and travelled from ear to ear until it became myth, and Uranus in his agony cursed his son:

'May the evil you have inflicted upon me be inflicted upon you. May you and your rule be ended at the hands of your progeny.'

Chapter Two

'Leipzig never used to be like this.' Tobias was staring at the throngs of men and women standing on the pavement outside the bars and cafés lining the street holding their bottles of beer and their glasses of wine. 'Back where I come from, everything shuts down after nine. Everyone goes home. Sure, we have bars, cafés and restaurants and people that visit them but nothing like this. Look at this, will you? The pavement is crawling with people.' He laughed, for some inexplicable reason. 'It's like we're in another country. Not Germany.'

Yıldız, behind the wheel of the Passat, took her eye off the road for a second to cast a quick glance at the crowds.

'You should see Istanbul then, Toby. There's a place there called Beyoülu. Heaving every night, it is. No room to swing a cat. This is nothing.'

'Were you born in Istanbul, boss?' her assistant asked. Yıldız shook her head.

'No, I was born and raised in Berlin. My parents lived in Istanbul before they came to Germany.'

Tobias was enjoying the conversation.

'What did they do out there?'

Yıldız smiled.

'They were activists working for a trade union. Haven't I told you about them before?'

Tobias tugged uncomfortably on his seatbelt.

'Actually, you haven't. I do know that you lost your mother... You bought some flowers for her grave the other day.'

Yıldız sighed.

'That's right. Unfortunately, my mother just couldn't get used to Berlin...' The memory was upsetting but she did not let it overwhelm her. 'But they didn't come here to work, my parents. When the 12 September military coup took place in Turkey in 1980, their party smuggled them out of the country.'

'Which party?' Tobias asked, his curiosity mounting. Yıldız answered without hesitating.

'The Turkish Communist Party. But eventually the party abolished itself. When the Soviet Union collapsed, the party collapsed too. Wait! Hold on a minute! I have more important things to tell you.' She shook her head, as though in regret. 'How could I not have told you this? When they came to Germany for the first time, do you know where they ended up?'

A few possibilities flashed through Tobias' grey eyes but he did not offer any guesses. His boss did not make him wait much longer.

'Your city, Toby. Leipzig!'

'You're joking?' Tobias said, fidgeting in his seat. 'What were they doing in Leipzig? And during the communist era too?'

Yıldız was surprised he could not make the connection.

'That's precisely why they went there, Toby — because the communists were in charge. The Soviet Union and Socialist Bloc countries were helping left-wing parties and organizations in capitalist countries so when my mother and father fled Turkey, which they did with fake passports, they came to the German Democratic Republic, via Bulgaria, because a great many high-ranking members of the Turkish Communist Party were in Leipzig at the time. After attending the party conference and meeting the directors, my parents were planning on returning to Turkey to campaign against the military dictatorship but mass arrests started taking place in Turkey and many of their friends were arrested. Unfortunately, some of them broke during torture and talked and my parents ended up at the top of a wanted persons list. Going back to Turkey was too risky and so the party decided to grant them the status of political refugees and they ended up in West Berlin.'

Tobias was listening on amazement.

'My father was also a member of the party at the time, but he was not what you would call a believing communist. He was a civil servant.' She paused for a moment before continuing. 'My grandfather was, though, and remained so till his dying day.'

A strange smile appeared on Tobias' face.

'Wow, boss. You and I seem to have so much in common.' He suddenly fell silent, and looked away in embarrassment. 'You know, I've never been to Turkey. Not even for a holiday…' Then he laughed. 'But I had a friend in high school. Herbert. Herbert Brigel… He went to Turkey many times. And not just Istanbul but to some other city. Somewhere deep in the heart of Anatolia.'

'Was it Ankara? The capital?'

'No, it wasn't Ankara. I know Ankara, boss. Some place called Kayzer or something. It's famous for making a kind of smoked meat similar to bacon. You know, like the stuff the Americans and the Brits have for breakfast…. This Turkish smoked meat is really spicy and really tasty, too.'

Yıldız knew exactly what he meant.

'You mean *pastırma*? And the city of Kayseri?'

Tobias thumped a large hand on his knee.

'That's it! That's the one. Herbert had only just finished high school too and he didn't know any Turkish either, apart from one or two words.'

'Why did he go?' Yıldız asked, fascinated. Tobias shuffled his large body around in the seat again.

'It's actually quite a nice story... Our Herbert was head over heels in love with this Turkish girl. Songül, her name was. A darker girl, though. Not like you. She was tall, with jet black hair and sort of brown, earthy-coloured eyes. Not hazel, but more....'

'Amber?'

Tobias thought about it.

'Let's say light brown. Anyway, she was a sweet lass, and she was our Herbert's first love. This Songül wasn't totally uninterested in him, either. They used to meet in secret, without her family knowing. But when Songül's father passed away, everything changed. The poor fellow had a heart attack one day and the family couldn't get him to the hospital on time and so he died. With the father dead, the family decided to move back to Turkey. Herbert was distraught, naturally, because he was head over heels in love with this Songül but there was nothing he could do. Songül, her mum and her two brothers moved back to Turkey but Herbert just could not forget about her so he worked hard all summer and saved up and in the autumn he hopped on a plane and flew to the city they had moved to. I could never have done it. Can you imagine? He doesn't know the girl's address, and he doesn't know anybody in the entire city either. But that was Herbert for you. Not only did he go over, he actually found her too! And he was still only eighteen. Nothing to do with luck or the Gods. It was pure chance. He told me all about it when he got back to Leipzig.

'So when our lovestruck Herbert landed, he booked himself into a hotel. Then he went down to reception and asked the guy there about the girl and her family. Of course, the receptionist didn't have a clue. In a city of hundreds of thousands of people, how the hell would he know this one particular girl? But Herbert was not one to give up. And what is love, after all, boss, if it isn't hope, eh? So, the next day, as soon he gets up, he writes the girl's name and surname on a piece of paper, goes to the town square and sits on a bench in front of some old castle they have out there. He shows the people that sit next to him the piece of paper and asks about Songül's family but of course, none of them have heard of them either but still he sits there and asks anyone and everyone that walks past. Eventually, some policemen nearby notice this strange kid who is clearly from out of town sitting in the middle of the town square showing random people a piece of paper and asking them questions so they call him over. They asked him who he was and what he was doing there but our Herbert didn't know Turkish so he didn't understand a word of what they were saying. Things were getting complicated until a young university student came along and helped him out. Herbert explained in English what he was doing, and she translated for him. The police were bowled over by the story and took him to the station, where they found someone that knew German and translated for the boy and the station Superintendent. The Superintendent was also moved by the story but he was a little more cautious than his officers.

"'Now look here, son," he said in an avuncular tone. "I admire your passion. But this is not Germany. Things are very different here. Our traditions and our way of doing things are not like yours. The girl's family may not take kindly to what you are doing here. You may wind up getting get hurt."

'But Herbert was so besotted, nothing could stop him.

"'Thank you for the warning but nothing will happen to me. All I ask of you is that you find Songül for me. Please."

'The Superintendent replied, "Kid, this is not a laughing matter. Fine, we'll find this Songül for you but let me talk to her family first. If they say they know you and that you can come and see them, then fine, we'll take you there ourselves. But if they don't like what you have done here and are angered by it, you're just going to have to accept it and go back to Germany. Got it?"

'Sensing the Superintendent's sincerity, Herbert agreed. The next day, they actually went and found this Songül's family and they called Herbert to the station. Unfortunately, when he got there, Herbert did not see Songül waiting for him but a middle-aged man instead. He shook Herbert's hand and introduced himself. "I'm Songül's maternal uncle. Welcome to Kayseri. But let me also tell you that what you are doing is not right. We like having guests, yes, but we do not like this sort of thing. I don't know what goes on in Germany, and I don't want to know. But the sooner you realize that what you are doing is both wrong and futile, the better for everyone. Songül is engaged anyway, and is due to be married in the spring. So you can go back home now, back to your own country, and find yourself a nice German girl. Otherwise things will get very unpleasant for you here."

'"So that's how it is, son," the Superintendent said kindly. "You had better forget about this girl."

'Herbert was devastated but he still wasn't ready to give in.

'"Fine, I'll go back to Germany but please let me speak to Songül, just once. If she says it is over, I'll be on the first plane back."

'The uncle was now showing signs of displeasure and he started walking menacingly towards Herbert, forcing the Superintendent to step in between them. After that, the Superintendent took Herbert to one side and, with the help of the interpreter, said, "Now listen up, son. You had better start thinking straight. You don't know what you're doing. You're actually in danger now. You are going to be on the next flight to Germany."

'But would he listen? No. He dug his heels in and proclaimed, "I don't care. Great. I'll go. But I won't leave this place without seeing Songül." The Superintendent and the uncle went into another room and talked for a long time. An hour passed, when suddenly Songül walked into the room Herbert was in. He was so excited, he could barely stand up but she was having none of it and acted as though she barely knew him.

'"Why are you here? Why are you harassing me like this? You've shamed me in front of my entire family," she hissed. That was it for Herbert. The poor lad slumped on his stool and sobbed while Songül walked out just as haughtily as she'd walked in. It was left to the Superintendent to console the poor devastated Herbert.

'"See, son? See how the girl you risked so much for treated you? You came all this way to see her and she doesn't even want to know you. She says you're harassing her. If this girl had any feelings for you, she would not have behaved like that. But look at this way; your journey has not been in vain. At least now you realize that this girl does not deserve your love."

'They were kind words from the Superintendent but Herbert was too distraught to notice. Nevertheless, the Superintendent made sure the adventure ended there. He took Herbert out to dinner that evening and the next morning he sent him back to Germany on a plane via Istanbul.'

'Then what happened?' Yıldız asked, who had been listening in silent amazement. 'Did Herbert manage to get over his Turkish lover and move on when he got back to Germany?'

'He did,' Tobias laughed. 'He found another Turkish lover.'

Yıldız began laughing. 'Looks like your Herbert knows his women. He got a taste of Turkish women and that was that. He never looked back.' Tobias did not laugh, though, and they both fell silent for a while.

'How's it going with that Samira of yours?' Yıldız eventually asked.

'We broke up last week,' Tobias mumbled glumly.

'No way!' Yıldız said. She was genuinely upset for him. 'She looked like a decent girl. Pretty, too.'

'She was a decent girl and she was pretty, yes, but I guess that's not enough...'

Yıldız knew that if she pressed him, Tobias would let it all out but she chose not to as she had no right or desire to probe a colleague about his private life. They drove on past rows of lit-up shop windows without speaking.

'So, is this Pergamon place far from Istanbul?' Tobias asked. 'Is it near Kayseri?'

Yıldız was glad the subject matter had changed.

'No, it's quite far from both. It's in Western Anatolia, one of the ancient cities founded by the Greeks on the Aegean coast. But it's very impressive. It's not just because of the Altar of Zeus. Even now, the ancient city of Pergamon looks incredible. It's built on top of a hill and overlooks a vast plain... The old palaces, the temples, the theatre and the library... They are all ruins now, of course, but the spot itself is still a sight to behold. Just imagine what it would have looked like with the Altar of Zeus still in place. It must have been a stunning sight.'

Because he had seen neither Pergamon nor the Altar of Zeus, Tobias, to his great embarrassment, was having trouble visualizing the scene.

'I really should go to Turkey and see this city,' he declared. Yıldız shot him a mocking glance.

'Before travelling thousands of miles to go all the way to Turkey, why not travel twenty minutes down the road to see the Pergamon Museum? Admittedly, it's closed at the moment as restoration work is being carried out on the Altar but it's not going to stayed closed forever.'

Yıldız went back to watching the road, while Tobias nodded in agreement.

'Absolutely. You're right, boss. I really should go and see this Altar…'

A strange smile appeared on Yıldız's face.

'That would be great. But don't see it as an Altar on which murders were committed. When you go, look at it as a peerless structure that was once considered the eighth wonder of the world. Pergamon belongs to all of mankind. It is part of our shared cultural heritage.'

Yıldız knew Oranien Street well as they had lived there for five years when she was a child. Due to the war, a number of buildings in the street had been abandoned and during the Cold War, it was considered a dangerous area as the Berlin Wall ran through the neighbourhood. As a result, rents were low and the municipality kept rent prices down in order to encourage migrant workers to move to the area. However, over time, rents and prices in the area began to go up and developers began eyeing up the buildings, only this time they were met with resistance. Protest groups began moving in and occupying the buildings. Their slogan was *'Housing is a right and will be taken by force if necessary.'* That is how the occupation of the buildings began, which then led to barricades and street clashes. The conflict lasted years, and in the end, the neighbourhood turned into one of Berlin's most colourful places, a self-made enclave of freedom that was an explosion of colour and culture in the middle of Kreuzberg, made up of Turks, Arabs, Germans and people from all over the world. As a child, Yıldız used to see men and women with wild and wonderful haircuts, dyed all sorts of manic colours, wearing bizarre clothing and sprawled in front of the bars with their bottles of beer, kissing openly without a care in the world.

Yıldız's mother's feminist friends' local association was housed on that street, a small room whose walls were covered in bright colourful posters proudly proclaiming and defending the rights of women, in German, English and Turkish. They liked Yıldız too, but she had never considered joining their group, for reasons she could not work out. Perhaps it was her mother's early death and her experiences of those trying events in Turkey. Moreover, as the daughter of a left-wing, activist family, she had made the rather sudden and unexpected decision to join the police. Her ex-husband Franz used to say that she had chosen that job because she was scared. 'So you can live more securely in Germany,' he used to say. Yıldız did not agree and would respond by saying, 'I was born in this city. Why should I be afraid of the country of my birth? I chose this profession because I love it.'

She was right. She had always had a fondness for the police and used to love the characters of female officers in television serials, especially in *Tatort*, a TV crime series that had been running in Germany for years. She always looked forward to the evenings when a new episode was to be aired. No, she had never wanted to be one of those old punks on Oranien Street or like her parents' left-wing friends, who could go months without leaving the house. She had simpler dreams, but they were also dreams that would have driven her father mad had he found out about them. In the end, she made the dreams come true. Interestingly, it was not a scene from a favourite TV show featuring a heroic policewoman but a real-life incident that took place in Dresden that made Yıldız decide upon her career. Years earlier, an Egyptian woman had been stabbed to death—in a courtroom, no less, and in front of the judge and lawyers—by a German citizen against whom she had filed a formal complaint. She was three months pregnant when she was killed. She was stabbed a full eighteen times and for months, argument and debate raged on as to how the killer had managed to sneak a dagger into a courtroom. There were news reports stating that he was given tacit support by xenophobes within the state apparatus but the ensuing investigations came up with nothing. Yıldız had been shaken to the core by the events and that same evening, while watching the news, she decided to become a policewoman. As such, there was more than a grain of truth in what her husband had said about her career choice, as being a police officer certainly did provide a level of protection for her. In fact, when things began to get messy in her marriage, she was able to use the advantages of being a police officer to send him packing, even though Franz happened to be a policeman too. But these were the effects of her choosing to join the police, rather than the causes. So, yes, it was confusing, which is why she had not been able to tell her parents. When they found out and expressed their disapproval, she left home and did not return. It was only when her mother died that she returned, as only an event that tragic could repair the rift that had opened up between her and her father.

It was midnight but most of the shops on Oranien Street were still open: people still thronged the bars, cafes, beerhalls, shisha cafes, pizzerias, kebab joints, sweetshops, off-licences and convenience stores. Only the *Dante Connection* bookshop, which Yıldız loved to visit and browse, had lowered its shutters. If Berlin was Germany's most unusual city, then Kreuzberg was its most unusual neighbourhood, and Oranien was its most colourful street.

'Isn't that the theatre over there?' Tobias asked, bringing her out of her reverie. 'See? Over there on the right…'

Yıldız had mistakenly thought they were at the end of the street.

'That's it, the door next to the sculpture studio.'

Tobias was excited.

'Great. We'll listen to some metal…'

'I never knew you liked heavy metal?' Yıldız asked in surprise. Tobias seemed vaguely upset by the remark.

'I did, and I still do. I even formed a band in high school with some friends. I played electric guitar.'

'Wow. That's great, Toby. Bravo!'

Her assistant turned his bulky body to face his boss.

'Why are you so surprised? I don't get it.'

Not wanting to upset him, Yıldız reached out and touched his hand.

'I'm sorry, Toby, it's just that when thinking of policemen, we sometimes get lazy and give in to stereotypes. You know, this idea of the rough and ready cop who has no sense of fun and only cares about his work. I'm sorry, really.'

'No need to apologize, boss,' Tobias said, looking ahead again. 'What about you? Do you like music?'

A modest smile appeared on Yıldız's lips.

'Actually, I do. I listen to all kinds. Anything except this damn techno music. I just can't get my head round it.'

Tobias' eyes lit up at the memory of something.

'You guys have this one type of music where these guys stand on the spot and spin around and around. Really powerful stuff, that is.'

'You mean the *sema*? The one with the guys in long white robes spinning around?'

'No, not them. This is men and women wearing insanely colourful costumes and dancing together in a circle. The music is really upbeat and it keeps getting faster and faster.'

Yıldız laughed and nodded her head.

'You're talking about the Alevis. That dance of theirs is known as the *semah*. It's actually a religious ceremony, depicting the circle of life.'

Tobias' mood had lifted.

'It's awesome. I love music from other cultures.' There was a pause before he went on. 'Are you a religious person, boss?'

Yıldız did not mind the question. In fact, she found her assistant's curiosity charming.

'Not particularly, as you can guess, growing up as the daughter in an atheist family. My mother's family were Sunni Muslims and my father's side were Alevi, but neither of them were interested in religion. They believed in morality. In goodness and truth. They were the most honest people I have ever known. Like I said, I am not particularly religious but I do like both the Mevlevi and the Alevi rituals. I think they're wonderful.'

Yıldız slowed the Passat down and steered it towards the pavement. They had arrived at the Tartarus.

'What the hell kind of door is this?' Tobias growled, staring at the theatre. 'They've drawn a picture of a hooded man dressed from head to toe in black. And look, he is holding a double-ended staff and there is a creature by his feet.' He squinted, trying to get a better grasp of what he was seeing. 'What the hell is this? It looks like a dog but it's got three heads. I swear, seeing this people would be too scared to even enter.'

Yıldız parked the car by the pavement and looked scornfully at Tobias.

'Didn't they teach you any mythology at school? You've been getting it wrong the whole night! Look, the figure in the painting on the door is Hades, brother of Zeus, God of the Underworld. One end of his staff represents life, the other death. The three-headed dog at his feet is Cerberus, the watchdog of the underworld. Don't tell me you haven't heard of them?'

Tobias looked away sheepishly.

'Erm, of course I have. Who doesn't know about Hades?' He scratched his neck. 'Zeus' brother, eh? So, another Greek God! Do you think this Alex really did murder Cemal?'

His voice came out a little muffled. Yıldız was not as flustered as Tobias.

'I don't know. What Pilar told us, all that stuff about mythology. It's hard to say right now. We've only just arrived on the scene.' She let out a sigh. 'As you can see, if Alex did do it, then it will soon be revealed. If he did, then it looks like he basically sacrificed Cemal to Zeus. He basically performed a ritual, almost as an example to others. As though he wanted everyone to know.'

Tobias blinked anxiously.

'If this is all there is to it, fine. What I mean is, if this is as far as the ritual goes.'

He was right. Killing someone with an accompaniment of art, music and a light show and ripping out the victim's heart and placing it in his hand seemed less like a gory final act and more the sinister inception of a sequence that could very well increase in violence and bloodlust. Yıldız hoped they would be proven wrong.

'There is only one way to find out,' she said, unbuckling her seatbelt. 'Let's go in and talk to this guy.'

On the pavement where they had parked their Passat, a waif-like girl with oriental eyes and dreadlocks and a man weighing at least one hundred and fifty kilos with blue beads in his beard were leaning against a wall drinking wine. They looked Yıldız and Tobias up and down and then went back to their conversation. Just then, Yıldız thought she heard a *davul* and *zurna*, the traditional instruments played during Anatolian weddings. She turned around. She wasn't wrong: a wedding party convoy, led by a black open-top BMW followed by a good seven or eight cars, rushed past. The music was coming full blast from one of the car stereos.

'Your lot,' Tobias chuckled. 'Announcing to the whole world that they're going to be getting it on tonight.'

Yıldız ignored him. She was focusing on the poster on the wall next to the Tartarus' front door. In gothic lettering were the words *The Gorgons' Grin*, while underneath it read *A Musical for Mortals about the Immortals*.

'Let's go, Toby. As mere Mortals, let's go and watch this show about Immortals and see what all the fuss is about.'

They opened the door with the painting of Hades and walked through. Inside, instead of a corridor, they found themselves face to face with a canoe. Or rather, a narrow entrance way painted jet-black that looked like a canoe. A huge, ugly man stopped in front of them and blocked their way.

'What is it?' Tobias asked. 'What do you want?'

The man held up two fingers.

'Twenty euros each. That's forty euros.'

'We're the police, we have come here to talk to someone.'

The man opened his eyes in surprise.

'Then you can wait here for the show to end.'

Tobias was about to object when Yıldız stepped in front of him and handed over forty euros. The man took the money and handed over four metal tokens, with a picture of Hades similar to the one seen on the door outside on one side and the name 'Tartarus' written in Greek on the other side.

Yıldız took the tokens, kept two for herself and gave the other two to her assistant, who stared down at them in bemusement.

'What the hell are these?'

Yıldız looked at him sardonically.

'I thought you said you knew your mythology?' She nodded

her head in the direction of the doorman. 'See? That's Charon, the ferryman. He carries the souls of the dead across the sacred river and takes them to Hades. These metal tokens represent the coins that were given to Charon as payment for his services. The theatre must have had the tokens specially made.'

The Conzemporary Charon who was listening also seemed indifferent to mythology.

'One of the tokens is for the musical, the other buys you a beer,' he informed them drily. 'Any brand you like.'

Yıldız let out a little laugh.

'You've destroyed all the charm and mystique of the ferryman, my friend. Charon carried the souls of the dead to the Underworld and here you are selling beer.'

Before the man could answer, she turned to Tobias.

'These coins were usually placed on the eyes of the deceased, who would then give them to the ferryman Charon so he would transport them across the river.'

Tobias looked at his two coins but still did not understand.

'Fair enough. So where is this Tartarus?'

'Walk down the stairs and you'll find the theatre two floors underground,' the doorman answered. Yıldız tapped Tobias on the shoulder.

'The mythological Tartarus was also many floors below the Underworld.' She turned to the living Charon. 'Has Alex started playing?'

Charon pointed to his ears. 'Can't you hear him? He's playing right now.'

As they began walking towards the staircase at the end of the narrow corridor, they heard such an intense wailing, it was hard to tell what was being played. 'Black Sabbath,' Tobias muttered when they reached the stone staircase. 'They're playing Black Sabbath. This track is a classic.'

Yıldız did not know the song. As they made their way down the stairs, a strong male voice could be heard screaming the lyrics: '*Big black shape with eyes of fire / Telling people their desire / Satan's sitting there, he's smiling…*'

'Satan's standing there and smiling?' Yıldız asked, bemused by the song.

'It is one of the first ever heavy metal songs,' Tobias explained. 'One day, Geezer Butler, the group's bass player, saw some people waiting in line at a cinema to watch a horror movie called *Black Sabbath* and he suddenly had an idea for a song. He went straight to Ozzy Osbourne to tell him about it and soon the two of them had a song. They also changed the name of the group they were forming to Black Sabbath.'

When they reached the bottom of the stairs, they found themselves in a huge basement, large enough to comfortably hold one hundred people. It had been converted into a theatre around a decade earlier but before that, during the Second World War, it had been one of the city's many bomb shelters. The theatre was now lit up by flashing red lights, just like the lights at the crime scene Yıldız and Tobias had just come from. Only around half of the seats in the theatre were occupied. While Tobias stood there looking disappointed, Yıldız narrowed her eyes to get a better feel for the surroundings. There were only a few youngsters in the crowd. Most of the audience were in their forties, and were headbanging in time to the music. There were just four musicians on stage in front of the temple-like stage prop. There were no actors anywhere, meaning it was probably an intermission. The musicians, like the audience, were middle-aged with long hair and long beards and were wearing leather clothing covered in metal studs and other such accessories.

The drummer at the back of the stage, the man they were looking for, caught both Yıldız and Tobias' attention. Although his hair and beard were an unkempt mess, he had a tough, stocky body which was pounding away at the drums and cymbals. His face was strained in concentration and his eyes were firmly shut, as though he was lost in an exhilarating dream. Could this really be the man who had carved open his lover's chest just a few hours ago, removed the heart and offered it as a sacrifice to Zeus?

'Incredible!' Tobias exclaimed, thrilled by the music. 'This guy really knows how to play! It's like he's in another world.'

Yıldız could barely hear him so she was forced to lean over and speak into Tobias' ear.

'They all are. It's like they're playing for themselves, rather than the audience.'

Tobias nodded in agreement.

'Absolutely. These guys are excellent musicians. Great musicians always play for themselves.'

While they spoke, the leather-clad old madman on stage was singing with an almost religious fervour : '*Is it the end, my friend / Satan's coming round the bend...*'

Alex's almost violet eyes, the softest part of his otherwise hard, stern countenance, were viewing them with suspicion. He had not been pleased to see these two strangers standing in front him when the show ended. They clearly were not fans of any type and he did not want to spend more time than necessary on them. 'I was in Cologne for a gig last night. I only just arrived today and I'll be setting off for Dresden in a bit. I don't have time for this,' he said standoffishly, hoping to get away as soon as he could. Of course, his wish was not granted. Yıldız, who only came up to Alex's chest, stood defiantly in front of him.

'You'll be on your way soon but we need to talk about Cemal first.'

Alex's indifferent expression turned to ice. The mention of the name was enough to throw him completely off balance.

'Don't tell me he's complained about me again?' he growled. 'I'm sick and tired of that guy!'

He looked so tense that Tobias feared he was going to lash out and he hurriedly stepped in. He stood between Alex and Yıldız and looked Alex straight in the eye.

'Calm down! We just want to talk. We have no intention in taking you in for questioning at this time of night. But of course, that's up to you. If you come with us to the bar in the foyer, we can talk there. After that, you'll be on your way.'

The drummer looked unconvinced. Yıldız opened up her hands in agreement with Tobias and said, 'That's all we want.'

The band's vocalist, a short man, was nearby and overheard the conversation.

'What's going on, Alex? Is everything okay?'

'It's nothing, Klaus,' the drummer replied coolly. 'Just a couple of mates joining me for a beer.'

So, Yıldız thought, *he does not want his friends to know that he is trouble with the police*. That was a good sign, this concern of his. She pointed to the narrow corridor.

'Let's go then.'

The walls of the foyer were covered in pictures dominated by red and black tones depicting mythological tales, all with the feel of a graphic novel. There were images of Titans buried up to their waists in the earth, as well as images of Giants and Gods. The darkness of Tartarus was depicted as a deep void at Zeus' feet. Yıldız chose the table at the far end of the wall with the painting of Zeus.

'Here, take a seat.'

She was watching the drummer carefully to see his reactions but Alex was indifferent to it all. He sat on one of the stools, his back to the wall, his mind clearly elsewhere. He impatiently eyed up the bottles of beer behind the bar.

'If it's no problem, can I have a beer?'

'Why would it be a problem?' Tobias asked, still standing. 'In fact, the beer is on us. We can't drink on duty and there's no point in letting these tokens go to waste. What would you like?'

'Flensburger...' Alex said, discreetly licking his dried lips.

'That's a nice, strong beer. I like that one too.'

Tobias walked off to the bar, while Yıldız looked at the King of the Gods on the wall and muttered, 'Children who do not kill their father are destined to never grow up...'

Alex turned to look at the picture.

'Zeus did not kill his father.' He pointed to the dark abyss at Zeus' feet. 'He sent him to Tartarus.'

Yıldız placed her elbows on the table, hoping to break the ice between them.

'You know your mythology.'

'I know a little. Just the basics, though. Cemal is the real expert. Listening to him, you'd think you were listening to an archaeologist. It runs in his family...' His gaze softened and his harsh features melted into a gentler expression. 'We met here, actually. At a cocktail organized by the company he works for.'

Yıldız was pleased at the way the conversation was progressing.

'What would an energy firm be doing holding cocktail parties in an underground theatre?'

Something akin to a smile appeared on the drummer's face.

'*Der Blitz* is not like most companies. It's in the renewable energy sector. You know, wind power, solar power, hydroelectric, that kind of stuff. They have flexible working hours at the firm. Staff are not required to come to the office so Cemal does most of his work at home. His boss is a weird guy. An East German, one of those that got rich when the Wall came down. But he's not one of those ghastly nouveau riche types. He's quite a sophisticated guy.' Even though he was praising the man, a shadow passed over Alex's face. 'He gets on well with his staff. Too well, in fact. That is why his business is going south.'

The recollection, Yıldız noticed, seemed enough to ruin Alex's mood.

'What is this unusual boss' name?'

'Peter,' the drummer replied, with a mixture of admiration and anger. 'Peter Schimmel.'

Yıldız remembered the way Pilar had said Alex envied Cemal. Yıldız had found the drummer's soft belly.

'As far as I know, he and Cemal also get on well.'

'Why are you asking me? Ask Cemal.' Alex replied angrily, the hostility he had displayed upon their first contact was now back. 'Let's cut to the chase, shall we? I don't know what Cemal has told you but I haven't touched him. Believe me.'

'So you admit that you have been violent towards him before?'

The drummer smirked.

'As if you don't know. It's all in the files. I'm sure you've read them. However, it is all reciprocal. He is violent towards me too.'

Tobias arrived carrying two bottles of Flensburger and, not knowing the topic of the conversation, inadvertently interrupted.

'Cheers!' he said, placing the bottles on the table, still in the role of the good cop. 'I got two, I hope you don't mind. I doubt it will be too much.'

'Thanks,' Alex said after a moment's hesitation before turning back to face Yıldız. 'Yes, we had a fight two days ago. But why has he waited two whole days to file a complaint?'

Seeing as there was no answer, he pulled one of the beers towards him, flicked the cap open and began drinking straight from the bottle, shunning the glass. After downing nearly half the bottle, he put it back on the table, wiped his mouth with the back of his right hand and exhaled deeply. The scent that is particular to beer wafted over the entire table.

'What did you fight about?' Tobias asked. 'Why did you beat Cemal up?'

'Beat up?' Alex laughed angrily. 'That's what I am trying to tell you. Who beat up whom is open to debate.' He reached out for the bottle again. 'He is no spring chicken himself. He is younger than me, after all. We hit each other all the time. Whoever is most sober is the one that does the hitting.' He downed the rest of the beer and put the bottle back, burping slightly as he did so. 'And do you want to know why we were fighting that day? Because we weren't getting along. The relationship has been fizzling out for some time. Perhaps we weren't right for each other from the start, what with the difference in culture and all that…'

Yıldız knew all too well how difficult cultural differences could be but something told her that Alex was not telling the truth.

'That's not what we heard. What we heard is that Cemal wanted to end it with you but you told him you would kill him if he tried.'

The drummer banged his hands on the table in surrender.

'I was furious that day. And anyway, it wasn't a fight, it was just a quarrel. A little tiff, that's all. If you don't believe me, ask Cemal's Argentinian neighbours. We were at their house when it happened…' He looked fed up. 'Cemal is lying. He's been very confused of late, and he's also been getting paranoid. Fair enough, we have odd fights, but I would never hurt him.'

He was so calm and so sure of himself, Yıldız could not wait any longer.

'Then who killed Cemal? Who sliced his chest open and cut his heart out?'

Alex froze. His hand, reaching out for the second beer, stopped in mid-air.

'What?' The look of complete assurance had gone. He pulled his hand back. 'What did you say?'

Both police officers were watching him intently, not wanting to miss even the slightest gesture or reaction.

'Yes, Mister Werner,' Yıldız went on in the same serene manner. 'Cemal Ölmez was brutally murdered in his flat in Neukölln this evening.'

The drummer had heard her but he was having trouble grasping what was being said. Or perhaps he had grasped it but did not want to believe it.

'And you threatened Cemal,' Yıldız went on. 'In the presence of your friends, you told him you would not let him live if he tried to leave you. Did you kill him?'

Alex seemed to be frozen on his stool.

'He's really... Cemal is really dead?' is all he managed to say. His eyes were wet with tears and his voice was shaking. 'Are you trying to have some fun at my expense? Is this one of Cemal's crummy pranks?' When he saw both police maintain their grim silence, his face fell. 'It's true? Cemal is really dead then, eh?'

There was a short silence, a silence that Yıldız had deliberately created as she wanted the suspect to have to deal with his feelings.

'Yes, Alexander Werner? You have not answered my question. Did you kill Cemal?'

The pain in the drummer's face, which had begun to show signs of aging, gave way to tension.

'What? Kill Cemal? Me? So now you're accusing me, is that it? Of course! We're the first people you think of, aren't we? A drummer in a heavy metal band. A wrong 'un. A devil child. A monster who would rip his lover's heart out. I get it.'

Tobias' deep voice cut through Alex's remonstrations.

'You should try and stay calm. If we were accusing you, you'd already be at the police station. We are simply trying to find Cemal's killer, that's all, and we've started with you because you're the first suspect. If you are not guilty of the crime, then help us and tell us what you know and we'll be able to find the killer more easily.'

Alex seemed emboldened by these words.

'Okay. Sure, I'll help you but let's get one thing straight: I'm no murderer. I did not kill Cemal.'

He reached out for the second beer but then Yıldız placed her hand on the bottle.

'What time did you get here?'

The drummer shrugged his broad shoulders.

'Same as always, around ten thirty. Around that time. The play starts at eleven thirty. We take the stage first, they come on after us…. What time was Cemal killed?'

It did not escape Yıldız's attention that he seemed to have recovered from the shock quite quickly and was now well enough to actually ask questions about the murder.

'Did you come here straight from home? Did you stop by anywhere else?'

Alex shook his head.

'I had no time to go home. I told you, we had a gig in Cologne yesterday. I got back to Berlin this evening by train. I had something to eat and then hung around here and there, killing time.'

The next question was ready.

'Do you have your train ticket?'

'No, I threw it away,' the drummer mumbled casually. 'I don't like carrying crap like that around in my pockets.'

He was speaking vaguely. Yıldız kept the pressure on.

'And where did you eat?'

He pointed to a far-off invisible place.

'At one of the buffets in the station. I wasn't even that hungry. Why do you ask? Look, this is my life, this is how I live. Wherever I find work, I play. That is how I get by. Like I said just now, I'm off to the train station once we are done here because we're playing in Dresden tomorrow. I won't have time to go home. I don't know why you keep hounding me. You're questioning the wrong man. I did not kill Cemal. I loved him. Do people kill the ones they love?'

Yıldız smiled wryly.

'Why, yes, they do… Most murder victims die at the hands of the ones they loved. And you have also been reported to have said that you were going to do it. There are two witnesses who can testify against you…'

He muttered angrily.

'That Pilar can't stand me anyway. But believe me, I did not kill Cemal.'

Yıldız stared at him for a few seconds.

'Then who did?'

'How the hell would I know?' Even though he was saying this, his eyes were darting around, a sign that he may be weighing up various possibilities. 'Hüseyin,' he said, with a hint of triumph. 'That's who. His older brother Hüseyin did it…. He hated Cemal. They all did, the entire family. But Hüseyin is the worst of the lot. He hated Cemal with a vengeance. And he has a criminal record. The guy is a madman.'

'Did Hüseyin hate his brother this much because of your relationship?'

Alex was not disturbed by the question.

'It's got nothing to do with me per se. They hadn't been talking for years. The family could not accept that their son was gay. Hüseyin went for him with a knife once. On another occasion, they almost threw Cemal out of a window.'

Such incidents were known to take place in Turkish families. Cemal's homosexuality could very well have been a factor in his murder.

'So, the whole family may have sided with the brother against Cemal?'

'The family disowned him. The only one that didn't was his grandfather, Orhan Dede. He was the only family member Cemal kept in touch with. And with his mother, secretly. They kept in touch over the phone. Neither his father nor his brother knew about these calls. Talk about bad luck, though; just last year, his grandfather came down with Alzheimer's so Cemal's visits stopped.' He nodded his head in conviction. 'Yes, it was that arsehole Hüseyin that did it. When he went to the hospital two months ago to visit Orhan Dede, he argued with Cemal and said he was not going to let him see their grandfather. Cemal didn't care, of course, and went ahead and saw the old man.'

This was something significant. The killer could well be this hate-filled brother. It was an exciting lead, true, but it was also never wise to concentrate on just one suspect in a murder investigation.

'Very well, we shall look into it. Did Cemal have any other enemies? People with whom he did not get on?'

Alex's eyebrows came together in a frown of concentration.

'No, he didn't have any enemies. But he had been acting weird of late. Like he was hiding something from me.' He paused, unsure as to what to say next. 'Don't use it against me, but I felt there was someone else. That is what caused the tension between us.'

'Another boyfriend?'

Finally able to drink his beer, Alex's face fell.

'Possibly. I think so. But if you ask me who, I really couldn't say because I don't know. Cemal seemed to be getting ready to break it up with me. That is what the fight at Pilar's was about. "Every day a love ends somewhere," Cemal had said to me. That we should be always be prepared for it. Of course, he was right, but I was blind drunk, and knowing he had been scheming behind my back just pushed me over the edge. I lost it.'

The clouds of suspicion had begun forming in Yıldız's hazel eyes again.

'But you managed to control your rage. You didn't kill him.'

'No, I didn't,' he replied, nodding his head firmly in assent.

Tobias wanted to change the subject.

'What do you know about the Zeus on the wall?'

The drummer turned around to look at the picture behind him.

'No, not this one. I mean the one in Cemal's house. The picture of Zeus on a throne.'

Alex narrowed his eyes, trying to work out in which direction the conversation was heading.

'Yeah, the picture of the statue of Zeus. Cemal painted it.'

'Did you want him to paint that picture?'

'No, it wasn't me,' Alex began, thinking a trap was being laid. 'Didn't you see the pictures of Zeus and the other Gods in the other rooms? Like I said, they were all into mythology as a family.'

'Well, I am into heavy metal but I do not decorate the walls of my house with pictures of metal musicians,' Tobias said disparagingly.

Alex took another large swig from his beer.

'Well, that makes sense. Neither do I. But Cemal loved painting. He always said he was an amateur but if you ask me, he was much better than that. He was really good. There is a museum over by the Spree River, the Pergamon Museum, which has these reliefs. I haven't been there, but Cemal described them to me. Said that the myths behind them were amazing and that he wanted to paint them in a more Conzemporary style. It was his way of proving himself. That is what he wanted to do. It had nothing to do with me. I don't know a thing about mythology or about art. I did not kill Cemal. I am not one of those monsters you described. Yes, we used to fight like cat and dog but then we always made up. Why would I kill someone I love?'

Even though it was almost dawn, the queue in front of Curry 36 went on and on, as though all of Berlin's revellers had decided to gather there. Elegant women in long evening gowns, men in tuxedos, youngsters in jeans and leather jackets, girls with piercings and mini-skirts, partygoers stepping out of all-night raves and blinking in confusion at the outside world, and drunkards and winos slurping on bottles of beer or wine as though they contained some kind of sacred elixir. People from all walks of life and of all shapes, sizes, colours and backgrounds mingling, joking and laughing as they waited patiently in line. Luckily for Tobias, there was only one person left ahead of him. When he saw his boss watching him from the car, he gave the V-sign, signalling an imminent end to their battle for currywurst.

Yıldız smiled back at her sweet assistant and then looked down at her smartphone screen to check up on her son. Once again, his blanket had slid off. She couldn't blame her father anymore as he must have gotten up God knows how many times to check up on the boy and make sure he was covered and warm. She knew what he would say, when she got home. 'That boy is definitely yours. He tosses and turns all over the place in his sleep.' Still, the weather was warming up so at least the kid would not be getting a cold. However, he had very sensitive tonsils and when he did fall ill, it lasted for days. His father was supposed to have spent this weekend with him but he had again come up with an excuse, the way he always did every week. This time, he had told her something important had come up and that he had to go to Hamburg for a Narcotics Department meeting. He loved his son dearly but when it came to his boat, everything else took a back seat, and she was sure that he had gone off on a boat trip again with his friends. Yıldız did not really care about his lack of responsibility. She looked up from the screen and saw that her assistant had arrived with two plastic plates topped with food and two cans of coke.

They had been working together for two years. At first, Yıldız had taken quite a dislike to this bulky young man. She even thought that Markus, her captain, an old-fashioned guy she did not trust an inch, had hatched a new plot against her. Markus was totally against having women in the force, and even more so on the homicide desk. 'They faint at the sight of blood,' he used to say. But by a strange twist of fate, a woman, and a Turkish one to boot, was placed under his command. At first, he had not taken Yıldız seriously but she turned out to be an excellent police officer, with eighty per cent of the cases she led being satisfactorily resolved. Despite her success, he would have had no hesitation in firing her but he was scared of angering the Greens and Socialists that made up the majority in the state legislature. So he decided to tolerate her, this admittedly tenacious woman, until the political situation turned in his favour. Naturally, Yıldız saw through Markus' schemes from the start and she had been dealing with chiefs like him ever since her first day on the job. When her partner Dieter, a tough, unflinching guy, had been left crippled in a car crash, Tobias was assigned as her partner and she began to suspect it was a deliberate ploy by Markus to assign her a bumbling fool to make her fail. But over the course of one particular investigation into the murder of an Albanian sex worker, she realized she had been mistaken about Tobias and that there actually was a keen mind behind his seemingly naïve and chubby face and that there was also a warm heart hidden behind those grey eyes that otherwise tricked you into thinking he was a cold, indifferent person.

Tobias, on the other hand, took to Yıldız almost immediately. Although most of the old East Germans did not take kindly to foreigners, he hit it off with his stern Chief Inspector straight away. Months into their partnership, Yıldız had asked him if he had ever had doubts about her but he had just shrugged his shoulders in response, as though the question was insignificant.

'Why would I? You're a great cop and you look after your men.'

'But you know I'm Turkish, right?' Yıldız asked, probing him to see if he would rise to the bait but he was having none of it.

'Don't even go there, boss,' he said in a lowered voice, as if giving away state secrets. 'I was born in a socialist country. Forget about those idiotic racists in the East. Our creed is universal humanity, not German nationalism.'

Seeing her assistant approaching with the food and drinks, she leant over and opened the door of the Passat. Tobias' face lit up when he saw the smile on his boss' face. He handed her food and drink.

'I thought the queue was never going to end. Must be because it's Friday night. Every man and his dog is in that queue.'

'It's like this every night, Toby,' Yıldız said, taking the plate and the can. 'Even people that dine in the most famous restaurants and most expensive clubs often get a sudden urge for currywurst.' She brought the plate up to her nose and inhaled. 'And who can blame them? It smells amazing.'

The Passat rocked a little when Tobias finally got in and sat down, causing several chips to fall off Yıldız' plate onto her lap.

'Easy! Do you have to sit down with such force?'

'Sorry, boss,' he said, with a sheepish smile. 'It's just that I've got all this in my hands…'

Yıldız had already forgotten about it and was busy biting into the sausage that was smothered in spiced ketchup. Tobias soon followed suit and the two of them sat and enjoyed their food without talking. After finishing the last of his first sausage and while getting ready to launch into his second, Tobias asked, 'What do you think of Alex? Do you think he was being honest with us?'

'What do you think?' Yıldız asked, sipping her coke, not even looking up. Tobias licked the crumbs clear from between his teeth and nodded.

'I'm not sure. But he really did look surprised at Cemal's death. You saw how shocked he was. Of course, it could all be an act, but he seemed genuine enough to me. If we could just nail down some fingerprints on a murder weapon, then everything would be different…'

'We can't get any prints because we have yet to find a weapon,' she said, although she still agreed with Tobias. She then thought of another possibility. 'What if he flew into a rage and lost control? Let's say he popped round to see Cemal before going to the theatre in the evening, which is not impossible, even though no one saw him. Let's say he went to his lover's house to sweeten things up between them, to make it up, although how he can sweeten anything with a face like his, I have no idea. So, he does what he can to win his lover back. He apologizes, tells Cemal he loves him and all the rest, but his young lover wants nothing to do with him anymore so they start arguing. Alex insists but Cemal is sick to the back teeth of the man and tells him he no longer loves him and that he has a new boyfriend. He tells Alex he is leaving him. Says it out loud. You saw Alex, right? You saw how hard it is for him to control his anger? He's like a powder keg just waiting for a spark. So, when he hears his lover has dumped him, he loses his mind, pulls out a blade and in a flash, kills him…'

Tobias has forgotten about his food and his coke and shook his head in disagreement.

'If that is what happened, he would have hacked Cemal to pieces but what we saw was a corpse that was so expertly sliced open, it may as well have been done by a surgeon. Not just that, the poor sod's heart was removed and placed in his hand at the feet of some ancient deity. The killer even set the music up so it would play the same song over and over again after he had left the building. I don't know the guy's motives but whoever he is, the killer is not a guy who went mad with rage. It's the complete opposite. He is a cool, calm monster who knows exactly what he is doing.' He shook his head one more time before reaching for his coke. 'I'm sorry, boss, but our metalhead does not fit the profile.'

It was a flawless analysis and was exactly what Yıldız was thinking. But there was something not right about Alex, something devious about him. His words, his behaviour, his feelings and his body language did not match up. Perhaps it was the shock that had been making him act so strangely. After all, it is not easy hearing about the death of a loved one. Additionally, he was being viewed as a suspect by the police, which can make anybody behave strangely. But it was still hard to be certain about anything with Alex. He seemed to be hiding something.

'What do you think about this matter of another lover?' Yıldız asked, probing another possibility. 'He seriously suspected another person was involved, this Alex. Do you think Cemal really had found another lover? Another lover who, it turns out, is a pervert, or a serial killer.'

Tobias was tucking into his second currywurst and hurriedly swallowed down the bite he was enjoying and washed it down with a swig of coke so he could respond.

'It's possible, sure. But we need to ascertain for sure the presence of this new lover. It could just be delusions on Alex's part. Once we talk to these Argentinians, we'll know for sure. Because if Cemal really had met someone new, then it's very possible that he was someone that moved in those art circles.' He took another sip of coke. 'Maybe one of those weirdo types from the squats. They've got all sorts of people over there.'

'Or someone from the company,' Yıldız said. 'When you went to get the beers, Alex was telling me about Cemal's boss. Some guy called Peter Schimmel.'

'Oh yeah, there was a Peter on the call. That must be him.'

'Yes, him. Apparently, he's an unusual guy. Gives his staff lots of freedom and all that. Not like your usual company directors. Alex looked a little jealous too. I'm just thinking aloud here but what if Cemal's new lover was this unusual, possibly libertarian boss?'

The possibility did not appeal to Tobias.

'I say let's concentrate on the family, especially on the brother, this Hüseyin fellow. If Alex is not lying, then this Hüseyin tried to kill Cemal once already, and in such a way that he could have said it was suicide, and with the rest of the family's approval too. I mean, just look at it. They had it all thought out. Rub out Cemal and then tell everyone it was suicide.'

'You're right,' Yıldız said, dipping her chips into the sauce. 'The family also knows about mythology, which means that the whole setup at the crime scene would not have been unfamiliar to them.' She paused before going on. 'On paper, it fits but…' She fell silent and helped herself to a couple of chips, thinking things over.

'But what?'

'But this: you won't get Turks involved in such sophisticated murders. You've been in this business for years yourself so I'm sure you've come across murder cases involving Turks. They don't arrange things like this. In such excruciating detail. They just fire away. Shoot first, ask questions later. They don't even feel a need to hide the body or what have you when they have killed. I'm generalizing, of course, but what I'm saying is, when they kill, it's because of a sudden bout of rage or because they feel they have been insulted and dishonoured.'

Tobias answered with a mouthful of currywurst.

'True. I looked into two murders involving Turkish migrants. In one of them, a guy killed his wife for cheating on him with his best friend. He shot his friend too but missed. In the other one, some fellow stabbed his cousin to death for not paying back money he had lent him. In front of everyone too. That was around two years ago. In fact, that was my last case before I started working with you. It happened on one of the backstreets of Spandau. In broad bloody daylight too… God, it was a mess. The perp stabbed his own cousin and then stood over him, waiting for him to die. Can you imagine? The guy just stood there in the middle of the street for minutes with a huge knife in his hand. Stood there and waited. When we got there, we had to shoot him in the shoulder so he would drop the knife but his cousin had already died by then due to massive blood loss. And do you know what the perp said? "Serves the bastard right. Now he knows not to try and pull a fast one on a relative." I still don't know if he did because of the money itself or because his cousin had tried to do one on him.' He reached for his coke. 'But we don't know Cemal's family. All we know is that they have some kind of interest in archaeology. We know nothing about what kind of people they are, their educational background, that kind of thing. They've been living in Germany for years so perhaps they've changed. Third generation Turks are quite an odd lot…' He was about to say she was a prime example but stopped, not wanting to be misunderstood. 'Isn't that so, boss? In our line of work, generalizing can be dangerous. We need to look at each case on its own terms.'

While Tobias drank, Yıldız realized a second sausage would be too much for her.

'You want it?'

'Well, if you're not going to have it…' Yıldız handed over her plate with a smile.

'*Afiyet olsun*, as we say,' she said, as Tobias dug in. 'This is just us talking. Let's see what Markus has to say. This case looks like it could be quite a tricky one. What do you think — do you think Markus will give the case to someone else?'

'No way,' Tobias said grimly. 'The deceased is a Turk. That means there is no one better suited to investigate than you. Not even Markus is that dumb.'

Yıldız was not convinced.

'Well, I guess we'll have to wait and see,' she said and turned the key in the ignition. 'On the Berlin Homicide Desk, you need to be prepared for all kind of surprises.'

As the Passat slowly moved off, the lights from the lampposts went off. Daylight was starting to take over Berlin.

3
This is I,
Zeus, King of the Gods, overlord of all creatures of the earth and sky

Even if you triumph today, the past shall haunt you. The spectres of the past shall follow you like a shadow. My father Kronos knew this. He never forgot this truth. Even when drunk with victory, he did not forget the curse of his father, Uranus. When he ascended the throne, when he rescued his siblings from the depths of the earth in which they had been entombed by their father and when he took my mother Rhea to bed, he did not forget his father's curse, for he was afraid he would suffer the same fate as his own father, Uranus. Yet he forgot the promise he had made to Gaia and he repeated his father's mistake, and even more callously.

Rhea, she of the luxuriant hair, bore him five children: three daughters and two sons. My beloved brothers and sisters, all sublime Gods and Goddesses: Hestia, Demeter, Hera, Poseidon and Hades. However, my father did not embrace them as a father. Not once did he hold them lovingly to his chest and inhale their scent. Instead, he swallowed them, one by one. Yes, he consumed his own issue, borne to him by our mother Rhea, all five children, savagely and without hesitation. His fear of losing his throne had twisted his mind and his body too and turned him into a tyrant. The siblings he had saved he imprisoned once again in the depths of Tartarus, whilst the others he freed on the condition of their subservience. And thus began the Golden Age of the Titans.

Again, it was the women that fought back against this tyranny of the King of the Titans. Just as our grandmother Gaia had severed her husband Uranus' power and presented it as a gift to her son, so my mother Rhea devised a plan with even greater wit, skill and cunning. The experienced Gaia assisted Rhea, as Kronos was not only tyrannizing her grandchildren but her own children too. Uranus, ever malevolent, approved of this righteous plot that would depose his treacherous son and satisfy his thirst for revenge. It was at this time that I, Zeus, was born, the sixth and the youngest of Rhea's progeny. As soon as I was born, I was taken away to Crete for the sake of the plan. When Kronos arrived, ready to ingest me rather than hold and behold me and rejoice in my birth, he was given a stone wrapped in swaddling cloth and, having utmost trust in his wife, the King of the Titans suspected nothing and swallowed the stone. That night, utterly sure of himself, he took his wife in his arms.

Our Mother Earth took me into the depths of a vast forest in Crete filled with mighty trees whose heads touched the clouds and she left me there in the care of a nymph, to whom she said, 'This child is not just a beautiful child, nor is he just a God. This child is the future of the world. Protect him with your life. Food, drink, a bed in which to rest and a garden in which to play; he shall want for none. You are responsible for this child's wellbeing.' The nymph obeyed Gaia's instructions and looked after me with a mother's compassion, fulfilling all my needs, and nourishing me with the milk of an enchanted goat. That nymph and that sacred goat have my eternal gratitude. Indeed, when the goat died, I had my armour and my shield, the Aegis, made from its hide. As my body developed and grew strong with the finest foodstuff, my greatest supporters, Gaia and my mother Rhea, emboldened me with words of justice. Day and night, they reminded me of my sacred mission, of the reason for my existence, of the righteous vengeance I was to enact. I believed in them, and I prepared for the battle against my father with pain, rage, love and hatred.

Time passed, like a mighty river splitting a forest asunder, and day by day I grew until I became what I was meant to be. One morning, Gaia summoned me and she looked upon me with love, compassion and pride. Then, in a voice sweeter than honey, she said:

'My son, most glorious and blessed of Kronos' progeny. My son, youngest, mightiest and most brilliant of the Gods. The time has come. The Gods, the Titans, the Giants, Man and all the creatures of the world call out to you. The Age of Kronos is over, yet he does not know it. Your time has come, my son, but it awaits your guiding hand. Shake off this guise of the exile, my son. Leave your cave. Grasp your rage as though it is a shield of steel, sharpen your courage like the blade of a sword, and remain ever vigilant. Remember, Kronos was powerful enough to overcome his father, the mighty Uranus. Remember, Kronos was cunning enough to entrap a strong and experienced foe. Kronos was bloody-minded and ruthless enough to castrate my own husband. Do not trust in your youthful energy alone, for the mind is stronger than raw strength. You must observe Kronos' every glance, his every breath, his every move, for he shall be observing you and your slightest mistake he shall punish with utmost severity. Should you err, your grave shall be your father's stomach, alongside your siblings. Should you err, there shall be no end to Kronos' tyrannical rule. Should you err, justice shall never reign. The time has come. The Sun of the Titans is ready to set. Now, the Dawn of the Gods shall illuminate the earth and the winds of freedom, not fear, shall blow through hearts. Sons shall not fear fathers, fathers shall love their sons, brother shall not hate brother, and none shall kill without reason or just cause. Son, do not delay. The time has come. Go, and do what you must. The time has come. Go, and stop the one that has obstructed the natural flow of life. The time has come. Go, and take what is rightfully yours. Drive Kronos into the underworld of Tartarus.'

Thus spoke our divine Mother Earth, she who gave life to us all. She sent me into battle against the Titan that was both my foe and my father. I listened to her words as sacred commands, which is indeed what they were. I left the darkness of my cave to face mighty Kronos, whom none dared look in the eye. At first, Kronos did not recognize me and simply stared at me with scorn, which then turned into amusement. However, when he saw my eyes and my brow and the lines of my face and my gait, the mightiest of the Titans was bemused. He thought he saw himself when he gazed upon me. And then the truth dawned upon him. He breathed in and roared:

'What is this? Another son of mine has been born without my knowing? What is this madness? Or have you made my own son prepare my tomb? What is this insanity? Have I been taken for a fool by a female, a female I myself have never betrayed?'

As my father howled in rage and confusion, I leapt upon him and before he could know what was happening, I unleashed a barrage of blows upon his face and broke my shield upon his shoulders. I grasped him by his thick hair and I struck his huge head upon the marble. Nor did I stop or pause, for I knew if I were to stop, he would be able to gather his strength and that he had enough strength to defeat me with a single blow. I knew that to let up in my attack would mean finding myself entombed in his stomach with my siblings. I struck his head again and again until the marble beneath us ran red with his blood and my own strength began to fade. When I was spent, so too was Kronos. He offered no resistance. He was still, without movement or sound. Had I not known he was Immortal, I would have taken him for dead. But his chest continued to rise and fall. I stood over him and bound his feet with the chains given to me by Gaia. I fed him an emetic, lay him down on his back under a cedar tree and then pressed down upon his stomach with my powerful arms. One by one, I released my siblings from their prison in his stomach — Hestia, Demeter, Hera, Poseidon and Hades. And with that, a mighty weight was removed from my mind and heart, and the sky, the earth and all the creatures of the world let out a huge sigh of relief. With all my strength, I roared:

'Here I am. Zeus, King of the Gods, overlord of all the creatures of the earth and sky. Zeus, vanquisher of the strongest of the Titans. Zeus, who sent his disgrace of a father into the depths of Tartarus. The storms are my fury, the lightning my roar, the thunderbolts my spears. I wander amongst the stars, I gather the clouds, I uproot the mountains, I drive before me all living things. Here I stand, King of the Gods, Titans, Giants and Men.

'Here I stand. Zeus, the mightiest, bravest, most brilliant and most accomplished of all the Gods. Zeus, whose sun shall shine forever. Let it be known, let it be said, let it be acknowledged: those that defy me shall be accursed and shall writhe in agony in the flames.'

Chapter Three

Markus strode into the police station right on time, not a second early or late, wearing his usual grey suit, white shirt and black tie. He had completed his morning run and had had a sound breakfast and so he was in high spirits. When he arrived, Yıldız and Tobias were at their desk staring at an image of a statue of Zeus on the computer screen. Tobias had just had his second coffee, while Yıldız was sipping a cup of tea. Both of their gazes were fixed on the image of deity.

'This is not the picture Cemal drew,' Tobias said. 'Okay, it's the same God, and we have the throne, the beard, the blonde hair, the nymph, the eagle and all that but it's a different picture. Is there more than one of this statue?'

Yıldız was about to reply when Markus butted in.

'What statue? What are you looking at on that screen?'

There was no greeting, no good morning. Just straight to the point. Yıldız peered at her boss caustically.

'And a good morning to you too. We're looking at pictures of Zeus. Well, a statue of him. If you're wondering, the statue was built in the fifth century BC in the ancient city of Olympus, the city in which the first Olympic Games were held. At the time, the statue was one of the Seven Wonders of the World.' She turned to her assistant. 'The statue in the pictures is the same, Toby, it is just the pictures that are different. There is nothing left of the original monument, so everyone just draws it the way they imagine it may have looked. Just read out what's that written at the bottom of the screen.'

Markus didn't mind the fact that Yıldız had not risen to her feet. He had grown used to her somewhat unruly behaviour. Moreover, he was intrigued by this Zeus business. He drew closer to his two officers.

'Go ahead, Tobias. Read it out.'

Tobias sat down on his stool and began reading the text under the depiction of the statue:

'Unfortunately, the statue of Zeus is no more. But this fabulous monument was described thus by the traveller Pausanias: "*The God sits on a throne made of ivory and gold and sports a laurel wreath. Perched on his right hand, in ivory and gold, is Nike, the Goddess of Victory, who also wears a laurel wreath. In his left hand, Zeus holds a staff made of hard metal, the end of which is fashioned into the head of an eagle. The deity's sandals and cape are also made of gold. On his cape are lilies and vibrant figures. The throne is adorned with gold, precious gems, ebony and ivory.*" This is the most complete description we have of the statue.'

After he had finished reading, Tobias fell silent, like a well-behaved schoolboy.

'Interesting,' Markus said, his voice marked by curiosity. 'This statue has something to do with last night's murder?'

Neither Yıldız nor Tobias was surprised at Markus being clued up on the case they were working on. Their boss, a man with green eyes sparkling with intelligence behind his brown bone glasses, was always on top of the job, even in his sleep.

'Well, yes, it seems both the killer and the deceased have some kind of connection to this statue,' Yıldız said calmly. 'The deceased's heart was removed.'

The Chief gave no reaction, meaning he probably already knew.

'A scene was set up whereby the deceased looked as though he was offering his own heart in sacrifice to Zeus.'

'A mise-en-scene, eh?' Markus said. 'Are we talking about a serial killer?'

His voice was tense, which suggested Kurt, the head of the Crime Scene Investigation Unit, may not have briefed him yet or had not briefed him thoroughly enough.

'Still too early to say. We currently do not have enough data to create a profile of the killer. As far as we know, there have not been any similar murders.'

Of course, Markus was not satisfied by any of this. Not bothering to hide his unease, he grabbed a stool and sat down next to the two officers.

'And we don't have any suspects? An enemy, someone who stands to benefit from this guy's death? Someone that would want to kill him?'

Yıldız stared at the Chief.

'Too many. His lover Alex and his entire family…. The deceased was gay.'

The unease on the Chief's face seemed to disappear.

'So you're saying this could be a family tragedy, rather than a case of a serial killer?'

'It's possible,' Tobias interjected, himself uneasy at how easily the Chief had changed his mind. 'But it is hard to say for sure.'

Barely noticing Tobias, Markus turned to Yıldız.

'The deceased was one of your lot, wasn't he?'

'When you say one of "my lot", what exactly do you mean?' Yıldız asked, pushing a lock of hair that had fallen over her forehead out of the way. She was far from happy at the wording of the question but she then realized Markus meant no harm by it.

'I mean, he was originally from Turkey,' Markus said, indifferent to Yıldız's displeasure.

'Yes, he was. His name was Cemal Ölmez. And one of the chief suspects so far is his lover Alex… Alexander Werner. Quite the record he has too. One count of possession, and arrested twice for battery.'

'Trifling infractions,' Markus said dismissively.

'Yes, that is true. Nor was he charged… However, in both battery incidents, he was arrested after his lover complained. His lover was the deceased.'

'So? Lovers always fight. It's no big deal. So long as they don't let it get out of hand, these squabbles can spice up a relationship. Okay, with these two it was a bit stronger, a bit rougher…' He then added, with a note of disapproval, 'And when they are both men…' The anxiety of moment's ago was gone. He looked almost ready to grin. 'Or should I say when they are both women?'

So now Yıldız was finding out that her xenophobic and misogynistic boss was also homophobic. She was not surprised.

'I wouldn't know about that,' she said in a slightly raised tone. 'The nature and dynamics of the relationships between gay men is not my area of expertise. What concerns me is the specifics of the relationship between the killer and the deceased. Just two days ago, Alex threatened to kill Cemal….'

'Threatened to kill him, you say? Well, did you bring him in?' he asked, now speaking with some conviction and authority.

'No, because we found out what we needed to. We'll take his statement after we have spoken to Cemal's family. We can't keep Alex in for long with the scant information we have.'

'So you don't think he's the perp?' Markus asked. He looked Yıldız up and down. She cupped her chin with her hand.

'I'm not sure. The guy is definitely hiding something but I don't think he is a killer.'

The Chief turned to look at Tobias, who was standing there quietly watching them talk.

'And what do you think? You've been very quiet this morning.'

'I agree with Yıldız,' Tobias answered, ignoring the barbed comment. 'At first, I thought Alex may have been the killer but there is very little evidence supporting that hypothesis. I don't think someone with such a messy past would be able to execute an operation as meticulous as this one. I reckon we need to focus on the family.'

Although he knew the answer, Markus still felt the need to ask, 'Why? Why do you suspect the family?'

'The homosexuality issue, for one,' Yıldız said. 'Cemal's family did not take too well to his lifestyle.'

Markus' expression grew serious.

'I can see why. It must be hard... But this removing of the heart thing is odd, don't you think? I get it when they are stabbed in the heat of passion but taking someone's heart out is a bit too much, wouldn't you say? And this Zeus thing, too. Why would a family that has killed their son to save the family honour go and create this whole sacrifice to Zeus backdrop? The guy was Turkish, for one. Not Greek.'

'That's beside the point, Markus,' Yıldız said. 'Greek or Turk, who still worships Zeus? No, what we have here is something downright absurd.'

As he usually did when stuck at an impasse, Tobias began scratching his neck.

'Let's not forget the family's ties to archaeology though, Chief… For years, they were involved with the excavations at Pergamon. How many generations did Alex say they were there?'

'Pergamon?' Markus asked. 'Like the museum Pergamon?'

Yıldız had not been planning on bringing it up with the Chief at this point but now that the topic had ben broached, there was no need to hold back.

'Many men of the Ölmez clan, including the victim's grandfather, worked on the Pergamon excavations. It wasn't just pictures of the statue of Zeus in the deceased's residence. There was also a painting of the Altar of Zeus, which is on display in the Pergamon Museum here in Berlin. Have you seen the Altar, Markus?'

'Of course, I have. It's quite a sight.'

Yıldız's eyes lit up.

'Well, you know the reliefs at the museum, the ones that have missing arms, legs and heads? Cemal wanted to paint the statues and figures in those reliefs. We saw the sketches.'

Markus was now thoroughly confused.

'And you're saying these paintings have something to do with the murder?'

'I don't know, Markus. That's why I think we should not be talking in certainties. Accusing the family and assuming Alex is innocent is also wrong. Who knows? Maybe they're all innocent. Maybe it will be someone else entirely that turns out to be the killer.'

The anxiety had returned. Markus rubbed his cheek with his right hand.

'Yes, maybe some deranged Zeus-worshipping cult carried out the murder,' he suggested. 'This is Berlin, at the end of the day. The city of extremes…. If that is the case, then there will be more murders. What do you think? Do you think there may be some whacko cult behind all this?'

'It's too early to say,' Yıldız replied. 'It hasn't even been twelve hours since the murder. Give it some time, then I can offer you something more substantial.'

Markus groaned, frustrated at the lack of compliance.

'Easy for you to say. The telephones are going to start ringing soon. Reporters from *Bild* and *Tagesspiegel* are going to be banging on the door wanting to know more. The press are going to be all over this. This will be huge for them.' He looked at them, almost pleading with them. 'We need to give them an adequate yet reasonable picture, otherwise they'll start making all kinds of stuff up. The deceased is a Turk, so all kinds of extremist and fringe groups will be getting ready to exploit it. Let's not start creating needless tensions in the city.'

Yıldız found his apprehension unnecessary but she kept it to herself. She was just pleased that she had been handed the investigation.

'Don't worry, Markus, I'll have a story ready for you tomorrow. However, we need to see the Crime Scene Unit's report first. Maybe not the autopsy just yet but we need toxicology reports. The deceased did not put up a fight so we need to know if he had any substances in his bloodstream. If I could have that information by tomorrow, then we can have a logical and acceptable account ready.

'Fair enough,' Markus said. He stood up, looking a little relieved. 'Well then, back to work I suppose.'

Yıldız called out to him just as he was leaving the room.

'I'll also let you know by tomorrow what we'll be needing. We're going to need some serious logistical support on this one.'

The Chief grinned wolfishly.

'Don't you worry about that. You just work out how you're

going to approach this case. Leave the rest to me. I'll give you whatever you need.'

Adalbert Street is where the heaviest concentration of shops and stores owned by people of Turkish origin can be found. In the little square at the end of the street, one can see the Namık Kemal Library, the Mevlana Mosque, a branch of Türkiye İş Bankası and the Black Sea Balıkcısı fish market. Anybody there would think they were in Turkey. As she parked the Passat, Yıldız laughed and said, 'You've always wanted to see Turkey, Toby. Well, here you are.'

As for Tobias, he was staring in amazement at the people sitting in and around the cafes and happily sipping their teas.

'I know, boss. Most of the shopkeepers around here are Turkish. In fact, it is the local Germans here who have changed and turned Turks.'

They got out of the car and began walking.

'Have you ever heard the story of Osman Amca of Yozgat?' Yıldız asked as they walked towards an arcade of shops further up ahead. 'He's the guy that built a *gecekondu* by the Wall.'

'What's a *gecekondu*?'

'You mean you don't know? It's a Turkish word for an illegally built house or structure. A shanty house, basically. The word has entered the German language. Anyway, this Osman Amca was a retired old man and he was bored out of his mind. This was around the beginning of the 1980s. He sees an empty plot of land by the Berlin Wall and so begins planting onions, garlic, tomatoes and cucumbers there, turning the spot into a mini-allotment. However, the land belongs to the German Democratic Republic and one day, soldiers stationed by the Wall notice him and start shouting at him, asking him what he is doing. Osman, somewhat brazenly, replies, 'What do you want me to? The land was not being used so

I started planting stuff here. And now look at what I have.'
And with that, he gives the soldiers some of the tomatoes and
cucumbers he has grown. As you know, when it came to the
Wall, the East German authorities did not show any flexibility
but oddly enough, they left this old man alone. In fact, as
a joke, they even had a document made out saying the land
was the "Property of Osman". As a result, a little green oasis
was formed by the Wall. Eventually, the Wall came down and
the unification took place, but Osman Amca would not leave
his little allotment behind. On the contrary, he had a two-
storey wooden structure erected in the middle of the plot. The
Greens run Kreuzberg Municipality so they don't interfere
with the old man's land, and now Osman Amca's allotment
is a part of Berlin's landscape. Tour guides include it in their
itineraries and visitors have their photographs taken in front of
it as souvenirs of Berlin.'

Tobias roared with laughter.

'Well, you have to give the man credit for his gumption. And
he had the right to do it too. As the old socialists used to say,
the land belongs to those that work it and the water belongs to
those that use it.'

Chatting amicably away, they eventually turned into
Kottbusser Square. They crossed the road at the traffic lights
and approached a group of people openly selling drugs in the
square. These were people that refused to go to a rehabilitation
centre, people lost in another world, wandering the streets night
and day, sometimes fighting each other, sometimes picking on
youngsters passing by, sometimes simply standing there staring
vacantly at unseen points in the distance. Their bodies and faces
were so worn and battered that it was hard to work out if they
were old or young. Indeed, with some of them, it was even hard
to work out their gender.

'Hey, pig,' a one-legged lady leaning against a tree called out. 'Yeah, you, cop. I'm talking to you. Give us a tenner, will you? I haven't had any all day and I'm gasping for a hit.'

Tobias turned around and was about to give her a piece of his mind but Yıldız stopped him. She took out two euros and flung them to the woman, who leant forward, caught the coins in mid-air and smiled gratefully.

'Thanks, sweet cheeks, I won't forget this.'

Yıldız carried on walking, her assistant following close behind and staring at her in amazement.

'You know her?' Tobias asked.

'I don't know her but she clearly knows we're pigs, either by our clothes or by our demeanour.' She winked at Tobias when she said *pigs*, and they carried on, towards the Bergama Baklava shop fifty metres ahead.

It was still early, before noon, so there were no customers in the shop. The walls were plastered with the blue banner of Hertha Berlin Football Club and the black and white banner of Beşiktaş Football Club. A young lad with a flat head and thinning hair sat behind a counter lined with rows of sweets: multiple trays containing walnut and pistachio baklava, bülbülyuvası, şöbiyet, kadayıf, künefe, saray sarması and a well-known sweet dish from Bergama known as zülbiye were there. The lad stood up when he saw Tobias and Yıldız walk in.

'Morning. What can I get for you?' he asked, trying to muster up a smile. Tobias flashed his badge.

'We would like to speak to Hüseyin Ölmez.'

'Oh, so you've found grandad?'

'No, we're here for something else,' Tobias said.

'What happened to your grandfather?' Yıldız asked.

'Orhan Dede has been missing for three days,' the boy replied nervously. 'We have informed the police so when I saw you walk in, I assumed you were here for him.'

It was possible that the missing grandfather had nothing to do with the murder but there was no harm in obtaining further information.

'Where do you think grandfather may have gone?' Yıldız asked.

'We don't know,' he replied, his green eyes blinking sadly under his long eyelashes. 'Orhan Dede is a forgetful one, though. He forgets things. Even forgets who he is sometimes.'

A voice from the back of the store called out.

'What's going on, Alper?'

A tall man emerged from the back and walked over to them. Despite his advancing age, the man was in good shape. He had a shapely nose, a heavy jaw, wavy hair with flecks of grey and white, a thick, greying beard and dark skin, all of which gave him a certain charisma.

'The police,' the youngster said. 'But they're not here for Orhan Dede.' He then turned to Tobias and asked, 'So what are you here for?'

Yıldız politely raised her right hand.

'Thank you, young man. We'd like to talk to the gentleman now, if you please.'

They approached the older man, who was watching them anxiously. The man looked familiar. Where had Yıldız seen him before? She tried to recall but could not place him.

'Hello. Are you Hüseyin Ölmez?'

The worry in the man's eyes turned to curiosity. Yıldız suddenly remembered the victim — Cemal's big black eyes, staring up at the ceiling.

'No, Hüseyin is my son. My name is Kerem. Why? What's happened?' And then, indifferent to what the young lad behind the counter had just said, he asked, 'Do you have news about my father?'

By way of an answer, Yıldız flashed her ID.

'Chief Inspector Yıldız Karasu, and this is my colleague, Inspector Tobias Becker.... We need to speak to you.' Yıldız scanned the shop. 'Why don't we sit down?'

Kerem sensed the gravity of the situation.

'Well, we may as well go inside. I'd rather we didn't talk out here.' Without bothering to wait for them to agree, he turned and went in through the back. He was not only tall but well-built too. In comparison, Yıldız was tiny, but she still stepped forward and began walking alongside the man, with Tobias following a short distance behind. As Yıldız watched the shop owner out of the corner of her eye, he reminded her of her father. Like her father, he was still good-looking despite his advancing years. But his eyes were not grey-blue like her father's but black and his hair was wavy, almost curly, and had more grey flecks. Moreover, she thought, her father was more easy-going and more light-hearted than this guy. But then she told herself to stop. She hardly knew the guy and was making all these assumptions about him, which was doing him a gross disservice. For all she knew, he had had previous run-ins with the police that had soured his taste for officers of the law.

'What's happened?' Kerem asked, disrupting the flow of her thoughts. 'Has something happened to my father?'

'The issue is not your father,' Yıldız replied, keeping up with him. 'But we would like to know what has happened to Orhan Dede.'

The man suddenly stopped and turned around.

'How do you know his name is Orhan?' he snapped.

'Alper told us. The lad on the counter.'

Yıldız grinned. The shop owner should at least have shown some contrition but he did not even apologize.

'Ah yes, of course,' he said and carried on walking. Yıldız realized she was about to impart terrible news to the man so she ignored his gruff demeanour.

'He's been missing for three days, you say?'

'That's right. He's gone missing before but we usually find him on the second day.' He sighed in despair. 'My father has Alzheimer's Disease. If you leave a door open, he'll be out. Gone, and no one will know where. The last time he went missing, we found him in Bahnhof Zoo, sitting on one of the benches watching the trains.' He almost smiled and his voice softened. 'When we first arrived from Turkey, that is where we got off the train. Mentally, I suppose he wants to go back home. That, or something else. Who knows? He lives in the past now. Sometimes he thinks I am his father. The doctors say he is only going to get worse and that we have to be prepared for anything.' They had reached an open door. He stepped aside. 'This way, please.'

When they walked through, they found themselves looking at the same picture they saw in Cemal's house, the photograph taken at the excavation site featuring fourteen workers posing with a European man in a suit and tie and colonial hat. Behind them were the same marble statues, broken columns and giant rocks.

'Is that Bergama?' Yıldız asked. Kerem looked pleasantly surprised.

'You know Bergama?' He was speaking Turkish now and asked the next question before Yıldız could answer the first. 'Are you from that part of Turkey?' For the first time, his voice contained some warmth.

'No, I'm from Istanbul.' Yıldız was pleased that Kerem had softened his stance but she still answered in German so as to preserve the formality implicit in their encounter. 'Or rather, my father was. I was born here.' She glanced at the photograph. 'Was this the excavation of the Altar of Zeus?'

Kerem was staring longingly at the photo.

'No, that was the Temple of Artemis… Right above the theatre.' He too had reverted to German. 'The Altar of Zeus was lower down. So you know Bergama well then?'

'Not that well,' Yıldız laughed. 'But I know Pergamon Museum. You seem to be very interested in archaeology.'

Kerem pointed to a tall, stocky man in a fez standing next to the man in the colonial hat.

'That is my great-great grandfather…. Pehlivan Efendi. He was the strongest man in all Bergama. He could lift three men in a wrestling match and pin them to the ground. He had a nickname too. They used to call him *Alman Pehlivan*. That's right. *Alman*. "The German".'

'Why did they call him that?' Tobias asked, confused.

'Because he got on so well with the Germans,' Kerem said, opening up a little now. 'He was one of the first men to join the excavations at Pergamon. Here, look. See this guy in the hat next to him? That's Carl Humann, the man who started the excavations at Pergamon. A really important man. He was the guy who brought the Altar of Zeus and other historical artefacts to Berlin. He wasn't actually an archaeologist. He was a highway engineer. He came to the Ottoman Empire in the 1870s from Germany to build the roads. Can you imagine? He was the one that began digging in Pergamon. My great-great grandfather worked alongside him, as a road digger. At the time, they were building the Ayvalık-Bergama highway. Humann had a great interest in historical artefacts and he was stunned when he saw Pergamon and so he started digging. He chose to carry on the work with the same work crew. Pehlivan Dedem was one of his men. For four generations, our family worked on the digs at Pergamon.' He swelled with pride. 'Our family knows more about that city than many of the archaeologists that have worked there.'

He pointed to another little photograph in the bottom left corner of the wall. 'See? There is a photograph of Atatürk here. Can you see it?'

Tobias was not interested but Yıldız stopped to examine the picture. The photo was of a large group of men, most in uniform, standing in what looked like an antique theatre. Mustafa Kemal Atatürk was wearing a light blue suit, whilst the soldiers and civilian administrators around him sat on small stools.

'This is Asclepion. It used to be a health centre in ancient Pergamon. A hospital of sorts, I suppose. It was named after Asclepius. He was the God of medicine, and the son of Apollo and grandson of Zeus. Asclepion was one of the finest hospitals of its age. This here is the hospital's theatre.' He pointed to a young man at the back of the photo. 'That's my grandfather. My father's father. He was around twenty at the time the photo was taken. Tall, thin and dashing he was. Atatürk noticed him rushing around and called him over. He asked him his name. "Cemal, sir, at your service," my grandfather replied. Atatürk looked my grandfather up and down and then asked what his duties entailed. "In the winter, I am the watchman, and in the summer when the digs begin, I am a manual labourer, sir. We have worked here as a family for three generations, ever since the excavations began, sir." Atatürk nodded his head. "So, you're the watchman as well one of the labourers?" "Yes, sir," my grandfather said. Atatürk stared at my grandfather with his piercing blue eyes. "This is not the way, Cemal. No son, this won't do. Seeing as your whole family has had such an important role in these digs, you should be working here as a scientist, not as a labourer. It may be a little late for you but your children should become archaeologists." Yes, that is what Atatürk himself said to my grandfather, who took his words very seriously. Saw it as his life mission.' He sighed deeply. 'Unfortunately, my father had to leave Bergama for financial reasons and come to Berlin. I could have fulfilled the undertaking given to us by Atatürk and I was actually going to as I love archaeology, but they wouldn't let me…' He sighed again and smiled a bitter smile. He only then realized his guests had been standing the whole time.

'Please, take a seat.' He pointed to the chairs in front of the table. Once the two police officers were seated, he sat on the chair behind the table. His initial harshness had vanished but he had not let his guard down completely. 'So, what can I do for you?'

Yıldız cleared her throat.

'We are here for Cemal…' Kerem's eyes immediately darkened in anger. Yıldız, unfazed, continued. 'For your younger son.'

'I have no such son,' he snapped. 'There is no Cemal in our family.'

'I understand. However, if you would just listen…'

'No. There is nothing to listen to.'

Yıldız decided upon a firmer approach.

'Sir, we have to talk to you about this matter. One way or another.'

The shop owner glared at them.

'Why don't you understand? I do not have a son called Cemal.'

His voice had hardened, as had his body, not that the Chief Inspector was worried.

'I am afraid you do. Biologically and legally, Cemal is your son. We need to talk to you about a matter concerning him.'

Kerem rose to his feet in anger.

'I do not want to listen to this. Please leave.'

'We are not going anywhere,' Yıldız said calmly, not budging. 'You had better sit down.'

'What? What the hell is this? How dare you! What, you think you can force me to listen to you? This is my property!'

Tobias was on his feet now. He looked the fuming shop owner in the eye and warned him.

'Sir, please calm down. We are just doing our duty. Please do not make it any harder for us or we shall have to take you down to the station.'

'Why?' he asked, opening out his arms in a gesture of helplessness. 'What have I done?'

Tobias answered slowly and clearly.

'Look, Mister Ölmez, I am afraid we have bad news for you so please try and stay calm.'

'I am calm,' Kerem said tetchily. 'Fine, fine, I'm listening. So what's this bad news then?'

'Your son has been killed. Cemal, whom you named after your grandfather, was killed last night. And in a quite brutal manner, too. His heart was removed with a knife.'

Kerem did not understand at first and simply stared at them. A single word eventually fell from his lips.

'Killed?'

'I am afraid so,' Tobias nodded. 'So please sit down.'

Yıldız could not decide if the man was in shock or was trying to work out how to react.

'I think you had better sit down, Mister Ölmez,' she said, repeating Tobias' suggestion. 'Please take a seat so we can talk in more detail.'

Kerem fell back into his chair, his black eyes staring blankly ahead.

'Who?' he eventually said. 'Who did it?'

Yıldız pushed back a lock of hair from her forehead.

'That is what we are trying to find out. If you help us, our search will become a whole lot easier…'

The Chief Inspector did not know what to make of Kerem's attitude. Or, to be more precise, she was not sure if this father sitting in front of her was genuine in his shock or not. Before arriving, she thought he was going to be indifferent to his son's death but that was not the case. He was rocked by the news of his son's death. Tobias must also have been confused as he was staring at the shop owner, trying to gauge his reactions.

'Cemal was a beautiful baby,' Kerem eventually said. 'Just like my grandfather…' Unwanted memories that had been suppressed for years now seemed to be surfacing. 'In Bergama, they used to call him *Güzel Cemal*. Beautiful Cemal… He really was a beautiful boy. He would turn heads wherever he went. Snow white skin, jet black hair and eyes with wonderful dark lining. The word *cemal* actually means "handsome". I did not want the family tradition to be disrupted and so I named my boy Cemal, both to keep my grandfather's name alive and as a description of the baby's beauty…' He could not go on. His eyes welled up. 'I'm sorry… I cannot imagine a worse pain than this. This is just horrible. I admit, almighty Allah is my witness, that I prayed for his death many times. I wanted him gone for good. Nor did I want him spoken of ever again. Not even a whisper. I did not want to hear people's barbed comments. It was shameful for us. Showing our face in public became an ordeal. People whispered behind our backs. Neighbours and relatives. We knew what they were saying. That's why they spoke. So that we would hear their comments. We are an honourable family…'

Tobias could not stand it any longer.

'Your son being gay does not make him dishonourable. Neither him nor you.'

Kerem looked on helplessly.

'Tell that to our relatives and our neighbours. And to my cousins, my uncle's children. They have always despised us. I am afraid it is not as simple as that, Mister…' He had forgotten the surname. Yıldız helped him out.

'Becker. Tobias Becker.' She put her hands on the table and leant forward. 'When you say relatives, I assume you are referring to your older son, Hüseyin.'

Kerem's ashen face tensed up.

'What's happened to Hüseyin?' he asked anxiously. 'You keep going on about him.'

'Please try to stay calm. Nothing has happened to Hüseyin. But we do know that he used to be violent with Cemal and that on one occasion he tried to throw him out of a window. Cemal only managed to save himself at the last minute.'

Kerem's shoulders slumped, the look of a man that knows his mistake and regrets it.

'Oh, that… That's not quite how it happened. You've got it all wrong. Hüseyin would never kill his own brother. He actually loved his brother dearly. It's just that on that particular day, he lost control. I was there. Cemal was being deliberately provocative. If he had just let it slide that day, things could have been resolved amicably but Cemal kept saying he was doing nothing wrong. I remember what he said: "I'm a thousand times more honourable than all those relatives and neighbours of ours gossiping about me behind my back. I am not stealing from anyone, nor am I hurting anybody. I have a good job and am a respectable person. But you guys; instead of sticking up for me, you listen to those evil gossipmongers. Am I not a member of this family too? Am I not your child too? Enough of all this! Where is your humanity? Where is your backbone?" That is when Hüseyin lost it. "Look! Now he's pointing the finger at us! You're the one lacking in humanity. Not only do you shame us in front of the whole world, you come here and insult us to our faces." Then Hüseyin grabbed Cemal's throat.'

Tobias had been watching Kerem and his calm demeanour all along. Now he spoke up.

'And you helped him. You were all going to throw Cemal out of the window together.'

Kerem was quick to object.

'Rubbish! That's a lie! Cemal was a strong lad. He had always been a sporting lad and he knew how to handle himself. I raised him like that. As far as I'm concerned, a man should be physically strong. He could easily have overpowered the both of us. It took hardly any effort for Cemal to squeeze out of Hüseyin's grip. He then picked his brother up and threw him to the floor. My wife and I together tried to protect Hüseyin and in the middle of the commotion when I pushed Cemal away, he bumped into the window. That's all. Cemal stormed off after that anyway.' He looked at the Chief Inspector, hoping she at least would understand. 'These things happen in families. No one actually considered harming Cemal, or, God forbid, killing him. We are not murderers. Why would we harm our own flesh and blood?'

'And yet just now you said you had prayed for his death,' Yıldız said, flinging his inconsistency back in his face.

Kerem did not know what to say. After stroking his white beard with his right hand, he said, 'I was just saying what was in my heart, and yes, I meant it. But the pain of losing a child is indescribable.' Tears formed in his eyes again and he shook his head in remorse. 'I was wrong... So very wrong. I was under pressure, you see. Everyone was talking about us, about my family. That is why I had those dark thoughts. And now look. Look what has happened to me. No, neither I nor Hüseyin would have killed Cemal, because he was our own flesh and blood.' He paused and then, shoulders slumped with the look of a broken man, asked, 'How am I going to tell his mother?'

He was saying this yet Tobias noticed that he did not appear overly distraught.

'I wouldn't worry about it. Who knows? Maybe she'll be pleased. Cemal was nothing but trouble to all of you.'

A flash of anger passed over Kerem's face but he held himself together.

'Do you have any children, Mister Becker?'

'No. No wife or children,' Tobias replied casually. 'And I have no intention of bringing a child into a world like this. Take you, for example. Your own son has been killed and yet we still have our suspicions about you.'

Yıldız realized her assistant had gone too far but thankfully Kerem stayed calm.

'You may not believe it but Cemal was the most beloved of my children. Over time, people begin to grasp the value of their children. He was our youngest and we doted upon him. I used to hold his hand and take him to the park. I even used to drop him off to school. He was such a smart kid. So very smart. Always got commendations from his teachers. They used to call him the computer acrobat. He was really into it, software or programming, whatever you call it… And he started earning good money too… But then he went off the rails. Instead of taking the family's reputation into consideration, he chose to live another way and removed us from his life. I told him not to and warned him of the consequences but he would not listen. Family is important. In a family, everyone has responsibilities. A father should be a father and a son should act like a son.' He stopped and swallowed several times, hovering between grief and rage. 'But to lose a child is a terrible thing. You do not know what to say or do. You would not understand, Mister Becker, as you do not have children. It doesn't matter how angry you may be with them, to lose children is simply awful.'

It was the second time he had mentioned losing children. Not a child but children, a detail that did not escape Yıldız's attention.

'Have you lost any other child?'

Kerem stared blankly at her.

'Huh…? Sorry, what do you mean?'

'You said children,' Yıldız said, thinking he had not understood. 'I'm wondering if you have lost any other child.'

'Oh no, thank God. I've already lost Cemal, what more do you want? Do you have children?'

The Chief Inspector pictured Deniz's sweet face. Naturally, she did not want to discuss her one and only child with a murder suspect.

'Yes,' she said quickly and changed the subject. 'You mentioned some people who despised you just now. Your cousins, if I remember correctly.' She looked into his eyes to glean his reaction. 'Were you just saying it or are there really such people out there with these hostile feelings for you?'

The change of subject was a relief to Kerem too.

'There was some ill will between my Uncle Recep and us. He was my father's elder brother. My father Orhan was his younger brother. When my grandfather died, he left behind a house and an olive grove. The olive grove was nothing spectacular, just this little patch of land by the Selinos River in Kozak, Bergama. The house is an old, two-storey building. At first, Uncle Recep wanted the land and my father agreed but then Uncle Recep changed his mind and said he wanted the house. My father agreed to that too. But then, one day, he turned around and said, "Our father helped you a lot. I want both." That was too much and we refused. The dispute ended up in the courts. In the end, we got the olive grove and they got the house. But they were not happy with the decision. They did not accept it.'

Tobias was having trouble grasping the situation.

'Why didn't they accept it? Didn't the court hand down a fair verdict?'

Kerem let out a frustrated sigh.

'It did, but my uncle is an obsessive kind of guy. All his life, since he was little, he has gone around complaining that he has been wronged. He always said grandfather Cemal loved my father more and that he treated his younger son preferably. Basically, Uncle Recep has resented my father for a long time. Even after the court issued its verdict, he wasn't happy. My uncle has three sons, while I am an only child. One day, they stormed our house…'

The Chief Inspector was confused.

'The house in Bergama?'

'Bergama?' Kerem said, confused as to why she did not understand. 'No, Berlin. Our house here in Berlin. My father and Uncle Recep came to Berlin together. Actually, the family had agreed that my father would come by himself and Uncle Recep would stay behind in the house in Bergama and tend to the olive grove. The archaeological excavations were to continue in the summers. But once it was agreed that my father would come to Germany, he insisted on coming too. Grandfather Orhan did not want to see both his sons leave but he had no choice and reluctantly gave his assent. At that time, Erich Boehringer was in charge of the excavations, while my grandfather was the foreman. He was a great craftsman too, and Mister Boehringer was very fond of my grandfather. When my father and uncle came to Berlin, Mister Boehringer helped them a lot. As a result, they did not struggle as much as the other Turks that came over at the time for work.' He fell silent and frowned. 'Why am I telling you all this?' he suddenly said angrily. 'My son has just been killed and here we are having a damn conversation about utter nonsense.'

'We can talk another time if you like,' Yıldız said, looking at him with understanding and a little tenderness. 'Whenever you are ready. But what you have to say is of great importance to us. Of course, it will not bring Cemal back but it may help us catch the killer.'

Kerem seemed uncertain at first but he then stood up and walked over to the window at the rear of the room.

'It's a bit stuffy in here.' He opened the window and stood in front of it for a while before coming back and rifling through a drawer for a bottle of medicine. He took a pill and then lifted his head slowly and stared at the Chief Inspector with eyes full of hurt. 'Are you really going to find Cemal's killer?' he asked in Turkish. 'I mean, this isn't all just grandstanding, is it? I'm sorry but I do not trust the German police.'

'You can trust me,' Yıldız answered in Turkish, nodding her head, before continuing in German. 'Rest assured, we shall do everything we can. One way or another, we will find the person responsible for Cemal's death.'

'Very well,' Kerem said, although his disbelief was still palpable. 'God, what has happened to us?' he muttered and then took a deep breath. 'Where was I? Ah, yes. I was telling you about the time they stormed our house. Uncle Recep rounded up his sons and grandsons and came over to our house in Wedding, where my father, my late mother and I used to live. Can you imagine? Some of your closest relatives all hop into a van. They drive over to your house, gather outside your front door wielding sticks and bats and then force their way into your house… They turned the house upside down. Made a complete mess and caused a massive amount of damage. God, it was so embarrassing. All the neighbours were watching, German, Turkish, everyone. My father sustained a head injury and I had my leg broken. Hüseyin was still young at the time and Cemal was just a kid but I raised them both to be men and not to run from danger. Hüseyin grabbed a knife and began chasing them away and Cemal, despite his age, flung whatever he could lay his hands on at them. However, a tragic accident then occurred. One of my uncle's grandsons, Ihsan, was hit by a truck. He died on the spot and his family has never forgiven us for his death. We never wished for such a terrible thing to happen. I loved Ihsan dearly.'

A family squabble... Yıldız continued with her questioning.

'How old is your Uncle Recep?'

'Uncle Recep, may he rest in peace, died fifteen years ago. He had a heart attack. He had always been an ill-tempered type of guy and he smoked a lot. Of course, his family blamed us. They said he had never gotten over Ihsan's death and that that is what eventually led to the heart attack. Twice his eldest sons Mehmet and Davut squared up to me in the middle of the street, and one night they opened fire on Hüseyin and Cemal in the dark. Cemal was wounded in the arm.'

'Didn't you go to the police?' Tobias asked. 'I mean, come on! What they did was a clear felony. An open and shut case.'

'Of course we went to the police,' Kerem said, tensing up at the memory. 'Mehmet and Davut were arrested and questioned but they were released as they were not found to be in possession of any weapons after the arrest and there were no witnesses.' He looked at Yıldız and continued in Turkish. 'You know how it is. It was a fight between Turks so the police couldn't care less. Let them beat ten shades out of each other, they thought. Just let them get on with it.'

'I understand but please, let's speak German,' Yıldız warned him. 'My colleague does not understand Turkish. Tell me, was Cemal's wound an accident or do you think they were really aiming for him?'

'They were aiming for him,' Kerem replied, anger and hatred beginning to form in his dark eyes. 'Because they knew how much I loved him.' He stopped and looked at Yıldız. 'Do you think they are the ones that killed him?'

The possibility would definitely have eased Kerem's problems to an extent, in that it would have at least taken him and his family off the suspect list, but it was too early to say. Moreover, the people who carried out such a sophisticated murder were probably highly educated. Kerem's family may have been familiar with Zeus and other ancient Greek Gods but the manner in which the killing had been carried out did not suggest a family feud.

'What do your cousins, this Mehmet and Davut, do?'

'Mehmet, the eldest, retired last year. He's around seventy. He bought a summer house in Dikili, and spends six months there and six months here. Davut is the same age as me. He is also retired. He has a nargile café in Neukölln. The Turks and Arabs love it. He's been raking it in for the last three years. He moved into the apartment above the shop. They say he owns the entire building now.'

It seemed meaningless for two cousins to keep an old feud going after so many years but nothing could be overlooked.

'What about children? Does he have any? What do they do?' Tobias asked. Kerem's forehead wrinkled up in a frown as he tried to remember.

'Mehmet has three daughters, all housewives. Davut has one daughter, Hülya, and two sons, Ihsan and Haluk. As I said, Ihsan died during that fracas, while Hülya married someone from Bergama and went back to Turkey. Haluk lives in Berlin. He is a good lad, like my Cemal was. Smart, hard-working and well-mannered. He is well-educated too.' He looked disappointed. 'He fulfilled the promise made to Atatürk. Fate works in mysterious ways, I suppose. Grandfather Cemal wanted me to be an archaeologist. I tried but I failed. Haluk, on the other hand, succeeded, and good for him. He works at the German Archaeology Institute. In the summers, he goes to Turkey and joins the digs at Pergamon. Who knows, he may become head of the excavations one day. We're all very proud of him, as you can imagine.'

It was quite clear that he was not proud and that he was jealous, not that it mattered to Yıldız. What did matter was the fact that this archaeologist Haluk was the closest match to the profile of the perpetrator. If he still held Cemal and his family responsible for the death of Ihsan, then he had a plausible motive for murder.

'Have you ever spoken to Haluk?'

Kerem threw his head back.

'No. Like I said, we have not spoken to my uncle's family since Ihsan's death. We hear about Haluk's successes through mutual acquaintances. You know how it is with Berlin Turks. If you are from the same town, then everyone knows everyone.'

'And was Haluk involved in that fight the led to Ihsan's death?'

'Oh no, Haluk was too young at the time. Two years younger than Cemal.' His eyes fluttered in suspicion. 'Why? Do you think Haluk did it?'

'We don't know yet,' Yıldız said, taking out her mobile phone. 'We'll have to look into it. What was Haluk's full name?'

'Haluk Ölmez', Kerem replied, now mulling over this new possibility. 'You think Haluk could have done this terrible deed?'

'Don't worry, we'll soon know,' Yıldız said, saving the name on her mobile phone's note app before turning to her assistant. 'We need to speak to this Haluk as soon as possible.' She placed her phone on the table and turned to look at Kerem again. 'What does your older son Hüseyin do for a living?'

The expression on Kerem's face went from suspicion back to nervousness.

'We have another branch of *Bergama Baklava* in Kudamm. He runs that store.'

'So you have two branches in Berlin?' Yıldız asked, wanting to be sure of the details.

'Yes, two. Baklava is actually Hüseyin's profession. He had a teacher from Gaziantep who taught him the trade. When I retired, we came into a bit of money and so we opened the shop. Praise to the Almighty, things went well and we managed to open another branch in Kudamm. Hüseyin runs that branch and I keep an eye on this one. Cemal, bless him, was always in his own world. My grandson Alper helps out every now and then too.' The worried expression returned. 'Listen, if you suspect Hüseyin, then don't bother. I know my son. He has a temper, yes, and he can be volatile, but he could never kill anyone. Especially not his own brother… Never.'

At that moment, Alper poked his head through the door.

'Grandad, there's a guy here. He says he wants to talk about Uncle Cemal.'

All three turned to look at the door. A tall man in his forties wearing a black suede jacket, black shirt and black trousers and with wavy hair that fell past his shoulders walked in past Alper.

'Good day,' he said in a hoarse voice. 'I would like to speak to Kerem Ölmez.'

'I'm Kerem Ölmez,' the shop owner said, getting to his feet. The visitor extended a hand.

'My name is Peter Schimmel,' he said sadly. 'I am afraid I have bad news for you, Mister Ölmez. Your son…'

'I know, Mister Schimmel,' Kerem said, blinking away the tears and pointing to his guests. 'The police have informed me.'

Peter looked momentarily surprised. He greeted the police and then turned to address Kerem again. 'Your son used to work for our firm. I am the manager of Der Blitz.' He grimaced. 'Please forgive me for my crudity when I say he worked for us. Cemal was a dear friend.'

His dark eyes were also tearful. As the Chief Inspector looked at him, she could not help but notice how good-looking he was. This must be the unconventional boss Alex had mentioned to them. Good, it saved them a trip to the company's premises. Yıldız got to her feet and offered a hand.

'Chief Inspector Yıldız Karasu, Berlin Police Homicide Desk. And this is my assistant, Inspector Tobias Becker.'

Peter shook hands with both of them.

'This is just terrible news. I liked Cemal so much. This truly is a terrible tragedy. Just terrible. I hope you find the perpetrators as soon as possible.'

Yıldız scrutinized the man carefully.

'With your help, we will. Actually, we were planning on talking to you, Mister Schimmel, but please go ahead and finish your business here with Mister Ölmez.'

'Please, take a seat.' Kerem offered.

'Thank you,' the new arrival said. He smiled graciously and accepted the seat. 'To tell the truth, I was unsure as to whether I should come or not. I know about the thorny issues that existed between you and Cemal but I felt I had to come in case you had not heard the news. Cemal was your son, at the end of the day, and I felt you needed to know.' His eyes flitted over to the police and then back again. 'But I see you have already been given the dreadful news. My condolences, first of all. I would like you to know that I share your grief. Secondly, there is one thing I would like to know.' He stopped, not knowing how to continue. 'My apologies for being so blunt at such a delicate time, really, but it concerns Cemal's last rites? How and where will they be conducted? What arrangements are being made?'

Yıldız was curious as to how Kerem would answer but he failed to answer so Peter went on.

'This is clearly not the right time to discuss such a delicate issue. Perhaps it would be better if you discuss it with your family first. However, I would be most grateful if you would inform once you have reached a decision.'

Kerem seem relieved.

'Very well, Mister Schimmel. I shall speak to my wife and son and then get back to you. I'll call you.'

A cold expression flickered in Peter's black eyes.

'Understood. However, let me just say that if you decide not to undertake the arrangements for Cemal's funeral, we would be honoured to do so.'

The late spring sun streaming through the branches of the acacia tree lit up Peter's sombre face. Tobias sat on a stool to the right and enjoyed a cigarette while Yıldız sat in the shade and sipped her coffee. She was staring at the Der Blitz manager and his stubble, which had taken on a reddish hue in the sunlight. It suited him. But the question on her mind was whether this supposedly unusual boss was the man whom Alex envied.

They were sitting in the Leylak Kafe in Kottbusser Square. Yıldız had not wanted to talk to Peter in front of Kerem and, as far as she had been able to intuit, Peter was of the same mind. Although this particular case had a significance for her beyond mere work, it was her opinion — and Peter's too, evidently — that Cemal's family had wronged him. As for Tobias, his main concern in the sweetshop had been to get out into the open as soon as possible and light up a cigarette, and now here he was at last, puffing happily away. After taking a large sip of coffee, Yıldız got straight down to business. 'Tell me, how did you find out? Was it when Cemal failed to show up for work?'

'No, we are not really into having fixed working hours,' Peter said casually. 'Even less so for those involved in the creative side of things like Cemal. Pilar told me last night…' He stopped to think. 'You must be the police officers she mentioned. She called me after you left.'

'How did she get your number?' Tobias asked, carefully tapping the ash from his cigarette into a metal ashtray on the table in front of him.

Peter answered as he reached out for his coffee.

'I know Pilar and Rafael. We know each other well enough to have one another's phone numbers. They are also friends of mine. In fact, after the baby is born, Pilar is going to start working for us.'

Yıldız admired the man's attitude.

'Do you always employ immigrants?'

Peter took a sip from his coffee.

'I don't employ them, I work with them. I work with people that will be of use to me. That is all. However, if a German and an immigrant with the same skillset and who can both be of use to me apply, I will opt for the immigrant because they have less chance of finding work.' He smiled sweetly. His white teeth shone and his black eyes seemed to turn dark blue. 'Why? Are you thinking of a change in career?'

Was he flirting with her?

'Oh no, we are simply trying to work out whether you are a killer or not,' Yıldız said, somewhat austerely. 'Until we find the perpetrator, anybody with any kind of link to the deceased remains a potential suspect. Tell us, why did you employ Cemal?'

Unperturbed, Peter gently put his cup down on the table.

'I'm sorry if I crossed any line,' he said and cleared his throat. 'I took Cemal on board because he was incredibly talented. The field of renewable energy requires highly advanced technology. Cemal created computer program and wrote software for us. He was fast, hard-working and very creative. He was also a painter. In fact, we met him at my older sister's art exhibition. Have you seen Cemal's paintings?'

'We have,' the Chief Inspector replied, but she did not want the topic of the conversation to be diverted. 'What has art got to do with renewable energy?'

Peter placed his elbows on the table and opened out his arms.

'If there were no visual arts, there would be no Der Blitz.' Seeing the looks of curiosity on the two officers' faces, he asked, 'Do you really want me to go on?'

'Please,' Yıldız replied, with a measured smile.

'Very well, if you want to hear it.' He looked up at the sky. 'It's getting quite hot. I hope you won't mind if I take my jacket off?'

Still smiling, Yıldız nodded and watched Peter take his suede jacket off, leaving him in a black t-shirt that was so tight, one could see almost the contours of his well-defined torso. Again, Yıldız find herself pondering the link between this man and Alex's jealousy.

'Art's importance to Der Blitz stems from my sister, Angela,' Peter said, hanging his jacket on the back of his chair. 'She was a great artist, my sister. You may have heard of her.'

'Angela Schimmel?' Tobias asked, as though he was someone with an abiding interest in the art world.

'No, she only used the name Angel.' He smiled. 'She had a nickname too: Dirty Angel. Indeed, when people talked about her, they just called her Dirty.'

'Why Dirty Angel?' Yıldız asked. For the first time, Peter looked affronted.

'It is not what you think. Angela was the cleanest person on this planet, both physically and mentally. She was sweetest, kindest, most selfless person I ever knew, as well as being the most talented…. They gave her that nickname because they thought her working methods were messy and disordered. Tins of paint and brushes scattered all over the place… It was impossible to set foot in her studio. I think they gave her that name out of envy, not that Angela cared. Indeed, over time, she adopted it. She was such a strong woman. So free-spirited. She lived the way she wanted. I am not saying this because she was my sister, nor because she left me an inheritance that allowed me to found Der Blitz. Everyone that knew her says the same about her. However, nobody knew her true worth while she was alive.' He reached for his coffee and took a sip. After licking his lips clean, he looked at Yıldız. 'How long have you been in Berlin?'

There was no condescension in his voice but Yıldız kept her guard up.

'Since I was born. Why?'

Peter's cheeks seem to flush.

'It looks like I cannot stop putting my foot in my mouth today. I am sure you know the Kunsthaus Tacheles. It was a living arts centre. A free art complex gifted to the world by Berlin.'

Yıldız knew the place very well.

'Did your sister set it up?'

Peter picked up the tiny hint of mockery in her voice but he was not bothered by it and went on.

'No, she was just one of the people that transformed it into the legendary arts centre it is now. Jews had been living there since the beginning of the last century. The building was actually a vast set of corridors and passageway and when the Nazis came to power, they turned it into a prison. After the war, the German Democratic Republic demolished part of it, leaving the rest just standing there unused. When the Berlin Wall came down, a number of artists — painters, sculptors, actors and filmmakers — came together and moved into the building, where they set up their own studios, clubs and workspaces. And as a tribute to the Jews that had lived there, they named this space "Tacheles", which in Yiddish means "straight talk", or "to speak frankly"… That is how the Tacheles Art House was born. There, a communal spirit was forged in which artists could live and work side by side, bound by no authority and impervious to the vagaries of the market. It was a utopian island of art in the heart of Europe that lasted from 1990 to 2012. That's right, a full twenty-two years. An earthly paradise in which artists could freely express their ideas. The most productive years of my sister's life were spent there. It is where she created her most important works. When I said it was an oasis of freedom in all aspects of life, of course it was inevitable that there would be some extremes, as one would expect from artists in such an environment. It was all there — casual sex, drugs, alcohol, whatever your heart desired. Being in the same space, seeing each other's work, witnessing each other's creative processes may have increased competition but that does not mean success always came easily.

'Back then, some of the people based there, not all of them of course but some, really did take their hedonism and experimentation to insane levels and as it turned out, my sister, unfortunately, was one of them. Her life was fast, intense and rapturous but at the same time it was full of disillusionment. It was a life that respected no rules, an exhausting life that took its toll on the body and mind and which eventually consumed her. We lost Angela five years ago to cancer. She suffered enormously.'

He tried to smile but the attempt failed as the emotions were getting the better of him. 'But she lived the way she wanted, not the way others tried to make her live. And that is what counts.' He reached out for his coffee again. 'Look at the irony. Within a year of her death, the people that labelled her work as kitsch and dismissed her paintings as garbage when she was alive began showering praise on her: "Berlin's Melancholy Artist." "A magician who lets us feel the meaning beyond reality with her use of colour." Yes, that is how they describe her now, and now her paintings are valuable collectables. Not just in Berlin either, but art lovers and wealthy collectors all over the world compete with each another to get their hands on a Dirty Angel painting to hang on their wall. The money started flowing in.' He averted his eyes, as though ashamed, and took another sip of coffee before looking despondently at Yıldız and Tobias. 'And because our mother and father have passed away, I became the sole beneficiary of Dirty Angel's legacy.'

Tobias, lost in the story, did not seem to understand.

'So, all the money ended up with you,' he said jovially, as though celebrating a friend winning the lottery. 'I mean, we're talking about a small fortune here, right?'

'We are indeed talking about rather a large sum of money. I studied environmental engineering but without the capital from that art, there is no way I would have been able to set up my company. That is why I picked Cemal. Because without art, without portraiture, there would be no Der Blitz.'

He was spinning a near-perfect story, full of profound goodness in a rotten world, which is why Yıldız was having difficulty believing him.

'So your finding Cemal attractive had nothing to do with you employing him?'

The owner of Der Blitz narrowed his eyes.

'What? Oh no, Ms Karasu, I am not gay. I like women. And nor am I bisexual. Just women. I don't know how else I can put it. Just women…'

For some reason, Yıldız was secretly pleased.

'I'm sorry, I just thought…'

He nodded his head genially.

'Many have. It's not a problem. We are in Berlin, after all. The most liberated and unconventional city in Germany. Adults here can live any way they choose.' He paused before saying, 'According to the law, at any rate.'

'Do you know Alex?' Tobias asked, stubbing his cigarette out into the ashtray. 'Alexander Werner?'

Peter scowled.

'Yes, I do. Alex is a miserable man, and what's worse, he infects everyone else with his misery. Cemal was trying to break free from him. Their relationship was on the rocks. But you know how it is. It is not that easy to just walk away…'

This explanation did not help dispel Yıldız's doubts.

'Apparently Alex was deeply jealous of Cemal. We spoke to him last night. He mentioned something about another lover. That is why Cemal wanted to end their relationship.'

Peter frowned again.

'As far as I know, there was nobody else.' He paused and blinked several times. 'No, I don't think so. But then again, it was his private life. He may have kept it to himself.'

'You and Cemal were colleagues and friends and, from what I can make out, you got on very well,' Tobias said, taking another cigarette from his packet. 'Do you paint?'

Peter's gaze seemed stuck on Tobias' cigarette.

'You smoke quite a lot. You only just put one out. It's not good for you.'

Tobias glared at him.

'I can move away from you if it makes you uncomfortable when I smoke.'

'No, please, don't get up,' he said with the same grating serenity. 'I just wanted to remind you, for the sake of your health. If it is not a problem for Ms Karasu, then it is not a problem for me.'

Seeing no objection from his boss, Tobias lit up. During those few moments of silence at the table, Peter watched him with an easy-going smile. As the smoke rose up into the spring air, he carried on.

'As for your question, I am not an artist. In our family, it was only my sister that had that particular talent. I do not practice painting or any other artform. But I do try to be a good viewer of art. Since my sister's death, you can say I have become quite knowledgeable on the subject.'

'And what about archaeology?' Yıldız asked. 'Are you interested in that?'

'Only as much as the next man,' he answered. 'If you were to ask me, for instance, about the story behind the reliefs on the Altar of Zeus, I would not be able to answer you. I think it had something to do with a battle between the Gods and the Titans. But Cemal was really into archaeology. He was working on something with an archaeological theme.' He sighed. 'Unfortunately, the project has been left half-finished.'

Yıldız was about to ask Peter if there was anybody at work with whom Cemal had argued or had a misunderstanding when her phone rang. It was an unfamiliar number. She pressed the green button.

'Hello?'

'Am I speaking to Chief Inspector Karasu?' a voice with an accent asked.

'Yes, speaking. How can I help?'

'My name is Rafael. Rafael Moreno. You came to our house last night. I am Pilar's husband.'

'Ah yes, Mister Moreno. Please, do go on.'

'I need to speak to you, but not on the phone. It's urgent. Can you come to our place?'

He sounded tense. Evidently, what he had to say was of some importance but Yıldız did not want to discuss anything sensitive in front of Peter.

'Fine, we'll be there. Thanks for calling,' she said casually and ended the call.

'What's happened? What did Rafael say?' Peter asked.

Yıldız brushed the question off. 'Oh, it was nothing. We wanted to speak to him yesterday but he was not at home. He said we can meet at another time if needed…' She placed her phone on the table and went on. 'Was Cemal liked at the company?' Even she did not know why her tone came out so harsh but she went on. 'Were there any people there with whom he did not get on? Anyone with whom he had disagreements or quarrels?'

'No, not at all, Ms Karasu,' Peter said, almost amazed at the absurdity of the question. 'Cemal was not like that at all. Everyone liked him. He really was a great person. His greatest misfortune was the people around him not being as sweet and as decent as him.'

'So what do you think? Who do you think could have done this to Cemal?'

Peter's coal black eyes dimmed.

'I don't know. It's just a guess and only a distant possibility but one of his family perhaps. You saw for yourself how ashamed they still are of him. It may also have been Alex. For all we know, the guy is a xenophobic and homophobic psycho. I really can't say because Cemal did not have any enemies.'

He stopped. He had tears in his eyes but Yıldız was quick to shatter the fragility of the moment.

'We would like to see his office,' she said. 'He has an office of his own at the firm, I assume?'

'Of course. Whenever you like. You can speak to his colleagues too. There may be a detail I have overlooked...' He took his jacket from the back of the chair, removed two business cards from a pocket and gave them one each. 'You can call me any time. Day or night, do not hesitate. We have to find this killer. I am willing to do whatever it takes.'

4
Twilight of the Gods

Until power has been seized in its entirety, victory cannot be proclaimed. Victory, however, is not gained with one battle. To capture the sacred crown, to sit on the holy throne, to be the ruler of the earth and skies, it is not enough to merely defeat the King of the Titans. True, no one rewarded me with the spoils of destiny or handed power to me on a golden platter. It was with tooth and nail, wit and valour and patience and determination that I attained this exalted position. When no living being dared face Kronos, I faced him. When no Titan dared challenge him, I challenged him. But to defeat my father was not enough.

And that is because the Titans needed Kronos. They were all the progeny of Uranus, the brothers and sisters of my father. Some resented my father, and others outright despised him, as Kronos had humiliated them all. Just as his father Uranus had been disgusted by his progeny, so too was Kronos disgusted by his siblings. He was disgusted by them, while he also envied them. For instance, the three one-eyed Giants Brontes, Steropes and Arges; Kronos despised these three spectacular creatures for they were stronger, better and more accomplished than him and they were the lords of thunder, lightning and the thunderbolt.

And not only were they masters of the sky, they were skilled in the ways of the earth too. They knew how to extract iron from the hearts of the mountains, they gave wondrous form to the hardest of metals and they built the most fearsome weapons.

And then there were the three other formidable Giants, the three extraordinary brothers, Briareus, Cottos and Gyes. Each with one hundred arms and fifty heads, they were the strongest and greatest of all the creatures of the earth. In contrast to their terrifying size, they were kind, loyal and faithful. But any goodness in my father's heart had been corrupted by fear, and he had never known or experienced the feeling of loyalty, and he therefore hated these three wondrous beings and sent all six into the depths of Tartarus. However, my father had other siblings: the Titans. All born of Uranus and Gaia, these brothers and sisters of my father were strong, brave, warlike and indomitable. To see them was to fear them, admire them and revere them.

The eldest was Oceanus. If the earth is alive, then Oceanus was its arteries. When seen from the skies, he appeared to the eye as a vast tree made of water. If you descended to earth and were to mount the swiftest horses and ride for days without stopping, you would still have not been able to cover his range. My uncle Oceanus was Gaia's eldest son and he never betrayed the blood relationship between us. Even though his heart was with his siblings, he never took up arms against me.

Tethys was the beauty, fertility and feminine power of water. Her vision filled those that saw her with tears, her shadow filled them with melancholy and her depths made their heads spin. Whatever she touched would sprout into life, stones would melt, solid rock would soften and the mountains themselves would open up and reverentially make way for her. Not only did she give life, she added beauty to life. If Oceanus was the trunk of the vast tree that encircled the world, Tethys was its branches, leaves and flowers. When the two met, the earth would bloom. She was of my blood, and she did not take up arms against me either.

And Themis, most beautiful, most virtuous, most honourable and wisest of the Titans. Symbol of divine justice, upholder of the ancient law and the Goddess of prophecies. Were it not for Themis, intelligence would not consult conscience and the mind would lack compassion. The Titans, the Gods and man would not have known how to behave and the winds of oppression would have blown over the earth. Themis was also my second spouse, the sharer of my bed and of my thoughts, and the mother of my children. Such was her virtue, she was the only Titan allowed to ascend Olympus.

And then Coeus, who drew his strength from his intelligence, Hyperion, who walked in light, Crius of incontestable strength, and Iapetus, who raised sons in enmity towards me. And then Theia, mother to the Sun and the Moon, sweet Mnemosyne who remembers all, and Phoebus, who banished weak pallor from all beings, living and non-living, and made them glow with life. These Titans and Titanesses, and their brave, resolute, warrior sons and daughters, did not bow before me, despite their animosity towards Kronos. They did not want to live under the yoke of the Gods, and so they fuelled rebellion after rebellion on earth.

This was the first of the wars. The battles were directed from two vast mountains. My siblings and I were on Olympus, whilst the Titans and their issue were on Othrys. In valour, intelligence and fighting spirit, they were our equal. Moreover, they were greater in experience as they had walked the earth before us, and they were more steadfast than us, as they did not wish to lose their paradise. They were also greater in their rage, as they felt betrayed. They attacked us without hesitation, and we fought back, with sword, with spear and with arrow, and, when we were without weapon, we fought with bare hands, with tooth and nail. Countless times they ambushed us and countless times we ambushed them, yet neither side prevailed. This situation was intolerable, for the kingdom of the Gods could not be left to fester in rebellion. The disorder demanded an answer, a final and lasting resolution.

And thus it was that during this war, for the first time, I learnt to acknowledge the importance of mercy, that feeling that was usually so destructive to both Mortals and Immortals. I released the Giants from their shackles in the underworld to which they had been sent by Kronos and brought them out of Tartarus, thereby winning the gratitude of the brilliant and skilled Cyclopes Brontes, Steropes and Arges. With great munificence, they presented to me the gifts of thunder, lightning and the thunderbolt, and with these gifts, I gained mastery of the sky. I wrought terror in the hearts of my foes and trust in the hearts of my friends. These three Cyclops presented to my brother Poseidon a gift of a trident with which he would cause the earth to tremble, the oceans to rise in tumult and crash onto the rocks of the shore, and the mountains to quiver in fear. To my other brother Hades, they fashioned for him a helmet, one of such power that its wearer became invisible and could thus enter his enemy's strongholds at will and wreak turmoil.

And so began our ascendancy over Kronos' siblings. But to defeat the Titans was no mean feat. They did not surrender, they did not give in, they did not tire. A bloody and seemingly endless battle was waged on the earth. Our swords, spears and arrows could not find the final, decisive blow that would grant us victory over our enemy kin.

That is when my mind was awakened and the path to victory appeared before my eyes. The war could not be won with brute force alone. Intelligence has always been superior to raw strength and to blind fury. To win this war, I needed to expand my allies and diminish the ranks of my foes. I remembered once more the favours I had granted, and so once again, I found refuge in the sagacity of mercy. I visited the Hecatoncheires, the three brothers with fifty heads and one-hundred arms, for I had rescued them from Tartarus, just as I had the Cyclopes. I approached them and, without speaking, I shared with them my food and drink. At first, they were unsure, but they then saw that I had approached them in friendship and bore them no ill and so they ate and drank my offerings. And I said unto them:

'Greetings to you, strong Briareus, virtuous Cottos and beloved Gyes, the three most powerful, awesome and loyal of the Giants of the earth, my powerful kin whose father and siblings condemned you unto the darkness. I gaze upon you in awe and I salute your presence and your strength. I know that I am at war with your brothers and I know you may say that it is not your fight and that it matters little to you who triumphs. However, you are wrong to think thus. If I lose this war, if my father Kronos and his siblings triumph, they shall consign you once more as shameful prisoners to the bowels of Tartarus. If, however, I defeat the Titans, you shall live free and respectably. None shall stain your honour, none shall belittle your formidable bodies, none shall dare imprison you behind impregnable walls. I need you. Come, join me. Let us stand shoulder to shoulder and end the tyranny of the Titans. Let us launch a new age, one that is just, free and Conzent.'

My words reminded them of their father Uranus and their brother Kronos' cruelty. My words recalled to their minds my kindness to them and awakened in them a burning desire for justice, and so they willingly joined my side. In battle, they uprooted the immense mountains and flung them at the Titans.

With their one-hundred arms, they rained down a hail of rocks upon our foe and they smote their closest kin in the fires of the volcanoes. That is when I assembled my brothers and sisters upon the misty peaks of Olympus and I said:

'The day has arrived. This is the moment the reign of the Titans shall come to an end. If we delay, victory shall slip from our hands. If we hesitate, this decade-long war shall continue for centuries more. If we do not attack now, the Dawn of the Gods shall never arrive. So, let us advance and confront the Titans. Let us fight our final battle and finally end this bloody war.'

My brothers and sisters obeyed my commands. Arm in arm, shoulder to shoulder, we wore our valour like the strongest armour and embraced our minds like the proudest of helmets, and we set off to face the Titans. With all my might, I made the skies growl with thunder, I rained thunderbolts down upon them and I scorched them with lightning. My brothers and sisters unleashed all their lethal powers with all their expertise, and once again, a bloody and brutal battle commenced in the clouds. The blue sky turned black, the seas turned to blood, the fertile plains were scorched, the mountains levelled, and the fields and meadows splintered and cracked. The earth had never seen such a war since its creation. The Titans were suffering great losses but still, they did not retreat and with all their fury and might, they fought back. But when the six Giants, their own kin, entered the field of battle, they began to waver and their assembled ranks began to fall apart.

In this moment of confusion, I rained thunder and lightning down upon their heads. Their eyes bedazzled, their hair aflame and their bodies contorted in pain, they buckled and so, with the help of my comrades, who were now filled with yet greater courage, we sent the Titans, one by one, into the dungeons of Tartarus. Before they knew it, they found themselves in the darkest pits of that hell. My powerful brother Poseidon slammed shut the bronze doors of Tartarus, and I posted Briareus, Cottos and Gyes in front of the gates as its guardians to prevent the Titans' escape. And with this final and absolute victory, I announced my rule. Once more I inscribed into the minds of all living beings that I was the greatest of all the God and to Kronos, who was now a captive of Tartarus, I roared:

'Those that despise their children shall forever be despised. Mortal or Immortal, it matters not; those that betray their own kin shall be punished with the most terrible of betrayals.'

Chapter Four

The old polar-lined street in which Cemal's house was located looked wonderful in the daytime. They parked the Passat on the kerb. When they were getting out of the car, Yıldız noticed the wall on the other side of the street facing the house. She narrowed her eyes to get a better look at the painting on the wall: a superbly executed painting of a huge rainbow flag held up by yellow, black and white hands. However, scrawled messily across the flag in large brown letters were the words *'Foreigners Out.'*

The Chief jerked her head towards the wall.

'Did you see this last night?'

Tobias looked at the picture and then the writing.

'No, I didn't. Do you think the old man we saw last night wrote that message on the flag?'

Yıldız did not respond. Instead, she took out her phone and took a photograph of the wall but it was not clear enough so she moved closer to it and took some more snaps. A voice suddenly rang out: 'You see it, don't you? You can see it! They've ruined our beautiful picture. Bastards!'

They turned around. A tanned, slender young man with curly hair was walking towards them from the entrance of Cemal's apartment block.

'Hi. I'm Rafael Moreno. Thank you for coming on time.'

He spoke German with an even heavier accent than his wife. He came up to them and extended a bony outstretched hand.

'Hello. I'm Chief Inspector Yıldız Karasu, and this is my assistant, Tobias Becker. I believe you spoke to him on phone.' She shook the outstretched hand and then pointed with her telephone to the wall. 'Did you paint this?'

'Cemal and I did it together,' he said with a pained expression. 'Can you see what they have done to it? It was here for days, and then a week ago, they wrote that horrible slogan over it. Give them half a chance and they would have lynched us. And they did, in the end. They killed poor Cemal.' He turned around and nervously looked at his apartment building. 'Please, don't tell Pilar. I don't want her getting even more frightened than she already is. That is why I waited for you outside. I don't want to talk about this in front of her. She is resting right now. She is in a state of shock. She really liked Cemal.' He pointed to the street, shaded by the rows of poplars. 'If you like, we can walk and talk...' His expression changed to one of anger and looking in the distance at a spot at the end of the street, he added, 'And I can show you the place where those bastards that killed Cemal hang out.'

He spoke with such certainty, Yıldız felt a faint flutter of excitement. Finally, they had found someone who could give them some really useful information.

'So you're saying you actually know who Cemal's killers are?' Tobias asked.

'Of course, I do,' he said, jutting his chin forward. His voice came out louder than expected and his right hand quickly went up to cover his mouth. 'But please,' he went on quietly. 'Let's not talk here.'

His consideration for his pregnant wife was admirable. He also had possibly crucial information to pass on to them.

'Of course, please. Let's walk,' Yıldız said calmly. 'We could do with stretching our legs a little anyway.'

This was not what Tobias had been expecting. Like his boss, he had been on duty for hours and he had been looking forward to sitting back on the cheap armchairs in Rafael and Pilar's cosy little flat and enjoying a nice cup of coffee while they indulged in mental, rather than physical, gymnastics. But after hearing what Rafael had just said, he also knew that the exertion would be worth it. With the Argentinian artist in the middle, the three began walking.

'So who are these people that killed Cemal? Are they the same people that defaced your painting?'

After looking back at the window of their flat to make sure Pilar could not see them, Rafael said, 'Well, of course they are. Who else could it be? It had to be that sly lowlife Otto and his friends.'

'Otto? You know the killer by name?'

'Absolutely. I even met him. Twice. Once, when he tried to kick me out of his pub, the other time when he threatened us with an SS knife. That's right, a real SS knife with a swastika on the hilt. And he had those two snakes, who were with him that day too. I bet they killed Cemal with that same knife…'

He was talking quickly and carelessly now and Tobias stepped in to slow him down.

'One at a time, please, Mr. Moreno. Why don't you begin with this mural? Is that where you first met this gentleman called Otto?'

'No, it was in a café. A place called Kafe 88, not far from here.'

'Heil Hitler,' Yıldız muttered. 'Kafe Heil Hitler…'

'No, Kafe 88,' the painter said.

'Kafe 88 means Heil Hitler,' Yıldız said gently. 'Neo-Nazis use that number as a way of saying Heil Hitler.'

'Really?' Rafael said, taken aback. 'It's the first time I'm hearing it.'

A gentle breeze caressed their faces. Yıldız breathed in the scent of linden again before continuing.

'In the German alphabet, the eighth letter is H. Two eights put together make up HH, in other words, the first letters of the phrase "Heil Hitler". They also use the code 18, as well as 88.'

The painter was no slouch and quickly did the maths.

'1 and 8 would be A and H. So that must refer to Adolf Hitler…'

'Exactly…. Neo-Nazis use those numbers because it is illegal to display or use any symbols related to Hitler.' She quickly looked at the painter walking next to her. 'You really didn't know?'

'I didn't,' he said sheepishly. 'Why would I? If I knew, I wouldn't have set foot inside that bastard's café. This was about two months ago. I had forgotten my keys at home and Pilar was out shopping and running late so I went to Kafe 88 to wait for her. The moment I set foot in that cafe, I knew something wasn't right. The walls were covered with pictures of soldiers, flags, drawings of double lightning bolts, eagle emblems and all the rest. But I had already entered and couldn't just walk out so I sat in a corner. The people inside were not happy at my presence, I can tell you. The way they were staring at me. As you can see, I'm fairly dark-skinned so they thought I was an Arab. One of the waitresses came over and said, quite politely, as it happens, "Please leave, we do not serve Arabs." I should have left but I felt affronted and stayed. I said, "I am not an Arab, I am an Argentinian, and even if I were an Arab, so what? I am not going anywhere. Since this is a café, you are required to serve me." Yes, that is exactly what I said. The girl turned and looked at the guy behind the counter, a bald guy in a leather jacket. He was short, only around one metre fifty in height. He heard me and when he winked at the girl, her attitude changed instantly. The coldness in her blue eyes vanished, her face softened and she gave me a big smile, showing her dimples. "I'm sorry," she said. "There was a misunderstanding. What would you like to drink?"

'I forced a smile and asked for a Berliner beer. When the waitress went off, the bald guy came up to me. He really was short but you could tell from how well-built he was that he worked out. The first thing I noticed about him were the tattoos on his biceps: swastikas on both arms. He extended a hand. "My name is Otto Fischer, I am the owner. Please accept my apologies. We thought you were one of those *kanake*."

'I knew what *kanake* meant and his use of that word angered me. I told him, "I'm a *kanake* too. After all, I'm also a foreigner." He sat at my table, even though I had not invited him to do so, and said, "No, we don't consider Argentinians *kanake*. We owe a debt of gratitude to Argentina. Your country opened its arms to our brothers in the cause…" By now, the waitress had arrived with my beer and was pouring the beer into a glass. The short guy was getting comfortable with me now. When he asked me my name, I felt compelled to answer.

'"What do you do for a living, Mister Moreno?" he asked, rather cordially too, I might add. When I told him I was a painter, I thought he would be put off but on the contrary, his eyes lit up. "Did you know that Hitler was also a painter?" Then, with a deep sigh, he added, "Our Führer was a true artist."

'I could not keep the pretence up much longer. I stood up and said, "I am sorry but I do not agree with the views of your Führer. If I had known this was a Nazi place, I would not have set foot inside." And with that, I left. You have no idea how relieved I felt when I stepped outside. I started walking but then turned around to look back at the café and I noticed Otto and two of his friends were watching me. For a moment, I panicked and thought they were going to chase me but they didn't. I waited for Pilar in the front garden and promised never to go to Kafe 88 ever again. Alas, that promise was not enough to keep me away from those murderers.'

He was so calm and spoke so specifically, neither of the officers wanted to interrupt him. Seeing Tobias lit a cigarette, Rafael asked for one. He then turned to Yıldız and, as though she had asked, felt compelled to justify his actions.

'I don't smoke at home but when someone lights up in front of me, I can't help it and have to have one myself.' After lighting his cigarette with Tobias' lighter and taking a deep drag, he went on. 'A week passed. The Nazis were quiet. Meanwhile, Cemal and I were busy trying to complete the painting you saw outside our apartment in time for Gay Pride Day. We had set up a scaffold and worked a set number of hours per day, and we were doing quite well. Our work was progressing nicely. However, one day, we felt the scaffolding shake. Before we could work out what was going on, Otto and two other guys had started chucking eggs at us from below and were shouting things like, "Germany is for the Germans! Queers and foreigners out! Islam kills!" I am neither gay nor religious but they were screaming "Islam kills" and trying to kill me! Cemal was not as weak as me, though. He was well-built and had done some martial arts when he was younger. He was a tough, fearless guy and he went straight down to face the Nazis. When they saw him, they shouted, "Come and get it, you filthy fag!" However, when Cemal was around two metres away from them, he leapt into action. The three Nazis did not know what hit them. Otto was pinned down by a *kanake* he wanted out of Germany and was swearing and screaming for help from his friends. But when Cemal landed two punches to his misshapen face, the screaming stopped. Meanwhile, one of the Nazis was back on his feet and he started throwing eggs at Cemal. Cemal ignored them though, even though the eggs were coming at his head and body. He strode over to the Nazi, grabbed him by the collar and, instead of punching him, slapped him hard across the face, twice, just to rub it in. But it was not enough so he took hold of the guy's leather jacket and headbutted him right in the face. Bang! There and then, right on the nose. The Nazi fell on his arse. As for the other prat, he had just been standing there watching what was going on, not knowing what to do. His confusion didn't last long. When he saw the blood and his two friends writhing on the ground, he turned tail and fled. Otto was coming round now and had managed to stagger back to his feet. He was feeling his face with his hands. When he saw the state his friend was in, he went berserk and took out a knife from his belt, the one I told you about, a long, sharp dagger with a swastika on the grip, and he began walking towards Cemal, who did not see him as his back was to him.

"'Cemal, look out! He's got a knife!' I shouted from the scaffolding. Cemal turned around just in time and managed to leap out of the way so Otto's knife only hit thin air. However, the Nazi would not be deterred and he immediately began to ready himself for another lunge when Cemal caught him by the wrist with his left hand and slapped him hard over the ear with the palm of his right hand. Otto staggered back but did not fall, but when Cemal followed up with two more slaps, Otto's short legs began to shake. Cemal let go of him but he kept on hitting him and in the end, Otto, backing away step by step, tripped over a stone and fell. The knife slipped from his hand onto the pavement and Cemal began walking towards him. Otto was scared now. He held his hands out and looked at Cemal in fear, pleading for mercy, but Cemal was in no mood to forgive. When Cemal bent down and picked up the dagger, I thought he was going to slice the Nazi up but he didn't. He just waved it and pointed to the road with it. *"Şimdi siktir git,"* he said. "If you don't, I'll cut you open and feed you your own guts."'

Yıldız smiled at Rafael using the Turkish expletive.

'So Cemal taught you Turkish…'

'Not a lot, just some swearwords,' Rafael answered, taking a long drag on the half-finished cigarette. 'German doesn't have that much by way of swearwords, as I'm sure you know.'

Yıldız suddenly thought of something else, quite unrelated.

'Tell me, how did your wife Pilar take all this?'

'Pilar was staying with some friends in Frankfurt,' he answered, blinking gratefully. 'She didn't see any of it. She only read the writing on the mural, and we didn't think much of it at the time. If she finds out, she won't be happy.' After a short pause, he muttered, 'I don't know. Maybe we should move away from here. I might be next…'

'Then what happened?' Tobias asked impatiently, not wanting Rafael to give in to morose thoughts. 'Did Otto run away?'

'He didn't. He got up, held out his hand and said, "Give me my knife." I think it was the idea of losing his weapon and his friends finding out and mocking him for it that made him ask for it back. But Cemal shook his head firmly. "I will only give this dagger up to the police. If you like, we can go to the police station together." Otto's face fell and he turned around and began walking silently away. But after just a few steps, he stopped, turned back and said, "This isn't over, you filthy foreigners. You'll pay for this." Cemal just laughed in his face. "Yeah, sure. Whenever you need some more, just come back.

We'll be here. Now, on your bike." Cemal really was fearless. When I told him that those guys had guns as well as knives and could cause us some serious problems, he just slapped me on the shoulder and said, "We have a proverb in Turkish. *A dog that is going to bite does not bare its teeth.*"

'But look. The dog did bite. First they defaced our mural and then they tore Cemal's heart out with that knife… And for everyone to see, too.' He fell silent, overcome by sorrow, and sought solace in his cigarette, taking two more drags.

'Why didn't you go to the police?' Yıldız asked. 'When they attacked you, that is. Why did you not lodge a formal complaint against Otto Fischer?'

There was no anger in Rafael's eyes when he looked at Yıldız. Just suspicion and plenty of helplessness.

'Don't get me wrong. I don't mean you but the police won't do anything to those guys. Some neo-Nazis also attacked us when we were living in the squat and some of our friends went to the police but instead of catching the thugs, they arrested our friends, claiming they were drug addicts or had links to terrorist cells or other such madness. Can you believe it? They were injured too when they filed the complaint. They went to the station all bandaged up.' He stopped, wondering whether to say what was on his mind. 'I'm sorry but I do not trust the police. If you ask me, you have a fair number of neo-Nazis hidden in your ranks. They are not open about their beliefs but they are there.'

The police officers did not know what to say and they all walked on in silence. When they reached a sycamore tree up ahead, Yıldız asked, 'Did Cemal keep the dagger at his place?'

The Argentinian threw his cigarette to the ground, stubbed it out and nodded.

'He did, on the desk with his computer.' He tried to smile. 'He said it was war booty. He did not even cover the swastika on the hilt. He used to use the knife to open envelopes and packages.'

'But we did not find any such dagger in his flat.'

Rafael was not surprised.

'You wouldn't have because Otto and his boys took it. You don't get it, do you? I'm telling you, they killed Cemal. They killed him and then they took the knife and ran off.'

Tobias was not impressed by the almost accusatory tone of Rafael.

'Do you have any evidence for this? Any eye-witnesses?'

'Better than that,' the painter declared. 'They were caught on Peyman's security cameras. He lives two building down from us.'

Yıldız's eyes lit up.

'A camera, you say?'

'Yep. Peyman told me this morning. Peyman Majidi. He's Iranian. He lives with his wife and son in a building a little ahead of us. Their apartment's security camera captured Otto and the two others as they were making off. I saw it with my own eyes. At exactly 23.37. Peyman saved the recording.'

This was an important development, one that could change the course of the investigation.

'What exactly did the camera show?' Tobias asked. 'Does it show Otto and his guys exiting your building?'

Rafael was beginning to tense up.

'No, that camera's range does not extend that far, but the recording does show Otto and his two friends quickly crossing the street and heading towards their café. They're running away in a panic. If you raid their café, I am sure you will find that dagger. Of course, they must have wiped it down and cleaned it up by now but there must still be traces of blood on it, right?'

'Most probably, yes,' Tobias said with a newfound optimism. 'If the murder was indeed carried out with that dagger, then we will definitely know. Who do you think told them where Cemal lived?'

'Nobody needed to tell them,' Rafael said and pointed to a spot not too far away. 'Look? There they are.' He lowered his voice. 'Sitting in front of their café.'

There really were two men sprawled out in the sunshine at one of four tables on the pavement in front of a café up ahead sipping beers. The painter was clearly alarmed at their presence there. Yıldız looked at him sympathetically.

'Thank you, Mister Moreno. You can go home now.' She paused and then went on, feeling compelled to say what was on her mind. 'And one more thing: you can trust us. We most definitely are not Nazis. If anybody threatens you or your wife, please do not hesitate to call us.'

Rafael stared back, wanting to believe her.

'Thank you. If there are any developments, I'll call you,' he said and then turned around and headed home. Yıldız and Tobias, meanwhile, carried on walking towards Kafe 88.

Sitting at a metal table under a sign with the establishment's name were Otto Fischer and a blond youngster with spiky hair who was at least twice his size. The two men had obviously seen the policemen and the painter staring and pointing at them but they had not budged. They had just carried on drinking and they were now staring with open hostility at the man and woman walking towards them. Once Yıldız and Tobias were close enough to hear, Otto pointed to Yıldız with his bottle and then addressed Tobias.

'Aren't you ashamed as a German, fucking a *kanake* like this? All of Berlin to choose from and you can't find another woman to screw?'

The youngster next to him let out an exaggerated laugh. Tobias said nothing. He just turned to look at Yıldız and saw that familiar sheen of fury in her eyes. He scanned the outside of the café. There were no security cameras. He nodded in Conzentment, smiled and walked serenely over to Otto's table. There was no menace or anger in his expression or his walk. He was so calm that Otto and his friend simply stared at him, not knowing what to do. When Tobias reached their table, he graciously held out a hand.

'May I?'

While the café owner sat there mumbling in confusion, Tobias grabbed the bottle and brought it down on Otto's head, making a sound like a mini-hand grenade as it broke over his bald skull, which ran first with amber liquid from the bottle and then red from where the glass has cut his skin. Otto staggered back under the blow, while his friend, shocked at first, shouted, 'You son of a bitch!' He tried to stand up but Tobias gave him two sound back-handers with the hand that was holding what was left of the broken bottle and sat him down. Yıldız stood back and calmly watched the proceedings. Tobias dropped the broken bottle on the ground, grabbed Otto by the collar of his leather jacket and smashed his face onto the metal table twice, leaving it covered in blood. Tobias ignored the blood, leant over and whispered gently in Otto's ear.

'As a German, I have decided to fuck you instead, Otto. What do you say to that, eh? As you can see, I like to play rough though. I hope you don't mind?'

He had just finished talking when Otto, quite unexpectedly, shot up, his grey eyes wild with rage.

'Just you watch. Now I am going to fuck you up!'

He drew a dagger from his waist and swung it at Tobias, who, in anticipation of just such a move, raised his left arm and brought it down on Otto's right arm, which was swinging the blade. Otto was knocked off balance but he soon regained his footing. He grasped the knife, this time more securely, and was about to lunge again when the police officer's right fist came hurtling into his face like a sledgehammer. Otto took a few steps back, but Tobias was not done and followed up with several more lefts and rights, which eventually forced Otto to drop the dagger and hold on to one of the wooden posts that held up the awning over the café's porch. His misshapen head resembled a potato that had been dipped in red paint.

'Ah! Help! Chris!'

That was indeed Chris' intention but Yıldız did not let him. She pushed the metal table onto the youngster as he tried to get up from his stool, striking him in the chest and sending him crashing onto the ground. Just when they thought they were getting the better of the two men, the café doors swung open and another youngster, a sandy-haired man, at least as well-built as Chris, darted out.

'Toby, look out!' Yıldız shouted. 'There's another one behind you.' But her warning came too late as the newcomer had already jumped her assistant. The two of them fell to the ground, Tobias face down and his attacker sprawled on top of him, lashing out and punching Tobias however and wherever he could. Emboldened by his friend's assistance, Otto was preparing to re-enter the affray when Yıldız leaned back and kicked him squarely and soundly in the groin, causing the little Nazi to buckle up in agony. In the midst of the commotion, Chris had spotted his opportunity and was trying to grab hold of the broken beer bottle on the ground. Yıldız spotted him and quickly pulled out her gun and pointed it at the blond youngster's face.

'Stop or I'll blow your brains out!' She turned to the others and shouted, 'Police! Nobody move!'

The Nazis froze. Otto's eyes widened in fright upon hearing the word *police*.

'Okay, okay, I give up,' he eventually said, raising his hands in surrender. 'Why didn't you damn well tell us you were cops in the first place?'

The interrogation room was sparsely furnished. Otto was seated at the sole desk in the otherwise bare room. The plastic glass filled to the brim with water on the table in front of him remained untouched. He was trying to convince the two cops with whom he had been fighting mere hours earlier of his good intentions. 'We're sorry, really we are. If we had known you were police, we would not have acted like that.'

The blood on his face had been cleaned away and his uneven head and crooked nose were streaked with white plasters. Because the plasters on his nose were thicker and tighter, they were affecting his voice and making it sound odd. Now that he had put his foot in it, he had let the hard man image go and was playing the respectable citizen.

'Oh no, we would never go against the state. We would never have any issues with the German police. Never.'

Looking at this new breed of Nazi, Yıldız was reminded of her father and how he used to say that the fascists in Turkey had always supported the state. Whenever they attacked workers striking for better working conditions or students marching in protest against repressive government policies, the fascists always stood with the police, saying they were defending the state and the flag against "troublemakers and traitors". It seemed fascists, whether German or Turkish, were all the same: devoid of any human values, and willing to commit any atrocity just to defend the state. Moreover, whatever the state did was justified too as the state was sacred and the leader — the Führer, in essence — was some kind of God. A brave, wise, powerful and cruel God… And speaking of Gods… Zeus… The King of the Gods… Cemal's painting. Could there be a link between the

Altar of Zeus brought to Germany from Bergama and the Nazis of Berlin? She paused to consider it but then dismissed the idea as ludicrous. Such a connection simply could not be made. She was dragged out of her thoughts by Otto, who was busy defending his actions.

'We got confused when we saw that bullshit fake painter from Argentina. What's his name? Rafael or something. Whatever it is, he's a degenerate artist and an enemy of Germany. He pointed at us and you were standing next to him so we got mixed signals. You were wearing leather jackets and jeans so we thought you were two of those commie-types who live over in those occupied apartments. I'm sorry, really. If I had known you were police officers, I would never have been so disrespectful.'

While he was saying this, he was looking at Tobias, not Yıldız, even though it was the puffy-faced and heavy-handed Tobias that had bust his face open. Moreover, the Chief Inspector was sitting right in front of him in the small interrogation room, whilst Tobias had pulled up a chair and was sitting to one side, next to his superior. Christopher and Matthias, Otto's two comrades, were being held in separate rooMs

The fact that Otto was acting as though he was an old friend of theirs was actually working in their favour. If he were to demand a lawyer and then choose to remain silent and let the lawyer speak for him, it risked dragging things on indefinitely. That is why it was important that they kept up the pretence of camaraderie with Otto for as long as possible and to do that, they needed to keep him talking.

'Well, it's water under the bridge now,' Yıldız said nonchalantly, keeping her true feelings hidden. 'Let us get down to business. Our conversation needs to be recorded. You do not have any objections, I trust?'

There was a momentary flash of doubt in Otto's grey eyes but it soon disappeared and was replaced by a look of compliance.

'Not at all… Why would I object?' He then asked, 'Why? Is there another problem? Seeing as you're…'

Tobias pretended not to hear and kept on looking vacantly at Otto. Yıldız pressed a button on the recording device, stated the time and the date into the microphone and began.

'Chief Inspector Yıldız Karasu and Inspector Tobias Becker have commenced questioning of the detained suspect, Otto Fischer.' She then turned to the man in question. 'Let's say there are certain issues that need to be clarified, and which we believe we may be able to resolve with your assistance.'

Otto smiled cautiously.

'I am ready to provide any form of assistance. My friends are too…'

'Thank you, Mister Fischer.' She then turned and looked at her laptop screen. 'How do you know Rafael? The man you called a 'pretend painter from Argentina.' Did he do any paintings for your place of business?'

Otto smirked.

'No, I would never do business with such an unrefined man. His paintings are terrible anyway. That's why he daubs his crap on walls — because no one takes his work seriously. He has this Turkish friend too…'

'Cemal,' Tobias offered. 'Cemal Ölmez… Do you know him too?'

Otto looked taken aback. It took him a few moments to compose himself.

'I do,' he eventually managed to say. 'He is as talentless and as impudent as that Argentinian. The two of them go around painting on whatever spare surface they can find. They ruin the scenery, those two.'

'What is your educational status, Mister Fischer?' Yıldız asked, raising a finger in the air to silence him.

'I completed high school,' Otto replied proudly.

'And have you completed any education or training since? In the fine arts, for example.'

Otto knew what the question was aiming at.

'No, I have not, but one does not need a degree to know when a painting sucks. And their squiggles suck. Anyone with eyes can see that. Even the neighbours were disturbed by their pictures. They came to us to complain.'

Yıldız's black eyebrows formed a frown.

'They came to you to complain? In what capacity? Are you the police? Are you state employees charged with maintaining public peace?'

The neo-Nazi realized he had made a faux pas.

'No, nothing like that, Chief Inspector. It was more a case of, coming to us…'

'Rather than troubling the local bureaucracy, is that it?' Tobias said, competing the sentence for him. 'And as concerned citizens, you take on the responsibility of bringing these foreigners that disturb the peace with their murals into line…'

Otto could not work out if Tobias was being serious or not.

'I wouldn't call it bringing them into line. More like taking the initiative.' He turned to Yıldız. 'Please don't misunderstand. We have nothing but the profoundest respect for people such as yourself that have integrated into German life. But as citizens, we need to warn those people that wander the streets of Berlin still acting as though they are in Africa or the Middle East.'

Yıldız looked down at her laptop. She felt no anger as she had heard such drivel countless times before.

'And to this end you organize neighbourhood patrols and intervene when you come across people behaving in a manner you deem inappropriate.'

Otto realized she was reading his file on the laptop but he did not back down.

'The Albanians have gambling dens on Museum Island, in the very heart of Berlin, the Romanians are scamming people left, right and centre, pretending to be charity workers, and the Turks are pimping hookers out in front of everyone in Artemis. We have hundreds of thieves, beggars and conmen from inferior races running wild on the streets, visually and spiritually ruining the city.'

'Painting rainbows on walls…' Tobias said. Otto picked up the sarcasm in his tone.

'That is not an innocent rainbow, Mister Becker. That is a perverts' banner. Those pictures symbolize every degeneracy man is capable of. Every sexual, religious and racial degradation.'

Yıldız was beginning to tire of his nonsense.

'Is that why you engage in acts of violence with the artists that paint those pictures?'

Otto noticed the anger in the Chief Inspector's voice and wanted to lighten the atmosphere but did not get the chance.

'Yet, ironically, one of those painters turned out to be even better at fighting than he was at painting. It seems you went over to flex your muscles with him but you ended up getting soundly battered and forced to flee with your tail between your legs. You also lost a knife in the fight.'

'Knife? What knife?' Otto said sourly.

'A knife you used to carry. One with a wooden grip that can be affixed to a rifle and used as a bayonet. You know, one of those knives the Führer's glorious army used in battle… You tried to cut my colleague's face open with it today.' She turned to her assistant before Otto had a chance to respond. 'Isn't that true, Toby? Wasn't Mister Fischer about to use that knife to sign his name permanently onto your face?'

'Unfortunately, yes,' Tobias said with faux despondency, looking at Otto as he answered his boss. 'And to an honourable police officer of the great state of Germany too, no less.' He turned and leaned forward on the table towards Otto. 'Is that not so? You were going to stab me, weren't you?'

The neo-Nazi was at a loss for words.

'It seems you are suffering from some form of short-term memory loss,' Yıldız offered. 'I can bring the knife here if you like. It's in an evidence bag inside. Would you like to see it?'

realizing he was being cornered, Otto began fidgeting.

'No, I do remember now, actually. Again, I apologize, Mister Becker. If I had known you were a police officer, I would never have behaved like that... And anyway, you att...' He was going to say Toby had attacked him first but Yıldız quickly cut him off as she did not want what Otto was about to say recorded.

'Yes, thank you, Mister Fischer. If you could please tell us where you were last night between 23.00 and 24.00.'

Otto narrowed his eyes and stared at the two people on the other side of the table. No, these two officers were not his friends, that much he had worked out, but he was curious as to what they knew and how much.

'Why? What happened?' he asked, crossing his arms over his chest.

'As I said at the beginning, something quite trivial. We are simply comparing accounts and your statement will be of a great assistance to us.'

'I see.' He cupped his chin with his right hand, as though deep in thought. 'At that time, I generally need to be at the café. So yes, I think I was at the café.'

'You need to be more precise,' Tobias said, playing the good cop. 'If you want us to help you, you cannot behave like this.'

'Help you, eh?' Otto grumbled. 'You're trying to entrap me.' But he knew he had little choice in the matter and that he had to grin and bear it. 'I was in the café. Christopher and Matthias were with me, in fact. We listened to some music and had a few beers.'

Yıldız looked at her laptop screen.

'Are you sure? Did you go out at all? Between 23.00 and 24.00, that is.'

Otto's grey eyes blinked nervously.

'I may have. I get bored sometimes sitting in the café all day and so I sometimes go for a walk for an hour or so.'

A silence fell over the table. The two police officers stared at the suspect. Tobias began rhythmically tapping the table with two fingers. Otto could not stand the tension anymore and said, 'Yes, now I remember. We left the café around 23.00.'

Tobias smiled indulgently.

'And were Christopher and Matthias with you?'

Otto could sense that this was not going well for him. His right eyebrow, already a little lower than his left, fell even further.

'They were. Wo what?' His voice was getting higher. 'Where are you going with all this?'

Yıldız laughed silently.

'Calm down, Mister Fischer. No harm will come to you from the police. As I said before, we employees of the state so we are on the same side. If you have not committed any crimes, that is.'

'I have not committed any crimes!' Otto shouted furiously. 'But if standing up against an invasion of foreigners infecting the country like a virus and trying to take over is a crime, then that's something else.'

The angrier Otto became, the calmer the two police officers remained.

'That depends on what you mean by being against foreigners. If you mean calling the police when you see them violating the laws of the German Constitution, then that's fine. But you do not have the right to intervene. You cannot attack people for painting a mural. You cannot go around threatening people, whether they are German, Turkish, Argentinian or anything else, as they are all protected by the German Constitution. Worse, you cannot enter a house by force and kill people because you lost a knife to them in a fight. You cannot cut people's hearts out of their chest with that knife as an act of revenge.'

Otto's pallid complexion seemed to be turning a dirty shade of green.

'Lies. All lies. False accusations. I have not killed anybody, nor have I cut out anyone's heart.' He looked around anxiously. 'I am not going to say anything else. I want my lawyer.'

'As you wish,' Yıldız said, with the assurance of a hunter that knows her prey has nowhere to run. 'We shall call your lawyer forthwith. However, please let me remind you that we have images that show you, as well as Christopher and Matthias, in the area at the time of the murder. There are eye witnesses too. We also know you appropriated the dagger from the scene of the crime. Instead of calling your lawyer, if you cooperate with us, we will do whatever we can to try to minimize your sentence.'

Tobias nodded in confirmation.

'Exactly. Your lawyer will just prolong things in order to command a higher fee and you will be strung along by a series of false hopes. You cannot wriggle your way out of this, not with the evidence and the witnesses we have. So, play ball, tell us everything and we will all be better off. You'll get a lighter sentence.'

Otto's shoulders slumped. He had the look of a prisoner that had been tried and found guilty and was now being dragged off to await sentencing.

'I did not kill him. Believe me, I didn't. We just wanted to scare that Turk and retrieve the dagger.' He shook his head ruefully. 'You idiot, Otto! You idiot! Why did you have to try and get that dagger back? Even Chris and Matze told me not to. "It's only a knife!" they said. In fact, they bought that replacement for me, the one in your possession, to persuade me to give up on the idea but I couldn't help it, I couldn't let it go. But I didn't kill anyone… Yes, we went to the house. When we reached the front gates of the apartment, we heard loud music. Heavy metal, a track I had not heard before. When we reached the flat, the front door was open so we walked inside. We saw that so-called artist Cemal lying in a pool of blood in front of a picture of a king on the wall. We turned and ran out.'

He looked to be telling the truth but the fact remained, most perpetrators of premeditated murder looked and sounded genuine during questioning. Insisting that he had carried out the murder often proved counterproductive. Focusing on details in order to uncover the lies was often the more prudent path, which is what Yıldız decided to do.

'We are going to perform a luminol test on the blade. If we find traces of Cemal's blood on it, you are in serious trouble.'

Otto's lips began trembling.

'You won't find any because the blade you have is a new one.'

'So where is the old one?' Tobias demanded.

'How would I know? As soon as we saw the guy lying there covered in blood, we legged it. Maybe the killer took it.'

At that moment, there was a knock on the door. Two men appeared in the doorway, a man dressed in a smart suit and a uniformed officer. The smartly dressed man looked haughtily at the two seated officers and said, 'Hello. I am Helmut Berger, Mister Fischer's lawyer.' He turned to the suspect. 'You are under no obligation to speak now, Mister Fischer. I shall answer for you henceforth.'

Otto looked even more surprised than the Yıldız and Tobias.

'Wait, who? Who sent you?'

Helmut Berger's winked playfully.

'Your friends, Mister Fischer. They are not going to abandon you in your hour of need...'

'What we don't know about them far exceeds what we do know,' Markus had said after the questioning. 'They have serious players in their corner. If we don't have enough evidence at hand, we're going to be giving ourselves a lot of trouble.'

He had not said it to protect Otto and his friends but it was clear he was wary of them, a not unfounded worry. Developments over the last twenty years suggested the presence of a clandestine but highly influential organization that was protecting Nazis within the apparatus of the German state and any notion of achieving justice without taking them on was out of the question, which is why Yıldız was in a particularly combative mode.

'We have enough evidence, Markus. We have camera recordings showing them fleeing the scene, an eye witness that saw the fight, Otto's statement today and, most important of all, a weapon that may have been used to carry out the murder.'

The Chief's green eyes seemed to turn a dark shade of blue.

'You say *may* have been used. You don't call it the "murder weapon", because you're not sure. We still do not have irrefutable evidence. Our eye witness witnessed a fight that took place days earlier, not the murder. Basically, to say Otto and his boys did this is a tough call. Do you know Helmut

Berger? Have you heard of him? He is a formidable lawyer. If the tests on the knife don't come up with something, he is going to make sure the press go to town on us. He'll cause a complete scandal and turn all of us, the entire Berlin Police Department, into a laughing stock.'

'Then you better make sure those tests get carried out as soon as possible,' Yıldız said. 'Because we have a lot less to work with when it comes to the deceased's family and lover. At the moment, it's the knife or nothing. That dagger is the most reliable piece of evidence we have so far.'

And with that, they had left the station. Yıldız was at home now. She had put Deniz to sleep and was thinking about the new investigation. Was Markus right? Cemal had not been killed in a fit of anger. Even if the murder had been an act of revenge, it had not been done in anger or haste but had been planned and executed with meticulous precision. She recalled Otto's coarse body language, his slow, witless face and his hostile, suspicious looks. She also recalled Christopher and Matthias's behaviour. None of them looked like people capable of ritually cutting a man's heart out and placing it in his hands unless there were other people behind the scenes telling them what to do and the fact that a famous lawyer had suddenly turned up to defend them seemed to indicate that these three jackals were not alone. If that were the case, the people that had sent Helmut Berger to the station had to be found. On the other hand, in terms of the crimes committed by Nazis in Germany over the last twenty years, this was the first time they were seeing a murder like this.

Deniz began stirring in his sleep, mumbling for his mother. She leant over and planted a kiss on his damp forehead.

'I'm here, sweetie,' she said, stroking his sandy hair. Safe in her arms, he went back to sleep.

'Don't worry.' A voice called out, startling her. She lifted her head. Her father was standing in the doorway, staring at her lovingly. He was wearing a light green t-shirt and faded jeans and his hair had been cut short. 'He does fret sometimes, even though he slept like a log last night. Yesterday morning on the way to school, he asked me if you would be coming home in the evening. I covered for you and said you were and then joked and asked him if he enjoyed his grandfather's company. He told me he was happier when we were all at home together. He's a smart cookie, your lad.'

Yıldız smiled impishly.

'Diplomatic, I'd say, rather than smart. I wonder whom he takes after?'

Yaman was standing next to his daughter but he was looking at Deniz.

'His grandfather, of course.' He smiled and then, with an exaggerated tone, added, 'His mother steers clear of politics, which is fine. But if the lad wants, let him take an interest in the world's affairs.'

'Oh Dad, you always say the same thing... Yes, I admit, we do not bring any solutions to the world's problems but we are, in our own way, working to protect justice.'

Yaman hugged his daughter. 'I know, Yıldız, my dear. I was just joking.' He looked at his grandson again. 'But one thing is clear, and that is that this boy is going to be a lot more good-looking than me... That's what happens with babies of mixed marriages. And the little tyke knows how to bring a smile to people's faces too.'

'So I was never like that?' Yıldız said, shaking her head as though offended.

Yaman stroked his daughter's head the way he had just stroked his grandson's.

'You were better… You were always a forthright kid. You always said whatever was on your mind straight to people's faces. No messing around. My girl, all the way.'

He leaned over, kissed her on the forehead and then recoiled.

'You stink of cigarettes! Don't tell me you've started again?'

'No, Dad,' Yıldız said, smiling despite her exhaustion. 'I haven't started again, and I never will. It's Tobias. He smokes, so the smoke got into my hair.' She turned to look at Deniz, who was now fast asleep. 'Come on, let's go inside.'

'That's why I came here, actually. The coffees are getting cold.'

They walked into the lounge. Yıldız took the saffron-coloured cup from the green tray on the table and sat down on the sofa by the window. Yaman stayed standing by the table.

'There is still some *lokum* left from the packet I brought from Istanbul last winter. Would you like some?'

'No thanks, Dad. Why don't you sit down? You have been looking after Deniz since yesterday. You must be exhausted.'

Yaman took his cup of coffee and settled down in the bergère chair opposite Yıldız. She never would have believed that her father would take such a keen interest in Deniz. When she was a child, he had never behaved so dutifully. Not that he was a bad father, but politics had always been his priority. Whenever there was a rally or demonstration, he felt compelled to go and he would take Yıldız's mother with him, leaving Yıldız with the downstairs neighbour. They would often be gone for hours too, so when Yıldız first asked him if he could keep an eye on Deniz while she worked, she was convinced he would refuse but instead, he told her without hesitation that he would be delighted to babysit. At first, Yıldız thought he was just pretending to enjoy looking after Deniz so as to not upset her and that in reality it was simply a grandfather's duty he was carrying out but after he agreed to keep an eye on Deniz three times in a row, she realized her father really did enjoy spending time with his grandson. Of course, this delighted her but it also made her a little sad as she could not help but wonder why her father had not been as attentive and as indulgent with her when she was young. But that would have been out of the question for Yaman. He adored his daughter, yes, but he had not been the type of man to simply ignore the suffering of so many other children in the world and he had felt an urge to stand up and fight for them. Yıldız did not resent him for it, though. She had long since made peace with it. In fact, she was now staring at him with love and gratitude. Here he was; an old firebrand now on the threshold of old age who was happy to make a coffee for his police officer daughter, despite his fatigue. With eyes half-shut, she took a sip of coffee.

'Mmm, wonderful, as ever... How do you do it? I'm a grown woman and I still can't make coffee as well as this.'

Yaman looked down sadly at the bubbling froth on his coffee.

'Thanks to your mother... I drink a lot of coffee, as you know, but I used to drink even more, and I used to love smoking with my coffee too. Coffee and cigarettes — a sublime pairing! In the end, your mother got fed up with my constant calls for coffee and told me to get up and start making my own. She was serious too, so I learnt how to make a decent cup.' His momentary grief vanished and he winked at Yıldız. 'It's actually quite simple, Yıldızcım. All you need to do is just put in the right amount of coffee. For two people, four rounded teaspoons. And then you heat it over a flame, but nice and slow, just like good food. Just get the ingredients and the quantities right and then let it simmer over a low heat.'

Yıldız shrugged and raised her cup to her lips.

'Well, I just can't seem to get it right.'

'Are you okay?' her father asked. He had yet to take a sip of his coffee. 'Franz isn't bothering you anymore, is he?'

Yıldız gently placed her cup on the armrest of her chair.

'Franz? Oh no. That's well and truly over, and he knows it. We have a hearing coming up in the next few months. Probably the last one. He realizes it's over now. He doesn't bother calling, unless it is something involving Deniz.'

Yaman gestured with a jerk of the head to the bedroom inside.

'But there is still a photograph of the three of you in his room… Are you having second thoughts?'

'Nothing of the sort, Dad. Deniz wanted a photo with all three of us together, that's all.' She sighed. 'Look, Dad. There is no longer anyone called Franz in my life. I'm just a little tired today, that's all. I was out on call for twenty-four hours and I'm dealing with a complicated case at the moment so I'm just a bit tied up with that.' She pulled herself together and hoisted her feet up under her legs. 'It looks like the Nazis are on the move again.'

'Nazis? Seriously? What's happened?' Yaman asked, his eyes gleaming with curiosity.

Yıldız did not know how much she should tell him at first but then said, 'Someone was killed last night. In Neukölln. Someone of Turkish origin. We think it may be neo-Nazis.'

'It wasn't arson, was it?'

'No, why?'

'A few years ago, they burnt down one of our friends' house so I thought they might be up to their old tricks.'

'But why arson?' Yıldız asked. She suddenly felt rejuvenated. 'Why arson and not, say, knives or guns?'

'Who knows? Maybe because it's easy. You just sneak into a building without anyone seeing you, pour petrol all over the place, light a match and away you go. You don't need to see your victims or look them in the eye. Maybe they like arson because it is so gruesome and makes for more deaths. Doesn't matter where you are in the world, fascists love making blood flow. They are always ready for a massacre. Remember what happened in Sivas back home? They did the same there. Burnt scores of people alive.'

'But arson is not their preferred MO nowadays. At least, not as far as I can tell. Last night, the victim was stabbed to death.'

Yaman was not surprised.

'You're right. Now that I think about it, the National Socialist Underground (NSU) used guns in their murders. There was no arson involved in the massacre in Hanau or in the Halle Synagogue shooting.'

'So the neo-Nazis have changed their tactics,' Yıldız murmured, weighing up a number of ideas. 'Perhaps they feel stronger now. That explains why they are bold enough to draw weapons in public and do not refrain from carrying out even more audacious acts. The way they killed that guy, they were as if saying, "We are here and we are going to wipe you out."'

The worry in Yaman's eyes was deepening.

'Since the Wall came down, they have become even more daring. Unemployment in the old East caused a spike in xenophobia... People began to ask why foreigners were living so well when they, as Germans, were suffering. And their numbers are growing daily. It's frightening, and they are only going to get stronger.'

'If I remember correctly, the first arson attack was in Schwandorf, wasn't it?' Yıldız asked.

'That's right. It was the winter of 1988. An animal by the name of Joseph Seller set fire to the building in which a Turkish family was staying. Osman Can, his wife Fatma, their son

Mehmet and a German by the name of Jürgen Hübner died in the fire.'

Yıldız stared at her father in amazement.

'How do you remember it all in such detail? All those dates and names…'

Yaman placed his cup on the coffee table. He had still not taken a sip.

'Your mother and I were on a commission back then that represented a number of Turkish associations. I remember it so well because we prepared a report for the commission. The arson attacks just would not stop. Four years later, a house in Mölln belonging to a family by the name of Arslan was set on fire and three Turks were killed. A year later, five Turks died when their house in Solingen was set ablaze. You remember the fire in Ludwigshafen in which nine people died? Arson was suspected then too. I went to Ludwigshafen. It was awful…' His eyes welled up. 'The burnt bodies were lined up next to each other. Truly horrifying.'

'Here, drink your coffee, it's getting cold,' Yıldız said, wishing she had not asked the question. Yaman's mood was spoiled but he did not want to upset his daughter and took a sip. Despite all the questions racing around in her head, Yıldız felt she had to change the subject. 'What's Brigitte up to? Hasn't she called?'

Brigitte was her father's partner. A good woman, she was an active member of the Green Party. Yaman had not married Brigitte, though, as he thought it would be disrespectful to the memory of his late wife, Nilüfer. 'I can be progressive on most topics but I am afraid in this matter, I am quite conservative,' he had said to his daughter by way of explanation. Brigitte had no real desire to tie the knot either. If anything, it was Yıldız who was building castles in the sky, trying to convince her father to remarry, but Yaman was having none of it. They did not even live in the same house. That way, they did not get bored of each other and the spark between them did not go out. Or so they said. But Yıldız knew her father was scared. The idea of living with a woman again and of making her a part of his life frightened him. It had taken him a long time to get over his wife's death. 'To be so dependent upon another and to shoulder life's challenges together with another person makes you weak,' he had once said. 'It was only when Nilüfer left that I grasped this.' He never used the words *death* or *die* when referring to Nilüfer; instead, he said things like *when she left*, *the loss* and *when she passed on*. After Nilüfer, he could not face the prospect of becoming so attached again to another woman, and so he kept a healthy distance between himself and Brigitte.

'Of course, she called,' he answered. 'She's gone to Heidelberg to see her son. She has only just become a grandmother. A blond baby with lovely curly hair and huge blue eyes. She's going to be there a week. If you like, I can look after Deniz for a few more days.'

'That would be great,' she said appreciatively. 'I'll drop him off to school in the mornings and you can pick him up in the afternoon. Tomorrow is going to be a frantic day. I don't know when I'll be home.'

'Don't you worry about a thing, I'll keep an eye on Deniz. Only, I have an appointment in the morning at 11. A solidarity meeting with Turkish dissidents who have come to Berlin seeking political asylum. After that I'm free. I'll take him to the park after school. He wants to go to the zoo but I cannot bear to see those poor animals in those cages. It's not a zoo, it's a prison, and it needs to be shut down.' After having spent two years in prison in Turkey before the coup, Yaman could not stomach seeing any living being held captive. He took another sip of coffee and then looked at his daughter. 'Are you sure it was Nazis that carried out the murder?'

She had to think before answering.

'I'm not sure. But we do know that these Nazis had had an altercation with the deceased and that they were caught on camera at the scene of the crime. The weapon we believe may have been used in the murder is being examined by Forensics. If any traces of the deceased's blood are found on the knife, then that may be proof that it was the Nazis that did it.' She took a final sip of her coffee. 'Tell me, Dad, were the Nazis interested in Greek mythology?'

Yaman blinked, not sure what the question meant.

'Greek mythology? What do you mean?'

'Like Zeus, for instance,' she replied, scratching her greying hairs. 'Did the Nazis try to forge a connection between Zeus and Hitler, for example? Is it possible they wanted to see themselves, and be seen, as Greek Gods or something?'

'Greek Gods? Zeus? I have no idea. I do not recall any attempted parallels between Zeus and Hitler in any of the texts I have read. But Hitler did have a lodge in the mountains of Bavaria. It was called the Berghof Residence and one part of the residence was known as the Eagle's Nest, so, as I'm sure you can guess by the name, it was built high up. And as far as I know, the eagle was also one of Zeus' symbols.'

Yıldız recalled the picture at the murder scene in front of which the deceased's body had been found. She pictured the eyes of the eagle perched on the end of Zeus' staff twinkling and glowing in the dark.

'The Eagle's Nest, you say? So, we have a house in the clouds and an eagle, one of Zeus' symbols. It does actually suggest Olympus, yes…'

'What does that have to do with the murder?' Yaman asked, confused.

'I'll tell you later. Now, the Altar of Zeus... The one in the Pergamon Museum, I mean... Did the Nazis have anything to do with that?'

Yaman leaned back in his chair.

'The Altar of Zeus? How would I know, Yıldız! What am I, an archaeologist? I have not researched the Nazis in that much depth. I mostly know the political angles. But tomorrow what I will do is check in at the City Library on Potsdamer Street and see what I can find on the subject.' His face suddenly took on a worried expression. 'But please, Yıldız, you need to be really careful. These Nazis are a vicious lot. And that is not all; they also have support within the state. I'm not joking. They have no qualms about killing people. Remember, one of the victims of the NSU murders was a policewoman.'

Yıldız was moved, seeing her father so concerned for her welfare.

'Nothing will happen to me, Dad.'

'Anything can happen to anyone, my dear,' Yaman said sadly, shaking his head. 'Most of these guys are sick in the head. They are filled with a hatred for foreigners.'

Yıldız smiled a sweet smile.

'Look who's talking! I was born in this country and am a police officer, whereas you're a foreigner and an old-school leftie too! In other words, they have two reasons to hate you. Tell me, Dad, have you ever thought about going back to Turkey?'

It was a difficult question. Yaman loved his country, and he had a particular affection for Istanbul. His eyes misted over whenever there was talk of Beyoğlu, Kadıköy or the Bosphorus.

'Of course, I have. All the time. But you're here, my grandson is here and your mother has been laid to rest here. And anyway, even if the xenophobia here is on the rise, Germany has a sound democratic tradition. Yes, the Nazis emerged from these lands but this country also has one of the world's largest anti-genocide monuments. Despite everything, they at least confront the evils that have been committed.' He sighed. 'The same cannot be said of our country. I think that may be one of the reasons why I don't want to go back. But don't let that make you forget that the xenophobia here is a very real danger. You are under a very real threat, Yıldız, and being a police officer is not going to help you. In fact, it puts you in even more danger. So please, my child. Be careful.'

A mischievous smile appeared on Yıldız's tired face.

'Don't worry Dad. The fascists can't do a thing to me. You seem to forget — I am the daughter of a true revolutionary.'

Yıldız was running late. When she dropped Deniz off to school, she stopped to speak to his teacher, Ms Hermine Krause, as Deniz had not been doing so well in class this year. He had been very close to his father and Franz's sudden absence had affected Deniz quite seriously. Yıldız knew she needed to take a greater interest in her son, as did her ex-husband. If possible, the three of them needed to get together. It was not actually out of the question as they were still on fairly amicable terMs Ms Krause told Yıldız about problems Yıldız was already aware of and informed Yıldız of what she expected of her. She was absolutely right, of course, and Yıldız listened to her respectfully, and then told her she would do everything she could. In the car, she called Franz but his phone was switched off. She knew she should have tried again as the situation with Deniz was worrying but all she could think of in the car was the murder case.

Her phone rang as she was walking up the stairs in the station. The number was not one of her saved ones. She answered while still on the staircase.

'Yes?'

'Ms Karasu?'

The voice was familiar but she could not quite place it.

'Yes…'

'It's me. Peter Schimmel. We met yesterday.'

For some inexplicable reason, Yıldız blushed.

'Yes, Mister Schimmel. How can I help you?'

'I can call later if this is not a good time.'

His courtesy made her even more self-conscious.

'Please. Not at all. I'm all ears.'

'I went into Cemal's office this morning.' There was a pause. 'I don't know, maybe I shouldn't have but I couldn't help it and I just went in. I found a letter in his drawer. A threatening letter…'

'What did it say?' Yıldız asked, disguising her growing excitement. The sound of rustling could be heard at the other end.

'It's not that long. Just five sentences in all. This is what it says, I'm reading it out verbatim: *You filthy Turk, don't think you're going to get away with what you're doing. You'll pay for it all. You'll pay for your disrespect with your own blood. Get ready. Soon, very soon…* In place of the signature is a swastika.'

This was good news.

'Thank you for this information, Mister Schimmel. However, it would be better if you did not handle the envelope or the letter any further. We do not want the sender's fingerprints to be corrupted in any way. We shall be there soon. Could you also take a photograph of the letter and envelope and send them to me via WhatsApp? Immediately, if you would be so kind.'

'Of course, I shall do that straightaway. I am in the office today so I'll see you when you get here.'

Yıldız hung up. She felt much better now and had a spring in her stride. However, when she walked into the office and saw the expression on Tobias' face, her good mood vanished almost as quickly as it had appeared. Before she could ask, he pointed to a document on the table.

'The blood on the dagger is not the victim's.'

Yıldız froze.

'What do you mean? There must be a mistake.'

Tobias shook his head.

'No mistake, boss. The blood found on the knife is not that of Cemal Ölmez… It's not even human blood. It's animal blood.'

Even though she trusted Tobias completely, Yıldız still hurried forward and began thumbing through the report on her feet. Markus must have insisted as the results on the knife and the autopsy report were both there. She went through the pages until she found what she was looking for. There it was, written in plain ink, just as Tobias had said. *The luminol and DNA tests carried out on the weapon suspected of being used in the crime indicate that the blood on the weapon in question is not that of the victim, Cemal Ölmez…*

'So Otto is telling the truth?' Yıldız asked disappointedly. 'He and his friends didn't do it?'

Her assistant saw the disappointment in her eyes and tried to put a positive spin on things.

'It's still too early to say. The evidence we have at hand still points to Otto and his goons.'

The phone rang, cutting him off. It was the landline.

'Hello? Yes, Chief, right away. We're on our way.'

Yıldız was annoyed. She thrust the files under right arm with a frown.

'Right, let's go. Now we have to deal with the Chief's bullshit.'

When they walked into Markus' office, however, he greeted them with an unexpected smile.

'This way, please. Come in. Please, take a seat.' He turned to address Yıldız. The reflection of the green of the leaves of the linden tree outside brushing against the window pane could be seen in his eyes. 'So, did you manage to get some rest?'

'I did, thank you,' Yıldız answered, settling into her seat.' She turned to look at her assistant, who didn't care about formalities and was itching to get down to business. Markus, however, was already there.

'The blood on the knife has not been identified,' he said. 'But according to the autopsy, there were traces of rohypnol and ketamine in the victim's blood. Cemal was sedated five minutes before he was killed. It's all in the report. Basically, what we can conclude from this is that the killer, or killers, went about it extremely professionally.'

Yıldız did not say anything and just listened, curious as to where Markus was going.

'Professionally and in a highly sophisticated manner too,' Tobias added. Markus narrowed his eyes and nodded.

'Definitely. The picture of the statue of Zeus, the removal of the heart, the music being played at volume on the computer — the killers are clearly sending out a message. However, there is no way that moron Otto could have done this by himself. Not only did he not have the physique to overpower and subdue Cemal, he does not have the brains to plan and implement such a complex operation. This was done by an organized group… The fact that that lawyer sauntered in only a few hours after Otto was arrested suggests that there are some powerful forces at play here.'

Yıldız listened on in amazement. What had happened to make Markus change his tack overnight? Whatever it was, at least they were now on the same team.

'But what is the connection, if any, between Zeus and the Nazis?' Markus went on. 'The neo-Nazis have made no such reference or allusion in any of the murders they have committed in Germany so far. Dozens of people are said to have been killed over the last forty years either by Nazis or by other xenophobes.'

Tobias stepped in and corrected the Chief.

'Not dozens. Nearly 200.'

'Two hundred?' Markus repeated, raising his eyebrows in surprise. 'Don't you think that's a bit of an exaggeration? Wouldn't fifty be more accurate? That is the number I have been given.'

Tobias, however, had done his homework.

'I'm sorry, sir, but the actual number is much higher. According to the Federal Bureau of Statistics, right-wing extremists killed forty-seven people between 1990 and 2009. In just nineteen years, that is. However, the Amadeu-Antonio Foundation says one hundred and eighty people have been killed since 1990. They don't just say it, either. They have names, dates and locations. I can have a copy of their report sent to you, if you like.'

Markus was impressed but still cautious.

'Please do. I would like to go over it.'

Yıldız saw the opportunity to make a telling point.

'The sad thing, Markus, is that the people researching the true number of people killed by racists should be us and not some foundation.'

Markus did not respond. He just looked away. Yıldız did not twist the knife any further.

'Anyway, what I meant to say was, in all these murder cases, there have not been any references to mythology or Greek Gods.' He looked at his two colleagues. 'Have there?'

'No, none,' Tobias said confidently. 'None at all. The Amadeu-Antonio Foundation also uncovered the methods used in the murders. The neo-Nazis shot, stabbed or beat their victims to death or they set fire to their homes or threw them off balconies.

But none of them removed any organs or offered them up to any deities or what have you. Nothing like this has been seen before.'

'Absolutely. If it had, we would have known about it,' Markus said in agreement. 'This is not something to be ignored. Even if we do drop it, there is no way the media will let it go. No, I do not think the neo-Nazis have anything to do with Zeus.'

'And what do the higher-ups have to say about all this?' Yıldız asked, not holding back. 'Are they going to let us do our job this time and carry out a full investigation or are they going to cover it up like they did with the previous neo-Nazi murders?'

Markus' face fell.

'Why do you have to put it like that, Yıldız? Do you really think it's right to smear the entire force on account of a few rotten apples? Look, the Chief of Berlin Police called me this morning to ask about the case and the Federal Minister for the Interior himself is taking a personal interest in this case. He says they have zero tolerance for neo-Nazis. We have the full support of local and federal government. So yes, we will investigate to the full.'

Yıldız smiled at the change in Markus' attitude, the reasons of which were obvious. The smile did not escape her Chief's attention.

'What? Why are you smiling?'

'Nothing,' she replied, looking away. 'All I can say is, congratulations. I just hope they're serious. If they are, then we can get rid of our rotten apples. Perhaps they will stop harbouring a secret sympathy for neo-Nazis this way.'

Markus' face went red.

'What do you mean? Are you insinuating something?'

'Not at all,' Yıldız said, unfazed. 'I'm not insinuating anything. On the contrary, I'm delighted that you have changed some of your opinions.'

'Don't even go there, Yıldız,' Markus fumed, clearly affronted. 'I want the killer to be caught just as much as you do. The fact that the victim is of Turkish origin does not in any way alter the course of justice. Despite the gossip that goes on in these corridors, I am not a xenophobe.' He nodded twice. 'Oh yes, I know what is said around here behind my back but you are all wrong. I have never had any sympathy for neo-Nazis. Never have and never will. My grandfather Wilhelm was killed by the Nazis in 1943. He was a member of the anti-fascist resistance in Berlin. He was killed on Prager Street.' He picked up his mobile phone from the desk, tapped on the screen several times and then held it out to Yıldız. 'Here, see? This is where my grandfather was killed.'

Yıldız was taken aback by the force of his reaction.

'Go on. Take it. Have a look. Take a good look for yourself. Zoom in, get a closeup.'

Yıldız took the phone and narrowed her eyes to get a better look.

'You can enlarge the image,' Markus said. 'Just tap the screen.'

She did as he suggested. A ground-level photograph of a street came up on the screen. Covering one of the paving stones on the ground was a metal plaque of the type used to commemorate the Jews, Communists and Social Democrats that were killed or sent to the camps during the Nazi era. The plaque was there to remind people of the horrors that had taken place in Berlin, part of a project had been started in 1996 by an artist called Günter Demnig to honour the memory of those killed by the Nazis. The project caught on and later spread to the rest of Europe. Yıldız had seen dozens of these plaques, and had stopped and stooped over them numerous times to read the names and the birth and death dates of the people commemorated on the plaque. The plaque in the photograph on Markus' phone read *Wilhelm Herder, 1914-1943*.

'He was twenty-nine when he was killed. My father was only six months old at the time. He was shot there and then, on that street in front of everyone, by the SS. On that very spot. The reason given for the execution was that he did not stop when he was told to. In his file, the Nazis registered him as a traitor. They then stormed his house and confiscated all his possessions. Everything he had. We do not have a single photograph of him...'

Tobias had leant forward and was examining the photo with great interest. Yıldız was moved by the story but his grandfather being executed by the Nazis did not automatically make Markus a decent fellow.

'I'm sorry to hear it. He was clearly a brave man. And a righteous man too, more importantly. May he rest in peace...' She handed the telephone back to the Chief. 'This is why we need to be extra vigilant in this case, Markus. So more children don't become orphaned the way your father was. So that the catastrophe that occurred last year is not repeated... So tell me, what are we to do with Otto now?'

Markus took his phone and put it back on his desk. When he replied, his voice seemed to have gained an edge. Clearly, he was upset at Yıldız's muted reaction to the photograph.

'What do you mean *what are we to do*? We arrest him. At the time of the murder, he was seen exiting the victim's premises, and he also told us he went there to reclaim a knife. Moreover, the murder weapon is missing. We have grounds for reasonable doubt.'

Yıldız was happy to hear it. It meant the people at the top really were intent upon catching the Nazis. Tobias, however, was not so optimistic.

'This evidence may not be enough for us to nab him. It all depends on the Public Prosecutor's interpretation.'

'The man attacked two police officers with a knife. What more do you want?' Markus said. 'Had you two not defended yourselves, he may have killed you too. Or at least seriously wounded you.'

Tobias smiled uneasily.

'Don't get me wrong. If it were up to me, I'd make sure that guy never saw the light of day again as he is obviously the type that is more than willing to hurt other people but you saw his lawyer. He was as sly as a fox, that one. There is no way he is going to let his client go down on such flimsy evidence.'

'Don't be so sure,' Yıldız said. We may have more evidence up our sleeve. Peter, the owner of Der Blitz, called me just now and told me he has just found a threatening letter sent to Cemal. If we manage to identify Otto or his goons' fingerprints on that letter, we may give the lawyer something to think about.'

Markus' mood had lifted.

'True. If their prints are on that letter, none of them are getting out. Right, let's make sure we get that letter and have it analysed.'

Yıldız was already on her feet and ready.

'We're on our way. We'll also get to see where the deceased worked. If there are any developments, we'll let you know.'

She turned and glared at Tobias, who was still seated, but when he saw the look in her eyes, he slowly got to his feet.

'We need to stop by at the scene of the crime first, Chief, and chat to this Peyman fellow, the guy with the security camera,' he said. 'Our lads got stills from the recordings but we have not spoken to the owner yet. He may have other material for us. Other suspects, perhaps…'

Yıldız nodded in approval.

'Very well. After that, we'll go to Der Blitz.'

Tobias, who was on his feet now, put a check on her enthusiasm.

'I'm sorry, boss, but after that we'll have to go to the German Institute for Archaeology. I called Cemal's cousin, this Haluk fellow, to arrange a meeting. Remember we said we would speak to him? He's expecting us.'

Although it was still morning, the smile on Yıldız's face betrayed her fatigue.

'Very well, Toby. It looks like we have a long day ahead of us.' She gave him a hearty slap on the shoulder with her right hand. 'Right then. Let's get going.'

5
Do not underestimate Man, Mighty Zeus

First there was the darkness. Then fate emerged. I was the one that wrote fate and allowed it to manifest in the world. When I dethroned my father and the Titans and sent them into Tartarus, I declared my dominion and my rule over the earth and the skies. However, although I was the supreme ruler, I did not flinch from sharing power with my siblings. The sky was mine and it was from there that I ruled the earth. Poseidon ruled the seas and was the controller of earthquakes. The greatest sacrifice fell to Hades, to whom I gave the kingdom of the underworld. The heights of Olympus now forbidden to him. If it may be considered a gift, then to him I gave the gift of the abode of the dead. The other eleven Gods I invited to the cloudy peak of Olympus. Although I never gave them my Great Seal, I aided them and they aided me. However, there were times when I became angry with them as they often conspired against me. With their half-minds, they laid traps for me and time after time, they betrayed me, but I still permitted these exalted beings to remain by my side, because the number twelve is a sacred number and it was our presence together there that held Olympus up.

My jealous wife Hera, she with the eyes of a doe and translucent skin, the Goddess of marriage; waxen-haired Demeter, the Goddess of Fertility who, with a mere touch, could make a dry twig flower and bloom; Aphrodite, the Goddess from Cyprus who could inflame the heart of any God, Titan or man that gazed upon her; my daughter Athena, greatest amongst the Gods, Titans and humans in virtue, who could slay the most experienced of commanders in battle; my precocious son Apollo, he who knew the unknown, the embodiment of the serene mind; my daughter Artemis, who sat upon a golden throne, the reflection of the light of the moon, greatest of archers, Goddess of the Hunt; my anguished son Hephaestus, who tamed iron with fire to make the most fearsome weapons, who tried to contain his endless wrath only for it to erupt like a volcano; my son and personal messenger Hermes, youngest of the Gods, most handsome of the guides, his winged sandals making him the swiftest of them all; my stalwart, brooding son Ares, God of War, destroyer of castles, chief enemy of man; Dionysus, my playful son, who lived by the dictates not of reason but of instinct, who transcended himself through wine, art and theatre to become one with nature; and, of course, my powerful older brother, exalted Poseidon, lord of the seas, of earthquakes and of the finest steeds.

All were with me. Each of the eleven Gods on Olympus and Hades in the underworld had a duty and a role to play in the sacred order I had established in the skies and upon the earth, and each was important, yet the last word was always mine. Because the word belonged to me. All the creatures, whether they be of the land, the sea or the air, looked to me. All owed their lives to me, because I was father to them all.

All the creatures, from the boldest to the weakest, and all mankind, from the brightest to the dullest, feared, venerated and adored me. I did not fear the emotions of animals, for they were too naïve of nature to lie. However, that Mortal creature known as Man was the source of all manner of malice and strife. He could not be trusted. Whether he was hero or traitor, cowardly or brave, destroyer or creator, he could not be trusted. Not satisfied with the evil he did unto his own kind, he also wrought misery and devastation upon the flora and fauna. Indeed, this destruction gave him pleasure. Neither the Titans nor the Giants tested me the way Man did.

However, despite his destruction, stupidity, hypocrisy, weakness and cowardice, I could not help but take to those creatures known as humans. It was baffling, the affection I had for them. When looking at them, I saw a piece of myself. I know it is folly to see the Immortals in Mortal beings but in gazing upon myself, I began to see much within me that resembled this Mortal known as Man. And although I did not disclose this truth to any other Immortal, I came to realize that we, the Gods, were as impulsive, stupid, weak, cowardly, selfish, immoral and voracious as these humans. And yes, we were also as intelligent, brave, strong, resilient, virtuous and selfless as they were. We, it seemed, were the Immortal versions of men.

To admit to this shameful truth was difficult, because none wish to admit to their own fault. Moreover, no Immortal would dare to draw parallels between themselves and a Mortal. Perhaps this is why most of the Olympians, Ares most of all, did not like this Mortal, Man. Indeed, when their numbers multiplied, Demeter, Goddess of Fertility, started the Trojan Wars so as to not upset the delicate order of the earth. To stop Man, any and all means were legitimate, and there was little in Demeter's preferred means that could be objected to. It was an act worthy of the Gods. The true problem lay with me. With I, with Mighty Zeus, son of Kronos, Lord of the Titans, Gods and Men. I could not overcome my fondness and thus my weakness for humans. Moreover, I did not know how and when these humans emerged. Perhaps they were there before the Gods, maybe even before our ancestors, the Titans. And although they were weak, pitiful, pathetic creatures, they glorified their short lives, which were really were nothing more than a few simple deeds taking place in misery in a series of dark, gloomy cities.

That is the truth. I speak with certainty for it is I that built those cities and I that decided how long those pitiful creatures were to live. It was not just me; sometimes, the other Olympians would intervene in the fates of people. We were the ones that dictated their joys and their miseries, their delights and their sorrows, their victories and their defeats. All their stories were written on Olympus, in our palace in the clouds. Whenever we grew bored of the course of their events, we would change it and intervene in human affairs with glee, turning good into evil, love into hate, cruelty into compassion. We created their loves, so they would have something with which to pass the time, we started wars so the cowardly could be separated from the valorous, we sent down famine and drought so they would know their own weaknesses, and we afflicted them with disease so they would not forget how dependent they were on our mercy. Indeed, we would fight one another over these people, for on Olympus, we each had our favoured cities, kings, heroes and tribes.

Mankind knew this too, and in order to escape the traps laid by one God, they would appeal to another, pray to him or her and offer up their precious sacrifices. If they did not receive a response, they would immediately turn to another. They would forget the God or Goddess in whose name they had built temples and offered sacrifices and turn to another in the hope that this new deity would help. Of course, these displays of hypocrisy always ended in calamity. When they incurred the wrath of Ares or Athena, or Apollo or Hermes, they would again come to me to beg, to plead with me to intervene and in most cases, I would answer their prayers. However, there were times when I would become enraged with them and scold them with thunder, threaten them with flashes of lightning and chastise them with thunderbolts. How they would tremble in fright! But they did not tremble for long. For forgetfulness is one of the most prominent traits of these humans. Whether it is good or evil, pain or bliss, fear or delight, all is eventually forgotten by them, which is why they always made the same mistakes. Such was the foolishness of men, yet they were also as cunning as our very own Hera and audacious enough to manipulate the naïve Titans, those like Prometheus, to do their bidding when they dare not challenge the Gods themselves.

That same Prometheus who believed he loved mankind more than I did. Who dared to reserve the choice cuts of the sacrifices on the Altar for mankind whilst leaving the worst parts for me. He planned to deceive me. He was impertinent, brazen and sinful. Moreover, he thought himself wise. What value could the flesh of dead animals have next to the benevolence I had shown men? Yet this basic truth, even he could not grasp. And so, he stole fire from us, the Gods, and gave it to mankind as a gift. But mankind is like a child, and one does not indulge a child by giving him a gift that he has not deserved, for such a child knows the value of neither the gift nor its giver. Young Prometheus was too inexperienced and too much of a romantic and a dreamer to know this, and so, like mankind, he needed to be soundly punished. I pronounced the punishment, and summoned my eagle. I chained Prometheus to the side of the steepest mountain in the snowy Caucasus and every day my eagle devoured his liver, and after it had been consumed, he would be given a new liver and the punishment thereby repeated.

This divine punishment was to last forever until my valiant son Heracles intervened and appealed to my conscience, rousing my mercy. I forgave Prometheus, but the torments he suffered on the mountains of the Caucasus must have driven the poor Titan mad, for he approached me once the chains that bound him had been broken and said:

'Do not underestimate Man, Mighty Zeus. He is a sinister creature. He may even have existed before you, and before Hera, Poseidon, Hades and all the other Gods; he may have existed in the time before us, before Kronos, Rheia, Gaia and Uranus, before the Titans. Perhaps the glorious Titans, the awesome Giants and you, the mighty Gods, all the Immortals; perhaps we are but the dream of that Mortal creature known as Man. Perhaps what created us was their minds, their logic and their dreaMs It is possible that we would not exist without their belief, and that we would lose our power without their invocations. Do not underestimate him, Mighty Zeus. There is a mysterious side to this creature known as Man. A dark side.'

Thus spoke Prometheus, and I roared with laughter. What mystery could that wretch Man possibly have? What dark side? He was but a Mortal, a simple creature with whom I toyed when the mood took me and one whose fate and life were under my control. A pitiful being under my heel, whether he be a king or a slave, young or old, male or female. That is why they were all so weak and dependent and why they worshipped me. That is why they called me 'Zeus, the Father'. And I did indeed look upon them as a true father. I was neither cruel to them the way Uranus had been to my father or without mercy the way my father Kronos had been with me. I was a good father to them, a caring father. When necessary, I was hard-hearted and when needed, I was compassionate. I rewarded them when it was required and I punished them when necessary. But I never abandoned them. They remained under my watchful gaze, always under my protection. It amused me to watch them from Olympus live their simple lives. That is why I did not heed the rebel Titan Prometheus' warnings. But a dream I then had, or rather, the words of the child with whom I spoke in that dream, began to gnaw away at me.

In the dream, there was a river, but this river did not run green and blue like those of Oceanus. This river was the colour of soil, a dark soil, and around this river, tall, imposing buildings rose up to the skies. Marble columns, domes piercing the skies, strange iron wagons on the street that even horses could not pull, and statues of Gods and Goddesses in the squares and forums fashioned by expert hands. It was like no other city I had ever seen. People were walking there but the clothes they wore were unusual. It was on a bridge over that river that I saw that child. He was with a tall, dark man, probably his father, and the father was pointing the buildings out to the child and talking to him with great excitement. It was clear that what he was saying was making him happy, and the child was listening intently. The love between them, even from afar, was palpable. I envied them, and as one that had never known a father's love, it tore at me. I could not stop myself from wanting to get a closer look at this virtuous father and his loving son. I approached them in silence, without disturbing them, to listen to what they were saying, but the child suddenly turned to me and, with an anxious look in his olive-black eyes, said:

'Be careful with these humans, Zeus. They are the most untrustworthy creatures on the earth. If you do not control them, they will condemn you to oblivion the way you did with the previous deities, and they will forget all about you, without feeling the slightest gratitude for you. Be careful with these humans, Zeus.

'Too much love and compassion will lead them astray, as will punishment that is too violent or forceful.'

'They forget even those that are closest to them. They abandon their own children wilfully. The tears of their loved ones mean little to them. Be careful with these humans, Zeus.'

I was stunned. I was about to ask the child why he said all this but then I awoke, bathed in cold sweat. Fortunately, Hera was not by my side, otherwise she would have mocked me, the Great Zeus, for having been startled by a mere dream. I sat up in my bed high in the clouds. I was thirsty, and I drank the nectar in my golden kantharos down to the last drop. This soothed me. I thought long and hard as to who that child was and what he was trying to tell me, but I could find no answer. But Prometheus' words rang ever louder in my ears: 'Do not test Man, Mighty Zeus. He is a sinister creature.'

Chapter Five

When they left the building, the sun was up and it was muggy outside. The scent from the three linden trees that shaded the courtyard was drifting through the whole street, as though trying to stress that life was not just made up of dull grey buildings and dreary official cars. But of course, human agendas are not the same as nature's. Yıldız was too busy pondering the case to notice the scent. She wanted to get back to the murder scene as soon as possible and from there move on to Peter's offices and see this threatening letter for herself. They needed that letter if they were to keep the neo-Nazis in custody, and if Otto or his friends' fingerprints were found on the letter or the envelope, then things would most definitely be easier. If their prints were not there, then there was a very distinct possibility that the Nazis would be able to wiggle their way out. They saw Kurt as they were hurrying towards their Passat. He removed his blue helmet when he saw his two colleagues and called out to them.

'Hey guys, how's it going? Did you read my report?'

They only had time to glance at it, not read it thoroughly.

'High levels of ketamine and rohypnol were found in the victim's blood,' Yıldız said walking towards him. 'As far as we can tell, the victim did not put up any resistance. Are there any signs of stress or forced entry on the front door or the front gate?'

He looked at them in disappointment.

'You didn't read it, did you? Well, thanks a million, Yıldız. The Chief was calling me non-stop, hustling me to write that report. I dropped everything to write it and you don't even have the bloody decency to read it.'

Yıldız wore the look of someone that had been caught out.

'You're absolutely right, Kurt. But these last two days have been so hectic. We were also attacked. You may have heard.'

'No, I haven't. What attack?'

'Oh, it was a right old dingdong. A proper brawl. Knives, bottles, fists, the whole shebang. Three guys had a pop at us in a café.'

She had finally gotten Kurt's attention.

'You're kidding? Who attacked you?'

'A bunch of neo-Nazis,' she replied, adding a dramatic pitch to her voice. 'You should have seen them. They were totally deranged, attacking us as if we were their sworn enemies. They almost had Toby in trouble.'

Kurt examined the bruise on Toby's face.

'Nasty. You're okay though, right?'

'I'm fine,' Tobias grinned. 'Don't you worry, they're in far worse shape. But it was touch and go at one point. Could have turned quite nasty. Those guys weren't messing around. So, you see, that's why we haven't been able to read the report in full yet.'

'I see,' Kurt said understandingly. 'But please read it when you can. It has all the information you need. We were there at the scene of the crime the whole night and went over everything with a fine-tooth comb. Down to the last detail.' He turned to Yıldız. 'What was it you asked me just now? Oh yeah. The doors.

No, there was no sign of any strain or violence on the doors or windows. The victim must have let the killers in. Either that or they had keys. But even then, the victim does not seem to have put up any resistance or made any effort to defend himself. The man either volunteered, willingly, to be sacrificed or he was given a very strong sedative…'

Yıldız only knew as much about the report as the Chief had told her.

'Like I said, traces of rohypnol and ketamine were found in the victim's blood.'

Kurt nodded, taking on board this information.

'Hmm, so they sedated him first and the victim would not even have known. If you put two tablets of rohypnol in somebody's drink they will fall into a deep sleep. But to carry out a complex surgical operation like removing someone's heart, you need a drug like ketamine. Ketamine is an extremely powerful anaesthetic.'

Tobias was mulling over something Kurt said.

'So if the victim actually wanted this surgical operation to take place; I mean, if he had volunteered to undergo it, would rohypnol still be needed?'

The sunlight seeping through the leaves of the linden tree lit up Kurt's eyes.

'Here, come this way, out of the sun,' he said, taking two steps back. 'We can talk more comfortably here in the shade.' They joined him in the shade. 'Cycling really makes you work up a sweat,' he said, wiping away the perspiration on his forehead with the back of his hands. 'So, what we were saying? Ah, yes. No, in such an instance, rohypnol would not have to be used. You've already given the guy ketamine. All it needs is a needle to the arm. Why drug a man twice? But we would still have to look at the Forensics Lab guys' report. Those guys are the real experts.'

Naturally, they were going to look at that report but while he was there, Yıldız still wanted to ask Kurt about some questions that had been bothering her.

'I know there was no weapon at the murder scene but there had to be other tools and instruments involved. Where did the killers remove the victim's heart? There was blood on the floor but surely there should have been more?'

Kurt shook his head in remorse.

'It's all in the report. If only you'd been able to read it. Still, not to worry. If you ask me, the operation was carried out in the room in which we found the body. It's not a small room so it's quite suitable for such an operation. The killer most probably covered the entire floor with a large plastic sheet so what we saw in that room is, as you correctly say, Yıldız, what was left after the linoleum sheets had been gathered up and taken away. Don't forget, the victim was still bleeding, which means there would have been footprints and other such evidence had there not been a lino sheet on the floor. Basically, the killer, or killers, thought this through properly and they carried out a very thorough job. Like you said, no murder weapon was found but, as you also said, other instruments must have been used. Shears, pliers, I don't know for sure at the moment. The guys at Forensics will know the correct technical terMs The killer would have needed such instruments because to access the heart, he would have had to cut the ties between the victim's ribs, but we did not find instruments for that specific task. The people that did this — they are true professionals.'

'And they were people Cemal knew,' Tobias murmured. 'Perhaps people he knew very well, and trusted. Otherwise why would he let them into his house?'

'It's too early to say,' Kurt said. 'The victim may have known his killer, he may not have. For all we know, the killer could be a travelling salesman or repairman, or even a neighbour. Just think about how many people knock on our day every day, and we let them in, for various reasons.'

'True, but why would Cemal let a Nazi who drew a knife on him into his house?'

Tobias' question was as logical as Kurt's explanations but there had to be an answer somewhere in the world of unknowns in which anything was possible. It was Yıldız's turn to speak up.

'Perhaps it was not Otto that knocked on the door. This is an organization we are talking about. A tough, no-nonsense organization. Otto may not be too bright but I am sure there are a number of highly intelligent people in his organization. If they decided to murder Cemal in this highly ritualized manner, then they must have thought all the details through. The killer could have entered in disguise. A pizza delivery guy, a postman, a TV repairman, anything. He may even have been someone local, someone Cemal knew and trusted. At the end of the day, the neo-Nazis are everywhere.'

Kurt had stopped fidgeting with his helmet.

'The killers were neo-Nazis?' he asked, surprised. 'The guys that attacked you?'

Yıldız did not want to share any more information with him.

'We're not sure but they do have a plausible motive for wanting to kill Cemal.'

'Well, that explains what was on the victim's computer,' Kurt muttered, his eyes fixed on the Chief Inspector. 'For the last month, the deceased had been reading up on neo-Nazis.'

'Really?' Yıldız said excitedly. 'This is actually a very significant development, Kurti. Did any names turn up in the victim's searches? For example, did you come across the name Otto Fischer?'

Kurt tried in vain to recall.

'There were names but I'm not sure if there was an Otto. He was reading about far-right parties like the German National Democratic Party and Alternative for Germany, as well as fascist groups like Combat 18 and the Oldschool Society. It's all written in the report…'

Yıldız looked at him gratefully.

'Thanks, Kurt, really. As soon as we get back to the station, I'm going to lock myself in my office and read your report. But I'm curious as to what your thoughts on this case are. What do you have to say about it?'

Kurt took a deep breath.

'Well, let's see. An elaborate ritual was carried out, for starters, which would suggest this is not a simple case of revenge or anger but rather the work of people who still have some kind of belief or adherence to ancient cults or religions. You saw the scene of the crime for yourselves. The way in which the victim was killed, the picture on the wall, the music that was playing. It was an ancient ritual performed in a modern setting… Now, are neo-Nazis capable of such a setup? Of a plan with such intricacy? I know they are nutters but I'm not sure they are capable of taking things to such extremes.'

'What if they wanted to deflect attention?' Tobias suggested. 'What if they do not want it to be known that they carried out this murder? That may explain why they created such an ornate, almost ceremonial atmosphere at the scene.'

'It's possible, yes,' Kurt said heavily. 'But why wouldn't an organization like this want their actions to be known? If you ask me, that is why the murder was performed with ceremonial aspect. To tell people that this was no ordinary event but something of significance. To draw people's attention to the murder. To get the organization's name out there. That's why, if the neo-Nazis are behind this, they will want this murder known and heard about, rather than covered up.'

Tobias was not convinced.

'Not necessarily. In most of the murders carried out by neo-Nazis so far, the killer or killers have not been caught. So for them to kill even one Turk must be something of some significance. There are hundreds of idiots in this country who think removing one foreigner is a grand victory for Germany. It doesn't matter if the murder was carried out by Otto Fischer or some other neo-Nazi. What matters is killing foreigners. Harassing them, scaring them, intimidating them. You remember what happened to Walter Lübcke. He was the governor of Kassel. One day, a guy just walks up to his house, takes out a gun and shoots Lübcke in the head. The killer was caught a week later. It wasn't a personal thing, a simple crime of revenge or hatred. It was later discovered that the killer and his instigators had connections to the National Socialist Underground. What I'm saying is, the neo-Nazis will not always assume responsibility for the murders they carry out.'

'I get it, Toby,' Kurt said, listening intently. 'What do you say makes sense but you have to remember, this is the first time we are coming across a setup like this. In previous murders, houses were set on fire or people were beaten or stabbed to death. More recently, they have started using firearms. But this is the first time we are seeing something like this, something so intricately planned and executed, almost as a spectacle…' He turned to Yıldız. 'Did they have human sacrifices to the Gods in the old pagan cultures?'

The Chief Inspector looked on helplessly.

'We don't know. But we did find some links between the Nazis and ancient Greek mythology.'

Kurt nodded approvingly.

'That's good. If what you say holds up, then yes, the neo-Nazis may be the ones behind this murder. You already have a suspect in custody. I just hope their crimes are all brought out in the open soon…' He took a few steps but then paused. 'If this is the work of neo-Nazis, then I'm afraid more will come. A mind that can come up with and execute something as elaborate as this will not stop at just one murder. This is going to go on so we better get ready for more cases.' He grinned. 'Be careful out there, guys. If what I say is true, you're in for a rough ride.'

Yıldız shot him a stinging glance.

'Not just us. I'm afraid you'll be on the ride too. You're one of us too, remember? Don't think you're not going to wriggle your way out of this…'

A surprise was awaiting them on the street. An angry mob holding up banners and placards had gathered in front of Cemal's apartment building. They made quite the sight, amongst the billowing white drift coming from the poplars. When the Passat got closer, the slogans being chanted by the crowd became clearer. 'United Against Fascism!' 'Down with Fascism!' they shouted. Yıldız pointed to a spot on the right.

'There. Park over there. We should keep a healthy distance between ourselves and the protestors.'

While Tobias expertly manoeuvred the car into position, Yıldız began examining the crowd. Several of the placards being waved by the assembled anti-fascist parties, trade unions and NGOs stuck out. The first one she noticed was one with the slogan 'Unite in the Fight Against Racist Attacks!' in yellow letters on a red background. Another said 'No Place for Nazis!' But the one she liked the most was being held by a dark young man and a young blonde that read 'Fascism—Never Again!' It reminded her of a photograph she had seen at home, one that had been taken during her father's youth, on 1 May 1977, during a rally in Taksim Square. In the photo, Yaman, right fist raised and eyes gleaming with exhilaration and fervour, was standing defiantly in the square in front of a placard that said 'No Pasaran!' One hour after the photo had been taken, the police opened fire on the gathered protestors, resulting in thirty-four deaths. Yaman's younger brother, Yücel, was one of the dead. The photo had been in the possession of a man who later arrived in Berlin as an émigré. He tracked down Yaman and gave him the photo as a gift. Yaman had no other photographs from Turkey. He had burnt or destroyed them all, even his wedding and childhood photographs, after the September 12 military coup so that his friends would not be in danger should the photos be seized by the government's police squads. The fascism condemned in the placards had, unfortunately, been established in Turkey by mutinying soldiers and had destroyed their lives, as it had the lives of hundreds of thousands of others, and had led to Yıldız's mother falling terribly ill and eventually dying in agony. Yıldız stared at the demonstrators, experiencing a disturbing déjà vu. Was the same thing going to happen here? Despite so many massacres, so much pain and so many millions of lives lost, was the dark shadow of fascism about to fall over this beautiful country once again?

'Well, it's clear now why our Chief is so hostile towards neo-Nazis,' Tobias said, snapping Yıldız out of her thoughts. 'He realizes Cemal's death is going to create a furore in the media. Just look at this, will you? Look at all these people. Our case was on the news on TV last night. Protests are being planned all over the country today.'

'Good. Let them protest,' Yıldız said, as though wishing to free herself from her own feelings of despair. 'Otherwise these lowlifes will cause us no end of grief.'

While two police officers began walking towards a group of protestors shouting 'Down with Fascism!', Yıldız scanned the unfamiliar faces in the crowd looking for Rafael.

'How are we going to find him amongst all these people?' Tobias huffed. 'He's not at home, either. Maybe we should come back later?'

But she had no such intention. For the first time, she felt a connection with the protestors.

'Don't give up so easily, Toby. Let's keep looking…'

She had only just finished her sentence when someone called out to her in Turkish. 'Yıldız Hanım, Yıldız Hanım…' She turned around and saw a dark man with a low forehead approaching them. He walked up to them and held out a hand.

'Hello! Özcan Mutlu. Remember? Ex-Green Party MP. We met last year. In Engelbecken. The incident with the corpse in the park.'

'Yes, of course, I remember,' Yıldız answered in German, her eyes lighting up. 'How are you, Mister Mutlu?'

He frowned and replied in German.

'As well as can be. Cemal's death has come as a real blow to us. The Nazis are becoming more and more audacious.' He looked to her for confirmation. 'It is the neo-Nazis behind this, isn't it?'

His gaze then wandered over towards Toby. Yıldız understood.

'Inspector Tobias Becker. We work together. As for your question, Mister Mutlu, it is still too early to say but there are neo-Nazis amongst our suspects, yes.'

He did not seem satisfied with the answer.

'These are important cases, Ms Karasu. This country is on a dark path. It feels like 1930s Berlin all over again. If the neo-Nazis gain strength, they will become even more ruthless. They need to be stopped.'

'I agree, Mister Mutlu,' Yıldız replied with a sad smile. 'I share your worries, both as a citizen of Germany and as an officer fighting crime. We are doing everything we can to find the perpetrators. Mister Becker and I are trying to get to the heart of this matter.' She emphasized the words *Mister Becker* in particular to stress that he was not amongst the racists that had infiltrated the police force. 'In that respect, you do not need to worry. Did you know the deceased?'

Özan narrowed his eyes in grief.

'He was not a friend per se but I did bump into him a number of times during meetings. He was a member of the Green Party. He was not an activist but he always supported us. He was a good man. He helped the squatters out a lot. We worked together on one of those projects.'

'We heard that his family disowned him?' Tobias asked. His voice carried a hint of suspicion but Özcan saw no need for dispute and looked for the middle ground.

'He lived his life the way he wanted, regardless of what others said. Let us just say that he paid the price for living the way he wanted.'

'He had a fight with some neo-Nazis… Did he ever mention it?' Yıldız asked. 'Did the two of you ever discuss it? Did he ever ask for help from the party?'

The politician seemed a bit taken aback.

'No, I'm hearing about it for the first time now from you. If he had appealed to the party for help, I would no doubt have heard…' He stopped to think. 'So, they had a fight… Then it must have been the neo-Nazis that killed Cemal. Why don't you go public with this?'

A tense silence ensued.

'It is still too early to go public. We do not have enough evidence. If we point the finger at people without the evidence to back it up, the right-wing press will have a field day. I am afraid we shall all have to exercise a little patience. I can tell you this though; we are making progress in our investigation.'

Özcan did not look convinced but he did not object either. He took out a business card from his pocket.

'We are also following this case very closely. After all, the deceased was one of our members and a friend. So, please do not hesitate to contact us if there is anything we can do.'

'Thank you,' Yıldız said, putting the card in her pocket. 'If we need you, we will definitely contact you.' She checked her pockets for her own business card but could not find one. 'Toby, could you give Mister Mutlu one of your cards please?' She turned to address Özcan again. 'And please call us if you hear anything. Day or night, it doesn't matter. We are available 24X7.'

'Actually, we were going to meet a gentleman called Rafael,' Tobias said, handing Özcan a card. 'He is one of Cemal's friends. You wouldn't happen to know him, would you? Have you seen him?'

Özcan's eyes lit up in recognition as he accepted the card.

'You mean the Argentinian? The painter? He is over there, under that placard. Yes, just over there, under the sign that says *No Pasaran!* His wife is with him. They're using the banner as shade. She's pregnant, you see.'

Yıldız spotted them.

'Ah, yes. Thank you. Well, good day, Mister Becker,' she said, and they began walking towards Rafael and Pilar.

Pilar was the first to notice them but she was not sure if it really was them and narrowed her eyes to get a better look. Once she knew it was them, she told her husband, who smiled broadly when he saw them. When Yıldız and Toby were just a few paces away, a girl with all her hair shaved off came in between them, making it difficult for them to talk.

'Here, this way,' Rafael said, moving to his right. 'Let's go this way.'

He took his wife by the hand and tried to move away from the crowd, watched by the two police officers. Moving out of that sea of people proved difficult, however, and it was a few minutes before they managed to find a quiet spot under one of poplar trees where they could talk.

'I was worried about you guys,' Rafael said anxiously. 'What happened? Have Otto and his friends been arrested?'

He both wanted to hear that Cemal's killers had been punished and to be sure that the threat to him and his wife had been nullified.

'They will be,' Yıldız said calmly. 'But we need to speak to the owner of this camera first.'

'You mean Peyman?' Rafael turned and looked at the crowd. 'He's here somewhere. Can you see him, Pilar?'

Pilar narrowed her eyes and scanned the crowd.

'There he is. Over there. With his son.'

'I'll go get him and be right back,' Rafael said, and kissed his wife on the forehead before diving into the crowd.

'Are we safe here?'

Her voice was so low, Yıldız could not make out what she was saying.

'Excuse me?'

'Will the neo-Nazis attack us too?' Pilar said, reframing the question. While talking, she placed her right hand on her stomach. 'Will you protect us?'

The Chief Inspector did not know what to say. Her assistant came to her rescue.

'To be honest, we cannot say with one hundred per cent certainty that you are safe. But the neo-Nazis are in serious trouble at the moment. It would be stupid of them to try and attack anybody again. I think they will keep their distance for some time.'

'Some time?' Pilar muttered. 'And then?'

Yıldız hated making false promises to people but she felt sorry for Pilar.

'Don't you worry. We will have them all locked up. We will make them sorry for killing Cemal…'

Pilar beamed with gratitude.

'Thank you so much. Really. Otherwise, Rafael and I would be back on the plane to Buenos Aires. Rafael would worry too much for us to stay here. Yet his future is here. His exhibition opens in November. He has been working on it for three years. I don't want to see his plans go to waste.'

Yıldız squeezed Pilar's shoulder gently.

'Don't worry. Rafael's exhibition will go ahead as planned.'

Pilar looked surprised. The same police woman that had been quite formal with her the other night was now trying her hardest to reassure them. She was about to thank her again when her husband came back. 'Here's Peyman.' All three turned around and saw a dusky gentleman, at least one metre ninety tall, with long grey hair reaching down to his shoulders.

'Hello,' he said, extending a hand. He spoke flawless German, without an accent. 'My name is Peyman Majidi. How can I help you?'

After Yıldız and Tobias introduced themselves, Yıldız got straight down to business.

'We are curious as to what happened on the night of the murder. Apparently, your camera recorded the suspects as they went past your apartment block but it did not capture them entering the scene of the crime. Did you or any of your family happen to see the suspects that night?'

Peyman did not seem to mind the question at all and was happy to answer. His silver locks billowed in the wind as he spoke.

'If by suspects you mean Otto and his friends, I had seen them before. We had had a few run-ins with them before with some goading going on but I did not see them the night Cemal was killed. They are extremely dangerous people, though. Highly unpredictable, and quite audacious too.' He peered at the two police officers. 'I say audacious because they always seem to get away with what they are doing. They have support from the inside.'

Yıldız knew what he meant but she kept her cool.

'Did you know Cemal? Were you friends?'

'He was our neighbour, yes. I knew him well enough to know he was a good man. I don't know what Rafael thinks but for me, he was a good artist. He was working on a big project, drawing the statues from the Altar of Zeus that depicted the battle between the ancient Greek Gods and the Giants. In fact, when he told me about the project, I told him not to.'

'Why?' Tobias asked. 'Why would you not want him to embark on such a project?'

'Because our very own Iranian artist Yadegar Asisi has already done it, and quite brilliantly too. It's on display here in Berlin, opposite the Pergamon Museum. Haven't you seen it?'

Neither Yıldız nor Tobias even knew about it. Seeing their silence, Peyman went on.

'Asisi created a panorama of the ancient city of Pergamon. Sounds from the Imperial Roman era have also been added to the panorama for added effect. You should see it. It's an absolute treat, really.'

Yıldız made a mental note to see it but right now she was too focused on the case.

'How did Cemal react when you told him not to go through with this project?'

'He didn't really care. I told him there was no point in doing something that has already been done and that a copy of a work that has already been done has no value and is just junk but he looked me in the eye and told me that, where Asisi's work depicts Pergamon during the Roman era, and he said it was amazing, his project was going to show Pergamon during the Hellenistic era. The statues showing the war between the Giants and the Gods depict the Greek Gods, the Immortals of Olympus and he said his exhibition was going to bring the whole of ancient Greek mythology to life, starting from the Gods on the Altar of Zeus. He sounded very determined too, like a guy who knew what he was doing. I did not voice any further doubts.' He paused, looked at the crowd and then turned back to address Yıldız. 'He was killed in front of his painting of Zeus, wasn't he?'

Instead of confirming or disconfirming the question, Tobias answered with another question.

'Does that matter?'

The Iranian stared at them, incredulous at them for not having noticed.

'Well, in the painting, Zeus has Cemal's face. In the drawings in the lounge, his drawings of Kronos have his father's face. In other words, he painted his own father as Zeus' father.'

The information was startling but Yıldız and Tobias were there to investigate a murder, not art and mythology, and it was Cemal's father, not Zeus', that was their focus.

'How do you know Kerem Bey?' Peyman looked at Yıldız in silence, awaiting clarification. 'Kerem is Cemal's father,' Yıldız went on, surprised that Peyman did not know. Peyman, in turn, shrugged his shoulders.

'I have never seen him. I didn't know his name was Kerem until now.'

Yıldız was, of course, ready with her next question.

'If you have never seen him before, how do you know it is his face in the drawings of Kronos?'

'Because Cemal showed me photographs of his father. He called me to show me the pictures in the lounge.' He then turned and spoke to Rafael. 'In fact, you were there too, weren't you, Rafael? Remember?'

'Yes, I do,' he said with a sad smile. 'Remember how excited he was? "These are just rough sketches, but the rest will be like this," he said…'

'He said the exhibition was going to have a personal significance for him as the history of his family was bound up with the ancient city of Pergamon,' Peyman said. 'He told us that all the men in his family had worked on the excavations in Pergamon since they had started, including his father, and that they had all witnessed the rebirth of that amazing city. That is why he was going to put his relatives' faces on the bodies of the Gods on his painting of those statues. He said he was going to make his grandfather Uranus, his father Kronos, and he would be Zeus. Then he took his father's photo out and showed us and asked us if the painting he had created was a fair depiction."

Rafael confirmed what Peyman was saying.

'Yes, that is what he told us. If he were still alive, it would have been an amazing piece of work. He said he was thinking of opening the exhibition in the Pergamon Museum, if it could be arranged. How sad that the project could not be completed.'

Yıldız was secretly furious with herself while listening to Peyman for not having noticed Kerem's face in the picture. How could they have missed it? She had seen it and it had struck her as familiar but she had not given it a second thought. Nor had she realized that the Zeus in the painting had been painted with the face of the victim. Tobias did not seem to mind this failing on their part, though.

'On the night of the murder, or indeed, earlier in the evening, did you see anybody suspicious on the street? Did you see anything out of the ordinary?'

Peyman's black eyebrows formed a frown while he thought about Tobias' question.

'There was a minivan,' he said eventually. 'Yes, a cobalt black minivan. I saw it in the evening, after sundown. I had gone out onto the balcony for a cigarette.' He looked at Rafael and Pilar. 'Didn't you see it? A black minivan…'

'I was at the squat,' Rafael said. 'When I got back home, it had already happened.'

'I was sleeping,' Pilar said guiltily. 'I wasn't feeling that good so I had a mug of camomile tea and then lay down and dozed off. It was that music that woke me up.'

'Did you catch the minivan's number plate?' Tobias asked.

Peyman shook his head sadly.

'I didn't even look… Had I known, then of course I would have looked. But at the end of the day, it was just a minivan. One of the many that park there every day.'

'Can you at least tell us the make and model? Any writing on it? Any signs, emblems or logos?'

A vague look of remorse passed over the Iranian gentleman's face.

'I didn't. If I did, I certainly can't remember now. All I can say is I saw a black minivan. Cobalt black. That is all I can say for sure. That, and those Third Reich clowns on camera walking past my house…'

'What say you, boss?' Tobias asked, keeping his eyes on the traffic flowing calmly around them. 'You haven't said a word since we got into the car.'

Yıldız still did not reply. She carried on watching the road, lost in thought.

'Or have we got this all wrong?' Tobias went on, looking at his partner this time. 'What if this has nothing to do with those neo-Nazis?'

'Why do you say that?' she asked nervously.

'I don't know,' Tobias answered, thinking he had been misunderstood. 'It's just that what that Iranian guy told us was quite interesting.'

Interestingly, it was the same thing that had plunged Yıldız deep in thought and made her silent up till now.

'Which part, exactly?'

Tobias was about to go through a red light and had to hit the brakes. The Passat shuddered to a halt.

'Sorry, boss. Didn't see it.'

Yıldız was too lost in thought to mind the emergency stop. 'You mean what Peyman was saying about that painting?' she asked. 'Why was it interesting?'

'Cemal giving Kronos his father's face and Zeus his own face. Don't you find that a bit weird? I wouldn't want the Gods to look like my father, or for my mother to smile down at everyone like some kind of Goddess…. And no way would I want to see myself as a God. That would be terrifying. Wouldn't it?'

It would indeed; it is what Yıldız had been pondering ever since they had gotten into the car. However, instead of sharing her thoughts with her partner, she wanted to know what her partner was thinking.

'So, what do you make of all this?'

'I don't know. It's just weird. I mean, think about it. Your family has disowned you. Not just that, they beat you up. They hate you so much that they even consider killing you. And what do you do? You go and paint their faces on the bodies of Greek Gods, basically Immortalizing them. Why would he do that? It doesn't make sense.'

Tobias' question actually helped shed some light on an issue that had been bothering both of them.

'Actually, it does make sense. I don't know why I didn't notice it. In doing this in the painting, Cemal is taking his revenge on his father. In ancient Greek mythology, the throne was fought over. Zeus defeated his father Kronos, but Kronos also defeated and castrated his father, Uranus.'

Tobias grimaced in pain.

'That's a bit brutal, isn't it?'

'Yes, but as I'm sure you know, men's battles for supremacy usually are brutal. If we examine Cemal's sketches again, we will be able to gain an insight into how he viewed his various family members, as well as himself, of course...' She looked at her assistant. 'Do you remember how you felt when you looked at the painting of Zeus?'

Tobias shrugged.

'Not really. I wasn't really paying much attention to the painting...' His face, sweating slightly, was tense with regret. 'Seriously, boss, how did we overlook such an important detail? How did we not see the similarities between the victim and the picture of Zeus in the painting?'

Yıldız already had the answer.

'Let's not be too harsh on ourselves, Toby. The God in that picture had three crowns on his head and a beard, whereas Cemal had no facial hair. Moreover, that figure in the painting was slightly older than Cemal. And let's not forget it was quite dark in the flat that night. I'm not saying we should make excuses for our mistake but we do have reasons for it.'

'I suppose you're right,' Tobias said. 'But we should go back to the scene of the crime after this protest breaks up. We need to check out that house one more time in the light of what we have learnt so far.'

'We can check it out later but we need to speak to Haluk first and see what he has to say. Then there's this threatening letter Peter mentioned. That is what I'm really curious about.'

They fell silent and stared at a dark, half-naked, dreadlocked man juggling five balls in the air in front of a line of cars. He was lean but extremely supple and was juggling the balls with great dexterity, garnering the attention of the people waiting in their cars at the traffic lights. Seconds before the lights turned amber, he stopped his show, hoping for some money rather than mere applause but nobody coughed up. Yıldız caught him looking at her with his big black eyes and was about to dig into her pockets for some coins but there was something harsh in the juggler's expression that put her off and she changed her mind. When the lights turned green, Tobias put the car into gear and they moved off. They watched the road ahead for some time before he finally broke the silence.

'Are the statues in the Altar of Zeus praising the Gods or damning them?

'As far as I remember, they are praising them. I don't think people created statues in order to damn or reprimand of the Gods. Humans' anger will always be outweighed by their fears and desired outcomes. The statues were made to gain the favour and the protection of the Gods. They were basically a form of worship. Of course, the sculptor himself may have had ideas that were at odds with society's, in which case he would have expressed those ideas secretly, in coded form. Don't get me wrong, I'm not saying there is a secret message hidden within the statues in the Altar of Zeus, but I see no harm in seeking the opinion of an expert. Haluk Ölmez may be able to fill us in on some of the details we're missing.'

Despite their conversation, Yıldız was still disturbed by Tobias' thinking. They had all this evidence pointing to the neo-Nazis as the perpetrators and yet Tobias seemed to be fixated on the family and the idea that a member of the family may be the killer. Perhaps this was why she was so keen to make sure they met Haluk Ölmez — so that the opposite of what Toby thought could be proven. Although she did not want to probe too much, she felt she had to ask.

'So you think the murder has something to do with the Zeus painting? You think Cemal may have been killed because he painted his face onto a figure of a God?'

Tobias did not answer straight away. He stared at the slow-moving traffic for some time first.

'Not exactly, boss… But I must say, I'm a little confused. This is a really wild case. I'm just saying that although we are focused on Otto and his boys, we do not want to overlook any details. He may have replaced Zeus' face with his own as some kind of fantasy thing but why would he paint the family that disowned him and kicked him out?'

It made sense but Yıldız still felt a need to discuss the matter.

'It seems Cemal's wish to show his family in a bad light has not convinced you. Okay, let's say he painted his mother, father and brother onto those figures not as an act of revenge but as an act of love. To immortalize them, as you said. His family may have mistreated him but Cemal may still have loved them dearly. Maybe he was planning on embarrassing them, in the hope that one day they would regret their actions.'

Tobias was not taken by the idea but he wanted to stay in his boss' good books so he nodded politely, his eyes still on the road.

'It's possible, sure. In fact, perhaps by putting his family members in that project, he was looking for a way to reach out to them. Anything is possible.' He turned to look at Yıldız. 'But admit it, boss. This is an unusual case.'

She was about to answer when her telephone rang. It was Franz, her ex-husband.

'Hold on, Toby... Hello, Franz. How are you?'

'Hi Yıldız, I'm fine,' he answered sleepily. 'I'm sorry, I went to bed late and didn't hear the phone ring... How are you? How is Deniz?'

'I'm fine but we have one or two probleMs I was at his school this morning. I spoke to Ms Hermine Kraus...'

'Ms Kraus?'

She was about to add a harder edge to her voice but decided against it.

'His teacher. You remember? We spoke to her last year.'

'Ah yes, I remember,' Franz grinned. 'That fat woman.'

'Yes, her. She says Deniz isn't doing well this year. That he's slacking in class and is having problems concentrating. He says we need to spend more time together with him.'

'I see...' He sounded upset. 'Well, I'm ready to do whatever it takes. I can even come back home if you let me. What do you say? Why don't we move back in together?'

There he was, twisting things again.

'Stop being flippant, Franz. We're talking about Deniz here, not our relationship.'

'The two are not unrelated. Deniz is our son, and it is our separation that is psychologically affecting him...'

'We have been over this. No need to go over it again.' She was tired and irate. 'You know what I mean. Ms Kraus says the three us of should be seen together, that we should do things together. If not, then we can at least go out for a meal together once a week.'

'We can go out more often than that, Yıldız. That would make me so happy.'

There was a hint of pleading in his voice. Yıldız ignored it.

'Once is quite enough. The issue is not what makes you happy but what gets Deniz through this phase without any lasting damage...'

'You're right. I'll do whatever it takes. I can even take him with me on a boat trip. You know how much Deniz loves boat trips on the lakes.'

'How about we manage a simple meal first,' Yıldız said stingingly. 'This weekend suits me. So long as you do not promise us and then cancel on him. That really hurts Deniz.'

'I'm sorry but we had an operation.' He waited for a reply but there was none forthcoming. In a hurt voice, he went on. 'You don't believe there was an operation, do you? But I'm telling the truth, Yıldız. I haven't slept properly for three days. I was in Hamburg at the weekend. We seized a large amount of heroin on a cargo ship on Sunday evening. The head of the network is a Russian living in Berlin…' A sigh could be heard at the other end of the line. 'My son is precious to me, Yıldız. I would never cancel a meeting with him without reason. Unless it's urgent work, I'd never break a promise to him… You know how it is with work. Come on. The same can happen to you too.'

Yıldız believed him but she was not ready to let him off the hook just yet.

'You could have at least called him to make up for letting him down.'

'I didn't have the chance. You know how these things work. It was a joint operation with the British police. Our phones were all switched off…'

No matter what he said or did, though, he could not convince her.

'Fine, that explains last week. What about all the previous times?'

'But…' he began but his voice trailed off.

'Whatever, Franz. So long as we agree about Deniz, there's no problem. Once you are fully awake, check your schedule and then WhatsApp me with a suitable day for dinner. And I'll write to you too. See you for now…'

'See you, Yıldız,' Franz said, in a resigned tone. 'Kiss Deniz for me. Remember, I am ready to do anything for you guys…'

Yıldız pressed a button on her phone to end the call and then muttered, 'Ready to do anything, he says. Why don't you learn to keep the promises you make your son first?'

The whole time Toby had been keeping his eyes on the road ahead in an attempt to avoid hearing the conversation but of course he could not help but hear. Yıldız looked over at him.

'I'm sorry to have to bother you with all that, Toby, but it was important.'

'No worries,' he replied awkwardly. 'It's no bother at all. Don't mind me…' They drove on in silence for a little while until curiosity got the better of Tobias. 'Why did you and Franz break up?' Then, realizing he may have overstepped the mark, he turned to Yıldız and added, 'If you don't mind me asking, that is. I mean, if you don't want to talk about, please don't…'

Yıldız looked at him as though to say she wanted to be understood, rather than have to explain. She did not mind the question. In fact, she found his concern touching.

'It's a long story, Toby. A long and complicated story. But I can tell you one thing for sure and that is there was no cheating involved. In that respect, Franz is very honest. He is one of a rare breed — a faithful man. He loved his mother very much. She died when he was young, before we met, but she raised her son very well. He is extremely kind and courteous to women. In fact, when he does manage to pull himself together, he can be very thoughtful.'

Toby turned and looked at her in surprise, as though to ask, *why split up then*?

'But his mother was so protective of him that he never got a chance to grow up. He has remained a child. That's probably why he gets on so well with Deniz. You should see them when they play. Not once has Franz grown bored of Deniz's requests. Deniz loves it too, of course.... But now... Now that Deniz is growing up, he needs a father, not a frivolous playmate.'

Tobias was listening intently but he did not quite understand.

'So he is the irresponsible type?'

Yıldız smiled uncomfortably.

'It's complicated, isn't it? Yes, it took me a lot of time and effort to work Franz out. Perhaps it was that aspect of his personality that attracted me to him in the first place. But then his true self emerged in all its naked glory. I was married to a man with the emotional age of a seven-year-old, someone who simply did not take life seriously and did not want to take it seriously either. Someone who just wanted to play all the time. Because his mother had made his life easy for him, Franz was someone that did not know what to do when he encountered probleMs He did not want to confront problems and whenever there was one, he fell to pieces. He looks like an adult but he has not grown up. He just wants to live like a teenager all the time with his head in the clouds.'

'Who wouldn't want to live like a teenager all the time?' Tobias laughed.

'Then don't get married, don't have kids, and live your life the way you want,' she said tersely. 'Of course, the fault lies with me, for going ahead and marrying a man like that. Okay, so we got married, but then why did I have to go and have a child? Love is the biggest delusion of them all, Toby. Oh my God, just listen to me. What am I saying? I'm still calling it *love*.' She sounded extremely agitated now. 'And now he says he wants to live together again! He hasn't got a clue, that man.'

'What's he like at work? He was Head of the Narcotics Division, wasn't he?'

'He is actually brilliant at his job. He is a great police officer. Really. It always surprised me how such a frivolous man could be so successful in his professional life. When it comes to work, everything stops. The playful Franz vanishes, and a disciplined pro takes over. Maybe it's because he looks at work as a kind of game too, I still haven't worked that part of him out. Nor do I really intend to work it out…. He's a fine police officer but not a man to live with and share a life with. The sad part is, he still loves me…'

Sensing her sorrow, Tobias wanted to console her but did not how and simply mumbled something along the lines of, 'Maybe you didn't get along because of cultural differences.'

Yıldız smiled disdainfully.

'Oh God, no! There was nothing like that. In a lot of areas, I'm even more German than he is. I think before I act, I plan, I maintain discipline in all aspects of life. No, it wasn't cultural differences. The man simply has the soul of a child…'

Realizing he had no solution to offer, Tobias chose not to speak.

'Anyway, my apologies again for bothering you with my personal problems,' Yıldız said. 'Back to work. You were saying we should not overlook Cemal's family, right?'

'Well, what I was saying was there are certain contradictions in the deceased's behaviour. I wonder if there are any other issues that we do not know about within the family.'

Yıldız was thinking along the same lines.

'Like what? Inheritance squabbles, stuff like that?'

'Possibly,' Tobias replied, turning the Passat into a narrow street. 'I mean, his grandfather fought his own brothers. One of the family, a kid, even ended up getting killed in the fight.

But there is something about this Altar of Zeus that is bugging me. If you were to ask me what it was, though, I really wouldn't know.' He paused and then, as though an idea had occurred to him, went on. 'Buried treasure, perhaps? Or a valuable antique? Who can tell…'

None of these ideas had occurred to Yıldız. Tobias' reasoning was sound. The Ölmez family had worked in Pergamon for a hundred years and in that time, it was perfectly feasible for one of them to have discovered a precious artefact during a dig and have kept it for themselves rather than hand it over to the archaeologists. Perhaps it was the money from the sale of that antique that had allowed them to open their two shops in Berlin. After all, opening two separate shops in Berlin was not easy. Perhaps Cemal was sending a message to his family by painting his relatives' faces on the bodies of the Gods. Perhaps that is why he was murdered… To silence the treacherous son… But this was all still speculation and conjecture, whereas what they did have in terms of tangible suspects were the neo-Nazis, who had plenty of reason and motive to kill Cemal. Of course, other possibilities had to be duly considered but the focus needed to be on the more credible suspects.

'Don't worry, Toby, we shall examine all possibilities. If necessary, we shall knock on every door, look into every room and question everyone. But first, let's see what this Haluk has to say.' She peered out towards the buildings at the end of the street. 'How far away are we from the German Institute of Archaeology? Is it far?'

Her assistant jerked his head forward.

'Not that far. We'll be there shortly.'

Haluk did not look like Cemal or like Kerem. There was a wild look in his green eyes as they stared out from behind his metal-framed glasses, and his aquiline nose, falling sharply over his thin lips, had a beak-like quality. He did have one thing in common with the relatives with whom he was at loggerheads though and that was his height and his impressive build. He greeted Yıldız and Tobias coolly when they walked in.

'We aren't that close,' he said gruffly. 'He called me two years ago and told me he wanted to have an art exhibition about the Altar of Zeus. It was an interesting proposal, to be fair. He said he needed information about the period and so I helped him out…'

While he spoke, Yıldız was staring at the colourful picture on the wall behind his desk. Three years earlier, when she had gone to Turkey with Franz and Deniz, they had seen the ancient ruins of Pergamon but what she saw now on the wall was another panoramic image: one with the Temple of Trajan up on the hill, the Temple of Athena a little lower down and then, behind that, the ancient world's second largest library and the theatre that was possibly the most vertigo-inducing built at the time, with the Temple of Dionysus next to the theatre and the Altar of Zeus down below in all its wonder. People were gathered in groups in front of the Altar, the Gods and the Giants fought their bloody battle in the friezes carved into the Altar, blood from the animals being sacrificed ran down the steps and a grand fire raged at the top the monument. While Haluk spoke, she could not help but imagine what it must have been like to live at that time.

'You still helped him, even though Cemal's family were responsible for your older brother's death?'

Tobias' voice was as cold as Haluk's. The archaeologist leaned forward slightly in his chair with his elbows on the table.

'Yes, it's true, my older brother Ihsan did die because of a stupid fight. I was too young at the time but I know there was no ill intention. He was hit by a car during the brawl.' He stroked his chin with his right hand. 'Had there been intent, the law would have dealt with him accordingly. What happened, happened, and there is nothing that can be done about it. Cemal was extremely courteous the day he came to visit me and I saw no reason not to help him. In fact, the proposed project would have been good marketing for the Pergamon Museum.' He peered at the two officers sitting in front of him. 'Why, was I not supposed to help him?'

He was completely calm, and was simply trying to attest to the ludicrousness of their suspecting him. Tobias ignored the question and asked, 'How did your family react to you helping Cemal? Your father, in particular. What was his name again?'

'Davut,' Haluk sighed. 'Davut Ölmez. I did not tell them. There was no need. Had I told them, they would not have understood anyway.'

'But they did find out, didn't they?' Yıldız asked, probing. 'Were they angry when they found out?'

'Someone saw Cemal and me together. My mother was very upset when she heard and asked me how I could fraternize with my brother's killers. I tried to remind my parents that Ihsan's death had been an accident but my father was having none of it. He was furious, claiming it was not an accident and that 'that animal Hüseyin' had had a knife in his hand and had pushed Ihsan in front of the lorry. He said they were all murderers. I do not know what happened that day but I don't think Cemal is capable of murder. He just isn't that type of guy. However, I was not going to go against my family either. They had lost their favourite son. So I stopped meeting Cemal, so as to not upset them. I haven't seen him for two years.'

This could be an important new lead.

'So your father loved Ihsan the most?' Tobias asked, digging away. Haluk smiled wryly.

'He did.' He paused before continuing. 'But after Ihsan died, his love for him turned into an obsession. There was no way I could compete with a dead person. Not that I bothered…'

Haluk spoke with self-assurance that Yıldız saw no harm in asking.

'Didn't your father want revenge for the son he lost? The son he adored?'

The archaeologist's expression changed instantly. He pulled his hands back from the table and sat up upright in his chair.

'What the hell kind of question is that? Are you accusing my father of murder? You said you wanted information but instead you have come here to insult my family! Maybe you think I'm a killer too. Do you? If you do, then please let me know so I can call my lawyer.'

'There is no need for that, Mister Ölmez,' Yıldız said apologetically. 'We may not have made ourselves clear enough. We are not accusing you of anything. We only want information. That's all.' Haluk sighed and sank back in his chair. 'We need your help.'

It did not seem enough to appease Haluk though.

'Who told you all this?' Seeing no answer forthcoming, he made a guess. 'It was that madman Kerem, wasn't it? Ha! Instead of throwing accusations our way, why didn't he tell you about his own insanity? Because your lovely Kerem used to think he was Kronos.'

Yıldız and Tobias exchanged glances. Perhaps Cemal had given Kronos his father's face because he knew about his illness. Haluk saw how intrigued his guests were by this information and, still irate, went on.

'Yes, that's right, I'm talking about Zeus' father, Kronos. Kerem completely lost his mind. Spent six months in a mental hospital. Back then, our families got on well. My father personally looked after him and used to visit him every week. "Welcome, Oceanus," Kerem used to say when he saw my father walk in. "Welcome, my brother. My Immortal brother. For we are all Immortals, are we not? Are we not from Pergamon? Pergamon is the mountain of the Titans and the Gods," he used to say.'

If what he was saying was true, the case had taken on yet another dimension.

'But he didn't look ill,' Yıldız said. 'When he spoke to us, he sounded completely reasonable.'

'That's because he is on medication. If he stops taking it, he will pick up his staff again and start wandering around saying he is Kronos, father of Zeus. Can you believe it? A man like that has the nerve to talk disparagingly about my family.'

This definitely had to be looked into further but there were other things they needed to learn from the archaeologist.

'This information you have given us about Kerem Ölmez will be very useful,' Yıldız said, trying to win Haluk over. 'Rest assured, we shall look into this. However, we would like to talk a little about Cemal first. How tragic that your cousin has been quite brutally murdered. His heart was removed and offered as a sacrifice to Zeus.'

Yıldız kept her eyes fixed on the archaeologist while she spoke. The reaction she had been expecting was not long in coming.

'What? His heart was offered as a sacrifice to Zeus? What is this nonsense? Is this some kind of joke?' His green eyes had nearly popped out of his head.

Yıldız sat back in her chair.

'Unfortunately, it is not a joke. Your cousin was found in his home with his chest sliced open and his heart removed and placed in his hands. He was found in front of a wall on which a mural of Zeus had been painted. The scene was arranged in such a way as to make it look as though Cemal was offering his own heart to the King of the Gods on Olympus. As a person who is an expert on such matters, were humans sacrificed in Ancient Greece?'

Still reeling from the shock of what he had heard, Haluk scrambled around, trying to compose himself.

'Iphigenia,' he eventually mumbled. 'King Agamemnon wanted to sacrifice his daughter Iphigenia to the Goddess Artemis.'

Yıldız had heard of neither the king nor the daughter but Tobias, unexpectedly, seemed to be familiar with the story.

'Like the king in the film *Troy*? One of the two brothers?' he asked.

'Yes,' Haluk said, giving Tobias a withering look. 'Agamemnon, King of Mycenae, and his brother, the Spartan King, Menelaus. But the film was not always right. If you really want to learn history, you need to read scholarly works. Artists' passions can often end up twisting the truth.'

'Wasn't Helen Menelaus' wife?' Tobias asked, unperturbed by the archaeologist's superciliousness. 'You know, the woman that was abducted and taken to Troy.'

'She was not abducted. She went of her own accord because she was in love with Paris, the Prince of Troy.'

'We were talking about sacrificing humans to the Gods,' Yıldız interjected, thinking the conversation was veering away from the key subject. 'You were telling us about Agamemnon's daughter.'

'Yes, the unfortunate Iphigenia. On a hunting expedition, her father Agamemnon killed a sacred deer belonging to the Goddess Artemis so in order to punish him, Artemis forbade the winds from blowing for the king, which meant Agamemnon's ships could not sail. Agamemnon, however, was preparing for battle and the ships needed to sail so he offered to sacrifice his own daughter to appease the Goddess and have the curse lifted. But he did not want to cut out her heart; he wanted to cut her throat. Artemis, however, felt pity for the girl and sent a deer down from the skies to be sacrificed in her place. Iphigenia survived and went on to live her life as a priestess.' He paused before adding, 'Iphigenia was a virgin.'

'So?' Yıldız asked, unsure to as what was being implied.

'So, when people were sacrificed to the Gods, they were usually virgins, as in this story, or they were boys or young men. Cemal had none of these qualities.'

Yıldız understood but there was another question on her mind.

'You said it was a story. In other words, mythology. But were people actually sacrificed to the Greek Gods in real life?'

'They were indeed. Human skeletons have been unearthed alongside the remains of animals that were sacrificed at excavation sites in Crete. The marks on the bones suggest that the people were ritually killed for sacrifice. Crete is an earthquake zone, you see, and in ancient times, people believed earthquakes were a sign of the Gods' displeasure so they thought by offering valuable sacrifices to the Gods, they could be saved from annihilation. The city's most beautiful virgins and most beautiful young men were killed for the Gods.' His face took on a grave expression. 'Was Cemal really killed as a sacrifice to Zeus?'

'It appears so,' Yıldız said softly. 'Or perhaps that is what the killer or killers want us to believe. We do not know for sure right now. As you said, there are inconsistencies.' She remembered what it was she wanted to ask. 'Were humans sacrificed on the Altar of Zeus?'

Haluk shook his head.

'No, I do not think they were. We have not come across anything during any excavations that would suggest so.'

'Maybe you will one day,' offered Tobias, who had been on the receiving end of the archaeologist's condescension ever since they arrived. 'King Agamemnon himself was willing to cut his own daughter's throat. Isn't that so? Just because there is no evidence now, that does not mean we can say for sure that humans were never sacrificed back then, does it?'

'I suppose not, Mister Becker,' Haluk said, still looking at him with disdain. 'But a thousand years separates the Trojan Wars and the construction of the Altar of Zeus. Animals, the finest wines and precious items were offered to Zeus on the Altar. We have evidence for all of this but nothing has been found to suggest that humans were sacrificed there.'

Tobias did not look convinced, something that had not escaped the archaeologist's notice.

'You don't look convinced. Well, let me put it this way: would you charge someone with murder without evidence or witnesses? Let's say that you did. Would you then dare to imprison that person? Of course not. You would need evidence. The same applies to us. We cannot say this or that happened in the past unless we have solid evidence, and there is no evidence to suggest that humans were sacrificed on the Altar of Zeus. In fact, sacrificing human beings would go against the entire philosophy behind the construction of the Altar in the first place.'

'How?' Yıldız asked, genuinely curious. 'After all, was it not a place in which offerings were made? And as far as I know, Zeus was hardly the most compassionate of deities.'

The archaeologist sighed in exasperation, wondering how he was going to explain all this to these annoying visitors.

'Please Mister Ölmez,' she said with a warm smile. 'What you have to say to us is of great importance. Even a seemingly insignificant detail may lead us to the killer.'

Haluk glanced at his wrist watch.

'I am giving a presentation in fifteen minutes on the floor below so if you allow me to speak without interruption I shall proceed.'

Tobias did not like the archaeologist's smugness and was aching to give him a piece of his mind but Yıldız knew how counterproductive this would be. They needed Haluk to be on their side so they could call upon his expertise if and when needed. Yıldız signalled for Tobias to be quiet and went back to facing Haluk.

'Please, go ahead. We're listening.'

'The history of Pergamon as a city goes back a long way but it truly began to prosper during the era of Alexander the Great, so we're talking about Anatolia around two thousand three hundred years ago. When Alexander died at a young age, his territories were divided up between his various commanders. Lysimachus was one of his most fearless officers and over many years of unrelenting warfare, he had acquired a fortune of 9,000 talents. He chose to keep this fortune in Pergamon because the city was like a fortress. It was built atop a hill that was incredibly hard to scale. He placed a eunuch by the name of Philetaerus, one of his most loyal men, in charge of the fortune. Nine thousand talents was a vast sum in those days, equivalent to around 225 tonnes of silver today. It was a massive horde then and a massive horde now, enough to make even the most honourable man stray. Philetaerus, however, was an honest man, not the type to betray someone's trust. Anatolia at this moment in history, however, was in turmoil, plagued by incessant wars, rebellions and raids, and Alexander's officer Lysimachus was killed during one of those wars. As a result, the governor of Pergamon and the city itself suddenly found themselves in possession of a vast fortune, and it is this amassed wealth that led to Pergamon becoming one of the foremost cities not just of Anatolia but of the entire ancient world.'

'So all those palaces, temples and libraries were built with that money?' Yıldız asked, staring at the painting of the city of Pergamon behind him. Haluk smiled indulgently.

'Not all of them. Some were built during the Hellenistic Period, others were built during the Roman Era.' He turned around and pointed to a building with white marble columns in the most spectacular spot in the city. 'The Temple of Trajan, for instance, was constructed during the Roman Era.' His finger moved to the right, past the Temple of Athena and the library, and moved down, coming to a stop at the Altar of Zeus. 'The Altar, however, is from the Hellenistic Period and was dedicated to the King of the Gods.'

'Did the guy who inherited the fortune have it built?' asked Tobias, now engrossed by the story. Haluk was more magnanimous in the way he looked at Tobias now.

'No, the Altar was built around a hundred years after Philetaerus. As I said, Philetaerus was a eunuch and he left Pergamon to his nephew, Eumenes I, who ruled for twenty-two years. He was succeeded by his cousin, Attalus. It was this Attalus' son, Eumenes II, that had the Altar built. The exact date is unknown but it was definitely built between 197 AD and 159 AD, because that is when Eumenes II ruled. He was an important ruler: shrewd and brave, a man with great vision. But he had another great quality, and that was that he had a great respect for artists and scholars. For example, he was accompanied on his travels by renowned bards and was also close friends with the artist Pythias and the judge Menander. He enriched the Library of Pergamon to such an extent that it rivalled the Library of Alexandria. And of course, he would also go down in history as the king that had the Altar of Zeus created.'

They were meandering off topic again. Yıldız stepped in to steer the course in the right direction.

'You said something about the philosophy of the Altar's construction,' she reminded him. Haluk seemed to appreciate the question. He quickly glanced at his watch before responding.

'Indeed, I was. Eumenes II had the Altar built to commemorate the victory of his father, Attalus I, the previous king of Pergamon, over the Galatians. The Galatians were a wild barbarian tribe that roamed across the land attacking and raiding as they pleased, living off the taxes, or, rather, the tributes, they took by force from those they subjugated. They were an annoyance to the kingdom of Pergamon, just as they were to a number of kingdoms across Anatolia. Attalus I, however, defeated them, dealing them a crushing blow.

'And so Eumenes II had the Altar of Zeus built to immortalize his father's victory. The story being depicted by the large reliefs on the Altar are actually a symbolic representation of Attalus' victory. In the war between the Gods and the Giants, the Gods of Olympus represent civilization, whilst the Giants represent barbarism. In building this stunning monument, the king was making a statement: "The Gods on the Altar are the people and soldiers of Pergamon, while the Giants are the Galatians. We fight against evil and we defend all that is good. We have fought against those without conscience and we have defended compassion. We have fought against ignorance and we have defended culture." Sacrificing humans to the Gods — a bloody, messy and brutal ritual — may have been something the Galatians or primitive tribes did as an act of worship but never civilized Pergamon. That is why humans were not sacrificed on the Altar of Zeus. Pergamon survived and prospered for hundreds of years as a centre of art and culture that rivalled Athens. None dared to defame the city. However, during the early years of Christianity, the Apostle John in the Book of Revelation in The Bible speaks of the throne of Satan being located in Pergamon.' Haluk turned to the painting behind him. 'And the Altar does indeed resemble a vast throne. But a throne for Zeus, not Satan, of course. However, it is understandable that John would identify Zeus with Satan for the purposes of spreading the faith but it is still a total misconception, one based on a specifically Christian worldview. Zeus, in fact, can be seen as a bridge, a transition, between polytheism and monotheism, as the forerunner to the notion of a single God that is found in current monotheistic belief systeMs Powerful, merciless and just, he is a being all unto himself.'

He was stopped by the ringing of a phone. It was Yıldız's. She looked at the screen. It was Markus.

'I'm sorry but I have to answer this.'

'By all means,' Haluk said affably. 'I had better be on my way too. My presentation is about to begin.'

Yıldız hurriedly answered the call.

'Hello? Markus? Yes?'

'Hey,' Markus said nervously. 'There has been another murder. Orhan Ölmez's body has just been discovered.'

For a moment, Yıldız was unable to comprehend what was being said.

'Cemal's grandfather. Remember? He went missing? His body has been found.'

She remembered. The old man with Alzheimer's. A second member of the same family had been killed. A member the first victim loved dearly...

'How? How was he killed?' she asked nervously.

'I don't know the details. The CSI squad are on their way. You better get there as soon as you can.'

'Understood. Where is the body?'

'On Teufelsberg.' There was a strange shiver of fear in his voice. 'That's right. I don't know why but the old man was killed and left on Devil's Mountain…'

6
Those that fail as fathers shall also fail as Gods

The Titans were not wise. The kings that drove them as a herd, my father and grandfather included, were not wise either. We Gods that have succeeded them are not wise either. It is true. Not every God knows all. Few amongst us have attained such wisdom. Wisdom begins with remembering what has passed, for those that do not know the past cannot know the present. This is why the oracles look to the past, rather than to the future, for the past is a mirror full of secrets that hides the future within itself. If you stare into the mirror long enough, you will see the secrets of time, as well as the meaning of life. And of course, when children look into that mirror, they encounter not themselves but their fathers. They may think they see themselves but in fact it is their fathers that look back at them through that sheen. In time, they come to understand this truth. Our fathers live on in our minds as a bitter memory that we think we have forgotten but which we can never erase. They are in our eye and on our brow, in our posture and our gait, in our hearts and our minds. Their strength gives us strength, their compassion softens our hearts, their tyranny makes us cowards or brutes, their courage lifts our spirits, and their cowardice disgraces and demeans us. Good or evil, selfishness or selflessness; in the battle between whatever opposites we have in our souls, it is our father's persona that determines the outcome. Whether one is a Titan, a God or a human is unimportant; if your father is evil, if he is a coward without love and compassion, if he is able to reject his own children without hesitation, then expect no good from those children.

As the King of the Gods, I know this and I say this. I have experienced it, as did my father Kronos. But fear often infects the heart and the mind. It turns us into those we condemn, into those we vanquished in bloody battle, into our forebears, into the predecessors that made our lives hell. Let this be my pledge to the born and unborn children of the world: in this matter, I shall never lie. Let this be a pledge to the blue sky, the green sea and the red earth: none that sit upon the highest throne of Olympus shall ever conceal this truth. Yes, let it be known that I too made the same mistake, that I too, like my father and my grandfather, was rash and cruel at times, so much so that I almost ruined the birth of my precious first son and first daughter.

I am a male. That cannot be denied. I have always adored the female, whether she be Titan, God or human. I have always taken pleasure in gazing at them in their sublime beauty, in stroking their hair, in drowning in the scent of their cheeks, in tasting their lips, in listening to their sweet sighs. And my every act of love was rewarded by the Gods with a child. With a new life and with the continuation of life…

My first love, my first wife, my first infatuation, was Metis, daughter of Oceanus and Tethys. Because her parents adorned the entire earth with veins, over every plain and over every mountain, she, Metis, my heart's companion, was witness to all that transpired. Her speech was profound, her actions wise and her body wondrous. I loved Metis the way a God should love a Goddess, and she was faithful to me as a Goddess should be. She offered me wise counsel when I was in need and showed me the path when I was lost in the dark. If I was able to balance my fury with prudence and my power with justice, it was for to her. She was with me from the start. She was the one that gave me the potion that I fed to my father Kronos in order to free my siblings from his stomach, and she was the one that gave me the gift of my firstborn, my one and only Athena.

I was young and raw and my heart full of fear. I had defeated the Titans but I had numerous enemies. I remembered what the black-eyed boy had said to me: *do not underestimate Man, Zeus. He is the most treacherous of the creatures.* But it was not just man that had his eye on my throne; those from the same bloodline as me also longed for my power. Those I had imprisoned in Tartarus continued to struggle to break free of their walls and try to force open the bronze gates of their dungeon seven levels below the earth and return to the surface to seize my crown. I could hear their sinister growls even on the distant heights of Olympus. And it was then that I erred. Like my father Kronos, I succumbed to fear. I fell foul of the same lie that undid my grandfather Uranus and began to fear that my own issue would destroy me. Uranus said unto me:

'Be vigilant, Zeus. All covet the throne. Be vigilant. You shall have a daughter by Metis, and then a son, and just as you dethroned your father and took his crown, and just as your father Kronos removed me from my throne and took my crown, this child shall do the same to you. Even if you do not love them, you must be with them as a father should be to his children. Leave nothing to chance; all possibilities, good and evil, must be taken into consideration and eliminated. That is why you must swallow your wife, your great love, the one and only Metis, wisest and most perceptive of the Titanesses, and the child she carries. Yes, she adores you and is utterly devoted to you, but when it comes to her child, have no doubt, she will act as your mother did. She will always choose her child over her husband.'

His words twisted my mind and filled my heart with suspicion. And I, raw, inexperienced Zeus, impudent, imprudent Zeus, listened to these words and complied. I deceived my one and only love Metis with sweet words and then I swallowed her. Even the King of the Gods cannot stop Fate. However, after this vile misdeed of mine, I was taken by a terrible pain in my head and before I knew it, a lump appeared in the middle of my brow. The pain was excruciating but I tried to resist, knowing such agony was fit only for a God, and consoling myself also with the fact that there was no death at the end. However, the pain only increased as the swelling grew until it became too much and I summoned the blacksmith.

'Come, Hephaestus! Come! Bring the sharpest and mightiest of your axes and strike me on my brow!'

The blacksmith was stunned and, at a loss as to how to react, said: 'I cannot, Mighty Zeus. For if I strike you now, you will then ask me how I dare do such an insolent thing and then you will expel me from Olympus and send me into the depths.'

I replied: 'I give you my word, you ill-starred cripple, that I shall do no such thing. It is the word of a God. Bring your sharpest axe and strike me on the brow.'

Who can defy Zeus? He came, the great blacksmith, and did as instructed, and when he struck me in the centre of my forehead, the blinding pain stopped. I closed my eyes, breathed a deep sigh of relief and offered my thanks to all that was sacred beyond me. When I finally opened my eyes again, a young girl with blue eyes and a clear face holding a spear stood before me.

I then understood my mistake. I took my child into my arms, embraced her and whispered into her ear:

'Welcome, my daughter. Welcome.'

I named her Athena, and once more, lovingly and with tender compassion, whispered into her ear:

'Welcome, Athena. Welcome, my daughter, to the world of the Gods.'

I breathed in her scent. I shall not deny it; of all my progeny, Athena is the one I loved the most, the one who, with her beauty, her valour and her acumen, filled me with the greatest pride. She is the one I adored most. When in strife, I came to her for counsel, and when faced with the greatest obstacles, I asked her to advise me. But I did not favour her or spoil her. I treated her as I did all the other Gods. Although at times I favoured her, I never upset the scales of justice.

For example, when she battled my exalted brother Poseidon for dominion over the Attican Peninsula, I did not decide alone but assembled all the Gods and then addressed the two rivals, my daughter and my brother, in their presence:

'Seeing as you both covet this city made by men, you must bestow gifts upon those that live there so you may be deserving of the city. Show your abilities to this sacred council so that they may decide who becomes the God of this city.'

Both Poseidon and Athena accepted my terms and presented their skills and talents. First, my all-powerful brother Poseidon stepped forward carrying his formidable trident. He stood boldly before the council and, without even looking us in the eye and with an assured wave of the hand, he conjured up the swiftest, strongest and most beautiful horse, which he presented to us. All of us, myself included, were entranced by this magnificent creature, one that would make its owner rightfully proud and would win any war or race for its possessor. As the horse reared up on its hind legs towards the sun like a commander victorious in battle, I thought that Athena was bested for sure and I was despondent for my daughter. Nevertheless, I waited with baited breath, eager to know how my sky-eyed daughter would show her skill.

Athena did not enter the council with spectacle and awe as her great uncle had done but strode in with utmost serenity. Moreover, she wielded neither shield nor spear. Instead, she carried in her two hands a green sprout. She smiled to the gathered assembly and said:

'I, too, stand in awe of my uncle Poseidon's horse. It is a truly glorious creature. Sturdy and strong, one that would be a mighty asset in battle and which would carry its master to many great victories. King or slave, all would wish to own such a steed. But it is not the destiny of all to ride such beauty. For to mount such a steed, one must be affluent and of noble blood. For such an animal to bring victory, war is needed, and war means suffering, death and destruction. I, too, see the beauty of this horse but humans need something greater, something that will benefit them all, young and old, male and female, rich and poor. Something that will remind them of peace, something that will evoke and commemorate peace. It should provide them with sustenance so they may eat, it should be a tree so they may rest in its cool shade, and it should be enduring so that it may survive through the centuries. And so long as people live, it shall be named the undying tree and sacred drops should fall from its branches.'

Thus she spoke and planted the seedling she carried into the fertile soil of Olympus. A tree suddenly appeared in the palace courtyard, its leaves a thousand shades of green and its branches bearing nourishing fruit. It was an olive tree, and, with the exception of Poseidon, it captivated the hearts and minds of every God present, even that of Ares, the sworn enemy of man. All hands were raised in favour of my daughter. And so she came to be ruler of that fabled city, the people of which erected a vast temple on their highest hill in her honour. As I gazed upon my daughter, I could not hold back my tears, and once more I cursed my grandfather Uranus and his son Kronos for failing to become the fathers they should have been. And so I engraved into the hardest marble with the deepest cuts this absolute truth: those that fail as fathers shall also fail as Gods. And they shall be deserving of every ignominy and every savagery.

Chapter Six

The summer breeze carried with it the scent of fresh herbs from distant places. The tall trees were huddled over under the blue sky, as though whispering a secret amongst themselves in their own tongue. The scent grew heavier and more intense and then changed into something else, into another smell. Was it the smell of flowers wilting in the sun? Or leaves submerged in water? No, it was something much worse. It was the stomach-churning smell of rotting flesh, of the final moments of what was once a living, of an organism whose life has been snatched away from it and is now being sent back into the earth. 'Looks like we're getting closer,' Tobias said, screwing up his face. A few moments later, they heard Kurt's pained cries.

'No! No! No! This is just ghastly! Horrific! Nobody deserves this! No, this should never be done to anybody. They have torn the poor man to pieces. Savages!' Kurt was standing above a ditch in an opening amongst the trees. 'I'm sorry but no human can do this, even if they wanted to. Nobody can be this lacking in conscience.'

'What's happened to Kurt?' Tobias asked in hushed tones, looking at Yıldız. 'I've never seen him looking so distressed before.'

It was also the first time Yıldız was seeing Kurt like this. She quickened her stride until she was standing by the ditch into which the victim had been thrown. The frail body, now pulled from the ditch and laid out on the grass, was naked and covered in mud, with only the face remaining clean. Yıldız narrowed her eyes and tried to get a better look at him. It was then that she noticed the bloody wound where the victim's genitals should have been. She thought about Kerem, the son who thought he was Kronos when alive and whose body was mutilated in death. Didn't Kronos castrate his own father Uranus? Did that mean it was the old man's own son that carried out this horror? If so, then did that also mean he had killed Cemal — his own son? The man was psychologically disturbed so it was possible. But they had only just heard about Kerem's affliction from Haluk and it was possible that the archaeologist had been lying to them. But why would he have lied? For the obvious reason — because of the enmity between the two families. For all they knew, Haluk was the perpetrator. Mulling over these questions, Yıldız took a few steps forward towards the corpse. The smell was almost unbearable but she needed to see the victim's face close up. Kurt had seen them arrive by now.

'Yıldız, over here! Just look at this! This is an outrage! I have never seen anything like this. The poor sod has been savagely maimed! And he was already an old man with one foot in the grave...'

Yıldız was in no mood to listen to Kurt's babbling and she raised her index finger in the air.

'One moment please, Kurt...'

She reached the body, fell to her knees and gazed at the corpse's waxen features. They were contorted in pain. The first thing she realized was how much he looked like his son Kerem. His mud-splattered hair was whiter, naturally, the lines on his forehead a little deeper and his eyes lighter in colour, a light brown bordering on hazel, but the resemblance was still there.

'His genitals were removed before he was killed.' Kurt could not stand the silence any further. 'But that wasn't enough. They body has been drained of all its blood too. Poor chap. See how pale he looks? And look at that look of horror on his face... I'm certain that it was done while he was still alive...'

It was possible. Perhaps the look of shock was because he had seen his own son coming towards him with knife. That is, if he had even recognized his son. After all, the victim had been suffering from Alzheimer's. She looked down at the crotch area again, and at the muddy and bloody wound... What she felt was sorrow, rather than horror. Not so much the disintegrating of a body into the earth but at a man's loss of his primal source of power before his own death. It was ancient punishment, one that had been meted out many times throughout history. Even though she was a woman, she could still empathize. Kurt must have felt it with even more intensity.

'He looks like a statue,' whispered Tobias, who was standing next to her. 'A statue of an old man made of mud.' He looked at Yıldız. 'What was Zeus' grandfather called again? Uranus, wasn't it? That's right. A wounded body that has turned into a statue of Uranus...'

His voice also seemed sad, rather than dismayed. Kurt was not impressed with the comment.

'This is a human being, not a statue,' he said tersely. 'An old man who was horribly mutilated before he died. And not just any old mutilation but the worst imaginable. God knows what that dirty pervert has done with them. And you stand there talking about a Goddamn statue.'

He was so upset by what he had seen that his tone was almost accusatory. But Cemal's death was more disturbing than Kurt's ravings. Yıldız remembered that Kurt's father, Fritz, had been in the hospital as a patient a long time, either with Alzheimer's or Parkinson's, she could not quite remember which at that particular moment, and Kurt must have seen the parallels between a corpse and his father, who had died a slow, drawn-out, agonizing death. She lifted her head to look at Kurt. He looked anxious, hovering on the verge of outright panic. Seeing the Chief of the CSI squad so affected by a scene was not a promising sign. Kurt, still in his coveralls, was still talking.

'We have a very dangerous killer here, Yıldız. The person who committed the previous murder is the same monster that did this. I'm afraid this is not the last we are going to see of this. This madness is going to go on....'

Tobias was upset not at Kurt's engaging in speculation but his dire pessimism.

'It's still too early to say, Kurt. Perhaps we should wait for the autopsy results.'

Kurt turned around and pointed to a spot behind Yıldız.

'Too early, you say? What do you have to say about that then?'

They both turned to look at the spot to which Kurt was pointing. Apart from the dark brown trunk of a large chestnut tree, there was nothing to be seen.

'What? What are you talking about, Kurt?' Yıldız asked. 'What's in that tree trunk?'

'I'm talking about the eagle in front of the tree, not the tree itself. Can't you see it? Look, just over there, just under the spot where the trunk splits in two.'

Looking more carefully, Yıldız saw it. It was difficult to see at first because it was similar in colour to the tree trunk behind it but there it was: a metal staff planted into the ground. They walked towards it to get a better look. On one end of the staff was a wooden carving of an eagle, its head, from the perspective of the onlooker, facing right and staring out with its left eye. Yıldız was reminded of the painting in Cemal's house and the eagle on the end of Zeus' staff in the painting staring at them with its keen, piercing eyes. She was not surprised by the news, and as soon as she heard that Cemal's grandfather had been killed, she knew the two murders were linked.

'See?' Kurt said, his voice snapping her out of her thoughts. 'Now do you see how serious this is? How big this is going to get?' He walked over to Yıldız, his eyes wide with dread. 'We need to take measures. Sound the alarm, make sure our lads are on alert.'

It was troubling for Yıldız to see Kurt so flustered. She looked at him reassuringly and tried to calm him down.

'Don't worry, Kurti, we'll do whatever needs to be done. They won't win. We'll stop them. But we need to get down to business. Every clue you find is going to be vital for us.'

Kurt was not convinced. Indeed, he was disappointed at how dismissive Yıldız seemed to be of his fears. Muttering to himself, he turned around and headed back to the corpse rotting on the grass.

Yıldız had already forgotten about him. She had far more important things to consider. Had she miscalculated? Had she got it wrong? Members of the same family had been killed in quick succession. Was this really the continuation of a decades-old family feud? Was it possible that this had nothing to do with the Nazis? Was a cousin taking revenge for little Ihsan, who had died in that brawl all those years ago? None of these questions were to be taken lightly. The symbols found at the scene of both murders were related not to Nazism but to mythology, and to Zeus in particular, and there was one person with a motive and expert knowledge in this and that was Haluk. Yıldız was lost in a maze of thoughts when Tobias spoke up.

'This eagle is different to the one we found in Cemal's house. That eagle was looking straight at us, whereas this one's head is turned to the right.'

And then, like a bolt of lightning, it hit Yıldız. She hurriedly got out her phone and began tapping on the screen. She looked at the results of her search and, with great excitement, held the screen up for Tobias.

'Look. This is the Nazi eagle.'

Tobias examined the picture. It was a picture, not a carving, of an eagle, and it bore a strange resemblance to the eagle found on the coat of arms of the German Police Force. There was, however, one crucial difference and that was that the eagle in the picture on the phone clasped a swastika in its claws.

'You're right, boss. That is the party's eagle. But if you get rid of the swastika, it's the same as the one on our badge. The eagle that is the emblem of the German State is the also the same.'

'No, Toby, they are not,' Yıldız said firmly, shaking her head. 'There is a crucial difference. The eagle on our badge and on the national coat of arms looks to the left.' She pointed to the carving on the end of the staff. 'Whereas this one, as you can see, looks to the right. To the right from where we are standing, of course…' She tapped on her telephone's screen a few more time with her slender fingers. 'And look, this is the eagle on Cemal's painting of Zeus.' The picture was too small, however, for details to be picked out so she enlarged the picture so the eagle's picture filled the screen. 'See? This is Zeus' eagle.' She then pointed to the staff a few feet away. 'While that one over there is the Nazi eagle.'

Tobias stood there, not knowing what to say, not that Yıldız was really expecting an answer. She put her phone back in her pocket and strode towards the staff. When she was close enough, she got down on her knees and began looking for any possible clues. Her face was so close to it that her hair, billowing in the wind, was touching the eagle's wings.

'Hey! Hey! Not so close!' Kurt warned her. 'You'll compromise the evidence.' Clearly still troubled by their conversation of a few moments earlier, his voice had come out more strained than necessary. Yıldız, on the other hand, was not pleased at being scolded like a child.

'Kurt, it's okay. We're just looking. Don't worry, we won't corrupt any of your evidence.'

It was the first time the Chief Inspector, whom he had known for years, had spoken to him so brusquely.

'No, what I meant was... I didn't mean it like that...' He stammered for a while but then he realized he was in the right. 'You are walking around a crime scene right now, Yıldız. You may even have compromised prints already, so I am simply asking you, politely, to please leave this area so we can get on with our job. Once we are done, you are free to return.' He sounded more assertive now. 'And anyway, the two people that found the victim are waiting for you.'

Knowing there was little point in causing any more unnecessary tension, Yıldız got up.

'Fine, Kurt, we're leaving. Where are they?'

'Over there, by our van,' he said, gesturing to a spot down below. 'A couple of youngsters. A boy and a girl. Girlfriend and boyfriend probably.'

Yıldız looked at Tobias to get him moving but he took his time, taking photographs with his mobile phone of the staff and then the corpse. Once he was done, and ignoring Kurt, who was also standing by the corpse and glaring at him, he slowly trudged off with Yıldız. They walked down the staircase wordlessly, each step taking them further away from the stench of the decaying body. When they were halfway down the steps, for some reason,

Tobias began whistling a tune, one Yıldız had heard before but one to which she could not put a name.

'What's that song?'

'Black Sabbath,' Tobias answered, reaching into his pocket and pulling out a packet of cigarettes. 'We heard it the other night when Alex's group was playing it in that spooky theatre. What was it called again? Tartarus, something like that.'

'*Big black shape with eyes of* fire,' Yıldız said, humming the tune. '*Telling people their desire / Satan's sitting there, he's smiling…*'

'Wow,' Tobias said admiringly. 'Those are the exact words. Satan's sitting there, he's smiling…'

'No, this cannot be a coincidence,' Yıldız said, more to herself. Her assistant stared at her and then took a cigarette out of his packet.

'What can't be a coincidence, boss?' he asked.

'This spot,' Yıldız said, looking around. 'Here we are on Teufelsberg, the Devil's Mountain, and you're whistling a song with the lyrics "Satan's sitting there, he's smiling".' She stopped, turned to Tobias and gave a playful grin. 'Don't tell me you're involved somehow in these murders?'

Tobias burst into laughter.

'Yes, that's right, I'm the real killer. The wild metalhead in me told me to kill these poor people and I have been embellishing the murders with mythological motives to add a bit of spice to the whole thing. The stuff I learn on this job has been a great help to me too.' His mirth died down. 'It's no coincidence, boss. I was whistling that tune on purpose. Because we are here on Teufelsberg.' He stopped, his countenance taking on a graver turn, and he looked out at the rugged woody landscape. 'And the killer leaving his victim here is not a coincidence either, I can bet you. He is obviously trying to send a message. Remember what Haluk said about the Altar of Zeus? How it is described in the Bible as "the throne of Satan"?'

He was making an important connection.

'And the Altar really does resemble a throne,' Yildiz said. 'A huge marble throne. Do you think that in leaving his victim here, the killer is hinting at or making a reference to the Altar of Zeus?'

'I wouldn't know, boss,' Tobias said, his mood now sombre and with none of the humour of a few seconds ago. 'What I do know is that this place has nothing to do with the Nazis. That is, of course, if we do not count that staff over there with the carving of the eagle on it.'

Yildiz looked at her assistant in amazement.

'You've got to be kidding, Toby? This hill is all about the Nazis. This is their hill.'

Tobias' face fell. Before he could answer, Yıldız went on.

'Berlin is located on flat ground. In fact, it used to be one giant marsh. This is a manmade hill, Toby.'

'I know. The rubble from the houses destroyed during the war was all brought here,' Tobias said, sensing he had overlooked an important piece of information and trying to rectify the situation. 'All the city's debris and the leftover from the ruins was piled up here. This hill was formed, in a way, by the bombardment of the city.'

'Yes, and who was responsible for that bombardment?' Yıldız said, busily tying up her hair, which was blowing in the wind.

'The Nazis, of course...' Tobias looked around, trying to join the dots. 'The eagle on the end of the staff, the corpse being dumped here, a threatening letter... You think the Nazis were behind this murder too, boss? But how could they have done it? We have rounded them up.'

'Didn't you sleep well last night, Toby?' Yıldız asked sarcastically. Tobias was growing increasingly uncomfortable.

'Why do you say that, boss? What has that got to do with any of this?'

'It has everything to do with it. If you had slept well, then you would have noticed that the victim we saw just now was actually killed a few days ago. The corpse has started to rot. What I'm saying is, Cemal was not the first victim. It was the old man.'

Tobias smiled in embarrassment.

'Maybe. But it's not sleeplessness that made me overlook it. This case has so many ins and outs, I just don't know where to start.'

She looked at him questioningly. What had happened to him? There was something odd about his demeanour today.

'We need to focus our attention on the Nazis. Yes, if you ask me, they are the ones behind this. Mark my words, that moron Otto's fingerprints will be on that threatening letter. I'm afraid Kurt was right. These murders are not going to stop.'

Tobias did not respond. Instead, he lit up and let out an angry plume of smoke. The mini ash-coloured clouds stung Yıldız's eyes but she didn't complain as she was thinking about what she had just said. Although she looked convinced, she knew there was something missing in her hypothesis. They had evidence but they were still unable to definitively prove that the Nazis were behind the murders. Yes, the Nazis were still their prime suspects and yes, they had committed numerous grisly crimes before and would no doubt go on to commit more in the future but the sophistication of these murders did not gel with the bungling incompetence of the neo-Nazis they had arrested. Moreover, Kerem used to think he was Kronos and now his father Orhan had been found castrated and dead and these were two events that could not be easily dismissed. If these murders were the work of the Nazis, they had to have a sound grasp of mythology and they also had to know the Ölmez family quite intimately but the question that was bothering her was why they felt a need for all this elaborate organization. If they wanted to get rid of the Ölmez family, all they had to do was storm their house and kill them or set fire to it, the way Nazis had done in the past to their other victiMs Perhaps the family had another secret. Why would the racists choose this family and not another? She thought about the war booty of 9000 talents that Haluk had mentioned. Was that at the root of this chain of events? She realized she was veering into the absurd, thinking like a wildly deranged treasure hunter. It would be a miracle for even one penny of a two-thousand-year-old treasure to have survived to this day. The Nazis would also know this. But there had to be another connection. If she could just uncover it, the mystery of the murders would be solved.

She needed time to think about it all, to go over it all properly, to consider all the possibilities, put them on the table, compare them and weigh them up. But when was she going to be able to do it? Events in the field were overtaking them, forcing them to rush from suspect to suspect. No, she needed to set aside some time so she could think things through calmly. The most complex cases were solved not when they were chasing the perpetrators but when all the details had been properly analysed and evaluated. Watching Tobias smoke next to her, she told herself to stay calm. She reminded herself that if she wanted to see the whole picture, she had to think things through and not let the incidents affect her emotionally or mentally.

The couple were sitting on a bench next to the CSI squad's van, under a weeping willow tree whose long branches were almost brushing their shoulders. From afar, they painted a pleasant picture but on closer inspection, one could see that they were bored out of their minds. A white English Setter with yellow spots stretched out on the grass by their feet, Conzentedly wagging its tail, until it saw the two unfamiliar people approaching, when it jumped up and began barking. The young man of the couple looked down at the dog.

'No, Diana! No! Sit! Sit! Now!'

The dog ignored the young man and began barking even more loudly, and towards Tobias in particular. Fed up and now pointing a finger at him to show him who was boss, his owner repeated the commands in a more assertive voice. 'Sit! Sit, Diana! Now!'

Seeing her master on his feet, the dog opened its big brown eyes as wide as they would go.

'Who am I talking to, Diana? Sit down! Sit down and be quiet!'

Diana reluctantly sat down on her haunches but she carried on glaring with bloody eyes at the large man walking towards her. She barked a few more times from where she was sitting but her owner's reprimands had taken the wind out of her sails and her growls were now closer to a whimper.

'She doesn't like you,' Yıldız said, ribbing her assistant. 'Let's hope she doesn't attack you later on.'

Tobias did not find it as amusing as Yıldız.

'I know. Dogs don't like me.'

'Don't worry, he won't hurt you,' said the young man, who had overheard their conversation. 'She's just bored and barked to tell me she wants us to go. That's all.'

Tobias was not convinced.

'What if she attacks me because she's bored?'

'Come on, Toby,' Yıldız said. 'Are you seriously afraid of this adorable little thing?' She quickened her stride until she reached the dog. 'Hello, Diana. How are you, my little beauty?'

Diana peered at Yıldız first and then began wagging her tail, warily at first but then more amiably. Yıldız crouched down beside her and stroked her head.

'You're a beautiful little thing, aren't you?' She looked up to her owner. 'She's very young, isn't she?'

'She's two,' grumbled the young man, still unhappy despite the interest in his dog. 'But she's frustrated. We have been waiting for the police for hours.'

Yıldız left Diana, stood up and looked at the two lovers. They looked like sweet kids. The boy had light brown hair that fell over his forehead and blue eyes that sparkled with vitality, despite the rather depressing situation he currently found himself. The girl had a petite nose, freckles, a broad mouth and bored-looking deep green eyes.

'Hi. Sorry we're late. We're the police you have been waiting for.'

Their faces lit up.

'Finally,' the girl said, sitting up straight on the bench. 'You took forever. We've been here for hours.'

'We left as soon as we got the news but this place is quite far away from our station and we have only just arrived. Anyway, we are here now so let's get this over with. Don't worry, it shouldn't take long. You just need to answer a few questions and then you can be on your way... By the way, I'm Chief Inspector Yıldız Karasu from the Berlin Police Homicide Desk and my colleague here...' She turned and saw Tobias still timidly standing a few feet away. She could not help but chuckle. 'Oh, come on, Tobias. This little thing is not going to hurt you.'

Tobias was still not sure but he also knew he could not stand far away from them for much longer and so took a few faltering steps forward.

'And this is my colleague, Inspector Tobias Becker,' Yıldız went on with a smile. She took a pen and a small notebook out of her pocket. 'If you could tell me your names, please.'

'My name is Martin. Martin Hitzfeld. My girlfriend's name is Hanna…' He seemed to have forgotten the rest and his girlfriend came to his rescue.

'Wuttke,' she said, putting her hand on his shoulder. 'Hanna Wuttke.'

'Thank you. I guess you came here to walk your dog.'

'Yes, Diana loves it here.' His face lit up and he looked down and smiled at his dog, who, ears outstretched, was impatiently waiting for them to go. 'The poor thing is cramped in the city centre. There is a park near our house but it's not big enough for her so we come here at least twice a week, sometimes more. Diana gets to run around as much as she wants and play with the other dogs and we get some fresh air.'

'When was the last time you were here?' The question was asked by Tobias, who was now standing a bit closer to them but who also made sure Martin was standing between himself and Diana. 'Before today, that is.'

The young man tried to remember and looked at his girlfriend. 'Three days ago, I guess….'

'No, it was four days ago,' Hanna said. 'Remember? You had an exam in the afternoon so we skipped a day.'

'Yes, that's right. We were here four days ago.'

'Did you see anybody or anything suspicious or unusual while you were here?' Tobias asked, still looking at Diana stretched out on the grass.

'What do you mean by suspicious?' Hanna asked.

The two police looked around and then turned back to face the girl.

'For example, people you would not normally see around here. Skinheads, for instance, or neo-Nazi types. Or people that stood out. People wearing odd clothing or acting or walking in a strange manner.'

'No,' Hanna said, pouting. 'We haven't come across anyone like that. Have we, Martin?'

'She's right,' Martin agreed. 'We haven't seen anyone like that. We actually like people-watching. Don't get me wrong, we don't go around harassing people. But we like looking at people and then trying to work them out, making guesses about them. We like to talk about people.' With a hint of pride, he added, 'We're both studying psychology. It may sound ridiculous to you but we like to observe people and then try and work out their personality. So if someone was acting in an unusual manner, we would have noticed. But this is a very calm, tranquil place. God knows why they call it the Devil's Mountain.'

'Because it is the work of the Devil,' Yıldız said, her voice reflecting the pain of the topic. 'Because it is the graveyard of the bitter memories of the war. It is not just a pile of debris here. That debris is the leftovers of the houses, schools, factories, theatres, cinemas and cafes in which the people of Berlin used to live, work and play. All the things that make a city are here. The remains of a bombed and destroyed Berlin lie beneath these beautiful trees and this green grass, kids.'

Hanna looked around as though seeing the place for the first time and, without realizing, clung on to her boyfriend's arm. Martin, however, did not seem so moved.

'Well, whatever,' he said. 'That all happened years ago. People come here to unwind now. You've seen them. They come here to have picnics and walk their dogs. Lovers come here looking for a nice corner to cuddle up and kiss. Trees everywhere, clean air, birds singing… You can see how calm it is.' He paused and then, probably remembering the corpse they had just seen lying on the grass up ahead, added, 'Well, most of the time.'

'You were the ones that found the corpse, weren't you?' Yıldız asked. Hanna looked at her boyfriend.

'Martin found it. With Diana's help, I should add. I couldn't look at it. Didn't even go near it. The dead really scare me. When my grandmother died, I could not look at her, even though my mother kept trying to make me look. And I adored my grandmother.'

'Can you tell us how you found the body?' Yıldız asked the young man. Martin did not seem pleased at his girlfriend being interrupted but Hanna did not seem to mind.

'Actually, Diana found it.' His gaze slid down to the dog resting by his feet. It was hard to tell if it was pride he felt or anger at the dog having gotten them into so much trouble. 'Diana goes crazy when we come here. She loves this place. It's really hard to keep hold of her. She runs and jumps about all over the place.' Hearing its name again, the dog lifted its head, wondering whether they were finally going. Her owner leaned over and patted her lovingly on the head. 'Diana is very smart. She never gets lost. She will run up the hill and run around the trees and jump over the ditches but in the end, she will always come back to us. She does not wander too far or stay away for too long. However, this time she did not come back and of course we started to worry. I looked up and saw her amongst the trees. We heard her barking but didn't think much of it as we thought she was just playing around with the other dogs. She came back to us but she would not settle down. She was clearly agitated, barking like mad trying to tell us something. Again, we didn't make much of it but she is a hunter by instinct and she grabbed my trouser leg and started pulling. It was clear she wanted to show us something and we were curious as to what it was so we got up and started following her. We climbed the hill but she ran on ahead impatiently and then came running back, pleading for us to hurry up. When we reached the trees, we noticed a foul smell. We thought it was a dead animal, a crow perhaps, or a hedgehog or rabbit. Whatever it was, it was not going to be pleasant and Hanna suggested we turn around and go back. So I called Diana so we could go back but she wouldn't comply. I called her again in my sternest voice but still she wouldn't listen. She was going mad. It was the first time I had seen her so restless. She ignored my calls and went back to the copse. I was getting angry now so I told Hanna to wait for me and went in after Diana. The deeper I went in, the worse the smell got. I eventually saw Diana standing by a ditch in a little clearing in the woods. When I got close to her, the smell had become unbearable. Then I froze. I thought I had seen a face in the ditch but I wasn't sure so I took a few steps closer to get a better look. Sure enough, it was a human face. An old man's face. His body was covered in leaves. The leaves were old, as they had already started fading and his face was showing because the wind had blown the leaves off his head and face. When I reached the lip of the ditch, I got a better look. The fellow had been buried right up to the neck, with only his head poking out. I made sure I didn't touch anything, got Diana and went back to Hanna. Then we called you. That's it.'

Yıldız turned to Hanna to see if she had anything to add.

'It's just as Martin described,' she said, her eyes filling up.

'What about the staff by the ditch?' Yıldız asked. The young man looked at her blankly.

'What staff? I didn't see anything like that,' he replied, feeling a little guilty at not knowing. 'Of course, I was in shock. If there was a staff there, I didn't see it. There may have been other details but I was in no state to notice. This is the first time I am experiencing something like this, you know'

Yıldız nodded understandingly.

'I have to ask. Did you notice a staff with a carving of an eagle on its handle?'

'No, I didn't see anything like that,' he said again after having thought about it for a moment. Yıldız made some notes in her notebook.

'Is it a murder?' Hanna asked, her voice trembling. 'Was that man killed?'

'What do you think, Martin? Do you think he was killed?' Yıldız asked.

'Probably,' he answered, his face falling. 'What else can it be? But then again, I only saw the face. It looked like it was in some pain. Whether he died of natural causes or was killed, I don't know but someone clearly buried him here.' Then, after an uncertain pause, he went on. 'I mean, he could hardly have buried himself, could he? Somebody must have dug the hole and put him in it. Even if he did die of natural causes why would they bury him here?'

Yıldız liked the way he was reasoning.

'Has anything happened today, that is, in the previous few hours, that attracted your attention? As my colleague said, have you come across any people you are not accustomed to seeing around here?'

'I told you we didn't!' Martin said, starting to show signs of frustration.

'That was when you were talking about when you were last here, four days ago but I am asking about today. Before you found the body, did you see…'

The two lovers shook their heads.

'No, everything looked normal. We did not see any skinheads or neo-Nazis.'

Martin sounded tense and it must have affected Hanna too, as she then nervously asked, 'Why? Was he killed by neo-Nazis?'

'We do not know, Hanna,' Yıldız sighed. 'That is what we are trying to find out. That is why we are combing through all the details.' She looked down at the dog. 'If only Diana could talk,

I'm sure she would have a lot of useful information for us.' She lifted her head again. 'Well, that's all our questions. Unless you have anything to add…'

'If we did, we would tell you…' Martin said, relieved. He looked at his girlfriend. 'Isn't that so, sweetheart?'

Hanna nodded her head.

'Very well. In that case, you are free to leave.'

'Hold on a minute, boss,' Tobias said. 'There is something else. The minivan.' He turned and looked at the two lovers. 'Did you see a black minivan around here? A cobalt black minivan… Today or when you were last here…'

'No,' Martin said firmly. 'We haven't seen anything like that. At least, not one that caught our attention.'

'When you say cobalt black, do you mean a minivan like this one?' said Hanna, her green eyes looking out at the road. At the same time, Diana sat up and began barking. All four turned to look in the direction of the dog's barking and sure enough, a black minivan was approaching them. Tobias and Yıldız exchanged bewildered glances and got ready while the two eyewitnesses stood fearfully rooted to the spot. 'You'd better get out of here, kids,' Yıldız said gravely, her eyes fixed on the approaching vehicle. 'Now. Get away from here.'

'Don't worry, we're off,' Martin said in a panic. 'Come on, Diana. Let's go, girl.'

Diana, however, did not want to go and was still barking at the vehicle. Martin quickly attached her leash and dragged her off, while Yıldız and Tobias stood where they were, waiting for the van, their hands ready on their weapons. They could not make out the person sitting in the driver's seat because the sun was behind them and was reflecting off the front of windscreen. As it got closer, the van slowed down before slowly coming to a halt in front of them. Two men rushed out of the vehicle, both in some distress. Yıldız recognized one of them. It was none other than Kerem Ölmez, the son of the man whose corpse was decaying up ahead in the woods.

'Why is he naked like this?'

Hüseyin was standing behind the yellow police tape that had been placed around the scene. He could not see all of the corpse but he could see that it was not wearing any clothes and he was furious. 'This is a disrespect to the deceased. You should at least cover the body!' He took off his coat and tried to cross the yellow CSI band but Kurt blocked his way.

'Wait! Stop! Don't come any closer. You'll corrupt the evidence.'

Hüseyin froze, but he could not contain his anger for long.

'What's that stench? This is an outrage! My grandfather despised bad smells! He made sure he always smelled nice. Even his cologne was carefully chosen. He had his cologne made and sent over all the way from Bergama.'

Kerem, looking on with tears in his eyes, nodded in affirmation.

'It was made with oils from tobacco that grew on the plains of Araplı Ovası. It was the only cologne he used. Ah, Dad! Which evil filth did this to you?'

Yıldız knew the scent. That tobacco plant had a particularly strong odour. Tobias just stood there listening, understanding nothing. Hüseyin's cries of grief did not last too long and he turned to the police officer in the coveralls standing by the body.

'How much longer will my grandfather be here like this?'

'Until our work is done,' Kurt replied coolly. 'We'll soon have him covered up. I'm afraid you are going to have to wait a little.'

Hüseyin was in no mood to wait but Kerem grabbed his son's arm, while Yıldız, realizing it would be better to let Kerem calm

Hüseyin down, held on to Tobias, who was also ready to spring into action.

'Take it easy, son,' Kerem said in a grief-stricken but calm voice. 'Let the police do their job. Let's go and have a cigarette.'

Hüseyin angrily pulled his arm away.

'Seriously, Dad? Grandad is lying there naked in front of everyone like this and you want to go off and have a smoke?'

Hüseyin was well past middle-age but apart from his pot belly, which caused to him to wheeze while climbing the steps, he still seemed to be in relatively good shape. He was shorter than his father but stocky like him. Like Kerem, he had hardly said a word since they arrived, except to inform them that they had bought the black van for Bergama Baklava, their business. Indeed, the company's name and logo were painted on the side of the van, and nobody in their right mind would think off driving off to commit a murder in such a conspicuous vehicle. Nevertheless, Yıldız told herself it would still be worth questioning Peyman again, before she turned to more urgent matters. The two Ölmez men that had just arrived had wanted to see the body and when they did, they were in a state of shock.

Hüseyin approached the yellow CSI tape again and glared at Kurt, his right hand on his hip in a rather challenging stance.

'How much longer is this going to take?'

Kurt did not bother responding but turned to Yıldız instead.

'Ms Karasu, could you please do something about all this? These gentlemen are making it extremely difficult for us to carry out our duties. Could you take them away from here?'

'We're not going anywhere,' the incensed grandson growled. 'You couldn't protect my grandfather and now you won't let us see his body?'

Had Tobias, Yıldız and two uniformed officers not reacted so swiftly, Hüseyin may well have jumped Kurt and started a fight but Tobias sensed the potential for trouble and gestured with his head to the two men on duty, one of whom quickly moved in to stand in front of Hüseyin.

'Please, Mister Ölmez,' Tobias said calmly but firmly. 'You're only making things worse. If you would just let our colleagues do their jobs, we will be able to cover your grandfather's body all the more speedily.'

The policeman standing in front of Hüseyin was staring at him with open hostility.

'Instead of handing out advice to me, why don't you go and find the men that killed my grandfather? But you won't, will you? Because you're collaborating with the Nazis.'

Tobias was too stunned to respond. Yıldız stepped forward and stood in front of Hüseyin.

'Which Nazis? Where? What are you talking about, Hüseyin Bey?'

She used the Turkish *Bey* for Mister, but Hüseyin was having none of it.

'As if it's going to make any difference if I tell you. It's not like you're going to go out and catch them if I tell you.'

'We will though. That's our job. Instead of standing here getting in the way, why don't you tell us what you know and help us find the perpetrators?'

'I'm not getting in anyone's way,' Hüseyin said stubbornly in reaction to her firm and authoritarian manner. 'I'm just asking you to show a bit more respect to my grandfather, whom you were unable to protect.'

Yıldız saw that his anger seemed to be subsiding a little. Wanting him to feel valued and important to the inquiries, she asked, 'Was your grandfather facing threats of any kind? Are neo-Nazis really involved in these murders?'

Hüseyin stared at Yıldız, trying to work her out. Was she being serious or was she just pretending?

'Yes, they are,' he finally said, although still with some doubt in his voice. 'Blind Rudolf is behind all these murders. The man has had it in for me for twenty-three years.'

'Twenty-three years? Why, what happened twenty-three years ago?'

'What else? We gave the neo-Nazis a proper pasting. Kicked them out of Kreutzberg. I was a member of the 36 Boys. That is why I went to prison.'

Yıldız seemed to remember something about a gang fight that had taken place years earlier but she did not know the details. Whatever it was, what Hüseyin had to tell them was interesting. Perhaps the eldest son of the Ölmez family was going to reveal the link between the murders and the neo-Nazis that she had been unable to uncover. She was eager to find out what it was, this unexpected information that may well prove to be the treasure they were hunting.

'Hold on a minute, Mister Ölmez. Hold on. What you have to tell us is extremely valuable so please come this way so we can talk more comfortably… There, that spot under that tree should suit our purposes just fine. You can tell us everything you know there. I don't want you to skip any details. Tell us everything, and while we are talking, the CSI crew can finish the work…'

Hüseyin, however, did not budge and was still staring at his grandfather's body lain out on the grass in the distance. Yıldız went on in a more conciliatory tone.

'I am afraid we cannot let you into that area, and there is no point in us standing around here waiting. But if you talk to us about this Rudolf, whom you say is responsible for your grandfather's death, we can begin investigating immediately.'

Hüseyin still did not respond. His father Kerem, who knew his son inside out, spoke up.

'Ms Karasu is right, son. We need to tell them about that business with Rudolf. '

'Fine. If you say so, Dad,' Hüseyin finally said, although he still felt the need to have a dig at the police. 'Even though I've told them so many times and they still didn't do anything about it… But I'll tell them one more time, Dad, just for you…'

The four of them walked over to a huge oak tree up ahead, the two members of the Ölmez family walking in front and the two officers following a few steps behind. While walking, Yıldız tried to picture Pehlivan, the man whose photo Kerem had shown her in the Bergama Baklava shop, one of the labourers that had worked alongside Carl Humann when he first began digging in Pergamon. Even from the photograph, it was clear he had been an imposing figure, just like Kerem and his son. Orhan, lying inert a few metres away from them, and Cemal were no lightweights either. They must have inherited the same genes, she thought. Meanwhile, Kerem had slowed down and was waiting for the police to catch up while Hüseyin carried on walking ahead.

'I apologize on behalf of my son, Ms Karasu. Seeing his grandfather like that has really hurt him.'

Yıldız had seen worse.

'Not to worry. I understand. But what I would like to know is why you did not mention this Rudolf character to us before? If he is somehow connected to your father's death, then he may also be responsible for the murder of your son.'

Kerem pulled his shoulders back and took a deep breath.

'It never occurred to me. Actually, I should have told you because when Hüseyin fought those Nazis, Cemal was there, in the fight with Blind Rudolf. In fact, Cemal was injured in that fight.'

While Kerem spoke, Yıldız watched him out of the corner of her eye. He had not mentioned Nazis before and now here he was accusing them.

'It wasn't a serious injury.' It was Hüseyin who spoke, so he had clearly been lending an ear to what was being said while walking up ahead. He stopped and waited for the others to catch up.

'Rudolf and the rat with him came off much worse. Cemal grabbed a chair and lay into them with it.' They were walking again, while the angry grandson told Yıldız about the events of the day. 'I'm telling you, he's definitely involved in Cemal's death because Cemal bought that chair crashing straight down onto Rudolf's head that day. He has a tough nut, that one, but the chair came down at such an angle that it split his head open. They had to give that bald bastard eight stitches.'

Tobias was about to warn Hüseyin about his language but Yıldız motioned for him to let it go. She turned to Hüseyin.

'And this happened twenty-three years ago, you say?'

'No, not this. This happened ten years ago. But ten years or twenty-three, that chimp will never forget it, nor will he forgive us. For twenty-three years, he has been brooding over it. He hasn't forgotten me and he won't rest until he has his revenge.'

'Who is this Blind Rudolf?' Tobias, quiet until now, asked. 'How can a blind man fight you?'

The same pride glinted in Hüseyin's angry eyes.

'Rudolf fights really well. They say he and his men were trained by Putin.'

'Putin?' Tobias asked in amazement. 'Russian President Putin?'

'Yes, Vladimir Putin,' Hüseyin beamed. 'He used to work for the KGB, and the KGB back then used to train the Nazis.' Seeing police staring at him in disbelief, he persisted. 'I swear, it's the truth. The KGB trained the Nazis in East Germany to stir things up on this side, in the West, that is. Putin was personally involved. I am not making this up. You can go on Google and look it up yourselves. There is even a book about it. Putin was also a member of the Stasi. I read about it in *Bild*. They had a photo of his Stasi ID card. So anyway, he trained Rudolf and his buddies over there. Trained them up as street fighters. Capable of taking out three men on their own.'

'Even while blind?' Tobias asked, still unconvinced.

'He is only blind in his left eye. His right eye works fine. Sees better than any of us. "Blind" is his nickname. His real name is Rudolf Winkelmann. He used to be able to see out of both eyes but then he came up against us and he got his comeuppance.' He noticed that the two police officers were still staring at him in astonishment and he calmly explained.

'Yes, that's right, I blinded him in his left eye.'

An awkward silence descended over them. Who was this guy standing in front of them — a psychopath, or an innocent guy who didn't know how to handle himself? Neither Yıldız nor Tobias knew what to say. For some time, the only sounds that could be heard were the squelch of their footsteps on the grass and the sweet song of a nightingale courting a female in the branches of an oak tree.

'What was it about?' Tobias eventually asked, breaking the silence. 'Why did you take out Rudolf's eye?'

'Because he would have ripped my heart out if I hadn't ripped his eye out,' Hüseyin said, showing not a trace of regret. 'The blade he had in his hand was so sharp, he sliced my left side up like a pickle.'

'He was in hospital for fifteen days' his father said. 'We thought he was going to die.'

'But Rudolf did a month in hospital,' Hüseyin added, eager,

or perhaps desperate, to prove his masculine credentials, like a teenager in a pissing Conzest. 'He was at death's door and believe me, I didn't feel sorry in the slightest for that prick. He should have died. People like that don't deserve to live. I mean, just look at him. He is still gunning for me. And he won't give up until one of us is dead…'

He was making some rather grand claims.

'Don't you think you may be exaggerating things just a little?' Tobias offered.

'Exaggerating? Don't you get it? The man is a killer. He tried to rip my heart out!'

It was the second time he was saying *rip my heart out*. Was it this a coincidence or was he deliberately trying to shift the focus onto Rudolf? Whatever his intentions, his haphazard account was beginning to complicate affairs.

'I'm sorry, this won't do. Can you start again, please? From the beginning?' Yıldız asked. 'What was Rudolf's beef with you, or yours with him? What made you go at each other with knives and chairs?'

Hüseyin took a deep breath, exhaled slowly and leant his bulky frame against an oak tree.

'Very well. The bad blood between Rudolf and I goes back a long way. We used to live in Kreuzberg. It wasn't the posh gentrified place it is now. We lived in a ramshackle old building that only just survived the war. The toilet was in the corridor and we had to share it with the neighbours. Because it was cheap, the place was full of migrant workers, not those snooty, intellectual arty types you see there now. My mother and father both worked at the time so there was no one at home to keep an eye on us. As kids, we were left to our own devices. I mean, we went to school but we didn't really take much interest in it. The German teachers all thought we were going to fail anyway so they didn't bother with us. I don't want to be unfair but there were very few teachers who took an interest in the Turkish pupils. But we were not failures. Anyway, we used to get home in the evenings, dump our school bags and then run outside to play. It was around this time that the Nazis began messing around with us. Yes, Kreutzberg was not the leftists' wet dream it is now. Back then, it had quite a few Nazis, and they were a serious threat, those guys. They used to corner us in the street and harass us, and sometimes they would stop us and beat the crap out of us. In the end, we got fed up with the beatings and formed our own gang. For our name, we used Kreuzberg's postcode: 36. We became the 36 Boys.'

Yıldız remembered her father telling her about an anti-fascist group that had been set up by a bunch of youths looking to defend themselves.

'Most of us were the children of migrant workers,' Hüseyin went on. 'But we also had some Germans in our gang. They were cool guys, politically in-the-know. They knew what they were doing and they also knew how to handle themselves in a row. They are the guys behind the squats you see today. As for us, we didn't have any political motives. We just wanted to defend ourselves. Soon, we started retaliating against the Nazis who were chasing us down the streets and hitting us. Anyway, that prick Rudolf was the leader of one of those fascist gangs. Like I said, he was handy in a fight and he also knew how to use a blade. No one wanted to come up against him. Despite the training we had all had, we were still amateurs, whereas Rudolf was a madman on those streets.

'So anyway, the Nazis used to win but then the tide started turning and we started winning our fights. Basically, we learnt how to fight the hard way — by getting the crap kicked out of us again and again. Over time, they began to fear us. It used to be the case that we were too scared to go out alone; now they were the ones too scared to walk around by themselves. We'd jump them wherever we saw them, but sometimes they'd ambush us. That is what happened that day. Me and two friends were walking past St Michael's Church. It had been raining and the ground was wet. Suddenly, Rudolf and two other fellas attacked us. No swearing or shouting. They just jumped us and began laying into us, without needing to say a word. We were three mates but that Rudolf was more than enough for all three of us. Luckily, my two friends weren't cowards. Neither of them fled, but as luck would have it, I ended up one-on-one with Rudolf. I had no choice but to try to defend myself but it was no good, he was kicking ten shades out of me. I tried to hit him back but I kept missing, and the more I missed, the more he grew in confidence. Anyway, he took a step back in preparation for a blow that I'm sure would have knocked me out flat. He came running at me to kick me in the chest but he forgot about the damp ground and he slipped and fell flat on his arse. I seized my chance and started kicking and punching him as hard as I could. I have a hefty punch too and I was giving him a good pounding but the guy was agile like a flea and once he got over his initial shock, he managed to wriggle free, get up and stand in front of me. "Now I'm going to show you, you filthy Turk," he said and he pulled out a dagger from his waist. It was a military blade, the type used by soldiers. We also used to make sure we were tooled up and I pulled out a blade a mate of mine from Trabzon had got for me from Sürmene. So there we were, the two of us in the church courtyard circling each other with knives in our hands, looking to inflict some serious damage on the other. Sure, I was standing up to him and all that but deep down I was terrified because I knew how good he was when it came to fighting. I had no chance, and he sensed it because he was smirking at me, switching the blade from one hand to the other just to demoralize me. I was hoping my friends would turn up and help me but no chance. There was nobody else there. Grandfather Orhan told us never to be afraid. "A real man can hand it out and he can take it too. Doesn't matter which one it is so long as you don't chicken out. Don't ever run away when you're in a fight." I looked around, sized up the situation and realized there was no way I could win. The guy was going to stick me one way or another. All I could hope for was that I come out of the fight with my pride intact and treatable wounds. *Screw it*, I thought. *If this is what it's gonna be, let's have it.* I got a good grip on my knife, dug my heels in and shouted out in Turkish, *"Gel lan, şerefsiz! Gel bakalım, ırkçı pezevenk!"* Well, it turns out Rudolf knew a little Turkish. He understood what I had just said and he was incensed by it. "You're the *pezevenk!*" he shouted and he came for me. Had I been a second late, his knife would have sliced my throat open but I moved to the right just in time. It wasn't far enough though because I felt a sharp stinging pain on my left side. I looked down and saw blood oozing out of a tear in my shirt. "I'm going to fucking kill you, you filthy *kanake*," Rudolf said. I'd heard somewhere that in order to scare your opponent, you should attack first. I didn't really know what I was doing and partly because of that, I went for him. Of course, Rudolf dodged me easily and my blade just went through thin air. Worse than that, I lost my balance and was about to fall over. Rudolf saw it and stabbed me in the chest again. The whole of my upper body was covered in blood. I must have looked a state because my two friends and the other two neo-Nazis had stopped fighting and were staring at us in horror. One of Rudolf's boys must have got the fear too because he said, "Let's go, Rudolf! Enough! You're going to kill him!" But

Rudolf was like a wolf that had tasted blood and now wanted to go in for the kill. He waved his friends away with his free hand. He wasn't going to go anywhere until he had finished me off. My two friends just stood there, rooted to the spot, like they were in shock or something. At one point, my eyes felt heavy, probably because I was losing a lot of blood. I must have been wobbling on my feet because Rudolf sensed an opportunity and came at me again but by some miracle, his foot slipped again. To stop himself falling, he had to put his right knee on the ground, which put his head at the same height as my waist. I didn't waste the chance and I slashed at him with my knife. I wasn't even sure I would get him because I couldn't even see properly but it just so happened that at that moment Rudolf was getting up. Put the two of them together — my slashing out at him with the knife and him suddenly trying to get up — and my Sürmene knife cut deep into the left side of his face, including his eye. He screamed, dropped his knife and brought both hands up to his face. Ever since then, he has been known as Blind Rudolf.'

'Then what happened?' Tobias said, intrigued. 'Didn't his friends attack you?'

'No, they just watched on in horror. The leader they had always seen as unbeatable was now covered in blood. Once they got over the shock, they wanted to get Rudolf to a hospital as fast as they could. As for me, I had already fainted anyway. When I opened my eyes, I was in hospital. Of course, the police were there too and once I had made a full recovery, I was tried and sent down for two years and nine months. But as soon as I got out of prison, the threats to my family started all over again…'

Kerem, who had been listening silently, nodded in confirmation.

'Back then, we didn't have our baklava shops. I was working as a security guard in the Museum of Egyptian Civilization.

That Rudolf and his boys stopped me in the street once but they couldn't attack me because the street was too crowded but they did threaten me. "We're going to set fire to your house and roast you all," they said. I told the police and they were arrested but it didn't last long and they were soon released. They tried on two occasions to set fire to our house but failed both times. All they managed to do was break a few windows. Then the 36 Boys began standing guard outside our house. This scared the Nazis off and they backed off. When Hüseyin got out of prison, they targeted him straight away.'

'I should have cut that Nazi dog's throat in that fight,' Hüseyin fumed. 'Rudolf would have done the same had he been in my position. He was going to anyway, in that church courtyard. He wanted to kill me. But I couldn't do it.' There was a wild flicker in his eyes. 'I wish I had. My grandfather would still be alive if I had.'

It had not escaped the police's attention that he had not mentioned Cemal's name. Yıldız could see Hüseyin's propensity for violence but she was listening to him with great interest. If what he was saying was true, then there was an even greater possibility that the Nazis were behind the murders. Nevertheless, she knew she must not rush things and that there were still gaps to be filled.

'And what about this fight with Cemal? What happened then? The fight in which Cemal saved you from Rudolf, that is. You said Cemal hit him over the head with a chair.'

'Oh yeah… Like I said, that was another fight, around ten years ago. We had just opened the shop in Kreuzberg.' He stopped and sighed. 'It's not right to speak ill of the dead but back then we did not know the truth about Cemal. He was living with us at the time and working for a computer firm around Potsdamer Square. Our shops are open on Saturdays so he would help me out from time to time. It was on one of those

Saturdays that Rudolf and this huge skinhead stormed the shop. That's right, in broad daylight, the bastard came at us in the shop. Cemal had yet to arrive so I was alone in the shop. The two of them went for me. They both had steel knuckledusters and were beating me senseless. My face was covered in blood, the window display had been turned over and there were sweets and desserts all over the floor. The locals had turned up and were watching on in amazement but they didn't get involved because they didn't know what the fight was about. Just then, from where or how I don't know, Cemal turned up holding a chair with metal legs and rushed in. Before Rudolf had a chance to defend himself, Cemal had brought the chair smashing down on his face. As soon as Rudolf fell away from me, I went after the other one, his friend. I was soon on top of him and I began beating him around the face with a POS terminal. Cemal had Rudolf in a corner and was beating him over the head with the chair. The last thing I remember was seeing Rudolf curled up on the floor in a pool of his own blood. He ended up in hospital, although how they got him there, I don't know. Had to have eighteen stitches in his head. This time, there was no punishment. Self-defence, they said.'

'Ms Karasu, Ms Karasu!' a panic-stricken voice suddenly called out. 'Diana has found something.'

She turned to look. It was Martin, he was holding a plastic bag up arm's length, as though he was repulsed by its Conzents.

'It may be a body part,' he said, and made a face. 'I'm not sure but it may be a male member.'

Standing in front of Martin and staring at Yıldız with her tongue out waiting for a show of thanks for her find, was Diana.

'What do you mean…' Kerem said, barely able to speak. 'Are you trying to tell me they… That his… That they cut his organ off?'

His shoulders were slumped and his eyes had almost popped out of their sockets. He was looking helplessly at the short CSI officer who was now walking away after having placed the bloody body part in question in an evidence bag. Yıldız felt sorry for Kerem.

'I thought it would have been better to inform you at a later time. But yes, unfortunately, I am afraid your father was castrated.' She paused and then, thinking now was the time to broach it, said, 'Just as Uranus was castrated by his son Kronos.'

While speaking, she watched Kerem carefully, hoping to capture a telling gesture or reaction, no matter how subtle. The colour drained from Kerem's face and he seemed to be short of breath. The reaction came from Hüseyin.

'Why the hell are you bringing Kronos into this? I've just told you, Rudolf is behind all this. This is the result of years of pent-up hatred. He is taking out his revenge on all of us.'

'Did Rudolf have any connection with or interest in mythology?' Yıldız asked, keeping cool. Hüseyin made a face and went straight into attack mode.

'Why are you asking such ridiculous questions? The man is a Goddamn killer with blood on his hands! He is a Nazi ringleader with a burning hatred for foreigners. Who cares if he is into mythology or not? He killed my grandfather.'

While speaking, he was gesturing wildly but Yıldız did not let it affect her and in the same cool, formal manner asked, 'So why is he using mythological symbols?

'What?'

Patiently, Yıldız tried to explain.

'Look, Mister Ölmez. In killing both your brother and your grandfather, the killer has employed numerous mythological motifs and has made multiple references to the culture of ancient Greece. Cemal was killed in a manner that suggests he was sacrificed to Zeus, whilst your grandfather has been mutilated in the same way Uranus was mutilated by Kronos. For this Blind Rudolf person to have done this, he would need to be well-versed in mythology. And to go to all this trouble, he would also need to know about your family's past.'

Hüseyin either did not understand or did not want to understand.

'And what's wrong with my family's past? Don't think I am going to stand here and let people insult my family.'

The breeze had caught Yıldız's hair again. With a firm sweep of her arm, she pushed the stray hairs back from her forehead.

'Nobody is insulting your family. All I am saying is, from what your father told me, your grandfather and many of your family elders worked on the excavations at Pergamon and had done since they first began. In both murders, the killer has alluded to this aspect of your family's past and used elements of the religious rituals of ancient Pergamon. What I am trying to say is that if this Rudolf character really is the one that carried out these killings, then he would have to have a substantial knowledge of both mythology and your family history.'

Hüseyin was preparing to stand up to her when his father stepped in.

'Ms Karasu is not saying anything incorrect, son. For all we know, Rudolf is interested in archaeology. Or maybe he learnt about it because he knows our family history. Remember, you're the one who says he will never forget what was done to him.'

He seemed to be validating Yıldız but he was actually trying to shift attention away from them and onto the half-blind Nazi. He turned to Yıldız.

'Is that not so? If Rudolf really has it in for us, then would he not find out as much as he could about us?'

'It's possible, yes,' Yıldız said, playing along. 'If his aim is to wipe out the entire Ölmez family, then he would have had to study you all very well and know a lot about you. He may have wished to add this layer of mystery to the murders after learning about your family's extensive connections to the excavations at Pergamon. We shall certainly ask him about it when we question him. We'll look into it.'

The father looked relieved but Yıldız had more up her sleeve.

'Well, there is one more area in which we need information.' She slowed down. 'We have obtained some important information about you. I say important, because it may be connected to the manner in which your father was killed.'

'What information?' Kerem said, trying to hide his growing concern. 'I am ready to assist in any way I can.'

'Years ago, you were treated in a psychiatric ward. You were under the illusion that you were the God Kronos and you spent six months undergoing treatment...' The more she spoke, the more Kerem's face fell. 'Apparently, you said that your family came from a race of Gods and that you used to call your cousin Davut, with whom you were feuding, Oceanus...'

'Fabrications,' Hüseyin snorted. 'Utter drivel. I see it now. Instead of the Nazis, you're going to let us take the blame for all this. And you call yourself a Turk...' He was also gesticulating now. 'But they're the ones that pay you, aren't they? They have bought you off, haven't they? I knew it. You work for the German deep state.' He was now standing dangerously close to Yildiz and Tobias had to step in between them.

'Stand back. Don't move any closer.'

'What the hell!' Hüseyin growled at the giant of a man standing in front of him. 'You turn a blind eye to the people that kill my grandfather and then you threaten us?'

'I said stand back,' Tobias repeated calmly. The two men stared at each other. Feelings were running so high that had Kerem not pulled his son back, fists would have started flying.

'Hüseyin, stop! Hüseyin! What the hell do you think you're doing?'

Hüseyin paused but did not give in straight away. He glared at Tobias with open Conzempt.

'You'll pay for this.'

'Sure. Whenever you want,' Tobias said breezily. 'But if you take one step closer to the Chief Inspector, I'll break your neck.' He stared at Hüseyin defiantly, all but inviting him to give it a go, and then turned to Hüseyin's father and said, 'Please tell your son, for your sake and for his, to control himself.'

'Calm down, Hüseyin!' Kerem said desperately, aware of the precariousness of the situation. 'Calm down, son. We're not going to accomplish anything if you carry on like this.'

'We're not going to accomplish anything anyway, Dad,' he said with a look of disgust. 'These guys aren't going to bother looking for Cemal's and Grandad's killers.'

'And when have you ever cared anyway?' Tobias said, arms crossed over his chest as he carefully assessed the situation and the men in front of him. 'You would have killed Cemal yourself had you been able to.'

Hüseyin was ready to turn on Tobias but his father held him back again.

'That's enough, Hüseyin! Enough! Let them do their job. Go and have a cigarette and let me talk to these officers in peace.'

But Hüseyin was in no mood to listen.

'Talk about what, Dad? These guys have already reached a verdict. Don't you get it? They're going to try and pin the blame on us.'

Yıldız could not bear it any longer.

'Damn it, enough! Who the hell do you think you are? For the love of God, pull yourself together, man! The days of the 36 Boys are over. We are not Nazis! We are police officers trying to find the people that killed your brother and your grandfather. If you don't believe us, then I am afraid that is your problem. But you are not going anywhere. You are not going off for a smoke. You are going to stand here and wait while we talk to your father. If you cause any problems, I will have you both placed under arrest. So watch your step.'

Hüseyin did not say a word but his father was eager to ease the tension.

'There is no need for anything like that, Ms Karasu, really. My son and I are ready to answer all your questions.'

Yıldız kept her angry gaze on Hüseyin, as though to tell Kerem where the problem was. Hüseyin looked away and, still incensed, bowed his head. Seeing this as an opportunity, Kerem began answering Yıldız's question.

'That is correct. I did suffer such an episode. And yes, it was a psychological disorder of a kind. Paranoid Grandiosity they call it. The final stage of megalomania, they say, in which the sufferer believes they are someone famous, a great statesman, or a prophet or even the messiah. Yes, you may find it funny or absurd but there is such an affliction. People can suffer from it or relapse when they are under pressure. At that time, I was severely depressed.'

Still silent, Hüseyin reached into his pocket. He pulled out a packet of cigarettes and took one from the pack. Yıldız noticed but said nothing, keeping her focus on Kerem.

'When did this happen? Which years exactly?'

'Eight years after Cemal was born... Cemal was forty so...' He stopped to work out the figure. 'So, thirty odd years ago. Yep, it was that long ago. My mind back then was in a mess. I had forgotten who I was. Actually, it's not really forgetting but...' He was having difficulty talking about his condition. 'More a case of escape. Escaping reality. We were having a lot of problems back then. Hüseyin was only fifteen and Cemal was still a young lad and I was missing Turkey a lot. Bergama, the Acropolis on the hill, everything. It was so different to Berlin. I had grown up in Bergama before moving to Berlin and I used to miss Pergamon so much that I often went to East Berlin to visit the Pergamon Museum. Yes, during the communist era. I used to feel at home there because all those pieces, those marbles and statues, they were all from my city. I only felt free from my worries when I was in that museum, and I used to wake up in the mornings thinking I was Kronos. It's hard to believe, right? But it's true. The young man who worked in the Museum of Egyptian Civilisation was gone and in his place was a fearsome Titan who had seized the throne of power from his own father.' Embarrassed, he sighed: 'The illness runs in my family. It surfaces during times of great stress.'

Yıldız did not miss this important detail.

'You mean Alzheimer's? Like your father's affliction?'

'No, this was not my father's illness. It was great-great grandfather Pehlivan's. I showed you his photograph in the shop, remember? He was one of the men that worked with Carl Humann when he began the excavations at Pergamon.'

'Pehlivan the German,' Tobias said. Something close to a smile appeared on Kerem's face.

'Correct, Mister Becker. *Alman Pehlivan*. The German. I remember telling you what a good worker he was but I didn't tell you how he died. He was actually a quiet, normal guy who worked hard and minded his own business at first but over time, he began talking too much and handing out advice to everyone, thinking he knew best on every topic. Then, one day, he said to Grandma Zöhre, his wife, that he had a secret to tell her. He told her he was the older brother of Zeus and that his name was not Pehlivan but Poseidon. The poor woman did not know what to do. Just imagine, this was at the end of the 1890s. They had a spiritual healer brought over to Manisa, a *hoca*, and he told them my father was possessed and so he performed his hokum, reciting prayers and such and then blowing over my great-grandfather to get rid of the unwanted spirits. None of it worked, of course. Seeing there was no cure to be found, the people in the village decided to humour him, because he wasn't actually causing any harm. However, he soon started having problems with the village *muhtar*, saying things like, "You are the leader of the Gigantes, you are the archenemy of Zeus." One day, he grabbed his pitchfork and attacked the *muhtar*, who only just managed to escape with his life, but they still let him be because no could be bothered to take him to the nearest psychiatric hospital, which was in Izmir. There is a rivulet in Bergama called the Selinos and back then it often used to burst its banks. When it did, the Jewish Quarter, which was on the riverbank, used to get the worst of it. Anyway, that year there was a lot of rain and the Selinos burst its banks again. The Jews of the village ran into their homes to save what they could. One young mother was too late in getting out and ended up getting trapped inside her house with her two young sons with the water continuing to rise outside. Grandad Pehlivan saw it and ran in to help. He managed to save the two boys, who at this point were treading water, but he could not find their mother. By now the water, was rising even further because of the water gushing down from the mountains. The villagers warned Pehlivan that it was too late to try and look for the mother and that she had probably drowned but he didn't care. "Nothing will happen to me, I am Poseidon," he said and dived back into the muddy waters. And that was that. He never came back up. When the water had subsided, the bodies of the mother and my grandfather were found under a fig tree in a field. Grandad Pehlivan was holding the poor woman's hand. So he had reached her but the water had proven too much for him.

'This happened around a hundred years ago. Nobody else in the family showed signs of the disorder until me. Thankfully, I was treated in time, before anything unpleasant happened. As you said, I received treatment in hospital for six months and made a full recovery.' There was an earnest look on his tired face. 'Look, it's been thirty years and that feeling has never come back. I have not had any relapses or any cases of delirium.'

Yıldız was moved. The vulnerability in his black eyes, the wavering voice, the pained expression on his face and his resigned body language all suggested he was telling the truth. But what if it was Kronos speaking — and lying — to her? What if Kerem had not recovered?

'Do you have dreams, Mister Ölmez?' The question was asked by Tobias, who, like Yıldız, was wondering whether Kerem really had recovered. 'For example, dreams about Pergamon... I ask because what you have just told us is so strange, it sounds like a dream. Or a nightmare, to be more precise...'

Kerem winced.

'I do,' he said in a broken voice. 'Not every night but when I am especially tired, or I feel particularly stressed or pressured, I have this one recurring dream. In the dream, a battle is taking place. Not a real-life battle but a fictional one I know well: a battle between the Gods and the Giants, the battle that is depicted on the friezes on the walls of the Altar of Zeus. In the dream, I am in the midst of the fight, surrounded by three Giants who draw their strength from their mother, Gaia. No matter what I do, I cannot kill them. I cut their throats with my sword, hack their bodies to pieces and cut off their hands and feet but it is no use. Mother Earth heals them every time and they come back stronger. We keep on fighting, but then Gaia points to Zeus, fighting the Giants, and says, "You, Kronos, cannot best my sons. You should seek help from your son and grandson." I am so desperate, I do what she suggests. I look up to Zeus, fighting shoulder to shoulder with Heracles against the Giants, and I want to shout, "Help me, save me from these Giants." I open my mouth try to say it but no sound comes out. Helpless, I stand there, waiting for those three human-like creatures with snake-like legs to destroy me.'

He looked and sounded like he was telling the truth but to what extent could a man who once believed he was a Titan be believed? Yıldız needed to know for sure that he was completely cured.

'Do you still use medication, Mister Ölmez?' she asked. 'Are you still undergoing treatment?'

Kerem had long since come to terms with his condition, however.

'Yes, I do still use medication and shall continue to do so till the day I die.' He then turned and looked in the direction where his father's naked corpse lay. 'But I have never been delirious enough to kill my own son and father.'

7
Dionysus has always been closer to the heart than to the mind

And they denounced me, without knowing, without asking, without thinking; they accused me, Mighty Zeus, the God of All Gods who decides what is and what shall be, Lord of the Earth and the Sky. But those that accused me of neglecting divine affairs by using my amorous escapades as a pretext are bereft of insight, unable to see the future and unable to grasp the fullness of my aims. My every breath, my every step and my every decision has a purpose. The business of ruling the world is one of regulation, of organization, of decision-making. I am, unarguably, the lord of the earth and the sky, but my siblings and my progeny also have a role to play within my rule. Every God and Goddess has his or her own duties, they each have their own affairs and missions. No God can govern the world by himself. No matter how powerful he is, he cannot carry the burden alone. This is why I was even willing to assign duties to enemies I had vanquished.

Atlas, for instance, son of Iapetus and Clymene, and brother of the unruly Prometheus, was one. The same Atlas that was the mightiest, most fearless and most selfless of all his siblings. In our war against the Titans, he fought heroically against us. I, Zeus, gatherer of the clouds, assigned this honourable foe with the task of upholding of the sky, for the sky and the earth are never to meet as this would destroy the divine balance. That blue expanse, however, was heavier than imagined, and it grew more burdensome with each passing day, yet Atlas, despite the agonies he endured, did not shirk from his onerous task. His legs did not buckle, nor did his back bend. Like the other Titans, Gods, heroes and men, he obeyed my command to the end, for the divine order required his strength and his compliance. Atlas was of my blood, it is true, but naturally my trust was greater in my siblings and children, which is why I had need for more Gods and Goddesses, and for more demigods and demigoddesses. This truth was revealed to me in a dream. Yes, we Gods also dream, and some of these dreams take root within our minds and, when the opportunity arises, are revived and begin to bud within the clear soil of our minds. And so, it was the second dream in which I saw that dark-eyed boy, who warned me of the impending danger and the need for me to procreate in order to counter the threat. He was standing in Olympus on the spot in which the Gods usually gathered but this time, there were no Gods there. No Hera, no other Immortals; just the boy and I. He held my father Kronos' staff and said:

'The Gods are alone, Mighty Zeus. This isolation is the source of their strength and their weakness. To be alone when strong is good, but if you become weak, it will lead to the loss of your power.' He insolently threw the golden staff down, where it struck the marble floor and fell at my feet.

The boy said: 'This is what happened to your father. None were there to come to his aid when he fought you. His terrible isolation led to his shameful defeat. You, too, are alone, Mighty

Zeus. You too may lose your throne as a result of a shameful defeat. If you do not wish to experience such dishonour, you must extend your lineage and multiply those that carry your blood. And you must love them and ensure their love for you.'

After this second dream, I followed the mysterious child's advice and continued in my amorous pursuit of the Titanesses and Goddesses. That is why I shared my bed with Metis the wise, with shimmering Themis, with Eurynome, the beauty of beauties, with Demeter, who makes all the world fertile, with silken-haired Mnemosyne, with sweet Leto, doe-eyed Hera, Maia, who was pure as water, innocent Semele, virtuous Alcmene, passionate Danae and countless others. I shall not pretend that I did not take great pleasure when making love to them. Just as we all came into being via the passion and ardour between our mother Gaia and our Father Uranus, so I held love, ecstasy and the pleasures of love higher than all other feelings.

Let it not be forgotten that all the Gods, Titans, men and women of Olympus and the earth are the offspring of nature and of love. The siblings with whom I shared a womb and those born of my seed were also like me, but with one difference: I gathered all the divine power unto myself, and gave but a portion of this power to the others. For instance, the God of reason and of art, Apollo, and his brother Dionysus, the God of feeling and art. Yes, both were Gods of art, but Apollo used reason to interpret dreams and transform the seen into art, whereas Dionysus was inspired by the mysterious and the unknown, and was aroused by that which was taboo. Apollo was wreathed in light, illuminating all thoughts and emotions with his light. Dionysus preferred to wander in the darkness and dwell in the hidden corners of the mind, experiencing the most forbidden of feelings, and he did not hesitate to tell all of the wondrous tastes of sin, for Dionysus was the strangest, the most audacious and the most rebellious of my children. Such was his audacity that, were it not for his fear of my wrath, he would have replaced the nectar that nourished the Gods and Goddesses and preserved their health with wines that would have clouded their minds, aroused their hearts and inflamed their bodies.

Wayward Dionysus' birth was unusual, just like him, the result of my dazzling nights of love with passionate Semele, the delicate princess of Thebes. Ah, beautiful Semele, the daughter of Cadmus and Harmonia! How we made love under the starry night skies! During those endless fragrant nights, when the warm winds embraced us like a silken sheet, we lay down on the cool earth and let the fires of our bodies intertwine. Ah, beautiful Semele, as soft and giving as her mother. When I gazed upon her, I felt I could see the snow-topped mountains, the deep wide seas, the fertile plains and the infinite sky. Such was her beauty, I was taken with her the moment I saw her. I appeared to her at first as a Mortal. I stole her heart as a man but made love to her as a God, with all my heart, all my mind and all my body. Of course, Hera, bane of my existence, learnt about our great love and also found out that Semele was six months pregnant, and so she hatched a devious plan to thwart her, a terrifying, brutal and devious plot. She twisted innocent Semele's mind by appearing to her one day as a friend and saying:

'If the one you love is none other than Zeus, the Lord of the Gods himself, the male that knows better than all others the loves of sky and earth, and if he is so infatuated with you, tell me, why does he appear to you in the guise of a Mortal when he appears as his true self, a God, to his wife Hera? Tell him to appear to you as Zeus, as Mighty Zeus of the shield, as Zeus your beloved.'

Semele fell for these words and after one of our nights of prolonged lovemaking, she began pleading with me.

'Mighty Zeus, Gatherer of the Clouds, greatest and most powerful of all males on earth and in the heavens, my one and true love — why do you not come to me as a God?'

No matter how much I tried to tell her that this was not possible, my simple and naive lover would not be convinced. Worse still, she made me believe her wild imaginings. Even if one is a God, the mind is of no use when it comes to matters of love. Moreover, I had promised Semele that I would fulfil all her desires, and so, in the end, her persistence too great for me to resist, I appeared to her in all my glory. But I am no peacock, a creature that charms and woos its female with colourful feathers. I am a God, and the mightiest and most terrifying of all the Gods. When I appeared thus before her, the skies began to rumble and thunderbolts began to clap. Before my sweet Semele could even comprehend what was happening, she was struck by a bolt of lightning from my hands and died on the spot, in front of me. Although beautiful Semele had died, I was still able to save our unborn child and so I took Dionysus from his mother's belly, sewed him securely into my thigh and ascended to Olympus. The child grew in my thigh and when the time came, opened his eyes and was born. I delivered him into the care of his brother Hermes, to be protected from Hera's wrath. Hermes, my loyal, dutiful son, carried out his duties without question and handed Dionysus over to the Nymphs, who cared for my son as though he was their own. They nurtured him, protected him and educated him so that he would grow up to intimately know the mysteries, miracles and dark secrets of nature.

But a scourge fell upon him, like a black cloud, and that scourge was my wife, Hera. The Queen of Olympus was never going to give up in her pursuit of this unexpected child. Had Dionysus remained a Mortal hero, then perhaps my vicious wife's hatred of him would have waned over time but Dionysus, although the child of the womb of a Mortal, was still my issue, the progeny of a God, and he soon became a God himself. Hera's bloody plot to kill Semele and thus cause me grief had come to naught. Enraged, the Queen of Olympus sent Dionysus to the Titans to be destroyed.

The treacherous Titans coaxed my son into a forest with an enchanted mirror and in that remote darkness, they tore the child into pieces, hiding his heart in a hollow. When the news reached me, it was too late. Nevertheless, I punished his murderers in a fitting manner. I taught them how grave a transgression it is to dare lay a hand on a son of Zeus and I struck them with lightning, incinerating them all. But my son's body was nowhere to be found. As I grieved, our Mother Earth, Gaia, took pity on me and on her grandson, and she told me about the hollow in which my son's heart was hidden. My brilliant daughter Athena immediately set off and found her little brother's heart and she pieced it back together with the rest of his body. And thus, Dionysus was returned to life.

This was my son's third rebirth. His first birth was in Seleme's womb, his second in my thigh and the third from his own heart. That is why my Dionysus has always been closer to the heart than to the mind, to emotion than reason, and to desire rather than will.

But my vengeful wife would not yield in her bloody quest and to protect him from her spite, I sent Dionysus across the endless oceans, to beyond the snowy mountains that were the roof of the world, where he saw places that no other Olympian had ever seen. He already knew the secrets of nature, thanks to his childhood growing up amongst the trees, the plants, the wild animals and the earth, but now he was with people. He began living amongst them not as a God but in the guise of an ordinary

Mortal. The foolish people did not realize at first that he was a deity, but when they stepped out of line, he showed them he was his father's son and made them pay for their insolence with their lives. Yet, at the same time, he loved humans, just as I love them. He gave them the gifts of the vine and of wine so they may better bear the difficulties of life, for he knew that the world was an unbearable place for Mortals and he did not want them to suffer, to constantly struggle with woes and worries and to only spend their days in pain and strife. And he said unto them:

'Listen to me, people! Drink this wine! Drink and be free of your minds. Forget the Gods, the kings and your fathers. Pay no heed to prohibitions. Listen to your hearts and your bodies, be yourselves, live as you are. Drink wine, and fear not the Gods! Do feel not sorry for yourselves, for poetry, music, love and dance await you. Drink, dance, sing, make love and return to nature…'

And they — women, men, kings, queens, princes, princesses, and even the oracles — heeded his call. In the palaces and houses, in the squares and the streets, in distant fields, on the banks of long rivers and on the slopes of the mountains, people sang and danced and made love, and they created new celebrations and rites with music, dance, wine and love. They discovered new ways to rejoice, and yes, Dionysus, just like the vine, just like the grape of the vine and just like the juice of the grape, gave them the gift of theatre, so they could laugh, learn and enjoy together. Those that believed in Dionysus became even more devoted to this God of ecstasy.

But not all greeted my unruly son's contrary ways with the same fervour. Some Gods and Goddesses, Hera most of all, kings whose thrones were threatened, fathers without love in their hearts and cruel husbands loathed and despised Dionysus. For him, they felt rage. They cursed him, they exiled him and they tried to destroy him, but my son did not waver or falter because, like his father, he was tenacious, steadfast and daring. The years he spent amongst men and their treacheries, plots and traps had helped him to grow and mature, and his divine gifts earned the admiration of both the Mortals and the Immortals. By the force of his hand, he had earned his place on Olympus amongst the Gods. I loved this mysterious, mischievous, playful son of mine as much as I loved my other children. Whenever I looked at him, I saw the other Gods as well as an aspect of the Mortals. Dionysus showed men and the Gods and Titans of Olympus, which was a divine reflection of the world, another aspect of life. He was the thrice born. He had defeated death three times and he had thus won his Immortality.

Chapter Seven

Peter Schimmel's firm, Der Blitz, was housed in a two-storey villa nestled amongst a clump of towering pine trees at the end of a perfectly narrow street lined with wonderfully cosy-looking houses. It was around noon when Yıldız pulled the Passat into the company's driveway. She had actually been thinking of taking Kerem and his son to the station to take their statements and seeing Peter Schimmel the next day instead but when Tobias warned her that they really needed to see the threatening letter he had described, she relented, and they set their course for the Der Blitz headquarters in Charlottenburg, which would at least give the Ölmez family a little more time to grieve in peace. She felt Kerem was telling the truth, and although her suspicions about the Ölmez family had not been completely dispelled, the neo-Nazis were still the prime suspects, even more so after hearing Hüseyin's story about this Blind Rudolf, whom they would soon be visiting. Perhaps it was Rudolf that was behind Otto and his goons.

After parking the Passat in the driveway, they walked across the garden towards the broad marble staircase. Passing through the cool swing doors at the head of the stairs, they found themselves standing before a vast mural of a glistening grey city.

Rain poured down over the Brandenburg Gate and the wan sky and the trees and buildings but somewhere in the background, a tired-looking sun was still defiantly trying to light up the cityscape.

'There is a signature here,' Tobias said, peering at the bottom left corner of the painting. 'But it's hard to make out what it says.'

'It says "Angel".' They turned around and saw Peter standing there. Once again, he was dressed from head to toe in black: a short-sleeved black t-shirt, black linen trousers and black shoes. 'That is one of my sister's paintings. It's called "The Death of Light". It was her favourite. I could not bear to part with it.' He smiled, even though the memory inspired by the painting was a painful one. 'Welcome. So nice to see you.' After shaking hands with them, he gestured to the building and said, 'Yes, these are the headquarters of our modest little firm.'

'Nice,' Tobias muttered, staring in admiration at the high ceiling. 'I've always wanted to live in this area. I even came here a few times to check out some flats to rent but nothing came of it.'

'*Kismet*, Mister Becker,' Peter said understandingly. 'Perhaps *kismet* is just waiting for the right time. When the time comes, perhaps you will have a house here.' He turned to face Yıldız. 'I pronounced it correctly, didn't I? Is that not what the Turks call it — *kismet*?'

'They do,' Yıldız said, remaining serious. 'How do you know that?'

'Cemal used it a lot,' Peter said sadly. '*Kismet değilmiş*, he used to say.'

'It's *kısmet*, not *kismet*,' Yıldız said with a smile. Peter blushed.

'I'm sorry. Turkish is such a hard language for Germans… Its structure is so alien to us. And it is not just language. Turkish people's way of thinking is also so different to ours. This word *kismet* alone highlights the difference between German and Turkish people's logic. As people, you are far more fatalistic than us. Please do not misconstrue what I am saying, I do not see it as something negative. It has its merits and its drawbacks.'

This meaningless drivel was beginning to annoy Yıldız.

'Mister Schimmel, I am a German citizen. I was born in Berlin, I was educated in German schools and, if we do not count a few holidays abroad, I have always lived in this country. So when you say *you*, I think you may be using an incorrect term.'

Realizing his *faux pas*, Peter looked to Tobias for help but Tobias was having none of it.

'I think I may have used the wrong choice of words. I was referring to your roots. To cultural differences... For example, my roots are in East Germany. I was born in East Berlin and grew up in that culture, and I am proud of it too. But I also know I am different to West Germans.'

The Chief Inspector was in no mood to take it lying down.

'I am also proud of my Turkish roots but I do not like these roots being discussed at every opportunity.' Peter was about to respond but Yıldız did not let him. 'Now, Mister Schimmel, let's get down to business.'

'Of course,' he replied, glad to be let off the hook. 'This way, please. Let's talk in my office. We can have some coffee.'

Yıldız shook her head sternly.

'We would like to see Cemal's office first.'

Peter was not happy at the way he was being spoken to but he remained courteous.

'Of course, Ms Karasu. As you wish.' His voice, however, did sound a little strained. He pointed to the right. 'Here. This way.' They began walking through a well-lit corridor, its walls lined with photographs of windmills, solar panels, hydropower facilities, hydroelectric power plants and geothermal power stations. Both officers examined the photographs with a cool, professional eye.

'Were all these installations built by your company, Mister Schimmel?' Tobias asked in amazement. Peter smiled a wry smile.

'Some of them. Some are joint ventures. Certain groups with very large amounts of capital at their disposal have been investing in the renewable energy sector recently. The competition has really intensified. We are going toe to toe with some very large companies.'

'They're pushing you hard, are they?' Tobias asked, coming across as an expert on the matter. Peter sighed.

'They want to buy Der Blitz.' He looked Tobias up and down. 'You are also an East Berliner, so you know how hard it is for us here in the West. You don't have time to breathe. They make it as hard for you as they can… But I don't want to bore you with my company's problems right now. Here we are. This is Cemal's room.' He pointed to a door. 'Cemal loved nature. The day he started working here, he jokingly said he wanted a room with a view of the garden.' He reached forward, opened the door and stepped aside to let them through. 'This way, please.' They stepped into a cosy room that was decorated in an ultramodern style one would expect from a company in the energy sector. The branches from one of a number of spruce trees outside hung low and almost touched the window. On a metal desk were a large computer, a few sheets of paper, some books and, to the right, a metal figurine of Atlas holding up the world. On the wall behind the desk was a cork board covered in notes. To the right of the cork board, was an etching of an ancient settlement on a hill. Yıldız immediately recognized the Altar of Zeus. The etching was of Pergamon. In the picture, a tall, muscular young man holding a trident stood in front of the gates of the city and stared defiantly out at the world. He must have been one of the Gods.

'Is that Zeus?' Tobias asked.

'No, that's Poseidon,' Peter replied nonchalantly. His two guests peered at the face of the God in the picture, hoping to see familiar features but they did not recognize the face.

'This man is not one of his relatives,' Tobias said.

'He is,' Peter said serenely. 'That is Pehlivan Efendi, Cemal's grandfather. The poor man used to believe he was Poseidon.'

So this was the man they had heard about earlier in the morning, the grandfather who drowned in the Selinos River.

'Why?' Yıldız asked. 'Why did he make this strange association?'

'I think you have found the exact word, Ms Karasu. It really is strange. Sinister, in fact. I also found it odd and when I asked Cemal, this is what he told me: "There is a photograph in my father's shop, taken in 1878, the year the excavations began in Pergamon. In the photo, there are fourteen labourers with Carl Humann, the man that started the excavations. One of those labourers is Pehlivan Efendi, my great-grandfather. Indeed, his nickname was *Alman Pehlivan*. I saw that photograph many times as a child, before I ever went to Pergamon. But then, I eventually managed to visit Bergama. While we were there, we climbed the hill, up to the old city. Just like my grandfather and great-grandfather, my father had a deep emotional tie to that ancient city. Even though I have been there twenty or thirty times now, whenever I think about Pergamon, that photograph of Carl Humann and Pehlivan Efendi taken at the launch of the excavations springs to mind. Whether it is the ancient city itself or the faces of the Gods on the Altar of Zeus, I am always entranced by it because many of the men of my family have worked in Pergamon so in a way, they served the mythological characters that are part of the city's story and identity. That is why I am putting the faces of the 'Ölmez' family men onto the Gods, the Titans and the heroes in my project. I shall make the Olympians 'Ölmez'. Or, if you prefer, I shall make the Ölmez men Olympians."

'As you know, the word ölmez means "immortal", or "undying". Cemal loved these little word games. You should have seen his face when he was telling me all this. The excitement, the passion, the belief it gave him. In the end, he began working on his project, and it would have been a fascinating work had he been able to complete it, but alas. I don't know what to call it but whatever it was, fate or simple back luck, something decided to stop this brilliant man.'

'And you find that explanation plausible, do you?'

The question came from Yıldız, who had been studying Peter through narrowed eyes the whole time, trying to work him out. There was a faint hint of mockery in her voice. The owner of Der Blitz did not know what she meant.

'Of course I did. Why wouldn't I? It's clear that Pehlivan Efendi's disorder had also infected his great-grandson, all these generations later. He too wanted to give the Gods and the Titans on the Altar of Zeus his relatives' faces.' Seeing no reaction, he went on nervously. 'Why, shouldn't I have believed him? Are you concealing something from me? Are there details about Cemal that I do not know?'

His voice was unusually strained, and Tobias, thinking his boss may react too angrily, stepped in and tried to change the subject.

'Do you go to Pergamon once every year?'

Tobias' tactic worked and Peter's black eyes softened.

'We used to, sometimes twice a year. In fact, he took me there last year. It really is a fabulous place.'

'So you were quite close then?' Yıldız asked, and then, in an insinuating tone that disturbed Peter, added. 'Was he going to give your face to one of the Gods?'

'Of course not. I'm not a member of the Ölmez family.'

'But you are a very unusual employer…'

'I am a friend, not an employer. We met on a professional basis but then we became friends. Very good friends. Our relationship went beyond work.' He had raised his voice slightly, clearly perturbed by his guests. He looked at Yıldız. 'And contrary to what you seem to think, it was not a romantic relationship. I loved him like a brother.' He took a deep breath and then gestured to the drawings on the panel. 'If I knew Cemal at all, he was not lying about this project. He had no reason to tell me about it anyway.'

'I agree,' Yıldız said casually, realizing that Peter was becoming tense. 'You are right, Cemal had no reason to hide the truth. But we have to take all possibilities into consideration, as I'm sure you know and can well understand.' She scanned the room. 'Speaking of which, where is this threatening letter that you told us about?'

Peter paused for a moment and nodded, as though trying to calm himself, then quickly moved behind the desk and opened one of its drawers. He was reaching into the drawer when Yıldız called out to him.

'Stop! One moment, please. Do not touch it. Please. We will handle it.'

She reached into the inside pocket of her leather jacket and took out a pair of plastic gloves.

Unhappy at being treated so harshly in spite of his courtesy and in his own company offices, Peter stepped aside and watched them with a disparaging look that did not escape Yıldız's notice. She felt the need to warn him.

'As I said on the phone, Mr Schimmel, we have to be very careful not to corrupt any possible fingerprints on this letter.

Fingerprints are judges' favourite form of evidence, and if the evidence is tampered with or compromised in anyway, not only will this end the investigation, it will make finding the perpetrators all the more difficult.'

She went over to the desk and smiled at Peter, who had graciously moved aside to make way for them. She leant over and looked inside the drawer. There was an envelope inside.

'Is that it?'

'Yes, that one, the one on top of the papers. I had put the letter back in the envelope after reading it.'

Yıldız picked up the envelope with a gloved forefinger and thumb. She folded back the flap, took out the light-yellow letter and read aloud:

'*You filthy Turk, you won't get away with what you are doing. You'll pay for it all. You'll pay for your insolence with your own blood. Get ready. It's going to happen soon. Very soon…*' She read it again, this time in silence, and then looked up. 'Yep, there is a swastika here for a signature.'

Peter's tension had turned into anxiety.

'Have they left a fingerprint?'

'I hope so,' Yıldız said, placing the sheet of paper back into the envelope. 'If they have, it will make our work much easier.'

After placing the envelope in a plastic evidence bag, which she then put in her pocket, she turned and smiled to Peter.

'Thank you, Mister Schimmel. You have been a great help.'

They had both been so formal with him since they first met that Peter did not know how to respond to this gratitude. He opted for caution.

'If you like, we can have some coffee in my office.'

'I'm afraid we don't have time,' Yıldız said, again maintaining a cool formality. 'We need to get this letter to the criminology lab as soon as possible. However, we would like to have a look around before we leave.'

Peter realized that a casual, friendly demeanour with these two officers was not the right approach.

'Of course. I'll leave you to it then…' he said and began heading for the door when Yıldız stopped him.

'Please do not leave. If you have the time, we would rather you stay for a few more minutes.'

Again, Peter was not overly happy with their demeanour but he did not want to appear rude

'Sure,' he said irately, leaning against the window frame. 'Whatever you want.'

'When did you last see Cemal?' Yildiz asked, rummaging through the Conzents of the drawer. Peter gave her a hostile look.

'The day he died. I gave him a lift home.'

Yıldız stopped what she was doing and straightened up.

'You gave him a lift home, you say? Why, had his car broken down?' She did not even feel the need to hide the misgiving in her voice.

'Cemal did not have a car,' Peter replied casually, almost insolently. 'He had never owned one. He did not like cars. He used to cycle to and from work. That day, he had a flat tyre on his bike so I told him that I would drop him home if he could just wait for an hour. I had dropped him home countless times before. But that day, my work just dragged on and we finally left two hours later. Cemal didn't mind though.' He pointed to a picture on the panel. 'He was busy staring at that picture of Poseidon. If you ask me, he would have stayed for hours more if I hadn't told him I was ready to go.'

'You do have security cameras, don't you?' Tobias' question came out of the blue. He too had stopped rifling through the papers on the desk and, like Yıldız, was staring intently at the owner of Der Blitz. At first, Peter did not understand and answered in a hushed tone.

'We have. There were thieves in the neighbourhood last year.' He paused and looked at the two officers incredulously. 'Why? You don't suspect me, do you?'

'Let's not call it that, Mister Schimmel. But what you have to tell us is vitally important. Just trying to get a clearer picture of what the victim was doing before he was killed.'

Of course, this did not prove convincing for Peter

'Rest assured, we have cameras. All the recordings of the last month are available. We can watch them now if you like.'

The umbrage in his voice was not hard to detect. Yıldız felt a little guilty at having caused him to feel so affronted.

'Please don't misunderstand, Mister Schimmel. We do not suspect you of anything.' She was going to say more when her phone rang.

'Hello, yes?'

'Hello,' an agitated male voice said at the other end. 'Is this Miss Karasu?'

'Yes. Who is this?'

'This is Alex. Cemal's boyfriend. Do you remember?'

'Of course. Yes, I'm listening. Has something happened?'

'No, no, nothing bad has happened, but we need to talk. It may be important.'

'About Cemal's killer?'

'It might be. Cemal left a message on my answerphone... I was at the train station in Leipzig a few days back and was mulling something over so I called my landline at home and listened to Cemal's message. The line was not clear though, and I didn't get to hear it properly. The message was left a few hours before he was killed. I think it might be important. I'm going to be in Berlin this evening but I thought I would let you know now…'

Cemal had most probably called to try and make it up with him after their fight. Alex may well have already listened to the message but was feigning ignorance to keep his hands clean. No matter what, they needed to listen to that message.

'Very well, you listen to the message and then give me a ring. If we have to, we'll meet somewhere. Got it?'

'Got it.' Alex then added, 'I don't really know about these things. Am I getting nervous for nothing?'

'No, you are doing the right thing. I am going to wait for your call. Thank you for letting us know.'

As she switched the phone off and put it away, she could feel Tobias watching her curiously. She gestured for him to let it go and indicated that they would talk about it later in private. She turned back to face Peter.

'Yes, where were we… Ah, yes. We do appreciate your cooperation with us. Please do not see this as something personal. However, we have to investigate everyone that knew the deceased, including you. This case is becoming increasingly complicated. Unfortunately, Cemal's grandfather Orhan Ölmez has also been murdered.'

Peter was stunned.

'What? The old man with Alzheimer's? What harm did that poor old man ever do anyone?'

'You knew him?' Tobias asked.

'We never met but I did see a video of him once. The poor chap thought he was back in Turkey, back in his childhood. He had forgotten German and was talking to everybody in Turkish. He looked like a sweet, sweet man. How sad. How terrible.' He was beginning to understand the gravity of the situation.

'Is somebody is trying to take out the members of the Ölmez family one by one? Is it the Nazis?'

'We'll soon find out, Mister Schimmel,' Yıldız said resolutely. 'Very soon, I hope.'

As dusk settled, the wind died down and the scent of linden was drifting through the police station again. It had a calming effect on Yıldız but the same could not be said of Markus. He did not like what he was hearing from his officers, who had just come back from the field. He had loosened his tie and unbuttoned two of the buttons on his shirt sleeves.

'And where the hell did this psychological disorder nonsense come from? Why didn't this Kerem tell you when he first spoke to you?'

They sat and watched their boss standing nervously in front of a large board featuring the names and photographs of the deceased and the suspects.

'Maybe it is because we didn't ask him,' Yıldız replied. 'Maybe he wanted to keep it from us. It's hard to tell right now. But it seems this disorder runs in the family. As I was telling you just now, the great-grandfather used to think he was Poseidon.'

Realizing this new line of enquiry was going to prolong their investigations and their resolution of the case, Markus was irate. He had been convinced that the culprits were the Nazis, with help from others further up, and had focused all his attention on them.

'Yeah, I got it,' he said impatiently, his green eyes flickering with agitation behind his glasses. 'If this illness is as intense as you say and affects people's minds this much, then you're saying it's possible that this Kerem could have killed his father and his son while he thought he was Kronos.'

On the way back to the headquarters, Yıldız had gone over all their hypotheses and scenarios over and over again and discussed them with Toby in some depth.

'That's not what we are saying, although it is a possibility, and one not to be taken lightly either. However, Kerem appears perfectly rational. He did not look like somebody suffering from a psychological disorder. We had more problems trying to control his son Hüseyin.' She turned to her assistant, who was sitting on a stool and watching on. 'What say you, Toby?'

Clearly tired from the day's events, Tobias shook himself awake.

'I agree. In fact, he sounded quite honest. I don't know. He may be hiding something but when it comes to this illness business, when he spoke about it, it sounded genuine. Of course, that is if he's not acting…'

It was not enough to pacify Markus, who had been preparing to wrap up the case as quickly as possible and gain acclaim from his superiors.

'Fair enough. So now what are we supposed to do?' he said, a hard edge creeping into his voice. He pointed to the photographs of Cemal and Orhan on the top row of the panel. 'Two murders have been committed, and a third one is bound to follow…' His gaze slid over to the photograph of Otto Fischer in the right-hand corner. He then turned and looked at his colleagues, almost pleadingly. 'Do you still think our prime suspects are the Nazis? Or have we given up on that possibility?'

Yıldız did not rush to answer.

'I have delivered the threatening letter that was sent to Cemal to the laboratory. The results should be ready soon. If we find Otto or his friends' fingerprints on the letter, it will be much easier for us to reach a decision. And let's not forget this Rudolf Winkelmann, either. If we can establish a connection between Rudolf and Otto, then we will be able to say with a lot more certainty that the Nazis were behind the murders.'

Markus' green eyes darkened in response to Yıldız's caginess.

'We will, yes, but you do realize that this mythology business has given the investigation a strange twist, don't you? And Kerem thinking he is Kronos has added yet another layer of complexity. Talk about throwing petrol onto the flames. What if one of the family is behind the murders? How the hell are we going to get out of this if it is?'

'You're right, boss,' Tobias said, seeing Markus' defeated look. 'If you ask me, both scenarios are plausible. One of the family may well be behind the killings, because we have yet to establish a link between the mythological elements found at the scenes and the Nazis.'

'That's what's confusing me,' Markus said, shaking his head despondently. 'If these murders are the work of some psycho who is obsessed with Zeus, then solving the case will be a piece of cake. It would also be a doddle if we knew for sure that it is some racist whackos who want to terrorize foreigners. But at the moment, I don't know what to think.'

Yıldız got up and walked over to the panel.

'Actually, there are four possibilities, not two,' she said, adding to the uncertainty. She pointed first at the photograph of the drummer and then the archaeologist. 'We're looking at the Nazis and the Ölmez family, but let's not forget Cemal's lover, Alexander Werner, and his cousin, Haluk Ölmez. Alex may be wanting to throw us off his trail. He called me today, saying he was prepared to help us. Apparently, Cemal left him a message on his answering machine. He's going to call me again this evening so let's see what he has to say first. Alex has sufficient motive to kill Cemal.'

Markus was now staring at the picture of the drummer.

'That's all well and good but why would Alex kill an old man who had never harmed him in any way? For what? Remember, both victims are from the Ölmez family. Once we take that into consideration, isn't it a bit pointless for this Alex to go and kill them both?'

'Yes, it does,' Yıldız said. 'But when it comes to affairs of the heart, and in the heat of passion, there is no evil a person will not do to inflict harm on their intended victim. Just look at all those men who kill the children of those women that dare leave them. And then all those bastards who kill their parents-in-law when their wives ask for a divorce. Cemal adored his grandfather Orhan. We may not know enough about Alex's mindset yet but we do know that he does not hesitate to use violence so who's to say Alex did not do this to take revenge on Cemal for leaving him? He told us himself that Cemal may have found a new lover. If so, would he not have wanted to hurt his lover for this betrayal?'

'Then why did he kill Cemal?' Markus' question was eminently reasonable.

'Maybe Cemal found out that Alex had killed his grandfather. Perhaps Alex told Cemal himself, boasted about and gloated to him to add to the pain. And then he decided to finish off the job by getting rid of his boyfriend too.'

Although she was trying to sound persuasive, there was little certainty in Yıldız's voice, something Tobias also noticed.

'I would say it is more likely that Haluk is the killer rather than Alex,' he said. 'The archaeologist has more plausible motive than the drummer for wanting to kill Cemal. Not just that, he also knows mythology and the story behind the Altar of Zeus very well. If the killer wanted to send out a message using the motive of the Olympian Gods, then nobody could have done this better than Haluk. Moreover, relations between him and Cemal had been strained for some time. He said he had stopped seeing Cemal so as to not upset his family. But then again, we can't know if he was telling the truth or not.'

'It's certainly a possibility,' Yıldız nodded, agreeing to an extent. 'We mustn't overlook Haluk. But I feel it would be better if we concentrate on the other two.'

'You're right, boss. Right now, we have four different suspects but I reckon we need to concentrate on Haluk Ölmez and Rudolf Winkelmann. And the sooner we talk to this Winkelmann, the better.' He pointed to a photo that had been taken out of the files and pinned to the board. In the photo, the scar on the left side of Rudolf Winkelmann's stood out and although the photo was not of the highest quality, anybody could see after a quick glance that his left eye was made of glass.

'Agreed,' Yıldız nodded. 'We need to talk to Winkelmann as soon as we can. To be honest, my money is still on the Nazis being the ones that carried out these killings. As Tobias says, we may not have established a link between Pergamon and the Nazis yet but the eagle that was left behind at the scene of the crime is a pretty obvious calling card. And remember what Haluk told us, Toby? That the Altar of Zeus in the Book of Revelations in the Bible is referred to as the Throne of Satan. If you ask me, it is the Nazis themselves using these mythological symbols. We know about the fight between Cemal and Otto, and today we found out about the feud between Rudolf Winkelmann and the Ölmez family. That fight between Cemal and Otto and his boys may not have been a coincidence. For all we know, it was Rudolf that steered Otto and his boys towards Cemal and it is Rudolf that wants to carry out his revenge on the Ölmez family, using this mythological theme. What I'm saying is, if we look at the evidence we have and at the people with whom the deceased had squabbles, everything still points to the Nazis.'

This is what Markus dearly wanted and was actually hoping for, but they needed to be sure.

'Was the eagle on the end of the staff left on the hill today really a Nazi symbol? I mean, what if the killer left it there as a symbol of Zeus?'

'The killer, or killers, have committed two murders and in both cases, they have been meticulous. The manner of the killings and the symbols used have all been consciously chosen. The killers, whoever they are, quite clearly want to be understood.'

'Have you heard of Albert Speer? He was the Nazis' national architect. He was given an important role in the party.'

It was clear to Yıldız from the tension in Markus' voice that he was about to tell them something important. Had Markus actually found a piece of evidence or picked up on a trail that led to the neo-Nazis?

'Yes, I've heard of Albert Speer…. He was one of Hitler's inner circle, wasn't he?'

'Absolutely. One of his closest confidantes. Anyway, Albert Speer began work on the construction of a military academy that would have stood on Teufelsberg, where the body of Orhan Ölmez was found this morning. Technicians who would design and build miracle weapons were going to be trained there. In fact, the faculty building was going to be part of a complex that in turn would be part of Germania, a grand city that was to be built when the Nazis won the Second World War and which was going to be the capital city of the world. Yes, if the Nazis had won the Second World War, they were going to redesign Berlin and rename it Germania, and it is from this new city that the entire world was going to be governed. The academy's faculty building was going to be a part of this mythical city. Eighty per cent of the building had already been completed too but when the Nazis were defeated, it remained uncompleted and was subsequently abandoned. The Allied Forces that occupied Berlin claimed possession of the structure but they did not know what to do with it. They wanted to destroy it but Speer had built such a robust structure that the Allied Forces' explosives had no effect on it. So what they did was they took the rubble from the buildings that had been destroyed by the Allied bombing campaigns and dumped it on top of the Nazis' Academy. A full forty million tonnes. And that is how Berlin's highest point, the Devil's Mountain, came to be.' He turned to address Yıldız. 'So you see, it's not just the eagle on the staff that is a possible reference to the Nazis. The half-finished building under the hill is also a Nazi symbol.'

Markus was intensely focused on the Nazis, which should have pleased Yıldız. Just a few days ago, she had been worried that the murders might be covered up to protect them—a perfectly reasonable concern, given that in previous investigations into murders by racist groups and individuals, neither the state nor the police had performed what could be described as passing with flying colours. But that is not what was happening now. On the contrary, the anti-racists within the force were becoming more visible. She still had her doubts but it was also possible that her doubts were groundless. Markus as well as Tobias were seasoned pros who were dedicated to their work and they were not going to go around locking people up on a whim. Moreover, going against the Nazis in this country was still a risky business. So what Markus was saying made sense but still, her doubts would not be dispelled. Instead, they just kept on growing, making it hard for her to see or think clearly, and she would not be free of this confusion until she had enough evidence. But she could not share these misgivings with her colleagues. There was little point in making Markus, who was already easy to upset, any more apprehensive, so she hid her doubts, smiled agreeably and said, 'You're right, Markus. The Nazis have to be our priority. The first thing we do tomorrow is speak to this Rudolf…'

The fact that the meeting had ended with something resembling a tangible decision and plan of action went some way to allaying Markus' fears.

'So, that's that then. You go and speak to this fellow. Go straight to his business, but act like you're there to get information rather to question him. Don't get me wrong, I'm not trying to tread softly or anything but we don't want to alarm him. I had a quick look at Rudolf Winkelmann's file earlier on. He's got a dark past, it's true, but he has been clean for the last five years. Not even a traffic violation. He runs a large sports complex in the east of Berlin so for all we know, he may have left all the nastiness behind. We have no evidence at hand suggesting that he is involved in any kind of criminal activity or is part of any underground organization.'

Yıldız was not so sure of his new-found innocence.

'Perhaps the circumstances themselves are the proof,' she said sternly. 'If he has reached a certain level with the Nazis, then he won't have to risk exposing himself in street fights. He can just sit quietly in a corner somewhere far from prying eyes and direct the mayhem from there. He may well be using Otto and his friends for the rough stuff.'

Markus grinned.

'Well, if we can prove it, then we will have covered some serious ground.' He looked at his two officers approvingly. 'Go and talk to this one-eyed Nazi. Let's see what he has to say. Meanwhile, I'll get in touch with the intelligence services and dig around a bit deeper to see what I can find out about him.'

'Deniz, sweetie, you're only eating the potatoes. Eat some asparagus too. Look, when you dip it in the sauce, it's delicious.'

Yaman had set up a dining table on the balcony and had cooked asparagus for his daughter. He was a good cook, and he used to cook even when his wife was alive. He had learnt his way around a kitchen from a convict friend who had done a long stretch in prison. His white beans with pastrami were legendary. Finger-licking good, as the saying went. Of course, many of the dishes he learnt were evening meals. For most Germans, dinner was a meal known as *Abendbrot*, which was a few slices of bread and butter with cheese and slices of salami, but that had never been enough for this little family from Turkey and after Nilüfer died, Yaman made sure he cooked a full evening meal whenever he could for his little girl rather than punishing her with a bland, tasteless sandwich. He kept this healthy tradition up until Yıldız was old enough to stay out and not have to come home for dinner. But even for Yıldız, her father's food was something she would not give up, especially when white asparagus season came around and the markets were teeming with that delicious vegetable. Yıldız loved asparagus but Deniz, funnily enough, could not stand it.

'Grandad, why don't you make *köfte?*' he griped in flawless German. 'Your *köfte* is much tastier.'

Yaman roared with laughter.

'I'm telling you, this child is going to become a politician. He doesn't outright say he doesn't like asparagus; instead, he tells me my *köfte* is much better.'

Yıldız could not help but laugh too. The balcony was her favourite part of the house and she loved sitting there, whether it was by herself, with her son or the whole family. And this was one of those precious moments. There was a slight breeze in the air, the trees were swaying gently, and a wonderful scent of burnt grass floated up from the earth. Yıldız felt a profound sense of peace and Conzentment. The stresses of the day–the running around, the corpse on Teufelsberg, the Ölmez family's litany of sorrows, the Nazis' murderous machinations–were all left behind. She looked at her son and her father and realized:

this was life. She picked up her glass of rakı and raised it with a smile

'To you. The two most important men in my life.'

Her father also raised his glass and Deniz, seeing his cue, raised his glass of apple juice and clinked it against his mother's.

'Şerefe!' he shouted in Turkish. 'Şerefeeee!'

Yaman immediately replied in kind.

'And *şerefe* to you Deniz, my lad! To you and your mother!'

Mother and father took a sip of *rakı* each while Deniz downed his juice.

'How about eating your asparagus now?' his mother asked with a groan. 'Look, there is still some left on your plate.'

'But I'm full,' he replied. He looked to his grandfather for help but Yaman was having none of it so Deniz looked at his mother instead. 'Mum, really? Do I have to eat it?'

Normally, Yıldız did not pander to such pleading and made sure Deniz ate whatever was on his plate but this evening, for whatever reason, she was feeling lenient.

'Okay, how about this — you eat half that asparagus and then you go to your room and do your homework for tomorrow. Deal?'

Although Deniz was smiling now, the negotiations were still not over.

'Deal. But when I've finished my homework, Grandad has to tell me a story. A Turkish story.'

'Why, of course,' Yaman said, before Yıldız had a chance to object. 'A story about sultans and viziers…'

'It has to have camels too…'

'Why, naturally,' Yaman said solemnly, raising his right hand. 'It will have a caravan of forty camels.'

Scared his mother may change her mind, Deniz wolfed down half his asparagus before jumping off his stool and rushing to his room. His mother and grandfather watched him go.

'He needs a little more discipline,' Yıldız sighed. 'He's really been falling behind in his lessons recently.'

'Well, we also need to make sure we don't put him off school. That would only make things worse.'

Yıldız reached out for some of the feta cheese in the middle of the table.

'He won't. He actually enjoys it when it is structured.'

'Well, his father is German, after all,' Yaman said drily. His daughter looked at him with a carefree look, her cheese still on her fork.

'I'm telling you, if I did not know Franz's parents, I wouldn't believe he was German. He's the most laid-back person I've ever met..'

'Don't complain. You chose him,' Yaman laughed.

Yıldız took a bite of cheese and then, with the serenity of someone that has accepted her mistakes, said, 'That I did. I chose him and then I sent him packing. Back to his freedom and his fun.'

They both raised their *rakı* glasses, which Yaman had had brought over especially from Istanbul.

'To your happiness, my daughter. To yours and Deniz's happiness.' After taking a sip, he noticed the expression on Yıldız's face. 'What is it, sweetie? What's bothering you? You look like you're in pain.'

Yıldız smiled.

'I'm not in pain. It's just that this *rakı* is just a bit strong.'

'Your mother used to drink it straight. She always said water ruined the taste.'

'I remember. Maybe that's why I'm making a face. Because I copied Mum and drank my first *rakı* straight.' She looked at her father with sadness in her eyes. 'I only added water to it when you told me to. Then I started liking it a little. But have to confess that I like wine and beer more than *rakı*.'

Yaman stared at the cloudy white liquid in his glass.

'*Rakı* is part of our culture, my girl. It's not just a drink, it's a way of life. But where it's drunk, how, with what and with whom are all critically important. If you get rid of *rakı*, love and conversation will lose all their allure.'

'Nor will we be able to save the world!'

He knew exactly what she meant.

'Absolutely! You should have seen some of the people I encountered during *rakı* sessions. Legends, those guys were! And the epics they orated. Such style, such verve, such panache! Of course, when it came to action, they weren't quite so adventurous.' He reached out to refill Yıldız's glass, but she placed her right hand on her chest and shook her head.

'That's enough for me. You carry on and enjoy.'

'To life, my girl,' Yaman said, raising his glass. 'To life, which gave me you and Deniz.'

Her father was getting old. Yıldız had begun noticing it this year. He was aging quickly, but she did not want to think about that now. Not tonight. Wanting to chase the thoughts away, she asked, 'How was your day, Dad?'

'I did a little reading around for you. I spent the whole day in the City Library. It really is an amazing place. More importantly, I got my hands on some important information about the stuff we talked about yesterday.' Yıldız frowned. 'I'm talking about the Altar of Pergamon and its connection to the Nazis.' He saw Yıldız stirring with excitement and got up. 'Hold on a sec, I'll tell you everything. I'll go and get my notes.'

He hurried off into his room, while Yıldız watched on with sweet surprise. He soon returned with a notebook with a green cover. He sat down, pushed his glass and plate a little to one side and placed his reading glasses on the end of his nose.

'Yep, it's all here. Yesterday you were asking me if there was any connection between the Nazis and mythology. Well, I did find some stuff. Ah yes, here we are. The German interest in mythology goes back to well before the Nazis, Yıldız, my dear. It was not just Germany. Many other western countries such as England and France began looking for what they thought would be their roots. What they wanted to proclaim to the world was that yes, they were powerful countries but that they also had deep, noble roots that went back a long way. First, they claimed Alexander the Great as one of their own, then ancient Hellenistic culture and then, naturally, the Roman Empire. They wanted to make these two grand cultures, which were a continuation of one other, the foundation of their own civilizations so they began conducting archaeological excavations in places like Italy, Greece, Anatolia, Mesopotamia and North Africa. They chose those areas because they were united by the Mediterranean and a wider Mediterranean culture that had been central to the aforementioned ancient civilizations and had formed their base. It was the philosophy, politics and art of the ancient Mediterranean which shaped the world we live in today. That is why the Germans established an Archaeology Institute in Rome as far back as 1829 and, intensifying their work, founded the Prussian State Institute in 1859. In 1871, this important institute became the German Imperial Archaeology Institute and since 1874, it has been known as the German Archaeological Institute and has conducted its affairs from Berlin.'

It is only until his last sentence that Yıldız finally realized what her father was getting at.

'Why, we were there only today. So the Institute goes back all that way, eh…'

Pleased at her reaction, Yaman went on.

'Yes, but the Institute does not only have a base in Berlin. It has branches in Istanbul, Athens, Cairo, Frankfurt and Madrid too. Basically, the Europeans grasped the importance of archaeology very early on. The English established the British Museum in 1759 and the French opened the Louvre Museum around thirty years later, in 1793. As for us, it was a full hundred years after the French, in 1891, that we finally created the Istanbul Archaeology Museum…' realizing he may be veering off topic, he looked up at his daughter. 'Okay, I'll get to the point. Now, as for the Altar of Zeus goes, work began in Pergamon on 9 September 1878.'

'I know,' Yıldız said, resting her elbows on the table. 'A German by the name of Carl Humann began the first digs.'

'I always used to say you would have made a great researcher. See? You've already started picking up the important pieces of information. It all started with Carl Humann's work. He was also the one to set up links with the German Archaeological Institute. But it was the Institute that ultimately put two and two together and realized what the findings in Pergamon actually were. While the Ottomans were sleepwalking, the Germans had stumbled across the eighth wonder of the ancient world, the Altar of Zeus, a monument whose grandeur is mentioned in numerous ancient texts. As soon as they realized the statues Humann had found were friezes that used to be a part of the Altar, they rolled up their sleeves and got to work. They were so fast that a year later…' He looked down at his notes. 'That's right, exactly a year later, in September 1879, they had already transported two hundred pieces of the Altar. On 28 November 1879, some pieces were shown in Berlin to archaeologists, historians, artists and the press.'

'In what is now the Pergamon Museum?' Yıldız asked. Yaman took off his glasses.

'No, that museum had yet to be built. Work on the construction of the Pergamon Museum began in 1910. The German Archaeological Institute waited for years but the most important thing was that construction work on a museum fitting for something as marvellous as the Altar of Zeus had begun. The work took a long time as the First World War broke out while work was still ongoing, and of course, the war ended in a crushing defeat. Anyway, the building that houses the museum we know today was finally completed in 1930 and opened to the public.' He raised his right index finger. 'Now the year 1930 was a critical year, for that is when the Nazi connection comes in. In the elections that were held in September 1930, the National Socialist German Workers' Party won a huge number of votes, enough to make them second only to the Social Democrat Party. Of course, this success was gained with the backing of major German industrialists like Thyssen, Krupp and Siemens, who realized there were huge profits to be made if Hitler came to power. The Nazis, however, were still not in control.'

Yıldız, who knew her father had a habit of linking most things to politics, felt her mind beginning to wander and asked, 'That's all well and good, Dad, but what does any of this have to do with Altar of Zeus?'

'A lot,' Yaman reassured her. 'Just imagine. A museum opens in 1930, a major event not just for Berlin but for all of Germany. At the same time, the Nazis are beginning their march to power. Three years later, they have gained control of the country and the new leader, a megalomaniac if ever there was one, wants to embark on a series of megaprojects so he calls on the Nazi national architect Albert Speer.'

'Are you talking about Germania?' Yıldız said, remembering the name Albert Speer. 'The Nazi capital that was going to rule the world for a thousand years?'

'No, no, not Germania. I know about that vision of the city. I'm talking about the Altar of Zeus. Or, more precisely, the Zeppelin Tribune that was built based on the design of the Altar. That's right. The Nazis used the Altar brought to Germany from Pergamon as a model for their massive rally grounds.'

Yıldız could barely believe what she was hearing.

'You mean the Nazis were so inspired by the Altar from Pergamon that they built a stadium based on it?'

'They did indeed. In Nuremberg. Hitler himself gave the order for the stadium to be built and Speer used the Altar as his model for the Zeppelin Tribune. I have seen the photographs and you can clearly see the influence and the traces of the Altar on the structure and design of the Zeppelin Tribune.'

Yıldız's throat was dry. She reached for her *rakı* and downed it in one go. What she was hearing was lifting her spirits but she could still not work out why the neo-Nazis had killed Cemal the way they had. She licked the last drops of rakı from her lips.

'So, the Nazis were inspired by the Altar to build the Tribune. But they did not kill anybody there, did they?'

Yaman looked at her in astonishment.

'Seriously? My girl, it was at Nuremberg that the Nazis gave the order to wipe out the Jews. With the help of some creative lighting and 150 strategically placed projectors, Hitler looked almost like a deity, like Zeus himself, when he took to the stage in that stadium and it was there that he stoked the flames of racial hatred in hundreds of thousands of his loyal, fanatical supporters. I'm talking about the Holocaust, Yıldız. The word *holocaust* itself comes from the Greek, meaning 'burnt offering', or 'burnt whole.' Burnt, just like the sacrifices to Zeus, Poseidon, Athena and Apollo… But this time, the creatures that were burnt as offerings to the Gods were actual living humans. So yes, the Zeppelin Tribune is not a stadium but an Altar, a bloody and savage Altar on which humans were sacrificed, and it was on that Altar that Hitler, in his speeches, began the slaughter of six million Jews. Men, women, young, old, it mattered not. They were all thrown into the flames.'

The weird music and the cool breeze blowing all over her body gave her the chills. It was an unfamiliar melody, a scream mixed with a moan, a cry of defiance. There were no words. Just haunting melodies coming from unfamiliar instruments. It was only then that she realized she was in the open. That explained the wind, the cries and the moans. Maybe she was in the clouds or on top of a hill or on a snowy peak, one high enough to let her see the entire globe and all its oceans, land, seas, fields, lakes, rivers, mountains, valleys, forests and deserts. She was sitting on one of the marble steps, staring at the world beneath her feet. She had experienced this feeling before. Not this feeling but this moment, but back then it was not the world beneath her feet but eleven marble steps, all identical to the one she was sitting on at the moment. To her right were colourful statues and reliefs that had been superbly carved by expert hands. The friezes depicted a bloody battle between Giants with huge heads, formidable bodies and snake-like tails on one side and the lords of Olympus, the Gods and Goddesses, on the other. She could almost hear the ringing sound of sword against sword, of steel sinking into flesh and of agonized screams as the Giants' heads were torn from their bodies.

'The Altar,' Yıldız muttered. 'The Altar of Zeus…'

'No,' said a voice that shook the heavens and the earth. 'This is not the Altar at Pergamon. This is my palace in the skies.'

The music stopped, as did the voice. When she turned her head, she saw an eagle with huge wings, a red beak and a jet-black body atop the entablature held up by rows of marble columns. The bird was staring at her the way a hunter stares at the prey it is about to tear to pieces.

'This is the sacred dwelling of the twelve Gods. This is the celestial house in which the fates of you Mortals are written. This is a shrine to valour, to justice and to power. This is a palace of honour.'

Yıldız was overawed. It was the eagle that was talking. It felt like a sick joke but it was real, of that Yıldız had no doubts. She believed what she was seeing, hearing and feeling and the more she believed, the more baffled she became.

'Why so surprised, Mortal?' the mightiest of the birds snarled. 'Even though your puny brain may not be able to comprehend it, a God can take on any form it wishes. Eagle, bull, swan or human, it matters not. I can take on the form of anyone and anything I desire. I can appear as anything I wish and I can become anything I want to be.'

It spread its vast wings and swept down towards Yıldız. She hid her head between her two arms and curled up in fear but there was no need for her to defend herself. The eagle did not sink its talons into her shoulders, or peck and stab at her with its beak. All she felt was a movement of air caused by the fluttering of its wings as it glided harmlessly down towards the top step. As it reached the ground, its appearance began to change and the mighty bird turned into a cloaked and hooded figure holding a staff in its left hand, with Nike, the Goddess of victory, perched on its right. A pair of golden sandals and a dress of the purest white studded with jewels could be seen glimmering under the cloak. Yıldız watched on in horror.

'This is Cemal's painting... You're... You're Zeus. But how is this possible?'

'Nothing is impossible for the Gods,' said the deity under the black cloak. 'The boundaries of your world have no meaning here. The prohibitions that have been put in place for you cannot hinder us; the rules you must obey do not bind us. We are the ones that created those boundaries and prohibitions. We are the ones that wrote those rules. But you... You cannot understand this, because your minds are shallow, your emotions defective and your spirits weak.'

With his staff, he pointed to the clouds surrounding the palace.

'Look, Mortal! Look, with those eyes of yours that will soon become one with the earth!'

The reliefs on the wall dissolved. The interplay of clouds and light gave way to a multicoloured infinity stretching away in front of them. Before Yıldız could work out what was happening, the figure turned to her and said, 'Is it not flawless? Is it not spectacular, wondrous and sublime? It has a purity those of your kind shall never be able to acquire. A beauty you shall never possess, a divine grace you shall never grasp.' He shook his head disdainfully. 'You humans shall never experience such a wondrous miracle because you are cowards and hypocrites, because you are lazy, because the foul blood that flows in your veins shall forever keep you at the basest level. The animal instincts that so easily overwhelm your minds shall always besmirch and befoul your actions. The outrages you commit for a handful of earth, for a piece of meat, for a glass of wine, will erode your wills like rust on iron. You can never overcome evil, you can never reject despotism, you can never challenge the unjust.

'But the Gods are different. For we come from the line of the Titans, from the mighty blood of the first to be created. But we believe in dignity rather than brute force, and in justice and nobility of action. That is why my father Kronos ended the rule of his father Uranus. Because Uranus violated the sacred law. With a scythe, he destroyed his father's power and threw his severed organs into the waters. The earth breathed a sigh of relief, and peace and love ruled over all. However, it was not to last. With each passing day, my father, sitting on his throne, began to resemble Uranus. Worried his fate would be the same as his father's, he swallowed his children one by one, imprisoning my brothers and sisters in his stomach. My grandmother Gaia and my mother Rhea found this barbarity intolerable and as soon as I was born, they saw me as a saviour and began training me in body and mind before I could even crawl.'

The powerful deity opened his arms out in fury. When the tip of his staff touched the clouds, darkness fell and shrouded all. The huge plumes of smoke that looked like red mountains danced and intertwined, red lightning flashed and dark blue thunderbolts coursed through the blackness.

'My father sowed the wind and now he was to reap the whirlwind. I bested Kronos, in a gruelling but fair battle. I did not lay a trap for him, the way he had with his father. Instead, I stepped forward and challenged him. He accepted the challenge and we fought and I threw him to the ground and drove his head into the marble floor. I showed the world, friends and foes, who the true king was, for neither my grandfather nor my father were true kings. Their bodies were flawed and their spirits lacking. One had given in to pride, the other to fear, and both were rapacious. Their minds were unrefined, they were bereft of nobility of feeling and their actions were wild and without restraint. That is why they could not stay on their thrones and why they did not become the sacred protectors of the Titans, the Giants, the Gods and all the creatures of the earth. That is why life produced me, Zeus, to face him down, for I was both bold and of noble bearing, and my body was strong and my spirit sound. I rescued my brothers and my sisters, I loved and revered them, and I protected them. I gave them a place in my palace, I gave them thrones and I let them share in my rule, for they were of the same blood as I, of the same powerful race. They were not like the brutish Titans or the primitive Giants. They were noble from birth, and in the era I was to inaugurate, nobility would be supreme. Our civilization and our rule were to arise from a foundation of intelligence, diligence, virtue, valour and beauty. Wherever there were living beings, an unrivalled new life was to begin. But first, I had to defeat the brutish Titans and show the witless Giants their place.

Purity is what we needed. Purity of body, blood and spirit. We needed to return to ourselves, to our purest state, to our wildest state, to our strongest state. We needed to free ourselves of needless mercy, of meaningless conscience, of pointless compassion. We needed to sever and discard with the keen blade of our ideals anything that stood in our way. We did not have the luxury to feel for others, to be so low of character that we would forgive others their mistakes or to be so helpless as to assist the weak. To help the weak is to sin against nature. We had to leave the powerless to their fates. Those that could not stand had to be left to fall, those that could not fight back had to be eliminated, the cowardly had to be destroyed. We could not allow the indolent to slow life down any further. We needed to be as merciless, as determined and as tenacious as circumstances demanded. We needed to shatter our enemies' ribcages with our steel claws and rip out their hearts...'

The unseen God's voice had taken on a savage timbre and was seething with hatred. A transformation then occurred: the ivory-white dress adorned with jewels under the cloak turned into military fatigues and the golden sandals turned into military boots. Lightning bolts flashed in a metal object where the belt buckle was supposed to be. She squinted to get a better look and then realized what it was. It was a swastika. The cloaked figure atop the marble steps let out a cry, as though affirming his appearance.

'I was going to establish a new world, a new Aryan world. A society comprised of strong and resolute people of high character. A civilization of superior people. The dark ages were to be left behind. Weakness, ugliness, stupidity, laziness and disability were to be erased forever from the face of the Earth. And I was going to destroy all the weak and pitiful creatures that symbolized these failings.'

Yıldız sensed the face hidden in the darkness under the hood had turned towards her. Although she could not see the face, she could feel the deranged eyes staring at her, not that the figure had any desire to conceal its intentions. It waved its staff threateningly at Yıldız. 'Yes, I am talking about you, woman. About you and your vile Asian race. About your useless and poisonous existence, which does nothing but corrupt life. About your ignorance, your cowardice, your mendacity, your deceptions, your filth, your duplicity and your vile inferiority complexes, which you do even have the decency to admit to yourselves.'

Yıldız realized this was it. The end. Such a grandiose speech had to have a bloody denouement. Just to hear the tone of his voice was enough to know death was imminent. Nevertheless, despite knowing this, Yıldız could not move. She wanted to; she wanted to get up and fight and defend herself but she could not. Meanwhile, the man continued to speak, overcome by his own zeal.

'I am talking about a rebirth, not of weaklings like you but of a new world founded by those of noble blood. Of that wonderful final moment when those like you who are born deficient shall be purged from the earth. When your weak soul, housed in that vile body of yours, shall writhe in pain and then be obliterated. In a moment, this ceremony shall begin, and it shall be consecrated with your blood.'

And with that, he raised his staff like a spear. He was summoning his strength to strike Yıldız with it, perhaps through the heart. She was running out of time. If she was to do something, she had to do it now. She gathered her wits and her will. Her plan was to leap up and grab him by the throat while he was momentarily dazzled by the lightning coming out of the tip of his staff but try as she might, she could not move. All she was able to do was let out a cry. A cry only she could hear…

'Yıldız! Yıldız!'

When she opened her eyes, she saw her father standing at her bedside.

'Yıldız, are you okay? You're caked in sweat.'

Panting for breath, she straightened up in bed and looked around, flustered. She calmed down when she realized she was in her bedroom.

'I'm fine. It was just a dream. A bad dream.' She looked apologetically at Yaman. 'Did I scream? Hopefully I didn't wake Deniz up.'

'No, you didn't scream. But your telephone rang.' He was holding up her walkie-talkie. 'Tobias is calling. That's why I'm here.'

Yıldız's breathing was getting back to normal.

'Why didn't he call my mobile?' Her father handed her the device.

'He did but you didn't answer.'

Yıldız remembered. She had switched her mobile to silent while putting Deniz to sleep and had forgotten to switch the sound back on. She took the walkie-talkie.

'Hello? Toby? What's going on?'

'It's Alex,' he said in a tired-sounding voice. 'He's been killed, boss.'

8

Whether you are a father, a king or a God, never stray from the path of justice

Being a father does indeed resemble being a God. Just as a father assumes responsibility for his children, so a God assumes responsibility for all living things, for all living things await governance, from a clutch of grass to the mighty trees, from a simple butterfly to the eagles, the great lords of the skies, from the tiny ant to the terrifying Giants, from the Mortals of earth to the Gods of Olympus. Were I, Zeus, Chief of the Gods, to relinquish my rule over them, chaos would engulf the heavens and the earth. I am the emissary of the divine order. My word is the law itself, the guarantor of life, the protector of existence. If my word were to fail, if my eagle were not to fly high in the skies, if my thunderbolts were not to growl, my lightning not to strike and my rains to not fall, the world would curl up and die like a dry leaf in the abyss. That is why, in my eyes, a God that only shows love to those whom he rules is a weak God, for life is far grander than just love. Grander, deeper and more complex.

Of course, love is necessary. Of course, tenderness, mercy and forbearance are required, but they are not enough. As the boy with the dark eyes that appeared in my dreams said, too much love and compassion will lead people astray. Whether you are a God, a king or a father, the fate of those that rule only with love and mercy is to be ridiculed by those they rule. Responsibility implies the need to be merciless at times. If the verdict to be passed is death, then it must be given, without second thought. Those that do not have the courage and the will to do this can never taste true love and they can have no place, not amongst Titans, Giants, Gods or humans.

Thankfully, I have never been one of those wretches. I have never forgiven sin, error or treason. Even if the one that has committed it is amongst my favourites or is one of my own blood, I have never overlooked such transgressions. Apollo was one. The lord of poetry and music, he was the God of Light, the one with whom I shared my secrets and consulted upon all matters. Even with him, I did not flinch from doing the right thing, even if it meant drowning in agony for me.

Apollo was my own son, born of Leto, the beauty of beauties, and twin to golden-wreathed Artemis. He was born under such trying circumstances, for my own wife Hera, Goddess of marriage and family, had discovered our forbidden love and did not want these golden children to be born. As was her wont, her insolent rage, her fury and her screams brought all of Olympus to its feet. Knowing her nature, the Gods and Goddesses of Olympus ignored her but this only made my jealous wife grow mad with anger, and she forbade Leto from giving birth on earth. Moreover, she imprisoned Eileithyia, the Goddess of childbirth, in her room, for she knew that without Eileithyia, there could be no birth.

The days passed and Leto's belly swelled and her pains increased. My twins were eager to set foot on the earth yet a place could not be found for the delivery for all feared Hera's curse. Eventually, the floating island of Delos opened its arms to my ill-starred lover. It was a dry, famished island, with but one palm tree, under the shade of which Leto lay, carrying her two sacred charges. All the females of Olympus, headed by my sage daughter Athena, were by her side, but Eileithyia was still Hera's captive, and without Hera's consent, my children could not open their eyes unto the world. After exhausting all possibilities, I sent Iris to Hera as an emissary to plead for help. At first, the cruel demoness stamped her feet and obstinately refused. 'I will never allow it,' she hissed. But when she saw the sparkling nine-yard long necklace made of the finest amber and the purest gold Iris had brought her, her heart yielded, for her weakness for such beautiful gifts was as strong as her fury. Freed from Hera's grasp, Eileithyia fled to the island of Delos in time and to Leto, who was writhing in pain under the palm tree.

Under that palm tree, Leto first gave birth to Artemis, and then, with the assistance of the daughter to whom she had just given birth, they delivered Apollo. As this wonderful event was happening, I ordered the sacred swans to circle the island, for I did not trust Hera.

A thousand thanks to fate, sweet Artemis and long-locked Apollo were safely delivered and they joined us with great joy and fanfare on Olympus. Hera eventually, albeit reluctantly, accepted these two beautiful children, and I held them to my chest and breathed in their scents. I knew they were of my blood and of my spirit. And with the sky and the seas and the earth as my witness, I swore always to protect them, just as I had protected my other children. I cherished them both but I must confess, Apollo, with his mind, his intuitions and his abilities, was always beloved to me. He knew the unknowable and he could sense the future; for him, time was not a dark well but a tunnel of light through which he could freely pass into the future and back. Although he may not have been my favoured amongst the many children I sired with the Titanesses, the Goddesses and with earthly women, he was still one of my favourites.

But the day came when my love as a father and my duties as a God clashed, for my beloved son Apollo's beloved son Asclepius would violate the sacred law. My grandson Asclepius was an erudite child. Skilled in the healing of the infirm and in the treatment of wounds, he was able to extend the lives of Mortals. At a young age, he had mastered all the secrets of medicine. Healing temples known as *asklepion* were opened in his name in Epidaurus, Athens, Kos and Pergamon. Had he been Conzent with this and with healing and curing Mortals with the consent of his grandfather, the mightiest of the Gods, then fate may not have presented us with such a stern test. But one of man's worst traits is his greed and his inability to know when to stop. Whether it be riches, fame or love, no matter how much you give them, they are never satisfied, and Asclepius' spirit was corrupted by the blood of his mother, which flowed through his veins. He was a famed and respected healer and yet, like the depraved Prometheus, he decided to challenge the Gods. Healing people was not enough for him; he wanted to make them Immortal. Immortality, however, is a gift reserved for the Gods. None, whether he be Titan, Giant, God or king, can dare to save that weak, pathetic, selfish, greedy, dithering creature known as man from death, and Asclepius, the son of Apollo, my own beautiful son, God of light and art, knew this. But he could not tame his ambition nor control his desire. He may have deceived that two-faced being known as man with lies and false praises. And with the blood he took from snake-haired Medusa's veins, he began to realize his foul dream. One by one, he began resurrecting the dead. Those that had been decapitated on the field of battle two weeks earlier were seen walking the streets of

Pergamon in good health and in fine spirits. Seeing that death had lost its power, the people succumbed to degeneracy. They declared they had no more need for the Gods. They stopped visiting the temples and they stopped offering sacrifices.

Yes, sweet Asclepius, my grandson and son of my beloved Apollo, violated the sacred law and disturbed the delicate balance of the world, and as the lord of all beings, I could not remain silent. Regardless of whether it is my son, my daughter or my grandson, those that contravene the divine law must face the severest punishment, and it must come from my own hand. I am the one to mete out that punishment, and that is what happened. This boy who played with fire I smote with fire from the skies. I destroyed him with scorching thunderbolts in the courtyard of one of his own *asklepion*.

Upon hearing of the death of his son, my son Apollo howled and writhed in fury and agony, as though he had been struck by the thunderbolts himself. Were he able, he would not have hesitated to avenge his son's life by taking mine. I saw it in his eyes and heard it in his cries, but the God of light is no fool. He knew that his father still adored him, and he also knew that the Lord of Olympus cannot be defied. He seethed and fumed. The rage in his heart had to be released and in his anger, he destroyed the Cyclopes, the creators of the thunderbolts, even though those poor creatures had committed no sin. Indeed, without the Cyclopes, we would not have been able to defeat the Titans. Apollo's act was unforgivable.

When I heard the news in Olympus of what had transpired below, I leapt off my throne, descended to earth and captured Apollo. I was as furious as he was, if not more. I hoisted him onto my shoulders and was about to sentence him to the same punishment I had meted out to my father and fling him into Tartarus when Leto, the sweet love of my heart, my moonlight, stopped me. Her sweet voice, gentle touch and seductive glances softened my heart and dampened my fury. But Apollo had flouted my law and he could not go unpunished and so I presented him as a slave to King Admetos so that he would learn to respect and uphold the sacred law. He was to toil under the command of this Mortal for at least one year. If he did not comply with the punishment and comport himself with the requisite humility, the sentence was to be extended; if he dared defy me, the punishment would be greater still.

As I said before, love, mercy, compassion and tolerance are required but a God, like a king and even a father, cannot rule with these alone. Duty at times necessitates ruthlessness, punishment and violence. Even if the penalty to be given is death, it must be handed down without hesitation. Whether you are a father, a king or a God, one must never stray from the path of justice. One must never favour one's kin over others. The law must be obeyed, and for the sake of harmony, the life of a son, a daughter or a grandchild must, if necessary, be taken. For without the law, there is no throne. Without the law, there is no crown. Without the law, there is no palace…

Chapter Eight

When they met by the canal, the June sun had begun warming the desolate streets of Treptow. Tobias was smoking a cigarette under the trees, whose leaves were still damp with dew, watching the still waters. When he saw his boss approaching munching on a pretzel, he straightened up.

'You're smoking again, Toby,' Yıldız said teasingly. 'How the hell can you enjoy that poison first thing in the morning?'

'And a good morning to you too, boss,' Toby said cheerfully before pointing with the cigarette to the canal. 'Look. Look at how beautiful they are on the water.'

Yıldız turned and saw two snow white swans gliding gracefully along the dark green water. They stopped in front of Tobias and stared at him, hoping he may throw them a bite to eat.

'If only we had some bread to give them.'

He is so soft at heart, Yıldız thought. She gave him the last piece of her *brezel*, which had earned the name 'German simit' amongst the Turks of the city.

'Here, I bought these from the bakery on the corner on the way here. You can feed your swans now.'

Tobias' face lit up like a child's and, cigarette balanced between his lips, he took the *brezel* and began throwing the crumbs to the swans. Before taking a last drag of his cigarette, Tobias jerked his head towards an ugly building by the canal.

'The drummer lived in that building over there. Shall we go up?'

'When did you get here?' Yıldız asked. She had already started walking. Tobias fell in behind her, blowing a huge cloud of smoke out of his mouth.

'Just now. I waited for you so we could go up together. The crew that responded to the call are still up there. The Crime Scene boys are on their way.' He threw the butt he had stubbed out on the sole of his shoe into the trash can at the entrance of the apartment. 'We should try and wrap things up here before Kurti arrives, otherwise he's going to give us another scolding.'

He was right. They quickened their pace as they climbed the steps at the entrance. Tobias pressed the topmost bell on the panel by the front door. While waiting to be let in, they tested the door. It did not show any signs of being forced open. The killer seemed to have gained access without any difficulty. Perhaps the victim had personally let him or her in.

'Did Alex call you, boss? Yesterday on the phone he told you he was going to call you. Remember?'

He was referring to the issue that Yıldız had overlooked. If only she had taken Alex more seriously when he had told her about Cemal's message on the answering machine.

'No, he didn't,' she replied. A metal click rang out in the morning silence as they were buzzed in. 'I didn't call him back either. I did not take him that seriously, if truth be told. My mistake.'

Tobias did not answer immediately but shoved the door open and stepped aside to make way for Yıldız.

'I didn't take him seriously either, boss. He was hardly the type to take seriously anyway.'

'Well, our killer clearly didn't share that sentiment,' Yıldız said, slipping into the building. 'They must have taken him pretty seriously because they have had no qualms about getting rid of him.'

Following Yildiz into the building, Tobias asked, 'You reckon this guy Alex was killed because of what he was going to tell you?'

'Hard to say at the moment, Toby. Maybe he was on the killers' list all along. There may be some important clues about the killer in the message on the answering machine.'

'But how would the killer know that?'

'I don't know. Maybe Alex told him. Maybe he called the killer instead of calling me back.'

Tobias' grey eyes lit up.

'Blackmail, you reckon?'

'Anything is possible,' Yıldız said, weary of the constant speculation. 'Let's take a look at this answering machine first and then we'll know.'

As they made their way to the lift, they could hear sounds stirring in the apartment. The residents had started waking up.

'Who found the body?' Yıldız asked.

'Some of our lads,' Tobias replied in a lowered voice. 'The night patrol guys. The downstairs neighbours complained about the noise. Apparently, Alex was always making a racket but the neighbours were usually too afraid to confront him because he was such a truculent guy but when the music was still blaring out at five in the morning, the neighbours couldn't take it anymore and called the police. When the squad arrived, the door was open so they walked in. Found the body lying there. Just like Cemal's'.

Yıldız pressed the call button on the lift panel.

'Was it music about Zeus again?'

'I don't know about that but seeing as it has got the whole apartment up in arms, something very strange must be waiting for us up there.'

The lift sped them up to Alex's floor. A baby-faced uniformed officer greeted them when they stepped out. The dismay in his large eyes was still evident.

'Inside,' he gulped. 'But let me warn you now, it's a horror show in there.'

'Thanks,' Tobias said, slapping him affectionately on the shoulder. Yıldız reckoned the officer may have thrown up upon seeing the body. The officer standing by the wooden door of the flat looked calmer. He was of medium build and had a nose like a boxer's, crooked and out of shape.

'Becker?' he asked, in a high-pitched voice that was at odds with his muscular physique. 'We spoke on the phone, didn't we?'

'You spoke with me, yes,' Tobias said, nodding his head. 'What's going on?'

The officer screwed up his face.

'It's a damn nightmare in there. A real mess. Like you said, we didn't touch anything. We just turned the music down because it was driving the neighbours round the bend. And it was Godawful music too.' He took a quick peep inside. 'The victim is in a real state though. The killer has torn the guy's face to pieces. Blood all over the place. I may be wrong but I think he peeled the skin off the guy's face.' He stepped aside. 'You had better see it with your own eyes.'

Yıldız walked between the two men and entered the flat. As soon as she had taken a step inside, that familiar smell hit her. Even if the officer at the door with the bent nose had not told her a thing, the smell alone would have told her that she was at the scene of a murder. There was a tiny hallway in front of her with a large wooden shelf on the wall to the right and a landline telephone on the shelf. She took out some plastic gloves from her leather jacket and put them on. She walked up to the answering machine under the telephone and pressed the 'Listen to messages' button. There was no sound. She lifted her head and saw Tobias watching her intently.

'The messages have been erased,' she murmured. 'It looks like your blackmail theory may be right.'

'Straight ahead,' the officer at the door said behind them. 'Straight ahead down the hall behind that door. In the lounge.'

The closer they got, the worse the smell became. When they reached the door, they stopped. Yıldız examined the floor, the wood and the glass. Nothing unusual stood out. She pushed the door open with her index finger, revealing a large, well-lit lounge. She took a couple of steps forward and saw it. Just like Cemal, the body was lying face up in a pool of blood by the wall but instead of a face, there was just a bloody piece of meat. She took a few steps forward and then saw the true scale of the horror. The face had been so violently mutilated that it was impossible to identify the victim as Alex.

'His face really has been flayed,' Tobias whispered in dismay. 'The poor guy has been stuck like a pig.'

Yıldız did not even hear him for she was too busy examining Alex's lifeless body. His heart had not been removed but there was a huge dagger sticking out of the left side of his body near his heart. After taking a few more steps, she saw the swastika on the hilt of the dagger. It was possible that this was the dagger Cemal stole from Otto during their fight. If so, then the killers were being very generous. But why? Maybe the killer had no more use for the dagger now. Perhaps firearms would be used in their murders henceforth. Pistols, rifles, automatic rifles, maybe even explosives.

'What's this picture?' Tobias said, bringing her out of her speculations. She lifted her head and saw the picture on the wall. A creature that looked like a goat, with huge ears and two horns sticking out of its head but with a human upper body, was leaning against a tree playing the flute.

'What's this? The Devil plays the flute now, does he?' Tobias asked, staring in bemusement at the creature's horns, tail and furry legs.

'It's not the Devil. It's a satyr.'

'What the hell is a satyr?'

She ignored his question because she was too focused on the picture.

'Isn't this Alex?' She took a step forward. 'What say you, Toby? Doesn't his face look like Alex's?'

'It does. It really does... You think Cemal drew this picture?'

'He may have. Here, look. There is some writing under the painting.'

They both stepped forward up to the wall and Tobias read the text out.

'*Those that challenge the Gods shall suffer the consequences.*' He bent over to get a closer look. 'This was written recently, boss. After the murder.'

Yıldız was not surprised. These ritualized murders were clearly going to continue. But there had been no writing in the murder of Orhan Ölmez, or at least none had been found. She cast her mind back to Teufelsberg. No, they would definitely have found writing had there been some. Why had the ritual carried out in the last two murders not been performed in this one? It was an important question, one whose answer was no doubt hidden in a detail somewhere. But now was not the time. She pushed the thoughts to one side and concentrated on the picture on the wall. Alex had been painted as a satyr, lost in his music. The ugliness of his facial features had a strange melancholy as he played the flute, almost making the creature look beautiful, as it leant against a pine tree. There were other figures in the background too. Yıldız noticed a tall, slender, handsome man holding a lyre, his long black curls lit up by blue light. He looked so impressive and so poised, that Yıldız thought it had to be a God. '*Those that challenge the Gods shall suffer the consequences*,' she said to herself. Is this the God being referred to in the writing? Just behind that figure was a group of about ten people, nine of them women. The only man in the group wore a crown on his head but he also had long straight ears, like a donkey's. She tried to remember who it was but could not.

'Who was that king with donkey ears?' she called out to her assistant. 'You know, the one that suffered the wrath of the Gods.'

Tobias was busy examining the body and was caught off guard.

'Sorry, what was that boss?'

She gestured to his pocket.

'Ask the smartphone, Toby. Who was the king with the donkey ears?'

Tobias did not understand but did as instructed and typed the request into Google's search engine.

'It was King Midas,' he said, oblivious to the detail in the picture and therefore still unsure as to why he had looked it up. 'Why? What happened? What's the connection?'

Yıldız pointed to the picture.

'If you look at the painting, you'll see that Cemal has painted a scene from legend. A mythological tale, perhaps.' She stopped to ponder what she was seeing and then asked Tobias to read out what he had found online about King Midas.

'Very well. A great number of legends surround King Midas, the king of Phrygia, the most famous being his punishment by Apollo. Upon angering the God during a musical Conzest, his ears were turned into those of a donkey's as punishment.'

'Apollo,' Yıldız said, still looking at the painting. 'Of course! The God playing the lyre is Apollo.'

'Hold on a second, boss,' Tobias said, looking at his telephone's screen. 'There is a picture here. What do you call these creatures again?'

'A satyr. Why?'

'Well, this rather handsome-looking God is peeling the skin of your satyr's face.' He held the screen up to show Yıldız. 'See? He has hung the goat up on a tree and is slicing the skin away.'

The picture on the screen was small and a little faded but the satyr on the tree and Apollo peeling the skin off his face with a knife could still be clearly made out.

'So, our killer has made a reference to mythology once again. Read some more, Toby. Let's see what this story was about.'

'It's a bit long…'

'That's okay. Unless we know the story, we won't be able to work out the killer's aims. Go ahead, read some more…'

Toby brought the phone a little closer to his face and began.

'Okay, here goes. Midas, King of Phrygia, had his ears stretched out and deformed by Apollo. This may be seen as a terrible punishment but when compared to what happened to Marsyas, Apollo's opponent in the same musical Conzest, it may be considered fairly mild. It is actually a satyr named Marsyas who is at the heart of this story. Marsyas spends his days wandering through the woods and the meadows, eating, drinking, making merry and chasing the nymphs of the woods. One day, he finds a flute in the forest and without a second thought, he picks it up and begins playing. The melodies that come out of the flute are so beautiful, Marsyas falls in love with the music and he claims the instrument as his own. He does not stop to think who has made it or why he does not discard it, for such subtle thoughts are not in his nature. For Marsyas, all that matters are love and pleasure.

'However, that flute has been made by none other than the Goddess Athena, daughter of Zeus. She created it from a stag bone and after making the enchanted instrument, she held a musical banquet for the Gods of Olympus. All the Gods, Zeus most of all, were delighted by her recital at the banquet, but Hera and Aphrodite, Athena's eternal rivals, turned up their noses and mocked her by saying, "You look so ugly while you play that flute; your face becomes contorted and you look ridiculous." Athena was stunned by what the two Goddesses said and so she quietly comes down from Olympus to the land of Phrygia and there, by a pure and still lake, she plays her flute and looks at her reflection in the water. When she sees that the two Goddesses were right and that her cheeks puff out while she is playing giving her an ugly expression, she throws the flute away. Not Conzent with that, she also places an eternal curse on the flute and on anyone that finds it and plays it.

'This is the cursed flute that Marsyas finds. Even if he had known about the curse, he would have still picked it up and played it, because a life without music, dance, love and pleasure has no meaning for a satyr. He plays his instrument throughout the forest and soon begins to draw the attention of everyone there; beast, nymph and man. As the flute creates ever more beautiful melodies, so Marsyas' reputation as an enchanted musician grows. The compliments and the praises go to his head and he begins to lose what little common sense he already had. Bursting with vain conceit, he begins to boast, amongst the people, at banquets held by nobles and even in the presence of the kings, that he is the greatest musician alive and that even the music borne of Apollo's lyre cannot compete with his melodies. Naturally, it is not long before these outrageous claims reach the ears of the God himself and a furious Apollo gives the command for a music Conzest to be held. Poor, unknowing

Marsyas haughtily accepts the invitation to the competition. A jury is quickly formed, consisting of the nine Muses, who were the daughters of Zeus, and King Midas. Eventually, the day of the Conzest dawns and the two Conzestants emerge. They begin to show off their skills and play music of outstanding beauty, Marsyas with his flute and Apollo with his lyre. All eyes then turn to the jury. The nine beautiful Muses choose Apollo, but King Midas objects to their choice and says, "You are all biased, for you are all the children of Zeus and are therefore helping each other." Apollo is incensed but hides his anger and replies, "Very well then. I have a suggestion. Let us turn our instruments upside down and play." Marsyas should reject the proposal but he is too blind to see and says, "Let it be, O Mighty Apollo. I shall defeat you in any manner." Apollo turns his lyre upside down and plays equally beautiful music, but when Marsyas turns his flute upside down, no sound comes out.

'As the winner of the Conzest, Apollo first turns to Midas and says, "You do not hear well. Perhaps if I enlarge your ears, you may hear better," and gives him the ears of a donkey. He then turns and glares in cold fury at Marsyas and says, "Those that challenge the Gods shall suffer the consequences." He then hangs him from a pine tree and flays him.

'Damn, these Greek Gods are just as brutal as humans,' Tobias said, after he had finished reading.

'Because they were created by humans. Whatever savagery and cruelty they had inside them, they ascribed to the Gods they created. But getting back to our investigation; things are a little clearer now. The killer sees himself as Apollo and saw Alex as Marsyas.'

'But Cemal did the same before the killer, boss. He was the one that drew Alex's face on a flute-playing satyr,' Tobias said, calmly putting his phone back in his pocket. His gaze slid down to the corpse. 'But Alex here was a drummer, not a flutist. Hold on. That reminds me. Why don't we give this music that drove the neighbours mad a listen?' He scanned the room and soon found what he was looking for. The music player was on a wooden table in the corner. He walked over to it and pressed the play button. A ghastly sound filled the room. Yıldız could only take fifteen seconds of the cacophony.

'For God's sake, turn it off! What the hell was that?'

Tobias' grey eyes lit up.

'*Raining Blood*,' he grinned. 'The original is by Slayer. This is a cover version, but with flute. Doesn't work at all! What a bloody racket!'

'If you ask me, the cover was done by our man here,' Yıldız said, pointing to the flute hanging on the wall to the right. 'It seems your drummer here didn't just play the drums.'

'And that's why the killer flayed Alex's face? Because he ruined one song?' Tobias asked incredulously.

'No, I don't think this butchery has anything to do with music.' She pointed to the dagger plunged in Alex's heart and, more specifically, to the swastika on its hilt. 'It has more to do with this. They want to create a wave of terror with these killings. A series of horrors that will be talked and written about for days on end on television and in the newspapers. They want to create a climate of fear that will terrify the foreigners and immigrants in Germany.' She turned around and faced Tobias. 'Do you happen to know the lyrics to the song?'

'Not that well, and not by heart, no. Let me look them up.' He tapped away on his mobile phone until he found what he was looking for. He tapped the screen a few more times. The song's harsh, abrasive melody erupted into the room, followed by the singer's dark, rasping vocals. But it was the words that Yıldız found even more chilling:

Raining blood from a lacerated sky / Bleeding its horror / Creating my structure / Now I shall reign in blood.

Any further postponing of the visit risked causing harm to the investigation so as soon as they handed over the top floor flat in that old building in Treptow and its dead resident to a very nervous Kurt and his CSI crew, they headed straight for Neukölln. They were certain now that the killer in this chain of murders was operating according to a mythological motif. Although they did not know exactly why, they knew that this grisly sequence of events had been started by Cemal and his fascination with the friezes and statues on the Altar of Zeus. Perhaps more concrete evidence of the link between mythology and the Nazis was concealed somewhere in the sketches and drawings in the studio in Cemal's flat. The swastika on the hilt of the knife sticking out of Alex's chest may have represented new evidence that would allow them to press charges against the Nazis but they still needed more.

By the time they pulled up in front of Cemal's apartment, the sun was high up in the sky. Before entering, they had a look around the garden through the tight fence. The randomness of the two metal stools, the wooden table and the dozen or so tins of paint lying around on the dried grass under an old acacia tree and a healthy poplar tree seemed to suggest that Cemal did not take much of an interest in this place. Tobias pulled out a packet of cigarettes while they were examining the garden.

'Smoke it later,' Yıldız said. 'Let's get this over with first.'

She sounded too stern for Tobias to object. They slipped under the yellow police tape in the doorway and entered the premises. They were both struck by an overpowering smell again but this time it was not dried blood but the musky smell of the paint and furniture in a house that had not been aired in days. They went into the room in which they had found

Cemal's body. As soon as they walked in, Yıldız noticed the dark bloodstain on the wall. When she looked up, she saw the painting of Zeus. The light coming in through the window seemed to be heading straight for the God's face, and his golden hair and beard glimmered in the sun. The painting looked even more magnificent in the sunlight. Cemal had painted him from such an angle that the deity's piercing black eyes were constantly on the observer.

'Cemal really has drawn himself here,' Tobias whispered. 'I mean, I don't know much about these things but the resemblance is uncanny. How the hell did we miss it that night?'

Yıldız had heard him but she was too busy looking at the sentence the killer had written under the painting.

'*Those that defied me shall remain accursed and shall be cast into the flames to writhe in agony.*' She read it aloud, enunciating each word clearly and carefully. After pondering it for some time, she began to see the link between the words and the latest chain of events. 'So, Cemal defied Zeus?'

Although Kurt had taken nearly everything back to the lab for analysis, including the computer, Tobias still checked the desk and, thinking Yıldız was asking him, shrugged his shoulders and laughed.

'I know. It's stupid, right, boss? If Zeus is Cemal, then that means he defied himself and was killed by... himself?'

The paradox inadvertently articulated by Tobias' word games triggered another possibility in Yıldız's mind.

'But what if it is someone else that thinks they are the King of the Gods and this person was upset about Cemal's latest project? Especially when Cemal painted himself as Zeus.'

'You mean Hüseyin?' Tobias said, walking away from the desk back towards his chief. Yıldız had not actually been thinking of anybody specific but Tobias' guess made sense.

'True, Hüseyin would have been one of the people disturbed by Cemal painting himself as Zeus. Seeing as their father thought he was Kronos, one of their sons had to be Zeus, and even if Cemal did not see himself as such, he still painted Zeus with his face for this project. If Hüseyin really did, or still does, see himself as Zeus, then he would not hesitate to kill his own brother, whom he did not like anyway. But then why would he kill his grandfather? Because according to the myths, it was not Zeus that deposed Uranus but Kronos. Taking Kerem's condition into consideration, Orhan Ölmez's son Kerem should have killed him, not his grandson Hüseyin. And by the same chronology, Huseyin should have killed his father, Kronos. But we both saw for ourselves that father and son get on very well.'

'And there would be no point in murdering Alex either,' Tobias said, also struggling with the problem. Yıldız tried to remember what the killer had written at the scene of the murder from a few hours earlier.

'What was written next to Alex's body?' she asked.

'*Those that challenge the Gods shall suffer the consequences,*' Tobias said, articulating each word carefully. 'It's a warning from the Gods. But like you say, boss, it doesn't match chronologically.'

'Our drummer's death has nothing to do with the chronology,' Yıldız said, getting ready to leave the room. 'Alex was probably killed because he stumbled upon important information concerning the identity of the killer. Most probably, there was a clue about the killer's identity in the message he left on Cemal's answerphone. Somehow the killer found out, or perhaps Alex inadvertently told him, and in doing so, he signed his own death warrant. The killer needed to get rid of Alex but he also prepared a scene replete with mythological motifs, just like in the other murders, to mislead us. The decoration was already there in the flat and he or she killed Alex in front of one of Cemal's paintings and then wrote his message on the wall.' She glanced around the room one more time. 'Let's go and have a look at that workshop again and those paintings.'

Falling in behind his boss, Tobias asked, 'And where do the Nazis fit in all this?'

Yıldız stopped and turned to look at her assistant.

'That is still a mystery I have yet to work out but there has to be an explanation. The Nazis sowed the seeds of the Holocaust, which they called the "Final Solution for the Jewish Problem", in Nuremberg in 1935, and the Zeppelin Tribune in that city was built by Albert Speer on Hitler's personal orders. The fact that the design of the stadium was inspired by an Altar cannot be attributed simply to Speer's admiration for Hellenistic architecture. The Zeppelin Tribune was not a stadium but an Altar, one on which Jewish blood was offered to the Nazis. However, the people that urgently need to be eliminated for the Nazis now are not Jews but immigrants. Of course, that does not mean that they have rejected their anti-Semitism, but the Jewish population of Germany now is so tiny as to be negligible, whereas immigrants, especially Turks, are everywhere. It is therefore the Turks and other immigrants who are now the Nazis' targets. We need to see these killings as sacrifices to the Nazis' high racial ideals. We do not have the whole picture at the moment because they have not actually accomplished anything yet but if you ask me, this is the goal. That is also why there have been chronological deviations in the murders.'

It was bewildering but not unreasonable. Tobias provided the missing piece.

'If this fellow Rudolf is in charge of the Nazis, then you're saying he started with his first target, his old enemy Hüseyin, the guy blinded him in one eye?'

'Definitely,' Yıldız said, nodding her head. 'But we need to make sure there isn't some madman who thinks he is Zeus behind these murders.' A flicker of doubt passed over Yıldız's eyes. 'Yes, I'm afraid that is still a possibility, Toby. That is why we need to get a real grasp of Cemal's project. And we also need to find out if anyone in the family objected to it.' She smiled before turning around. 'Basically, our business with Zeus is not over.'

'So what happened to Zeus, boss? I mean in the myths. Did one of his sons also defeat him?'

'I don't think so. But I do know that he was known as Jupiter in the Roman Empire. It was the same God but the name changed. Then Christianity became the official language of the Roman Empire. When I say then, it wasn't overnight. It took hundreds of years. Jupiter gave way to the Father, the Son and the Holy Spirit.'

Tobias looked at Yıldız to make sure she wasn't joking. No, she was deadly serious. Yıldız noticed his quizzical look.

'Do you have any religious beliefs, Toby?'

He thought about it for a few seconds. before answering.

'I have a conscience. That is what my father used to say when people asked him if he was an atheist or not. Years later, I began thinking like him. But I'm serious about it. I don't care what you believe in. What matters is how conscientious you are.'

It was an evasive answer but Yıldız could see his discomfort and so did not press him any further.

'You're absolutely right. I didn't mean to be disparaging of any faith, anyway. But I think Zeus, or Jupiter, as he was later known, was the last truly powerful pagan God before Christianity.'

'In that case,' Tobias said with a relieved-looking smile, 'Let us move ahead to the studio in which the last pagan God's story is being told.'

Again, when they opened the wooden door, they were struck by the familiar smell of paint and paint stripper. The sunlight was trying to sneak in through the door and the wide windows that looked out onto the garden but the thick curtains blocked its way. Tobias walked over to the windows and opened the curtains, letting the light flood in. The studio looked much bigger in the sunlight, as far as Yıldız could make out. Piles of boxes on the huge table in the centre of the room, sketches pinned haphazardly to the wall, tins of paint in the corner, painting materials... She saw a large easel in front of the wall facing the window. On the easel was the outline of a man's face, the features yet to be filled in. From a distance, it was hard to make out who it was but then she noticed the three sketches pinned to the wall, just as they had been when they first came here. Three bearded men... She did not recognize them but she could guess who they were. She took a few steps closer and narrowed her eyes to get a better look. Yes, it was just as she had guessed: grandfather, son and grandson. Uranus, Kronos and Zeus. Orhan, Kerem and Cemal.

'It's better depicted here,' Tobias said. 'I'd be jealous too if I were Hüseyin. I'm the oldest son but it is my younger brother who declares himself Zeus.'

'But Zeus *was* the youngest son.'

Tobias stared at the Gods with human faces in the picture more carefully.

'Well, that does change things. But it still wouldn't sit well with me.' He narrowed his eyes too and began looking around at the other pictures on the wall. 'Speaking of which, where is Hüseyin? Which God has he been painted as?'

Yıldız was wondering the same. She looked not at the pictures on the wall but at the one on the easel. In the foreground in the picture was a strong, powerful man. He had to be a God of some sort. In the background was the old city of Pergamon, with the Altar of Zeus, the Temple of Athena, the Temple of Dionysus and the vertigo-inducing theatre. Looking at the face of the figure in the foreground more carefully, she finally worked out who it was: it was Haluk. It was actually not that surprising. After all, Haluk was also a member of the Ölmez clan. But the question on Yıldız's mind was, on which mythological figure had Cemal transposed his cousin's face? She looked at and around the sketch hoping to find a note of some kind or some writing but there was nothing.

'Here, come and see who is over here,' she said, calling out to Toby. 'Let me introduce you to an earlier version of the archaeologist Haluk. A much earlier version, in fact. Thousands of years old.'

Tobias walked over and examined the picture.

'That's him alright. That's our archaeologist. I wonder how he took it when he saw it?'

'I don't know. What matters is which mythological figure his face has been given to. What say you? Which God is this? Any ideas?'

Tobias shrugged and held his hands out.

'Like I'm the person to ask. How on earth would I know, boss? I could ask Google if you want, but the figure in the picture doesn't have any specific characteristics. I suppose the best thing to do would be to ask Haluk himself.'

Yıldız looked long and hard at Tobias.

'What if it is Haluk that thinks he is Zeus?' She turned back to face the picture. 'Maybe this mythological figure is not Zeus. Whatever we have surmised and speculated about Hüseyin is just as valid for Haluk. What if it was Haluk that was upset at Cemal for not painting him as Zeus? The guy was an arrogant jerk anyway. You saw for yourself.' As ever,

Tobias did not know what to say. Yıldız continued with her hypothesis. 'Wouldn't you say, Toby? This Pehlivan Efendi who drowned in the Salinos River, the one known as Alman Pehlivan, was grandfather to them all. What I'm saying is, if Kerem's condition is hereditary, then it may also have been passed on to Haluk.'

'Which considerably weakens the Nazi hypothesis.'

There was a strange tone in Toby's voice. Yıldız could not work out if he was happy or sad about that particular possible outcome.

'What's your take on it then?' she asked.

'I don't know, boss. It's hard to say with the little evidence we have at hand.'

'Well, let's keep looking then,' she said, and went back to the picture on the stand. The figure in the picture was half naked. He held neither sword nor shield, nor did he have a crown on his head or a gown covering his body, or any footwear. Who could he be? She looked at the wall behind the easel, where there were a number of other drawings. As she was moving closer to get a better look, Tobias shouted out, startling her.

'I've found him, boss. I've found Hüseyin.'

He was pointing to a picture on the wall.

'See? Here. It's Hüseyin. Holding a spear in one hand and a shield in the other, helmet on his head. He's got a really nasty look in his eyes.'

She recognized Hüseyin's face as she soon as she was close enough to the picture. The body was not as imposing as the one in the picture on the easel but there was no denying who the face under the helmet belonged to.

'Ares,' she said gently. 'So, he has painted his brother as Ares, the God of War.' She smiled. 'Well, hats off to him. He made the right choice.' She scanned the pictures and etchings on the wall showing Gods and Goddesses with muscular physiques and what looked to be Titans and Giants caught up in the heat and fury of battle. However, because neither of the two officers knew all the family members well enough, they did not know who was who.

'Hold on a minute, boss. Isn't this the young lad we saw in the baklava shop?'

Yıldız looked at the painting Tobias was pointing at. It was a picture of a God sporting a winged helmet and wielding a staff with an eagle at one end and two snakes entwined down its length.

'It actually does look like him. Alper was his name, if I remember correctly.' She narrowed her eyes and looked at the painting more carefully. 'So, on which character did Cemal paint young Alper's face?'

Tobias got his phone out and typed 'Greek God with winged helmet.' The answer arrived immediately.

'Hermes. Son of Zeus and Maia. The God of merchants, thieves and gamblers. The messenger of the Gods...' When he had finished reading, he nodded. 'Cemal really has painted all his relatives' faces onto the figures of the Gods. What the hell was going on in his head?' He too stared at the wall as though staring at an intractable problem. 'This family is seriously troubled, boss. They are all head cases. I reckon this Pergamon business has driven them all nuts.'

'I wouldn't be so sure, Toby. Maybe it is this city that has gotten to them. I don't know if it is the Pergamon of thousands of years ago that has disorientated them so severely or the Berlin of today.'

Her telephone rang. It was Markus.

'Hello? Yıldız? Are you there?'

'Hi, Markus. Yes, I'm listening.'

'Good news. We have confirmed Otto's fingerprints on the letter.'

'Excellent. Are his friends' fingerprints on it too?'

'Better than that. A detailed report on Otto Fischer and Rudolf Winkelmann has arrived from the Federal Office for the Protection of the Constitution. The two men know each other. They go back a long way. There are photographs of them together on demonstrations. The photographs were taken by secret service lads.'

'Wow. The Federal Office for the Protection of the Constitution working *against* Nazis…' Yıldız was astonished.

'Policy changed after the NSU murders. Anyway, ask no questions, hear no lies, as they say. From now on, they're going to give us whatever information we need. Or so they say.'

'That's great news! We're in Cemal's flat. It may not be as important as your news but we have found some information that may help us better understand the killer's ritual.'

'Is Tobias with you? Just say yes or no.'

His tone was hushed and guarded. After a short pause, Yıldız answered.

'Yes. Why?'

'There have been some developments. We'll talk about it when you get back. When you do, come to my office. Alone.'

'Very well, Markus,' Yıldız said uneasily. 'As soon as we're done here, we'll head back.'

'No, you need to go to Germania first and speak to Rudolf Winkelmann.'

'Germania?' Yıldız asked, not sure she had heard him right.

'Yes, Germania. It means Germany.'

'I know what it means. But what is this Germania? A bookshop of some kind or what?'

Markus laughed.

'Ha, as if. No, it's not a bookshop, it's a fitness club. Somewhere in Köpenick. The club has been named after the old name for Germany. I'm sending you the address and the photographs of Otto and Rudolf together. Go and check this guy out. See what he has to say. What you, in particular, make of this guy is crucial. We'll have him arrested and bring him in if necessary.'

The Germania Sports Club had been built on land which used to house an old iron foundry and which had been sold for next to nothing after the collapse of the German Democratic Republic. Although it was modest in size, it still boasted state of the art fitness and sports equipment. As they made their way up to the second floor to Rudolf Winkelmann's office, Yıldız even noticed a small ice rink.

Rudolf was nothing like Yıldız had envisioned. He looked younger than in the photographs they had seen at headquarters. After hearing Hüseyin's account of their bloody fight, she had pictured a tough, ugly brute of a man, a scarred and battle-hardened monster, but what she saw was a handsome middle-aged man who was still in great shape, despite his advancing years. Where his left eye should have been was a highly sophisticated and convincing false eye and were it not for the vivacious bright blue of his right eye, it would have been impossible to tell the left eye was made of glass. The scar above his left eyebrow had been expertly covered up, leaving only the hint of a line. Rudolf greeted his two visitors warmly.

'Our doors are always open to German police officers,' he said, extending a hand. Although there was clearly a subtext to these words, which were directed at Yıldız, there was nothing untoward or hostile in his expression or in his behaviour. With the utmost courtesy, he gestured to two leather chairs in front of the wooden desk in his office and invited them to sit. He then told his two security guards, who had the same colour eyes, the same haircut and identical outfits, to wait outside. Aside from the large painting of an eagle looking to its right hanging on the wall behind his desk, nothing hinting at Nazi sympathies caught either officer's attention.

'Would you like some coffee?' he asked, making every effort to appear affable. 'We have our own coffee. We get it from Colombia and roast it ourselves.... To be honest, I am a bit of a coffee addict.' He looked at the Chief Inspector. 'I'm afraid we do not have Turkish coffee otherwise I would have gladly offered you some. Interestingly, the Greeks call it Greek coffee. Either way, we do not have that particular type I'm afraid.'

Here we go, Yıldız thought to herself, but she hid her feelings. Instead, she copied Rudolf and adopted a friendly exterior.

'Thank you but not for us while we are on duty.' She looked up and read out the writing above the eagle in the picture behind him. '*The Germania Sports Club*. Tell me, what exactly do you mean by "Germania"?'

Unaware of her aims, Rudolf looked at her with a quizzical smile, surprised that she did not know.

'It means Germany. Surely you were taught that in school. It is from the Greek.'

'I know what it means, Mister Winkelmann. What I was referring to was your club having the same name as the city Albert Speer was to have built for the Nazis and which was to have become their capital for a thousand years.'

Rudolf now realized the woman sitting in front him was not as slow as he had first assumed. Nevertheless, he managed to keep up the façade of amicability and maintain his smile.

'And there I was wondering how you could not know its meaning. Now, as to your question, I was actually going to call the club Teutonia. Teutonia also means Germany but in Latin... Personally, I would have preferred the Latin but my friends wanted to name the club Germania. Not because they were admirers of Greek but simply to keep alive the ideal that had emerged years earlier. That ideal had nothing to do with Speer, by the way. Speer did not have such broad vision.'

'The idea was Hitler's, was it not?'

'Indeed, it was,' Rudolf said, without hesitation. 'Nowadays, a voluntary amnesia has become the norm amongst us Germans. People are afraid to discuss history. They are ashamed of the past. I, however, am not one of those people. I prefer looking at the past with more courage. One may of course criticize Adolf Hitler but one cannot deny that he was a man of astounding vision.' He stopped, thinking Yildiz would respond, but when there was no response forthcoming he continued. 'The idea of building a world capital known as Germania was of course Hitler's. Chief Architect Albert Speer simply followed the orders he was given. He was trying to actualize this vision to guarantee a long and prosperous future for the German nation. I am not saying Speer was a bad architect, don't get me wrong. I, too, admire his completed works, of which there are, however, few.'

'And do you admire the Zeppelin Tribune?' Yıldız asked, sensing the opportunity. 'The design was based on the Great Altar of Pergamon.'

'Perhaps it would be more appropriate to call it the Altar of Zeus at the Pergamon Museum,' Rudolf said playfully. Yes, when Speer saw the friezes on the walls of the Altar depicting the battle between the Gods and the Giants, he immediately realized that this was a war between two distinct races, between a superior and an inferior people. In my opinion, it was those friezes that inspired him to create that incredible Tribune in Nuremberg. How unfortunate that it was destroyed. However, I don't care what anybody says. For me, the Zeppelin Tribune will always be Speer's masterpiece. It has a majesty worthy of the Gods.'

The conversation was proceeding just as Yıldız had hoped.

'When you say worthy of the Gods, are you by any chance interested in Greek mythology and ancient Greek culture?'

'Of course, I am,' Rudolf answered, unaware of the true purpose of their visit and Yıldız's question. 'I am not only interested in ancient Greece; I also find the Roman Empire fascinating. They are the two greatest civilizations mankind has ever created.'

'This must have contributed to the choice of a Greek word when naming your club.'

For the first time since they had arrived, not that he allowed it to show, Rudolf sensed something was wrong. Why was this Turkish police officer so interested in ancient history?

'Actually, I had never thought about it. Maybe my subconscious came into play when I was choosing the name. However, the main reason we named our club Germania is our deep love and profound reverence for the German nation and our unshakeable faith in this nation and its people. Just think about it. Which other nation on Earth could formulate a one thousand-year plan?' He brought his fingers together under his chin and smiled coldly. 'As Germans, that is our most notable characteristic: planning. A thousand years may be a little over the top but planning is most definitely required for long-term goals. If you want to control the course of history, then you have to make plans for a thousand years, or, indeed, for even longer.'

Tobias was sitting silently in his chair. It was hard to work out if he was watching the man or mulling over what he was saying.

'But that plan was a party's plan, not the German nation's,' Yıldız said. 'In fact, to be more precise, it was a single leader's plan. A plan that ended in catastrophe, because the plan was based on the assumption that the war would be won. Is that not so, Mister Winkelmann?' Rudolf was about to respond, but Yıldız did not let him. 'The Germans' peacetime plans were all accomplished. In peacetime, the impossible was achieved. A devastated country was revitalized and went on to become the most powerful in Europe. But whenever it went to war, it lost, and all the plans that were based on a victorious outcome in the war were ruined. Forget the creation of a world capital; the country could not even preserve its independence. The dreams of a thousand-year Germania were crushed and swept under the rubble of a bombed and broken city.'

There seemed to a be a flicker of anger in Rudolf's right eye. Yıldız was waiting for him to react in anger but he did not.

'You're talking about Teufelsberg. Well, that place should be turned into a monument like the Zeppelin. A monument to Berlin's rebirth from the ashes. My personal opinion is that that place needs to be cleaned up. No matter the cost, the rubble should be gathered up and removed and the academy underneath brought to the surface.' A knowing smile appeared on his lips. 'Who knows, when all that filth is cleaned way, maybe the old dreams will be revived and all the old plans can be put back into action. Losing a battle is of little consequence, Ms Karasu. What matters is winning the war. What is a hundred years, after all, to a man? What matters is securing the next thousand years.' Now that he had given the police a piece of his mind, he could go back to pretending to be a genial host. He tried to smile and hide the unease in his voice but he couldn't. The cat was out of the bag. 'But I assume you have not come here to discuss history with me. How may I be of assistance?'

This is exactly what Yıldız wanted.

'Do you know Otto?' she asked with her usual directness. 'Otto Fischer. He runs a bar in Neukölln.'

Before answering, Rudolf blinked, leant forward over his desk and picked up a pencil from his desk pad. He wrote the name in a notebook on his desk and answered drily.

'No, I do not know anybody by that name. Who is he?'

The battle had begun. Yıldız knew she needed to keep her emotions in check.

'A suspect in a murder case. He may be linked to two murders.'

A look of Conzempt appeared in his right eye as he put the pencil back on the desk and leaned back.

'Somebody dangerous then? Tell me, what business would I have with such a person?'

In lieu of an answer, Yıldız took out her mobile phone, found the photographs that her Chief had just sent and placed the mobile phone on the desk.

'You were together on a number of demonstrations. You were arrested together, you were released together, and there are also photographs of the two of you getting into a minivan that is associated with this sports club together.' Rudolf did not pick up the phone. He simply gave the screen a cursory glance, but Yıldız insisted he take a closer look. 'No, please. Take a good look. If you look more closely, you will see the name "Germania Sports Club" on the side of the van, as well the eagle that is your club's logo. Have a look at the other photographs too, please. You are the one in the lead role, while the supporting actor is Otto Fischer, whom you claim to not know.' She looked at Rudolf with faux-confusion. 'Tell me, Mister Winkelmann, why would you allow somebody you do not know into your minivan?'

The neo-Nazi was unfazed.

'Things were chaotic during that demonstration. Extremely chaotic. There were a lot of people there. We were simply exercising our democratic right to protest. The man in question may have wanted help from us, or he may have been a friend of one of my employees. I wouldn't know. But I most definitely do not know this Otto gentleman.'

'And what if he remembers you?' Tobias asked. Rudolf, without displaying any signs of anxiety, grinned, showing off a set of teeth that were too big for his mouth.

'So what if he does? I forget things sometimes. I may not look like it but I'll be fifty soon, and I have memory probleMs The doctor has prescribed me pills but they do not always work.' He turned to Yıldız and, with more than a hint of insolence in his tone, asked, 'So who did this barman Otto kill then?'

Not only was he lying, he was even going on the offensive. Yıldız was having none of it.

'Do you know someone called Hüseyin? Hüseyin Ölmez?'

Rudolf was visibly stunned. But only for a second. His ironclad self-confidence soon returned.

'Should I?' His voice was beginning to crack. 'Please don't take this personally, Ms Karasu, but I do not really like talking to Turks.'

'You didn't talk to him anyway,' Yıldız said calmly, not showing any emotion. 'You attacked him without saying a word.'

Rudolf swallowed several times and cleared his throat.

'Ah yes, of course. That incident with the 36 Boys of Kreuzberg. We did not attack them. They attacked us. There were just two of us and they outnumbered us quite considerably. See? It's been so many years, I'd even forgotten the guy's name.'

'Twenty-three years, to be exact,' Yıldız said. 'But I do not think you have forgotten Hüseyin Ölmez, Mister Winkelmann. You lost your left eye in that fight. No man would forget the name of the person who caused him to lose one of his eyes. You, for one, would never forget.' She pointed, almost playfully, at

Rudolf's false eye. 'I must say, your surgeon did a wonderful job. He really did fix your face up well.'

Rudolf's right eye flashed with fury.

'Mocking a person's disabilities is most unbecoming,' he said with barely concealed venom. 'Even more so for a lady.'

'Lying to the police is also unbecoming for someone that claims to respect the state and the nation. Why do you deny the fact that you know Otto Fischer? Why do you pretend not to know Hüseyin Ölmez?'

While Yıldız spoke, Rudolf had turned back into the assured businessman.

'I am not denying anything. I really do not know anybody by the name of Otto Fischer, and I have forgotten all about this person known as Hüseyin Ölmez. It has been twenty-three years since that incident. Look, my political views are no secret. I am in love with the German nation and I am willing to sacrifice everything for the future of my people. Yes, I confess, when I was younger I was wild and reckless. And yes, I may have become involved in some unpleasant events, some altercations that I would not approve of today. But I paid the price for them. I am an older, wiser man now, with a business to run, and I try to actualize my political ideals via legitimate political parties.'

Yıldız smiled a dry smile.

'So you're saying you have nothing to do with the National Socialist Underground or with organizations such as Combat 18…'

Rudolf lowered his head, then looked up and shook his head, as though deeply offended.

'As if, Ms Karasu! Terrorists such as the National Socialist Underground and Combat 18 only harm our cause. Our ideals have a much broader scope now and are gaining mass appeal. With each passing day, more and more Germans are beginning to appreciate and adopt their national identity and their national values. Parties that defend the true principles and values of the German people are making ever greater strides.'

Yıldız knew she needed to avoid becoming entangled in a protracted argument on this issue but she could not help it.

'By stoking xenophobia.'

Rudolf was quick to object.

'I don't think so. It is actually your people that are unhappy here and want to go back to their own lands. You live here but your hearts and minds are still in Turkey, and you take a much greater interest in the political affairs of Turkey than those of Germany. If you don't mind me asking, Ms Karasu, which party did you vote for in the last election in Turkey?'

'I did not vote for any party,' Yildiz said sternly. 'I am a German citizen and I do not vote in Turkish elections. There are those that do but I do not find it ethical.'

Rudolf was not convinced.

'You must be joking! The Turks I know are all at each other's throats when it comes to elections in their own country. Turkish political parties spend millions in Germany on their election campaigns. But this is the odd thing: while your people vote for left-wing, green and liberal parties here, they vote for conservative parties in Turkey. What I am trying to say is we, the people defending the values of the German nation, also want you to be happy. You are not happy here. People are happy in their own countries. You Turks, for example, have been friends with us for years. In the last century, we fought side by side and we shed blood together. We fought, we won and we lost shoulder to shoulder. We are basically brothers-in-arms. Our friendship has firm foundations. But ever since you started coming over here in droves, the relationship has turned sour.'

Yıldız managed to force a smile, despite her rising anger.

'Those people did not come here by force. The German government of the time invited the guest workers over due to a chronic labour shortage in the country. The foreigners came and were a great help to the German people in healing their war wounds. Everyone knows this.'

'Fair enough, I accept that,' Rudolf said. He did not look Yıldız in the eye and instead fiddled with the blue stone in the ring on the little finger of his right hand. 'Yes, that is what happened. But the plan was that they would go back to their own countries. That is also what your people assumed was the deal. To fill their suitcases with the deutschmarks they had earned and go back home and settle down. Set up their own business, buy houses, fields, land, whatever. But for some reason, they did not go back. They did not go back, but they did not integrate either. And please do not point to yourself as an example. You are clearly quite different. You openly state that you are a German citizen and you speak flawless German. You are also clearly a fine police officer who carries out her duties diligently and assiduously. But how many Turks in Germany are like you? The majority have not integrated into German society. That is the bare truth. They feel they belong more to Turkey than to Germany. There are people in this city that have lived here for years without learning German. Forget leaving Berlin to explore other cities; there are people that have never left their own neighbourhoods.'

It was all true but Yıldız was ready with her answer.

'And whose fault is that? The people that came here and ended up in the middle of an unknown culture, most of them from the rural backwaters of Turkey, or the government that tried desperately to get rid of them as soon as possible, instead of helping them and educating them?'

Rudolf smirked.

'Let me tell you a story. I have a friend who was a regional manager for the Social Democrat Party. Jochen was his name. Jochen Reuther. We have known each other since we were kids. He used to be a staunch supporter of immigrant rights, to the point that in his work and daily life he would actually discriminate against Germans and favour immigrants and then defend his actions when questioned by claiming it was needed. Anyway, one day, a pipe in his bathroom burst and blood, yes, blood, came pouring in, flooding poor Jochen's house. And do you know why? Because his Muslim neighbour upstairs slaughtered a sheep in his bathroom for the Muslim festival of the sacrifice. The blood had flowed into the pipes and congealed there, blocking them and eventually causing them to burst. After that day, Jochen's views began to change. He soon came to the realisation that these two cultures could not live side by side. The only solution, for the Germans and for the immigrants, was for everybody to live in their own country.'

Yıldız watched in amazement as the man sitting in front of her expressed such callous ideas with such a calm and natural demeanour. 'Everyday fascism is the scariest of them all,' her father often used to say. 'For fascist thoughts to be articulated as commonplace, for them to be believed and defended by everyday folk is more frightening than anything else…' What was worse was people like Rudolf now having the courage to openly defend these opinions. She could feel her anger intensifying, which was not good. A change of subject was needed but she could not pull herself away.

'So all those people that came here sixty years ago and their children who were born here should now just gather up their things and move back, is that what you're saying? Sixty years of work, labour, effort and adapting; in other words, sixty years of life should just be erased at a stroke, is that it?'

'With all your rights preserved and intact, yes,' Rudolf said, nodding his head. Tobias, uncomfortable with what was being said, was beginning to stir, something that had not escaped Rudolf's notice.

'Take you, for example, Mister Becker. You too are from the East, like me. Do not deny it. It's quite obvious. I imagine most of your friends and relatives are unemployed. Unfortunately, yes, the gap between East and West Germany has yet to be eliminated. The damage created by communism has still not been repaired. Tell me, why doesn't the government spend some of the wealth, energy and effort it spends on immigrants on its own people? If it did, the gap between East and West would have easily been resolved.'

Tobias looked on uneasily.

'There are taxes for this in the West, Mister Winkelmann. Everyone that lives in the West pays for the people in the East. But that is not what we are here to discuss. Nor are we here, as you said, to talk about history or politics. We were talking about your fight with Hüseyin Ölmez.'

Rudolf shrugged his shoulders.

'That was twenty-three years ago. Over and done with. Plenty of water has passed under the bridge since then. I am not that Rudolf anymore. But Germany is no longer the country it used to be. It is no longer weak and lost.'

Yıldız was finding it hard to stay calm.

'You're right, Mister Winkelmann, a lot of water has flowed under the bridge in the last twenty-three years. But you know as was well as I do that that fight was not the last. Soon after that altercation, you attacked Hüseyin Ölmez's father too. And please don't pretend to be confused as we have Kerem Ölmez's written statement. Nor are these baseless accusations. The statements and recordings are all on our records. When we call you to the station, we can show you the statements if you like. You also tried to set fire to Kerem Ölmez's house twice after that fight but failed on both attempts.'

Rudolf was scowling now, making the scar on his head stand out.

'Irrelevant details. Minor incidents. I have not denied any of this, so why are you raising these issues now? Enough!'

'If only it were enough,' Yıldız said calmly. 'But unfortunately, there is more. Ten years ago, you stormed the Bergama Baklava shop, which is run by Hüseyin Ölmez. His brother Cemal was there at the time and it seems he gave you quite a beating... Now, you may say this is of no concern of ours but this Otto Fischer, the man you let ride in your minivan, is currently under arrest on suspicion of involvement in Cemal's murder... Moreover, Orhan Ölmez, grandfather to Hüseyin Ölmez, the man you have hated for twenty-three years, was murdered a few days ago. Not just that; Cemal's best friend, the same Cemal that beat you senseless, remember, has also been killed. Evidence suggests your minivan companion Otto Fischer was involved in all three murders.'

Rudolf could not take any more. He jumped to his feet and pushed his seat back in anger.

'That's it! I've had enough. This conversation is over. Don't come here again. If you are going to charge me, then you can come back and formally arrest me. But if you do, I will have my lawyer with me. You can talk to him.'

Yıldız calmly got up, watched by her assistant. Before heading for the door, she looked once more at Rudolf's face, which was contorted with rage.

'We shall indeed talk to your lawyer, Mister Winkelmann,' she said sternly. 'But you may want to have a long, hard chat with him before we do. Because if you are in any way involved in these murders, he is going to have a very hard time saving you.'

'You were rather quiet at Rudolf's?'

Yıldız was driving the Passat and Tobias was eating a ham baguette with lashings of mayonnaise when she asked him the question. He hurriedly swallowed his food before answering.

'I was watching, boss. Observing his behaviour. You already had him cornered and I wanted to see how he would react. I was trying to work out his state of mind.'

She was asking not because of what Markus had said on the phone about Tobias but because Toby really had been quieter than usual at the Germania Sports Club.

'And? Did you work out Rudolf Winkelmann's state of mind?'

There was no insinuation in her tone but Tobias knew he would not be able to brush her question off with a few casual answers. He looked down at his sandwich, took a large sip of coke, wiped the crumbs away from his mouth and began. 'Well, not exactly. But he struck me as genuine. Of course, he was lying when he said he didn't know Hüseyin and Otto. But I'm not talking about that. What I mean is, I believe what he told us about his political beliefs because there are a lot of people like that in my circle too. Reckless and prone to violence in their youth but calmer now that they have matured and have careers. Now, they use more sensible and acceptable methods to accomplish their aims. And anyway, Rudolf didn't bother hiding his political beliefs from us. He was quite open about his admiration for Hitler and his dislike of foreigners.'

Yıldız glanced at him from the corner of her eye.

'And what do you make of him lying about Otto and Hüseyin?'

Coke in one hand and sandwich in the other, Tobias shrugged.

'I can see why he hid the fight with Hüseyin as it is a humiliating incident from his point of view. He got into a fight and he got beaten up. But it was weird how he told us he did not know Otto…'

'And continued to deny knowing him even after we had shown him photographs of the two of them together,' Yıldız added. 'But you're right. He struck me as quite candid. He thinks his people will to come to power via the vote, and if you look at the continuing rise of the far-right parties, you can't blame him. That may be why he thinks violence harms their cause.' She fell silent and stared at the road for some time before continuing. 'Having said that, when exactly did the Hanau attack take place? You know, the one in which nine people were killed, five of them Turks?'

'Last year… Last winter… February, I think. Yes, it was the middle of February.'

'So, around a year and a half ago. And before that, there was the attack on the synagogue in Halle. It was Yom Kippur and a massacre had been planned for the synagogue that day but when the attacker could not get into the building, he opened fire outside, killing two people. If I'm not mistaken, the Halle attack took place a few months before the Hanau shootings.'

'So you're saying the neo-Nazis are willing to use both legal means and violence to get foreigners out of the country?'

'Absolutely,' Yıldız said with a sigh. 'But when they use legal channels, it is not to frighten foreigners into leaving the country but to gain power. Xenophobia is fertile ground for them, one they can exploit to their benefit. Rudolf and his friends are not the type to forego violence completely just because they stand a chance of gaining power by legal means. They have used all available means before and they will continue to do so. You've read about Hitler; you know what he did. He used every available democratic instrument to get to power, and once he was in power, he set about destroying those very same instruments that had helped him become Chancellor. Even then, he did not hesitate to use violence and terror, and he used every dirty trick in the book to defeat and eliminate the opposition.' She watched her assistant as he wavered between taking another bite of his sandwich or not. 'What I'm saying is, yes, despite his supposed seeming openness, Rudolf would not baulk at getting his hands dirty. He has done it before and he is capable of doing it again.'

Tobias did not look so sure.

'Are you sure him and his cronies are being directed by the same people, that they are all of the same mindset? While Rudolf and others like him choose to distance themselves from violence, is it not also possible that other neo-Nazis think that violence is key?'

'Of course, it's possible but it is also a distinct possibility that Rudolf is the man guiding Otto and his boys. The data we have at hand only reinforces this possibility. If it is neo-Nazis carrying out these murders, if there really is such a terror group behind all this, then you can't get a better guy to head it than Rudolf. He has years of accumulated experience, he does not shirk from violence, he is calm, tough and level-headed, and, what's more, he seems to know a lot about ancient Greek culture. Remember what he said about the Altar of Zeus.'

She had put forward so many convincing points that all Tobias could do was agree.

'I agree, boss. And not just the Altar; he knew a lot about Teufelsberg too. What he said about Germania is also worth remembering.'

'And so that is why this Rudolf fellow should stay at the top of our list of suspects, Toby.' She stopped and noticed her assistant was still holding his drink and half-eaten baguette. 'Oh God, I'm sorry, look at me, holding you up like this while you're trying to eat. Go on. Eat up.'

'No worries,' Tobias said, although he was glad to get back to his meal when he saw Yıldız's focus go back to the road. They carried on that way to the station, Yıldız driving and Tobias making the most of his less than spectacular meal.

As soon as they were back at the station, Yıldız was told Kurt had asked for her. They both made their way down to the ground floor, where the CSI divison was located, and found Kurt hunched over his computer tapping away, too busy to even notice his two guests arrive.

'What's that you're writing, Kurt? A love letter?'

He looked up over his glasses and saw his two colleagues standing in front of him. Without bothering to reply, he opened the bottom drawer of his desk and took out a metal-coloured flash drive.

'There is a video on here. I got it from the computer in Alex Werner's flat this morning. I hope you find it interesting.'

There was no enthusiasm in his voice, just the bored tone of a man doing his job. He handed the flash drive over and then went back to his work on the computer. Yıldız laughed.

'And a good day to you too, Kurt.'

He was already lost in his writing and did not even give them a cursory wave of the hand, not that Yıldız or Toby minded for they were too curious as to what was on the flash drive. They picked up two coffees from the drinks machine in the corridor, went over to Yıldız's computer and inserted the flash drive. It opened without any hiccups, and a folder with last year's date on it emerged on the screen. They clicked on the icon. A photo of a plain appeared on the screen. The soil was brown and the lie of the land a little uneven but it was still a fertile plain. The word 'Pergamon', written in slapdash purple lettering, appeared, descended slowly over the image and then faded away. The camera then began roaming, zooming in on yellow fields, the odd walnut tree, green vines bearing plump grapes, and then over a dry riverbed towards a hill in the distance, on the peak of which gleamed a series of white marble columns. When the camera stopped, the ruins of the ancient city could be seen in the background. A male voice, in German, said, 'Hello. This is my town. Pergamon.'

They had not heard the voice before. The camera angle changed, showing the speaker. He was a handsome man with a light beard and curly hair that reminded both officers of the painting of Zeus on a throne.

It was none other than Cemal Ölmez.

'It is no secret that I am proud of two cities in this life: one is Bergama, the city of my roots, the pearl of the ancient world, also known as Pergamon. The other is Berlin, the city of my birth and the heart of Europe. Everyone on earth should see these two cities before they die. As it is, the Altar of Zeus, which was the heart of ancient Pergamon, was taken to Berlin, which is why every year I bring my friends from Berlin here. So they may see what is left of the body of this legendary city, the heart of which is on display in the Pergamon Museum in Museum Island.' He turned to the right. 'This year I have four guests.' Upon his signal, the camera moved, showing Alex's pockmarked face. The drummer nodded his head by way of acknowledgement, while Cemal's voice could be heard over the image. 'One of my guests this year is Alexander Werner, my beloved partner and musician extraordinaire. The finest drummer in all of Berlin.' The camera hurriedly panned back to Cemal, who had a twinkle in his eye as he spoke. 'I have been asking him to come for years and Alex Efendi has finally honoured us with his presence. We also have with us another beautiful friend from Berlin who is an outstanding artist and sculptor.'

The camera moved around again, stopping at a woman's thin face. She had thick lips reminiscent of wild fruit, a petite nose, light freckles and dark blue eyes with a soft, sweet look. Her hair, the colour of wheat, was blowing gently in the wind.

'Hello, I'm Kitty, and I'm so excited to be here. What an amazing trip this is turning out to be. We will be going to the Acropolis up on the hill soon. I am finally going to see the city from which the fabulous Altar I have seen so many times in Pergamon Museum was taken. I shall walk its streets, sit in its theatre's seats, wander around the spaces where its ruined temples used to stand and feel the spirits of the people that once lived and breathed here. It really is going to be a unique experience, and for that I would like to thank Cemal and my darling Peter.' Kitty approached the camera. Half her body appeared on the screen and the sound of a kiss was heard, after which her beautiful face reappeared on the screen. 'This trip is going to be one of the best gifts I have ever received.'

The camera panned back to Cemal.

'And my next guest. Not just a friend but a relative too. Yes, we have with us someone that loves Pergamon even more than I do for he comes here every year to take part in the excavations. It is with great pride that I introduce my cousin Haluk Ölmez, who also works as a researcher for the German Institute for Archaeology. Like me, he was born in Berlin but his heart beats in Pergamon, the city of his ancestors.' The camera came to rest on Haluk's dark features. He gave a measured smile and spoke to the camera. 'Hello, or rather, welcome. As Cemal said, this city is ours just as much as Berlin is. However, Pergamon also represents the ideal to which I have dedicated my life. The

Acropolis on the hill, the Asklepion, the temples, the palaces and the Altar all have profound importance for me. It feels as though they are my streets and that this is my neighbourhood, my house and my garden… And let us not forget the Altar of Zeus and the stories therein… "The War between the Gods and the Giants". I often feel I am taking part in that war, fighting alongside the Olympians against the barbarians. The story of Telephus, founder of Pergamon, feels like my life story. So once again, welcome to Pergamon, capital of ancient Anatolia.'

As the camera was about to pan back to Cemal, someone seemed to lose their balance but then managed to stay on their feet. Peter's face appeared on the screen. His hair was longer and there was some stubble on his tanned face but he was still his handsome self. Cemal's voice could be heard over the image.

'My apologies for the shaky image just now. The camera was being handed over to me. Yes, standing before you now is the incomparable director of Der Blitz, my amazing sponsor, my dear friend and the most handsome of all German men, the one and only Peter Schimmel.'

Peter smiled, showing two rows of immaculate teeth.

'Hello everyone. This is my first trip to Pergamon and I am also delighted to be here. And that is because Kitty is here with me.' He extended a hand and the beautiful sculptor appeared on the screen. With his right hand around her waist, Peter went on. 'Don't get me wrong, I also adore Pergamon. It has an extraordinary history and an incredible story. But I must confess, this moment right now is of greater interest to me than any two-thousand-year history. Yes, Hera, Athena, Aphrodite and the other Goddesses on the reliefs on the Great Altar are wonderful but I would not swap any of them for my Berlin Goddess Kitty.' He turned and kissed his lover on the lips, and she responded amorously. As they watched, Tobias grinned and said, 'Looks like the guy isn't gay after all then, boss.'

Yıldız smiled wryly. 'Looks like it. And she's a stunner too.' She reached out and pressed a button on the computer's keyboard. The kiss between Peter and Kitty froze. 'It says 2020 on the video file, right?'

'Yes. *Pergamon 2020*. So it was taken last summer,' Tobias said, not sure where his boss was going.

'But Haluk told us he had not spoken to Cemal in two years.'

'He did indeed. He said he stopped speaking to Cemal so as to not upset his parents. Hmmm. Why did he lie to us?'

Rather than tire themselves out speculating, it would be easier to ask the man himself.

'Call Haluk, Toby. If possible, we'll pay him a visit today.' She paused. 'No, wait. First, let's talk to Peter about this trip, and then we will go and see the archaeologist.'

'So I'm calling Peter then?' Tobias was not sure as to what he was supposed to be doing. Yıldız looked at him in amazement, wondering why he was struggling to understand.

'Call them both, Toby. We'll speak to both of them today, if we can.'

While Tobias busied himself with his phone, Markus' voice rang out.

'What's this then, Yıldız? We're into watching romantic films now, are we?'

He was standing just behind them, staring at the frozen image of Peter and Kitty kissing.

'No, this is an important video related to the investigation. We have just caught one of our suspects lying.'

Markus' face lit up.

'Good. Then why don't you tell me you're making progress? I have some good news too. Cemal's DNA has been detected on the knife that was used to flay Alex's face. They were both killed with the same weapon.'

'That really is good news. We really are making progress.' Yıldız was genuinely pleased but Markus quickly put a dampener on her good mood.

'Can I see you for a moment?' he said formally. 'I need to speak to you about tomorrow's press conference.'

He emphasized the singular *you*. Yıldız realized he wanted to speak to her about Tobias.

'Sure. Let's go.' She turned to Tobias and said, 'Toby, could you go ahead and arrange those meets, please? It's vital that we speak to them today.'

She left the room and followed Markus down the corridor.

'We were watching a video taken in Pergamon last year. Both victims were there.'

'So you reckon the perpetrator may have been there too?' Markus asked. Yıldız was not happy about what was happening but she could not bring herself to say so.

'That's not what I'm saying. We don't have any evidence in that direction. I still think we should remain focused on the neo-Nazis. Rudolf may still be behind these murders. We need to bring him in for questioning.'

'Very well. Bring him in. Do what you have to do, Yıldız. We need to bring this to a close before there are more casualties.'

Markus increased his stride but Yıldız had run out of patience and asked him in the corridor before they had reached his office.

'What's going on, Markus? What is all this business about Tobias?'

Markus had a quick look around before answering.

'Tobias' grandfather was a Nazi. Ernst Becker was an SS officer; one of the men behind the Night of the Long Knives in 1934, when the Nazis staged a violent purge of what they considered their dangerous internal elements. That night, they basically created mass terror amongst SA members they believed were harming their cause and ended up killing eighty-five SA members. After that night, Ernst Becker remained a loyal SS officer. When the Red Army invaded Berlin, he was charged with arming children and the elderly and directing the street fighting. He was killed by the Soviets in a clash by the Brandenburg Gate.'

Tobias had told her that his grandfather was a diehard communist who had been loyal to the party until his final breath. Not just that; he had also used this information to point out how much he and Yıldız 'had in common.' While Yıldız quietly pondered this strange turn of events, Markus went on, oblivious to her growing discomfort.

'Of course, such things are possible. After all, we all have parents and grandparents, we are all someone's son or daughter, and someone's grandson or granddaughter. It is hardly out of the ordinary for somebody in Germany to have a Nazi past. What matters is that Tobias kept this hidden from us.'

Yıldız did not want to tell her boss what her assistant had told her.

'How did this information get out? And how on earth did he manage to keep it hidden for so long?'

'I have no idea how he kept it hidden and nor do I wish to speculate as to why. Maybe somebody decided to cover it all up. It's no secret that the drive to protect the Nazis in the West began as soon as the war ended. They were all protected. Even the English and then the Americans joined the bandwagon. They made use of the Nazi scientists' vast accumulated knowledge in their fight against the Soviets. And of course, this became a widespread feature of the new German state. However, the increase in the number of racist and xenophobic attacks over recent years has meant that the security services have had no choice but to investigate any and all Nazi activity. Basically, an order from above says everyone has to be put under the microscope. I don't know how healthy such an order can be but the fact remains, something has cropped up with Tobias Becker and legal proceedings will take place. He is going to be taken aside and questioned.' He shook his head in remorse. 'I shouldn't have assigned him to you in the first place but I thought you'd get on, seeing as he knows Turks well and has been to Turkey countless times. He even speaks a little Turkish.'

'What?' Yıldız stared at the Chief in astonishment. 'Are you sure, Markus? Because Toby told me he has never been to Turkey.'

It was Markus' turn to be surprised.

'Is that so? Well, he was more than happy to tell me about his experiences in Istanbul. He even got into a fight with a bunch of Brits in Fethiye. He told you he has never been to Turkey, did he?' He turned and looked at the door of the room they had left Toby in. 'Why did he hide all this from you. What do you think he's playing at?'

Yıldız was thinking the same but she could not find an answer.

'If you like I can have him removed from duty,' Markus went on. 'I'll find you a new assistant. A woman, if you like. Might be a bit tricky at first but you'll get used to it. She can stay on with until the investigation ends. It's up to you.'

Yıldız did not know what to do. *Why, Toby? Why? Why did you hide this from me*? She thought about his baby face, his sweet, innocent countenance, and his voice, so bereft of malice. No, she said to herself. No. Toby cannot be such a man. No, he has no ulterior motive. There had to be a logical explanation for all this.

'Give me a bit of time, Markus,' she eventually managed to say. 'Let's just keep this quiet for now. Try and delay the legal proceedings a little. Tobias does not have to know we have found this out. Let's take our time and think things through properly. In the meantime, we'll just have to keep a discreet eye on him.'

It was a dirty business. Even Markus was at a loss.

'You sure?' he asked nervously. 'You'll be working alongside someone you no longer trust. Someone you cannot turn your back on.'

'We don't know that for sure,' Yıldız said, narrowing her eyes and shaking her head. 'So far, Toby is simply a police officer who has withheld some information from us, that's all. It's his grandfather that was the Nazi, not him, and naturally he would not want that information to get out. But hiding the fact that he has been to Turkey and that he knows a little Turkish… That is odd. Really odd.'

9

The one that will destroy you is the one that created you

Only the Gods and the oracles, such as Apollo and Pythia, the High Priestess of Delphi, can know the future. However, only an almighty deity such as myself has the ability to alter the future. And there are such events that, in order to alter them, one must prepare for today.

When my father Kronos overthrew and mutilated his father Uranus, it never occurred to him that one day he would lose his throne, and because he did not consider the possibility, he did not take the necessary precautions. In contrast, I knew all too well what I could one day face. I knew for sure that the Titans would not willingly give up their power to us, the Gods. That is why I rescued my siblings from my father's stomach. For the war, I took from the three Cyclopes Arges, Brontes and Steropes thunder, lightning and thunderbolts, and I forged an alliance with Briareos, Kottos and Gyes, whom I accepted into my ranks. I eventually defeated the Titans and I punished them and the other rebels. But even then, when my power was at its peak and I had proclaimed my rule over the earth and the skies,

I knew a new threat was taking root in the bowels of the earth. I knew, because the mysterious child with the dark eyes had told me of this danger in the third of my dreaMs

In my dream, I was in a vast chamber. No, it was not the Palace of Olympus. No palace of any king that I knew had a dwelling such as this. There were no windows, and no balcony or terrace; just two doors, with a huge dais in the centre of the room, a space in which sacrifices were made to the Gods. Reliefs depicting a war had been carved into the walls of this structure. Looking closer at the reliefs, I saw myself there, with my eagles and my thunderbolts, fighting three terrifying figures, huge beings with thick manes... Eventually, I realized who they were. One was Porphyrion, and the others were two young Giants. In another relief, I saw Athena; she had captured Alcyoneus, the leader of the Gigantes, by the hair. Gaia too was there, distraught at the imminent defeat of her son by her granddaughter. Indeed, her sorrow at Athena's pending victory was all too clear and she dearly wished for her son to best my daughter. But Nike was already spreading his broad wings and declaring my daughter Athena victorious. I then saw Hera of Argos, wondrous Poseidon, Apollo the bringer of light and my heroic son Heracles. For a moment, I thought this was our war against the Titans but there were no Titans anywhere to be seen. No, those we were fighting were the Gigantes. They were Gaia's terrible progeny, immense in strength and size with serpentine lower bodies, and they drew their power from the soil, from their mother. No, this was not our battle against the Titans but the war we were going to wage against the Giants. But there were arms, trunks and heads missing because most of the reliefs had been damaged so some I could not identify.

I lifted my head and scanned the vast room but there were no priests or sacrifices, there was no sacred fire or incense. All I saw were people wearing bizarre garments speaking languages I did not understand, all with their eyes fixed on the reliefs, wandering around them in amazement and awe. Some were climbing the steps, hoping to reach the Altar where the sacred fire burnt. I too began climbing the steps alongside those people. Of course, they could not see me, for they did not possess the jewel that allows one to see a deity. That is when I saw the mysterious child with the black eyes. He was with his father again but he let go of his father's hand for a moment, came up to me and stared at me. This time, I was the first to act, and I said:

'Who are you? Where do you come from?'

He looked disappointed and said:

'Do you really not recognize me, Mighty Zeus?'

'Should I?' I scowled.

He looked me up and down with a hurt expression and said:

'One day, maybe not today, you will know who I am.'

He was not going to escape my clutches so easily. I demanded:

'Who are you? Why do you talk in these riddles?'

He looked at me defiantly and said:

'I come from the future but I was born in the past. It is not as complicated as you think. I come from the unknown, but what I say shall make the future knowable. However, I do not bring joyous tidings, Mighty Zeus. A great reckoning approaches.'

'What reckoning?' I growled, angered by the child that spoke with the conviction of a God. 'What nonsense do you spout, child?'

His gaze slid over to the reliefs on the walls of the Altar.

'It is not nonsense, Great Zeus. I have come to inform you of a coming war. I have come to tell you about a perilous trap that has been prepared for you. Yes, Master of All, I have come to tell you of a bloody battle that will end in your defeat if you do not take the necessary measures.'

'None dare go to war without my consent,' I said, my anger with the child churning within me. 'A creature strong enough to defeat the Olympians has yet to be created.'

He looked at me in sorrow, almost as though he pitied me, and said:

'The one that will destroy you is the one that created you. This time, you have a powerful enemy.' He pointed to the relief of Gaia on the walls of the Altar. 'She that gave you your strength shall take it from you. But you can avert this catastrophe. I am not talking about allying yourself with the other Gods. This you must and will do anyway. I am talking about a human. About a Mortal taking his place beside you in battle. About a Mortal that carries your blood.' He raised a small hand and pointed to another relief on the wall. It was Heracles. 'If your Mortal son does not fight in this war, you will never defeat the Gigantes.'

His supercilious, conceited tone infuriated me.

'You are beginning to anger me,' I warned him. 'How dare you! Who are you to counsel me?'

'Mighty Zeus, I do not offer you counsel, nor do I dare overstep my remit. I am simply informing you of what is to be. Do not see me as a stranger. Consider me your own reasoning, your own thoughts, your own voice. And I implore you to listen. They are preparing for a great war. A bloody war that will cost you your throne.'

As he spoke, his voice began to taper away and he and the colours of the chamber began to fade.

'Who?' I roared. 'Who dares go to war against me? Ha! Tell me who these impertinent fools are!'

But my demands went unmet. My voice echoed around that grand chamber, bouncing off the broken arms and legs of the marble reliefs on the walls before coming back to me.

'Who? Who dares wage war against me?'

I awoke to my own shouts. When I opened my eyes, Hera was looking at me anxiously. Recalling the dream, the answer to the question I had asked the child came to me in all its clarity and the future began to unfold before my eyes. The truth I already knew but had been too afraid to accept suddenly caught me in its clutches. Our war against the Titans was not going to be the last; a bloodier and more brutal war awaits us. But was Gaia behind this war, as the child in the dream had foretold? Or were the Titans going to mutiny of their own accord? I was unsure, which is why I decided to speak to Mother Earth.

When she saw me, she stared down at me and said:

'Greetings, my son. My strong, powerful son whose wisdom cannot be questioned. So you finally remember your Mother Earth. You finally remember Gaia, who placed you on your throne. I was beginning to think you had forgotten the one that created you all.'

I ignored the resentment coursing through her voice and said:

'Greetings Mother Earth, most exalted, most virtuous and most wondrous of all females. I offer you my veneration and my love. How can I forget you? You are always in my mind, but you of all should know the tribulations that come with being the greatest of the deities, with being king of the Gods and the protector of all living things. You have always been on my mind but these humans do not leave me in peace. Always they beg me for help, from war, disease and famine. I am constantly on their lips, even on those of simple villagers that have lost their cattle. Nevertheless, here I stand before you. Do not close your heart to me. Know I love you and that there is no other in my heart.'

She did not relent, however. For she looked not at the words but at the actions.

'I know your tasks are hard and that governing the world is the greatest of burdens. As such, I can understand why you have not come to see me, why I have not been in your thoughts or, indeed, why you no longer love me. But injustice I will not abide. For you became Zeus to bring justice to the world. The world has no need for another Uranus or Kronos, yet you behave like them. You indiscriminately imprisoned my children in Tartarus. You loaded the entire weight of the sky on the shoulders of my Atlas and you feed your eagle my Prometheus' liver. You torture my children mercilessly and make their lives hell. This I cannot stand. My wish is for you to remember what you were before you became Zeus. My wish is for you to become the bold and intrepid rebel you were then. My wish is for you to once more become that youth who stood for justice.'

Had it been any other than our Mother Earth, I would have obliterated her before she had finished speaking but Gaia was creator of us all and even I did not know the full extent of her powers. And so I opted for deceit and denial. I feigned ignorance and said:

'Exalted Gaia, mother of my mother, wisest, most wondrous and most powerful of the Goddesses, how glad I am to have come to you, to have seen and spoken to you and to have heeded your words. You have told me how I have erred; I have seen my failings and I have seen the destructive consequences of my rash actions. And you are right. The world has no need of another tyrant. I shall become a more just, a more merciful and a more compassionate Zeus as of now. I shall treat all equally. Not just the Gods but all that are of your blood and of your line.'

Of course, Gaia did not believe me, but she did not challenge me either. She stayed silent the whole time I was there with her. When I left, I realized the child in my dream had told the truth. I realized that I had seen the one that had provoked the war in the statues around the temple. I now had no doubts; the one trying to destroy us was the one that had created us. We had no choice. In the impending war, we would have to fight against none other than the greatest of the Goddesses, against our grandmother Gaia herself, Mother Earth, she that had created the Titans and the Giants. Just as she had trained her own son to dethrone Uranus, with whom she had shared a bed and with whom she had also shared her body and spirit, and just as she had mentored my mother and prepared me and trained me to vanquish my father after he had assumed power, so now she was stirring the barbarians under the earth to revolt and dethrone me, Zeus, by telling them that I had insulted them and that I had abused their progeny. Yet it was true; the Giants were primitive beings, far beneath us Gods, both in body and mind. They were the emissaries of death and evil, capable of bringing only darkness and chaos to the earth. Gaia, too, knew this, but she had become blinded by her lust for power. She cared not for Titan, Giant or God. All our Mother Earth wanted was to reclaim her power, which had been usurped by men.

This is why she ousted my grandfather Uranus and this was why she brought to an end my father's reign; her female authority had been seized by underserving males, and the time had come for her to end this and to reverse the flow of time. Her wish was that the Giants, the Titans, the Gods and all the creatures of the earth would once more worship her and live under her reign. For she was there before us all, and she was the one that would remain after we were all gone. But for this to happen, she had to defeat me. This was unavoidable. The only divine force that could stop her was the lord of the earth and the sky, the God of all creatures, the king of kings, the terrible son of Kronos; I, her own blood, her youngest grandson, Zeus. And so she prepared for a mighty war that would end the reign of the Olympians once and for all, which meant I, too, had to prepare. And so I did, silently and patiently.

I had seen in my dream those whom I could trust. Apollo, possessor of the golden bow, Hera of Argus, Athena, possessor of the shield, Ares, possessor of the shimmering helmet, Artemis the archer, Hermes of superior intellect, Dionysus, Immortal born of a Mortal mother, dark-haired Poseidon, waxen-haired Demeter, master blacksmith Hephaestus, and all the other Gods and Titan allies that would stand steadfast with us, never to abandon us, not even during the bloodiest and most brutal battles. However, such was the magnitude of this looming conflict, even this array of powerful allies would not be enough. As the dark-eyed boy in my dream had said, to defeat the Giants, who drew their strength from the earth itself, a Mortal needed to be in our ranks, fighting alongside us. This was a command, a divine injunction. It was decreed that for the Giants to die, they had to be slain by a God and a Mortal, and that Mortal was none other than my own son, Heracles, a Mortal who carried my own blood. Without Heracles by my side, I could not win this war.

Yet my son was ready neither in body nor in spirit for such a clash. To fight alongside the Olympians, he needed to experience setback and sorrow, and to suffer indescribable torment whilst keeping his spirit pure. In body, Heracles was the strongest of the Mortals, strong enough to punish tyrants, hunt down monsters and tame wild beasts. But this was not enough. He needed to learn how to defeat wise Gaia's monstrous children, the Giants, and I, naturally, would be the one to instruct him in this. I needed to train my son in such a manner that he would leave this world in which he was born as a Mortal and take his rightful place in my palace on Olympus in honour as one us. However, it was imperative that no one knew of this plan, including Heracles himself. For if anybody caught wind of my plan, Titan, God or man, then Gaia too would learn of the plan. And so, for better or worse, whatever I did to Heracles had to appear as though it had been done unto him by others. More is the pity that in this scheme, Hera, my jealous wife, was to be the key.

Chapter Nine

It was vital that Yıldız not let on to Tobias what Markus had said and so on the journey from the station to Café am Neuen See, the meeting point Peter had given to Tobias over the phone, she said little. While they were passing over the Landwehr Canal on their way to the beer garden, she did mention an interesting chapter in the canal's history.

'Did you know Rosa Luxemberg's lifeless body was thrown into the water around this point?' Her voice was distant and sad, as though she was a relative of the woman that had been killed on that winter's day around a century earlier. 'Wait, why am I even asking you?! How can you not know? You were born in a communist country and your father and grandfather were both communists!'

She glanced at her assistant out of the corner of her eye as he drove but it seemed Tobias was just as good as an actor as Yıldız.

'That was a terrible thing to happen,' he said with the same sadness. 'They found her body days later. They say she was beaten to death.'

Tobias had to know the story of this eminent German revolutionary but whether he genuinely respected her or not was another matter. Yıldız could not help but press him further, even though she knew she had to avoid the topic.

'I first came here with my mother. There is a monument down below by the canal commemorating Rosa Luxemberg, a metal plaque with her name on it. My mother showed it to me and said, "Don't forget this name. Rosa was a great woman. She was not just a communist. She was a lover of freedom. She fought for freedom her whole life, even when it meant risking conflict with her comrades. That is why the militants did not let her live." I didn't know exactly what my mother meant but I did get an inkling that this Rosa Luxemberg woman was a hero. Years later, I came back with my father. That was after my mother's death and after the collapse of East Germany. I remember my father staring at the murky water flowing silently below and saying, "If Rosa Luxemberg and her comrades had succeeded in 1919 and the Spartacist Uprising had resulted in revolution, socialism would never have failed. Capitalism would never have defeated socialism because the blueprint of the society of our ideals already existed in Germany. It did not exist in Czarist Russia, which was still comparatively undeveloped. The socialist revolution was too complex and too big for Russia, which had yet to industrialize." Well, something on those lines anyway.' She turned to her assistant and, as though suddenly curious, asked, 'Didn't your family ever bring you here? Your grandfather or father?'

Tobias was so composed, he did not even take his eyes off the road.

'I never saw my grandfather. He died before I was born, defending Berlin from the Nazis. Even my father didn't really remember him as he was only five when my grandfather died. I did not visit the memorial but they did tell us about Rosa Luxemberg and Karl Liebknecht in school. Apparently, they were both summarily executed.' He laughed. 'Look at us. Two officers of the German police force sitting in their car talking about a female revolutionary leader who was killed years ago by the state. Not just talking about her but praising her unreservedly.'

Yıldız saw her chance.

'And yet this same police force is full to the brim with officers that have nothing but admiration for Hitler and the Nazis. Not only do they revere the Nazis, but they are also trying to complete their murderous unfinished business. What could be more natural than us talking about a woman who defended her rights and the rights of all women, even at the cost of her own life?'

Tobias' face went bright red.

'You're right, boss. But at least the state acknowledges its mistakes in this regard. Who knows, maybe the Nazis in the force will be brought to account one day…'

He was lying through his bare teeth but Yıldız did not react. They had two men they needed to question and she did not want either them to be distracted while they were working.

'Hasn't Peter gone to work?' she asked, changing the subject. 'Why did he want to meet by the lake?'

Tobias took a deep breath.

'He has another meeting at the Café am Neuen See. He told me he could see us if we came at the specified time. I told him we would be there. We're on a tight schedule ourselves too. After speaking to Peter, we're meeting Haluk in the café at the Pergamon Panorama.'

'Nice. So, after talking to Peter, we get to talk to Haluk immediately afterwards. That's good. How did Peter sound on the phone? Because he sounded a little tense last time.'

'No, he seemed quite relaxed and was quite courteous too. No showboating.' He smiled mischievously. 'He asked after you. When I told him you were coming too, he sounded quite pleased.'

Yıldız could not work out if this was just casual chitchat or Tobias attempting to further deflect from the conversation about his grandfather but she was still quietly flattered.

'And we'll also have a reason to be pleased if he gives us something on Haluk', she said, ending the topic.

The Café am Neuen See was one of the finest beer gardens in the city. Yıldız had come here many times before; first with her parents, then with Volker, her first boyfriend in high school, then with her ex-husband and then with Deniz. She had also come several times on her own. The view of the lake, the water, which turned green with the reflection of the branches of the trees hanging over it, and the sweet chirping of the birds in and around the trees made it a wonderful place to relax. One had to visit on a weekday though, as there was no room to swing a cat there at the weekend and finding a nice table by the lake was out of the question. It was quiet there today and they found Peter at one of the wooden tables by the lake where the kayaks were moored. He was poring over an Excel spreadsheet and did not notice his two guests until they were standing right in front of him.

'Don't work too hard, Mister Schimmel.'

Seeing Yıldız standing there only a few feet away, Peter's face lit up.

'Why, hello! I didn't see you there. Sorry.'

'A particularly tricky problem?' she asked, pointing to his tablet. Peter looked in frustration at the tablet and the spreadsheet on the screen.

'It looks like I am going to sell Der Blitz... I don't know if I mentioned it last time but we have been holding meetings with various large corporations, so yes, it is somewhat tedious. It's hard conducting business here when you are from the East.' He smiled a bitter smile. 'The collapse of the Wall didn't just bring freedom, it also caused a considerable amount of pain and misery, but sadly, that aspect of the reunification is rarely articulated... Still, don't let me bother you with my personal problems.' He switched the tablet off and gestured to them. 'Please, take a seat. Mister Becker, please.'

Yıldız sat facing him and Tobias sat to the right. They had departed on a slightly bitter note during their previous encounter but Peter seemed genuinely pleased to see them this time.

'What can I get you? Beer?'

'Thank you but we have to politely decline,' Yıldız said, smiling gratefully. 'We do not drink while on duty.'

'However, I wouldn't mind a cigarette,' Tobias added. Seeing no objection, he fished out his packet and placed a cigarette between his lips. Peter had already turned around to face Yıldız.

'I was actually going to call you and ask you about Cemal's funeral. Are his family making the necessary arrangements? I'm asking because I have not heard from Mister Ölmez.'

Yıldız had not thought about it. Even if he did not want to bother with Cemal, Kerem would still want to take his father's body back to the city of his birth.

'I don't know. I'll ask him when I see him.'

'Thank you. It's very important for me to know because Cemal told me he wanted to be buried in Bergama. If his family fulfil his wishes, then naturally I will not interfere but if they are not prepared to make the necessary arrangements, I would like to take charge of Cemal's funeral and fulfil his last wishes. However, having said that, I need to be in London in a few days' time as I am speaking at a conference on renewable energy but I can still have people help organize Cemal's funeral. We can have him laid to rest where he wanted.'

Yıldız was surprised not at Peter's generosity of spirit but at Cemal wanting to be buried in Bergama. Generally, it was the older immigrants in Germany that wanted to be laid to rest in the old motherland. For someone born in Berlin to want to be buried in his ancestral homeland was odd. Cemal must have been truly in love with Pergamon.

'It's because of his father,' Peter said, almost reading Yıldız's thoughts. 'Yes, I can see your surprise, Ms Karasu, but it's true. Cemo's love for Pergamon is due to his father's dream of becoming an archaeologist. Kerem Ölmez loved the ancient city to the point of madness. *Loved* is perhaps the wrong word. What he felt for the city was an unbreakable and incurable passion. I think it was his grandfather's dying wish, or something on those lines, for Kerem to become an archaeologist. Before the reunification, when the Pergamon Museum was still in the East, he used to take his little boy by the hand to the museum. Every weekend he was in East Berlin and if he did not visit the Altar, he would feel terrible.'

Yıldız was stunned.

'Incredible! From what I have heard, the Turkish guest workers in West Germany used to go to the East for fun and pleasure. This Kerem really is a strange character.'

'So it would seem,' Peter said absent-mindedly. 'They went to the museum so many times that his grandfather's passion was passed on to his own son, who became equally obsessed with the Altar of Zeus. He knew all the reliefs and friezes by heart and could describe the Gods, Goddesses, Titans, and Giants depicted in them with such detail that he might as well have been the one to unearth them himself in the digs.'

'Like his cousin Haluk?' Tobias said, after taking a deep drag on a cigarette and letting out a huge plume of smoke. It took Peter a few seconds to understand.

'Sorry? His cousin? Ah, yes, of course. You are referring to Haluk, the archaeologist. No, not like him. Haluk is a scientist.

He works on Pergamon too but for him it is just work, not a passion. His attachment to the ancient city and to the Altar is a scholarly one, a dispassionate interest, whereas Cemal's was totally emotional. An obsessive love, like his father's, so deep that he came to see himself and his family as one with Pergamon. Remember how I told you during our last meeting that he was going to paint a picture of the Gods and Goddesses on the Altar but with the faces of members of his family? Well, now you know why. He was so into the Altar of Pergamon that he began to see himself as Zeus. I am not talking about insanity here but an artist's imaginary world. He never lost complete touch with reality, but he did like to see himself as Zeus. That is why he compared his grandfather to Uranus and his father to Kronos.'

They both knew all this but what they needed to find out was whether Haluk saw himself as Zeus or not.

'What is Haluk like?' Yıldız asked. 'Have you met him?'

A frown formed on Peter's face.

'Why? Do you suspect him?' He shook his head. 'No, I doubt it. Haluk is a decent chap. And he loved Cemal.'

'Loved?' Tobias asked. 'What kind of love?'

Peter narrowed his eye and stared at the hefty policeman.

'No, not in the way you seem to be implying. Haluk is heterosexual, as far as I know. They were like brothers. Haluk is a very distinguished archaeologist. He works for the German Institute for Archaeology and spends his summers on the digs at Pergamon. Cemal went to him for support on his Altar project. Haluk gave him some technical help and provided him with detailed information about ancient Greek mythology and the Olympians.'

'But this creates a somewhat contradictory picture,' Yıldız said. 'Because Haluk's family had not spoken to Cemal's family for years. They had something akin to a blood feud going on.'

'A blood feud?' Peter asked, startled. 'Why? Did someone die?'

'Yes. Cemal and his family had a huge fight with their uncle and his sons and one of the cousins ended up dying in the scuffle. Haluk's older brother, to be precise. That is why the two families stopped talking. There was even an attack involving guns at one stage.' Peter looked quite stunned, as though he was hearing this for the first time. 'Cemal never told you about this?'

'No, he didn't,' Peter said, looking disappointed before regaining his composure. 'The matter was never raised. Maybe he didn't want to talk about it. It seems personal, after all. A family matter.'

'Can you tell us what you know about Haluk?' Yıldız asked. 'Did you meet him often?'

'Oh yes, we bumped into one another many times. But as to what kind of person he was...' He paused to think. 'Like I said, he struck me as a decent fellow. Smart, too. Most of the men in the Ölmez family are well-built but even for us Germans, he is a tough-looking guy. Really, he has an amazing body. He probably works out. In fact, last year he and Cemal stayed with me and we swam together in the lake at Wannsee. I work out too but he is in really good shape. I remember joking around with him and telling him he looked like a gladiator but he wasn't having any of it and laughed. He said, "We are not gladiators, we are from Pergamon and come from the line of Zeus. Better to call us Greek Gods." But he's got a weird face. He always looks sad. I don't know why. Maybe it's those hooded eyelids of his that make him look so forlorn. He's not like the other Turks I know. He's more civilized, like Cemal...' As soon as the words had left his lips, he realized his blunder. 'My apologies, Ms Karasu. I do not mean to belittle any minorities but Cemal and Haluk really are a breed apart.'

Yıldız did not mind. The topic at hand was far too important for her to be aggrieved by a casual comment.

'Would you say Haluk was prone to violence? Would you call him the aggressive type?'

'I do not know him that well,' he said, tensing up. 'He's a quiet one. Very measured in his demeanour. I do not recall any angry or threatening behaviour on his part. He is like Cemal in that respect. Calm most of the time. To be truthful, we have not spent that much time together. Whenever we have met, it has only been for a couple of hours. Some food, a conversation, that's it.'

It was Tobias that reminded him of something he had either forgotten or did not want to mention.

'But didn't you spend several days with him and others in Pergamon? You were in Turkey last summer. Weren't you?'

Peter paused and nodded his head sourly.

'Yes, it is true, we all went to Pergamon together but Haluk only stayed with us for a day. He was there with the research team working on the digs there. He showed us around the Acropolis, showed us the bare dais of the Altar and gave us some information about the temples, palaces, theatres and gymnasia of the ancient city. Then he treated us to lunch at a local workers' café. That's all there was to it. He didn't really spend that much time with us. Indeed, when Kitty asked him to stay with us for dinner, he asked if he could be excused as he had to wake up early the next day, before sunrise.'

'Who's Kitty?' Tobias asked. Peter's expression clouded over.

'My girlfriend at the time. My ex now. We split up two months after that trip.' Yıldız was about to tell him that he did not have to go into any uncomfortable personal details but Peter saw no harm in continuing. 'Oh no, I don't mind talking about it. There is nothing to hide. Kitty wanted to get married and have children.' His eyes misted over and he smiled what looked like a smile of futility. 'I didn't. Marriage is not for me.' He frowned.

'Well, marriage perhaps, but not kids.' What looked like profound grief, or pain, flickered in his eyes and he held his hands up. 'I will not bring children into a world such as this. I do not want such a weighty responsibility. That's too much. Way too much.'

She may not have agreed but Yıldız still felt sorry for him. Peter's grief, however, meant nothing to Tobias.

'Did they ever argue in front of you?' Peter looked at Tobias, not sure what he meant. 'Cemal and Haluk. Did they ever argue in front of you? During your trip to Turkey or at any other time.'

Peter stared at the still waters of the lake.

'No, I never saw them argue. I do not remember any unpleasantness while we were together. Cemal was a pretty laidback guy. Only one person could get him mad and that was Alexander Werner.'

'Well, he can't now,' Tobias said gruffly. 'Unless they bump into each other in the next world, of course.'

Peter frowned again.

'What do you mean?' He turned to face Yıldız. 'Has something happened to Alex?'

'Unfortunately, Alexander Werner was murdered in his flat last night. With the same weapon used to kill Cemal.'

Peter recoiled in horror.

'What? How?' His hand went up to his mouth. 'So... Was this a lover's tiff or what?'

'Possibly,' Yıldız said, not wanting to disclose too many details. 'That is one possibility.' She looked at him understandingly. 'Not everyone is as civilized as you are, Mister Schimmel.'

They parked the Passat by the pavement in front of Berlin Cathedral. As ever, the Lustgarten was packed. Some tourists were soaking their tired feet in the black waters after having spent the whole day wandering the city, whilst others, although clearly fatigued, were still happy to wander around and gaze at the historic buildings in the vicinity. Scantily-clad youngsters were stretched out on the grass sipping beer and enjoying the last of the setting sun. Yıldız looked on in envy and, to herself, muttered, 'Beautiful June'. There was a time when she too used to kick off her shoes and laze around in the sun like the young girls in the park but that was a long time ago. She was now a serious, stern-faced Chief Inspector with the Berlin Police and there were murderers that needed to be caught and murder cases that needed to be solved. She turned away from the youngsters to speak to Toby.

'Let's get away from here, Toby. It will be quicker if we use the bridge behind the Altes Museum.'

The piece of land that cleft the River Spree in two through the middle was known as Museum Island. The Pergamon Museum was one of its most important buildings but unfortunately, it was undergoing renovations so the Pergamon Panorama had been built to make up, however much it could, for its absence. The building housing the Pergamon Panorama was on the other side of the river and to get there, they needed to get off the island. Yıldız's phone rang while they were walking across the bridge. She recognized Kerem Ölmez's voice immediately.

'Hello? Ms Karasu? Are you free to talk?'

He sounded flustered.

'Of course. What's happened, Mister Ölmez?'

'We need to talk. Urgently! I do not trust anybody else apart from you.'

Yıldız needed to be careful and make sure her assistant did not hear their conversation.

'I see, Mister Ölmez. Go ahead, I'm listening.'

'No, not on the phone. It has to be face to face. Can't you come here?'

Speaking with him could actually be helpful but Yıldız still played it cool.

'What's the problem?'

He answered breathlessly, as though he was running out of time.

'It's our Hüseyin... You met him. My eldest. He's going to do something stupid. I can't talk about it on the phone. You need to come here or give me a place so I can come to you. But it has to be just us. Nobody else.'

Did he mean Tobias?

'Very well, that can be arranged. I'll get back to you shortly.'

'They're having problems with the funeral arrangements,' she said, switching the phone off and blurting out the first lie she could think of when she saw Toby staring at her. 'It must be hard on the poor guy. Two deaths in quick succession in the family.' She looked up and around. 'There it is. The Panorama. They built it facing the Pergamon Museum. Smart move.'

They did not find Haluk in the Panorama Café. They moved inside the museum to look for him amongst the statues built in Pergamon two thousand years earlier. They saw Athena, the protectress of the city, along with a marble bust of a king from the Attalid Dynasty. They searched for him by the wall beneath a scale model of the Pergamon Acropolis, where the history of the city had been summarized. They eventually found him in one of the smaller rooms staring at some friezes on a wall and talking into a handheld voice recorder. He noticed them as soon as they stepped into the salon. However, he did not smile but looked at them with exasperation, clearly annoyed at having to set aside precious time from his busy schedule for them. Despite his hostility, Yıldız managed to muster up a smile.

'Hello, Mister Ölmez.' She gestured to the reliefs with an exaggerated admiration. 'These are the friezes from the Pergamon Altar, are they not?'

He switched off the voice recorder, put it back in his bag and then in a condescending tone asked, 'Do you know the Pergamon Museum?'

'I may not be an expert like you but I have visited it many times. I have also been to Bergama. I am not even an amateur when it comes to archaeology but I do know a little about the Altar.'

Haluk smiled for the first time, although his eyes were still distant and aloof.

'I see. Well, if you have seen the Altar, you'll know that when you climb the steps you reach the upper terrace, which is where the actual sacrificial Altar is located. That is where the offerings used to be made to the Gods. Well, these reliefs were part of the inner wall of that space.' He pointed to one of the friezes, which was mostly damaged. 'See this? Telephus is ordering the creation of an Altar. Not this one, don't misunderstand. The Altar this hero commissioned was not the Altar of Pergamon.'

It was the second time Yıldız was hearing the name.

'Who was this Telephus? A God?'

Haluk pointed at the heavily damaged statue of Telephus.

'No, he was not a God but he was the son of a hero strong enough to take on the Gods. His father was Heracles and his mother Auge. His is an epic tale. These friezes tell his story.'

'Why would Telephus' stories be told here?' Yıldız asked, genuinely interested, which pleased Haluk.

'Because it is believed Telephus was the founder of the city of Pergamon.'

Yıldız was confused.

'But during our last encounter, you told us about another guy. A eunuch. What was his name again? Philip…'

'Philetaerus. Yes, historically, the city's foundation can be traced back to Philetaerus and its subsequent rulers, the Attalids.

But like every city in the ancient world, Pergamon had its own beautiful and powerful foundation myth and according to that myth, tales abound of Telephus' heroics, before Alexander the Great, before General Lysimachus and before the 9,000 talents he gave to his eunuch Philetaerus. That is why his tale is told in the reliefs you see here. These friezes formed part of the upper terrace, which was the heart of the Altar.'

Yıldız gazed at the reliefs on the wall, lost in thought, as though she had forgotten the actual purpose of their visit.

'But these statues have seen substantial damage,' she said, confused. 'You can't make out what they are trying to say.'

The coldness in Haluk's eyes seemed to vanish.

'You should have become an archaeologist, rather than a police officer, Ms Karasu. Very few people are actually interested in what the friezes depict but you have a historian's eye.'

He sounded like her father, not that Yıldız minded. She watched the archaeologist stride to the spot in which the friezes began. Tobias stayed where he was, wondering when the niceties would end and the actual questioning begin. This time, however, Haluk did not seem as rushed as he had been last time as he began his narrative.

'It is actually quite an interesting tale, the story of Telephus.' With his left index finger, he pushed his glasses further up his nose and turned to one of the reliefs. 'Here, can you see this? A kayak is being made.' In the foreground in the relief four carpenters were indeed working hard on the construction of a kayak, while three women stood in the background with their heads bowed in sorrow. 'As you can see here, the kayak is being made to transport Telephus' mother Auge across the sea, possibly to drown and die in the turbulent waters. Auge's father Aleus, the king of Arcadia, no longer wants to see her in his kingdom as he is afraid a terrible prophecy may be fulfilled.'

He turned his green eyes towards Yıldız. 'This is mankind's fear of the future, stemming from his own ignorance. The fear that something terrible will definitely happen to us. This is one of our primal anxieties, a trauma, perhaps, resulting from our knowing we are Mortal. But no less powerful nonetheless, as I am sure you know.

'Anyway, one morning Aleus, the king of Arcadia, made one of his regular visits to the temple, where he asked the oracles what the future held for his country and his dynasty. The answer he received was shocking. The oracles told him that his sons would be killed by a warrior born of his daughter Auge, and they were unequivocal in their statement. "Your own grandson shall slay your sons," they proclaimed. King Aleus was stunned. Who, after all, would dare question or defy the mighty oracles of Apollo? He thought long and hard and eventually found a solution — he would make his daughter a priestess. Nobody would dare touch her, and she would never marry. And so, Auge, whose beauty was legendary, became an exalted priestess of the Goddess Athena. However, the Gods, as cruel and as merciless as ever, were displeased with this act of cunning and so they conspired to make Auge and Heracles meet in a wood. The inevitable happened and Auge was soon pregnant, with the father of the child-to-be none other than the strongest man alive. It did not take long for Aleus to find out what had happened. At first, he was terrified, but then fury took over. How could his daughter do something so heinous?' Haluk pointed to the kayak on the wall. 'That is why he sent his daughter, accompanied by his loyal man Nauplius, on this kayak across the sea. However, he had a secret plan. Once they were in open sea, Nauplius would kill Auge, and thereby also kill the child she was carrying. However, Nauplius, it transpired, was not as loyal as Aleus had assumed. When Auge's labours began, they found land and climbed ashore, and Auge ended up giving birth to her son Telephus on Mount Parthenion and instead of killing mother and child, Nauplius sold them to merchants. The merchants, however, did not want the child and abandoned him on a mountainside. The Gods saw this and could not leave one of their own to such a fate and so they sent a deer to watch over him and nurse him. Heracles later found his son on the mountain. Meanwhile, Telephus' mother Auge was brought by the merchants to Mysia. The King of Mysia, Teuthras, rescued her from the merchants, adopted her and treated her as his own daughter.

'In time, Telephus grew to become a strong, brave and skilled warrior. Hearing from his father about his mother's fate, he decided to look for her and, after consulting the oracles, he set out for Mysia. On the way, he encountered two people, with whom he began arguing, and the argument soon turned physical, and Telephus ending up killing them both. Unbeknownst to him, the two people he had killed were his mother's brothers, his own uncles. And so the prophecy revealed by the oracles years earlier had finally been realized and King Aleus' worst fears had been confirmed. Not knowing the men he had killed were his uncles, Telephus reached Mysia, which was on the brink of war. When the fighting began, Telephus helped King Teuthras win the war and as a reward, Teuthras offered his daughter Auge to Telephus in marriage; in other words, Telephus' own mother. The marriage was duly performed but on their way to the bridal chamber, a serpent managed to tell the newlyweds they were in fact mother and son. Thus, a shameful tragedy akin to the one that had befallen King Oedipus was averted and Telephus ended up marrying the beautiful Hiera instead of Auge and King Teuthras gave Telephus half his kingdom as reward. Telephus began searching for suitable and fertile land on which he could establish his reign and eventually chose the hill on which modern-day Pergamon is located, a spot that overlooked the entire plain and which would be extremely difficult to conquer for any enemy.

'Since then, there have been numerous tales of Telephus' heroism, the most of important of which was the one that tells of him being wounded by a blow from Achilles and subsequently being healed with the dust from his assailant's own spear. It is this Telephus, Heracles' son and Zeus' grandson, who is the founder of ancient Pergamon. The most important figure here is Heracles, as he would emerge as a key character in the war between the Gods and the Giants. According to the sacred law, the Gods could not win the war if they did not have a Mortal warrior fighting beside them, and that Mortal was Telephus' father, Heracles. That is why Eumenes II had friezes depicting the war between the Gods and Giants on the lower levels of the structure and reliefs of Telephus placed around the central Altar on the upper levels. In doing this, he was proclaiming to the world that they were the sons of Heracles and that they came from the line of Zeus himself.'

'And you believe all this?' Tobias asked, his voice ringing out around the small chamber. The conversation had bored him at first but as the story developed, he began to realize that the legends being described may have a significant role in the investigation. 'Your roots go back to Pergamon too, Mister Ölmez. Your grandfathers were present on the digs there from the start and you are maintaining the family tradition, not as a labourer but as an eminent archaeologist. It is almost as though Pergamon is your city and the Altar of Zeus is your home. I mean, one of your own relatives, Kerem Ölmez, even began to believe he was Kronos and Cemal drew his relatives' faces on the bodies of the Olympian Gods on the walls of the Altar. What do you have to say about this? Do you also believe you descend from the line of Zeus and that you carry the blood of Heracles?'

Tobias had approached the issue from the right angle but Yıldız could not help but have doubts. In asking this question and putting the Ölmez family in the spotlight like this, was Tobias trying to deflect attention away from the Nazis? Haluk, oblivious to the silent tension between the two officers, answered with a scornful shake of his head.

'And you expect me to believe such nonsense, do you, Mister Becker? We are talking about mythology here. Legends. Belief systems that are outdated, yes, but which also happen to represent the evolution of mankind's psychological configurations. For thousands of years, people believed in these legends, legends that we today find outlandish. They created those Gods and then they built temples in their names, prayed to them, established laws based on them, and killed and died for them. Of course, I do not believe I come from the line of Zeus, because there is no such being. Zeus and the other Gods of Olympus are the products of the minds of people that lived back then. They are the external projection three thousand years ago of the fears, hopes and expectations of a species that will never be able to grasp reality in its entirety. The same process continues today. We have different religions, different Gods and different rituals. So long as humans are unable to grasp the truth of the world and are unable to come to terms with the miracle known as life, they long for a protector, a powerful being that will determine their fates, a divine scriptwriter who will give them the gift of happiness. And I am afraid this will continue until mankind realizes the most precious phenomenon on the planet is reality itself.

'As for Kerem Ölmez, like I said before, he is a sick man. A seriously sick man, who lost his mind over Pergamon. But

Cemal was an artist. Painting his own face on the figure of Zeus and his relatives' faces on the figures of the other Gods was mere artistic expression. It was simply artistic licence on his part.'

'To which God did he give your face?' Yıldız asked, a question that had been dogging her for some time. Something approaching a sour look passed over Haluk's face before it gave way to a smile and he pointed to the statue of Pergamon's founder.

'He was going to paint my face on his. See? The poor guy is already horribly disfigured.'

'We noticed, but we did not know who it was,' Yıldız said softly. 'We saw your face in an etching in Cemal's studio. So that must have been Telephus.'

'I told him not to,' Haluk said with a scowl. 'He had no right.' Then, after a pause, he asked, 'Did he paint anybody else from my family?'

Yıldız was taken aback at the ire in his voice.

'We do not know anybody from your family, Mister Ölmez. There were a lot of drawings in that studio but we would not know who was supposed to be whom. What is it about those drawings that so disturbs you?'

'What is it about them that disturbs me?' he asked incredulously. 'The man was using our faces without permission. It was an infringement and a violation of our privacy. I had warned him many times, and quite explicitly, that he was not to use my face or the faces of anyone in my family in his project.'

'Is that why you stopped talking?'

Haluk nodded his head angrily.

'I was risking angering my own parents when I was helping him but he didn't care about anybody except himself. All he cared about was the success of his project. People's right to privacy and their sensitivities meant nothing to him.'

There was a short silence until with his usual calmness, Tobias said, 'In that case, you were lying when you said during our last encounter that you stopped speaking to Cemal so as to not upset your parents.'

'What the hell is this? Are you accusing me of something?' Haluk asked, his voice raised.

'Please try and remain calm, Mister Ölmez,' Yıldız warned him. 'Nobody is accusing you of anything. We are simply trying to understand. As Inspector Becker says, the last time we met, you told us you had cut all your ties with Cemal out of respect for your parents, whereas now you are giving us different reasons. Could you perhaps explain this contradiction? And please, there is no need to respond with such anger. We are conducting a murder investigation here. Three people have been killed so far and there is every possibility more will follow…'

Haluk's face turned white.

'Three? Not just Cemal?'

There was little use in concealing the truth much longer.

'Cemal's grandfather Orhan Ölmez and Alexander Werner, whom you know. They were all most probably killed by the same person or people. If you do not answer our questions truthfully, it is very possible that more people will die.'

'I didn't know,' Haluk said in a low voice, dropping his guard. 'That's terrible. So, Grandpa Orhan and Alex are dead too, are they?' He hurriedly thought it over. 'It must be someone with a serious enmity towards Cemal that is carrying out these murders.'

'And someone with a serious knowledge of archaeology,' Tobias added with complete self-assurance. 'Because in all three murders, there have been clear references to mythology.'

The archaeologist looked stunned.

'You don't seriously think that I am the killer, do you? That would be ridiculous. Why would I kill Cemal?' Seeing the two officers staring at him disbelievingly, he went on. 'Now look, I may not have given you the full picture as to why I stopped speaking to Cemal but that is because this issue concerns my family, and Grandpa Pehlivan's affliction makes it even more sensitive. The fact that Kerem suffers from the same condition means it can affect any of us as we are all of the same blood. That is why I was so disturbed by Cemal putting my mother's and father's faces on his paintings of the Gods. The moment Cemal started talking about his planned project, I was against it but it is not something I wished to talk about with anyone, yourselves included. You had no reason to know about it. However, I am telling you the truth when I tell you that my family were upset at the fact I was speaking to Cemal and they asked me to cut ties with him. And so, for these two reasons, I stopped talking to him.'

'Is that so?' Yıldız asked drily. 'And did you? Did you really cut ties with him? Because you say you had not spoken to him for two years, yet a video we saw today shows us that you were with him only last year in Bergama. Not two years ago but a year ago, almost to the day…'

He had been caught out. He shook his head in embarrassment.

'That meeting was forced. I had no choice. I was already in Pergamon on a dig when they turned up. Cemal called me and apologized for everything that had happened between us and told me he had important guests with him, friends from Berlin that I also happened to know, and he begged me to set aside just one day for them so I could show them around. He told me they were all interested in the Altar and wanted to see its original location and learn more about it and that he could think of nobody better to show them around and inform them than me. I agreed. I could hardly refuse such a request. So yes, I showed them around and then they did some souvenir shopping. Kitty bought a statuette of a Goddess for herself and Peter bought a length of Bergama parchment from which he said he was going to have a notebook made. After that, we went to the olive orchard, the one bequeathed to us by our grandfather. The one that caused the family feud in the first place. There is an old cistern there that Cemal wanted to show his guests. He said he was going to use it at his model when painting Tartarus. Peter and Kitty insisted but I did not join them there. Peter, however, is a true gentleman. It's mainly because of him that I agreed to show them around Pergamon. If you like, you can speak to him. But believe me, I really did cut my ties with Cemal two years ago.'

When they stepped outside, the sun had started to set but the Lustgarten was still teeming with people. This time, Yıldız took a longer route, walking along the riverbank towards the Schloss Bridge. Just as she had predicted, Tobias started talking about Haluk instead of Yadegar Asisi's painting. After they had finished questioning the archaeologist, Yıldız had insisted that they stay and view Asisi's panorama, a massive painting of the ancient city painted on the inside of a cast cylinder with a raised platform in the centre for viewing. The city had been depicted not during its Hellenistic period but during the Roman Era, on the day of Emperor Hadrian's visit. The palaces and garrisons of which now only a few columns and ruins remained, the magnificent marble temple to Emperor Hadrian, the library housing 200,000 parchments given as a gift to Cleopatra by Marcus Antonius, the second largest library of the ancient world, the Temple of Athena in front of the library, the world's steepest theatre built to honour Dionysus and the wonderful temple built in the name of that same extraordinary deity, and, of course, the Altar of Zeus in all its splendour were all in the painting. The friezes on the wall of the Altar depicting the battle between the Gods and the Giants, smoke billowing up from the sacrifices on the Altar on the upper level and the people of Pergamon bringing their animals and their offerings to Zeus to the Altar... The light dimming and the colours fading as evening approached the city and the sound of the wind, of people, of animals, of work tools... Pergamon was there in all its wonder and vivacity. Even Tobias, after huffing and puffing his way up the platform, was left speechless. Haluk stayed with them and filled them in on all the details of the structures in the painting, their own personal tour guide. That is why they had not had a chance to talk about the archaeologist until they had said their goodbyes to him and left the museum. As soon as they were out of the door, Tobias began. 'What happened to him? That arrogant prick suddenly came over all sweet and friendly.' Before Yıldız could respond, he went on. 'I don't know what you're thinking, boss, but if you ask me, this guy is hiding something from us. That's why he got so angry when we exposed his lies. As you said before, for all we know, he's struggling with the same condition his great-grandfather Pehlivan had. If Haluk sees himself as Zeus, then naturally he would have been furious at Cemal for painting him as Telephus. A hero instead of a God, and not a hero like Heracles, one whose fame has lasted for thousands of years, but an ordinary hero... Maybe it was those paintings we saw in Cemal's house that triggered these murders. The painting of Telephus with Haluk's face... Look at how angry he was at Cemal using the faces of his family members.'

Rattled off without pause, it was all perfectly plausible. But it was still possible that Haluk had told them the truth. He may not have cared about Cemal's death at first but when he heard Orhan and Alex had been killed too, he realized this was no joke and that his name could also be on the killer's list of targets and so he decided the best course of action would be to cooperate with the police. Moreover, there was no law stating that everyone in Grandpa Pehlivan's family would suffer from the same condition. Amongst all his children and grandchildren, it was only poor Kerem that had drawn the short straw. Yıldız did not share these thoughts with her assistant, however, because just as she could not trust the archaeologist, so she felt she could no longer trust Tobias. It was still possible that she was suspecting him for nothing, and she hoped with all her heart that this would turn out to be the case, but she could not ignore any details or possibilities that could endanger the investigation. This is why she was not going to bring Tobias to the meeting with Kerem.

'It's possible, Toby. What he told us didn't make sense. But then again, he strikes me as an odd guy. If you ask me, we should still focus on the neo-Nazis. All the evidence at hand points to them.'

'So you reckon we should not bother investigating the family?' Tobias asked, surprised at the topic of the Nazis being raised again so soon. Yıldız played it cool.

'That's not what I'm saying. I'm just saying we should prioritize the Nazis. Which is what we're doing anyway.' She looked at her watch. 'I need to go home. My dad is busy tonight so I'm looking after Deniz. If you wouldn't mind, can you go ahead and question Otto? We never spoke to him about Rudolf Winkelmann. Can you show him the photographs we have of the two of them together and ask him where and how they met and whether they are still in touch or not? But you need to do it asap.'

Toby was surprised, not at the decision to question Otto again but at Yıldız having to go home early. It was the first time this had happened. She had had similar emergencies before but had always found someone to look after Deniz. He told himself that maybe this time she really was stuck and had not been able to find anybody.

'Sure thing, boss. Don't worry, I'll take Otto in for questioning.'

'But it has to be today, Toby. Doesn't matter how late it is. It cannot wait for tomorrow. Every second counts.'

'Understood, boss. I'll see to it.' She was saying every second counted yet here she was going home early. It didn't add up.

They carried on walking in silence. When they reached the Schloss Bridge, lit up by a row of lampposts, Yıldız raised her head and looked at the statues set on the tall pedestals lining the bridge.

'Do you know who this is?' she asked, pointing to a statue of a Goddess holding a shield in one hand and guarding a young warrior with her spear.

'How would I know? Who?'

'This is Athena,' she replied, ignoring his glib response and continuing to gaze at the statue in admiration. 'The guardian Goddess of Pergamon, the city we just saw in the Panorama.' She pointed to the other statues. 'Here, look. We have three different Goddesses in these eight statues: Athena, Nike, who is the Goddess of Victory, and Iris, the Messenger of the Gods. They all assist humans, and the humans they are helping here are all male warriors. Heroes fighting for sacred causes.'

Tobias' dark grey eyes seemed to haze over with the boredom of it all.

'At this rate, we'll all be archaeologists soon.'

'A little knowledge of mythology never hurt anyone,' Yıldız laughed. Tobias looked up sheepishly at the statues.

'You know, I've been over this bridge so many times and not once have I wondered who these statues were supposed to depict.'

'We were taught in high school. One of the benefits of living in Berlin…. But I should confess, I had forgotten that there were so many statues of Athena. Four on this bridge alone.' Her hazel eyes lit up. 'The guys that built these statues one and hundred fifty or so years ago probably wanted Athena to be the guardian Goddess of Berlin too.'

Tobias did not answer as he was still wondering why Yıldız was rushing home like this. He dared not ask, however.

'Mind if I take the car?' Yıldız asked when they reached the Passat. 'I'm in a real rush and need to get back before my dad has to leave. If you could take a cab…'

She sounded so insistent that Tobias could not even bring himself to offer to drive her home.

'Sure. No problem. I'll call you after I've spoken to Otto.'

She smiled broadly but without the usual warmth.

'That would be great. Please do. Doesn't matter what time, make sure you call.'

'See you later then,' he said and began trudging off. What was happening? Why was she acting like this? He wanted to know but could not ask her so he consoled himself by telling himself he would find out sooner or later. He crossed the street towards a waiting taxi.

Yıldız did not care what Toby may or may not have been thinking when she got into the Passat. She was too concerned with what Kerem Ölmez had to say. What had gotten into him? Why was he calling her so urgently like this? She started the engine and hit the gas, ready to find out.

She found Kerem sitting in the backroom of the Bergama Baklava shop. As soon as he saw Yıldız, he got to his feet.

'Thank you so much for coming. No one can help me except you. I'm scared Hüseyin is going to do something stupid. I cannot lose him too. Please, I'm begging you. Please stop him before he does something insane.'

He was speaking in Turkish, and so quickly too that Yıldız was having difficulty following.

'Please calm down, Mister Ölmez,' she said firmly in German. 'I will help you but you need to compose yourself first.' She pointed to the chair on which he had been sitting. 'Please sit down.'

He complied meekly, while Yıldız sat on the same chair on which she had sat during their last visit. The poor man was a wreck. His face had fallen. His cheekbones were sticking out and his black eyes were dark with dread. Yıldız, however, was not in a rush and watched him for some time first. No, Kerem was not putting on an act. He was in pain, and he was worried sick.

'Now tell me, what sort of madness are you afraid Hüseyin is going to perpetrate?'

Kerem, still speaking Turkish, came straight out with it.

'He is going to kill Rudolf. Or at least, that is what I think he is going to do. Hüseyin is rounding up his old friends, some lads that used to be in the 36 Boys. I heard him talking on the phone. They're all amateur hunters too. They like to go out and hunt. Wild boar, deer, that sort of thing. That means they all have guns. Powerful rifles.'

She recalled Hüseyin's stern face and his reckless, gung-ho attitude. And now, to top it all off, he was a hunter with access to guns.

'Where is your son now?'

Kerem pointed to a far-off, unseen place.

'In Rudow... We have a house and a garden out there in the woods. Like one of those old colonial cottages but a bit bigger, in a remote part of the woods far from prying eyes. That's where he is. I spoke to his wife this morning and she told me he went there last night. Told her he wanted to be alone. He came here at around noon today and asked me when we were going to pick up the body. But it was the way he asked me. Like he had something planned. His friend Raif called while Hüseyin was here. Rummenigge Raif, one of his old school friends. They used to play football on the same team. While they were on the phone, I heard Hüseyin say, "Get the lads together and bring the rifles tomorrow morning."'

'Maybe they're going hunting,' Yıldız suggested, hoping Kerem's fears were groundless. 'A hunting party they have been planning for some time. Maybe that's why he asked about the body and the funeral.'

Kerem frowned and then looked at her with a hurt expression.

'Yıldız Hanım, please. Do you really think my Hüseyin would go off hunting when the bodies of his dead brother and grandfather are still warm? I know he can be rash and impulsive but my son would never be that disrespectful.'

She knew from her own family and her own experience how important funerals were to Turkish families. But she also knew that there was an even greater chance of Hüseyin planning an attack on Rudolf if he knew the latter was a suspect in the death of his brother and grandfather. If so, she also knew she had some time, seeing as Hüseyin had asked his friend to bring the guns the next morning.

'I see, Mister Ölmez. Don't worry, we will not let your son do anything rash.'

Kerem shook his head in despair.

'You have to talk to him. If police officers who do not know him get involved, he'll get it all wrong and react. He sees them all the way he sees Rudolf. Thinks they're all the same. But he respects you. If you speak to him, he may still stop before it is too late. Otherwise he may end up opening fire on any German police that turn up, and if that happens, they will be forced to return fire.'

He was telling her to go and see Hüseyin alone. To go and see his son, an armed man who could not control his temper and who was burning with a desire for vengeance. It was highly dangerous but Kerem did have a point. A police raid on the house could have unwanted and tragic consequences.

'What makes you think he respects me?'

'We were talking after parting ways with you the other day. He said, "Our people should be more like her. See that lady? See how well she has done? She has only gone and become a Chief Inspector with the Berlin Police." Hüseyin does not talk so admiringly about people that easily. I could see he respected you. If you tell him you are going to catch his brother and his grandfather's killer, maybe he'll stop doing whatever it is he has planned. Please do something. He's the only child I have left.'

Kerem was truly distraught.

'Very well, Mister Ölmez. I shall go to Rudow directly and speak to your son. Can you write the address down for me please?'

'Thank you so much, Yıldız Hanım. I don't know how I will ever be able to repay you for this,' he said, taking a sheet of paper from a notebook on his desk and writing the address of the house on the outskirts of town.

'How long will it take to get to Rudow from here?'

'There's a bit of traffic right now but no more than forty-five minutes.'

It had already grown dark but Yıldız had time. Kerem finished writing the address and handed the sheet of paper over. 'Hüseyin's telephone number is there too. In case you need it.'

She thanked him and put the note in her jacket pocket.

'Actually, I had meant to ask,' she said. 'The funeral arrangements… When will you claim the body? Where will the service be held?'

'They said they would let us have the body when the autopsy is completed, so within a few days, I guess. I'm taking both of them to Bergama.'

'That would seem to be the right thing. Cemal's boss said he had always wanted to be buried in Bergama.'

'I know. He said the same to his mother,' Kerem said, a lump in his throat.

'Very well. If you are taking charge of the funeral arrangements, I'll tell Mister Schimmel that there will be no need for him to go to Bergama.'

Kerem looked annoyed.

'Why should he? I am going to bury my son and father there. With my own hands. We will have a religious service, with prayers. Mister Schimmel is free to come as our guest but we can take care of our own dead.'

'And no one in the family will object?' Yıldız asked, wanting to understand.

'I don't give a damn,' Kerem snapped. 'Cemal was meeting with his mother in secret but she did not tell us because she was afraid we would disapprove. That's a mother's love for you… She is inconsolable, the poor woman. She blames us. Keeps saying Cemal died because I had not been a good father to him and that Hüseyin had not acted the way a brother should. And she's not wrong.' His lips quivered. 'Had Hüseyin not been so vehemently against him, I wouldn't have minded but you've met Hüseyin, you've seen what he's like. He simply does not listen.' Tears began rolling down his cheeks. 'Ah, Cemal, my son! My beautiful boy! How could they do this to you?'

His love for his son was clear to see.

'You instilled a great love of mythology in him too, I believe,' Yıldız said. 'It seems you used to take him to East Berlin every weekend to see the Altar of Pergamon.'

Kerem was startled and rubbed his eyes dry with his large hands.

'What? What was that?'

'I said you used to take Cemal to the Pergamon Museum. Before the reunification of Germany, when the museum was still in the East.'

Kerem looked at her wondering how she knew this and why she was bringing it up. He leaned back, staring at her coldly.

'Who told you this? The secret service?'

He was speaking German now but it was the Conzent of what he said and not the language he was using that stunned Yıldız.

'The secret service? What do they do have to do with all this?'

The anxiety in his eyes deepened and took hold of his entire face.

'Everything. Back then, the East German police noticed my presence there during my visits. They began to have doubts about me so during one visit, they took me aside for questioning and asked me why I kept coming every week. I told them I was from Bergama and that my family had contributed to the discovery of the Altar and that the museum represented a link to my homeland. They found it fascinating, and they also appreciated my courtesy and so they told me I could visit the Pergamon Museum whenever I wanted but on one condition, and that was that I had to help them. Basically, they wanted me to spy for them. I was held and questioned in that room for a full eight hours. I asked them to give me some time to think it over and told them I would inform them of my decision during my next visit and they agreed. However, when I got back to West Germany, that was not the end of the ordeal. The West German Police had found out that I had been arrested and questioned in the East and they asked me what it is they had wanted and what I had been offered. I told them everything. I was then held and questioned on the Western side of the city for another five hours. The West German Police wanted me to accept the offer from the East Germans but to actually work for them, in the West. "They won't notice, don't worry, we'll protect you, and you'll earn tens of thousands of marks in the process," they said. For a while, I was in the middle of an espionage war. Of course, I refused and until the Wall collapsed, I never went back to the East. I never saw the Altar I loved so dearly again. It was a matter of life and death.'

For sixty years, everyone that lives in Berlin has had their own stories and their own traumas about the Wall, Yıldız thought to herself. She had heard many stories about forbidden loves between Turkish men living in the West and women in the East, of people caught trying to escape over the Wall, of soldiers expressly prohibited from rescuing children that had fallen into the river and who subsequently drowned, of families divided by a mother or a father who had managed to escape to the West. But this was the first time she was hearing a story like this.

'How did you explain this to your son? Didn't he want to see the museum again?'

Kerem's eyes misted over.

'He dearly wanted to go back. He loved the Altar. I used to hold his hand and show him every part of that monument, every nook and cranny, every minute detail, and tell him the stories about the Gods and Goddesses depicted in the statues and friezes. He was so smart, he memorized all the stories straightaway. The Altar of Pergamon for him was like a magic park. He loved the story of Zeus most of all. I remember the way he used to proudly say, "When I grow up, I am going to be Zeus. I shall ride my golden chariot driven by my flying horses towards my enemies and rain thunderbolts down upon them."

But after that day, for years, he could not go to the museum with his father. My eagle… My poor unlucky eagle…'

'Your eagle? Is that what you called him?'

Kerem did not avert his teary eyes.

'Yes. I used to call him my eagle. My eagle of the winds.' He was sobbing now and struggling to get the words out. 'Yıldız Hanım, please, I am begging you. Please save Hüseyin. I have suffered too much. I cannot lose my last son as well. At least let him live.'

A sweet, aromatic coolness was falling over the dark streets of Rudow. Yıldız parked the car under a sycamore tree whose branches were fluttering gently in the summer breeze. She had called Hüseyin twice on the way over and both times his phone had rung but without answer. She called him again when she got out of the car, with the same result. He was obviously too angry and too busy to look at his phone. She put the phone back in her pocket and began walking along the fenced path. Procedure demanded that she let Markus know she was here and to call for backup but she hadn't, not because she did not trust the Chief but because she was afraid of what may happen were Hüseyin to come face to face with unfamiliar police. Sometimes things could be resolved without clinging stubbornly to the rules and she believed this was one such case. Of course, she could be mistaken, but a voice inside her told her this was the best way to go about things. The address she had been given by Kerem was a remote place far from her headquarters, out in the middle of nowhere, with the nearest neighbour a good 250 to 300 metres away. A prime location for Hüseyin to use as a base.

She listened out to her surroundings as she neared the house but there was no sound other than the melancholy chirping of a chorus of crickets that had made their home on the branches of the trees in the area. A few steps later and she saw the two-storeyed house. She walked on until she had reached the garden gate and stopped. There was nobody in the garden. A single light shone in the lower floor of the stone dwelling. She narrowed her eyes to see if there was anybody inside but there was nobody there either. She opened the gate and entered the garden. She was struck by the wonderful scent of wind-kissed fresh basil. She heard a vague crackling sound, as though somebody was dragging a heavy metal object along the ground. After taking a few more steps along the dirt path, she stopped and shouted out, 'Hello? Hello! Mister Ölmez, are you there?'

The sound stopped. She waited for Hüseyin Ölmez to step outside but she saw no one and heard nothing. All that could be heard was the monotonous sound of the crickets in the evening darkness. Something strange was afoot. She unbuttoned her holster but kept her gun there. Maybe he was not at home or had gone to the shops, or, for whatever reason, had not heard her. It would be dangerous for him to see Yıldız holding a gun. But what was that dragging, scraping sound? A broke refrigerator perhaps? An unsteady washing machine? It was hard to tell. Keeping her right hand close to her gun, she approached the house. She berated herself for not informing Markus but it was too late now. She walked slowly towards the house, eyes on the door, ears peeled for any sound. She stopped when she reached the wooden door.

'Mister Ölmez!' she called out. Again, there was no reply. She tried again, in Turkish this time. 'Hüseyin Bey? Hüseyin Bey, are you there?'

Still no response, she made a fist with her hand and knocked on the door, gently at first, then harder and faster. It really did seem there was nobody at home, which was all well and good, but why was he not answering his phone? He could be driving, she thought. Had she seen his car? She looked around and noticed that the shape of the fences around the garden changed near the rear. She decided not to hang around by the front door and began walking to the right and sure enough, there was a gate there wide enough for a car to pass through, and a driveway leading to a garage. She noticed a shape by the door. It was a car. She moved closer and saw a white BMW just beyond the white fence. If his car was here, where was Hüseyin? She quickened her stride. When she turned the corner, she saw a garage, its shutters open. Why hadn't Hüseyin parked his car in the garage? She did not hang around any longer. She drew her gun, loaded it and, grasping it firmly with both hands, walked cautiously towards the garage. In the darkness, it was difficult to see what was going on inside. She suddenly realized how dangerous her position was. If somebody was hiding in the dark depths of the garage, he or she would have no trouble seeing Yıldız standing outside in what would be comparatively light surroundings. She clung to the outside wall of the house and called out.

'Mister Ölmez! Is that you? Are you inside?'

Of course, there was no answer. She stayed outside for some time by the wall listening carefully for any sounds but there was nothing. No breathing, no rustling, nothing. Hüseyin may have gone out for a walk and had put his phone on silent. The only way she could find out was to enter the garage. She crept in. Holding the gun tightly with both hands, she waited for her eyes to adjust to the darkness. It did not take long and she was soon able to make out the objects inside. Holding the gun with her right hand, she felt along the wall with her left hand for the light switch. It did not take long for her to find it. She flicked the switch and a fluorescent white light lit up the garage's interior, causing her to shield her eyes for a couple of seconds.

When she opened them again, she saw a man wearing the white overalls of the CSI crew walking towards her.

'Kurti!' she cried. 'What are you doing here? What are you looking for?'

At the same time, she saw a crowbar being raised into the air and quickly moved to her left. The crowbar came down but missed and glanced off her arm. It was not a heavy blow but it was enough for the gun to fall out of her hands. While she tried to get back on her feet, she saw the man in the white coveralls raise the crowbar again. She swiftly moved to one side again, causing the crowbar to miss again; it skimmed off her shoulder and thudded into the wall. Leaning back into the wall for protection, she felt the light switch protruding into her back. She leaned back with all her strength. In an instant, the fluorescent light vanished, burying the garage in darkness. Her attacker did not give up, though, and lashed out at the spot in which he had just seen her. Yıldız, however, had crouched down. She was one metre seventy and her attacker was tall and he was aiming for her head. Crouching down, Yıldız began sliding along the wall, which put her out the crowbar's range whilst also letting her see where her attacker was as the dim light coming in under garage doors was making his silhouette visible. Her advantage would not last long, though, as the attacker's eyes would soon become accustomed to the dark too. Yıldız looked down and began searching for her gun but the light was too dim and she could not make anything out on the floor. She began feeling for it with her hands. She heard a click. Before she had had a chance to find her revolver, her attacker had found the light switch. The harsh fluorescent light flooded the garage again and before Yıldız could find a place to hide, she was kicked in her stomach, causing her to double over in pain. As she struggled to get her breath back, she saw her gun. It had slid across the floor and was under a small cabinet a few steps away.

Reeling from the force of the kick, she fell towards the cabinet, colliding with it and sending a glass bottle that was resting on top of it crashing to the floor. It shattered, releasing a pungent tobacco aroma. She turned around and saw her attacker staring at her behind a pair of large glasses that covered much of his or her face. Thinking he had gained the advantage, his movements had slowed down and was now walking slowly towards her. Yıldız stayed where she was and waited for him to make his move. When he was close enough, he lifted the crowbar. At that moment, Yıldız reached for her gun. The hooded figure paused, and then hurriedly brought the crowbar down but again, he missed. Yıldız grabbed her gun and aimed it at her assailant.

'Freeze! Don't move!'

The garage was plunged into darkness again. Hearing footsteps racing away, Yıldız fired in the direction of the door, five quick shots in succession. Had she hit him? She stopped, narrowed her eyes and looked around. Then, ignoring the pain in her arm, she got up and, grasping her gun with both hands again, edged towards the door. She did not step outside, though, for she knew her attacker could well be waiting to jump her. She reached the garage door and listened, hoping to catch a sound from outside, but complete silence reigned. The crickets had ended their concert, scared into silence by the shots from the gun. Just then, she heard a car door opening and closing and an engine starting up. He was getting away. Yıldız rushed out. Around fifty metres ahead of the white BMW, the lights on a dark car under a cluster of trees by the roadside came on. Yıldız leapt over the fence.

'Stop! Freeze, or I'll shoot!'

At the same time, shots were fired in her direction. She threw herself to the ground just in time. The attacker did not seem to be alone. She lay face down on the ground and waited. It was not long before the firing stopped. She peeled back her ears, trying to get a grasp of the situation. Again, she heard a car door being opened and closed. They were getting away. She raised her head to have a look. The car was quickly lurching forward. She squinted, hoping to get the car number plate before it got away but it was too dark to make out the car's make and model, let alone its number plate. She watched the car as it sped away. Suddenly, she remembered Hüseyin. She had forgotten all about him.

She turned around and ran back into the garage, where she was met by that pungent scent of tobacco again. She switched the light on. There he was. He was bound hand and foot on a stool, gagged and with blood pouring from a wound in his forehead. Putting her gun back in its holster, she removed the gag from his mouth. Hüseyin let out a cry and started sucking in the air.

'Did you see his face?' she asked as she untied his hands behind his back. 'Did you see the attacker's face, Mister Ölmez? Please, this is crucial. Did you recognize him?'

Hüseyin stared at her groggily.

'What? What are you talking about?'

Before bending down to untie the ropes around his ankles, she looked him in the eye and repeated the question.

'Who attacked you? Was it someone you know?'

Hüseyin finally started regaining his senses.

'Rudolf,' he spluttered. 'Rudolf and his guys…'

'Rudolf? The guy you fought twenty-three years ago?'

'That's right. Blind Rudolf,' he said slowly, in a voice dripping with hatred.

'Did you see his face?'

He blinked and swallowed several times.

'No, I heard his voice.' His hand went up to his forehead. 'My head hurts.'

'How can you recognize the voice of a man you have not seen for decades? Mister Ölmez, what you tell me is of critical importance. The person that has just attacked you is most probably the killer we are looking for. Are you absolutely sure it was Rudolf Winkelmann?'

He focused his eyes on Yıldız. He was looking with greater clarity now.

'Hold on a second,' he said and took out a packet of cigarettes from his waistcoat pocket. He placed a cigarette between his lips, lit it with trembling hands and took a deep drag. He then exhaled, letting the smoke out with a loud groan. 'Damn,' he said looking at the woman that had saved his life and smiling almost like a naughty schoolkid. 'I thought I had copped it.' He stopped and looked around and saw the shattered bottle of perfume on the floor. 'That's my grandfather's cologne. He loved this smell. It's made from tobacco from the Araplı Ovası plain back home. Only grows in Bergama, that strain. Nowhere else.'

Hüseyin's slushy sentimentality did not interest Yıldız in the least.

'Are you sure it was Rudolf Winkelmann?' she asked again impatiently.

'Of course, I am,' Hüsyein replied, blowing smoke out of his mouth and nose. 'It was him alright. He called me a filthy Turk. He said, "You filthy *kanake!* You've been infesting Berlin for years and have stolen everything that is ours. Well, not any more. Enough! We are going to clean this place up and get rid of all you filthy barbarians!" He took another drag and jerked his chin down towards his feet. 'Could you untie my feet, please? These ropes are starting to sting.'

She did as asked and untied him. As she straightened back up, she asked, 'You're not making a mistake, are you? It really was Rudolf Winkelmann that attacked you, wasn't it?'

Hüseyin scowled and pointed to the wall.

'Can't you see the slogan?'

On the wall in red lettering, flanked on both sides with swastikas were the words *Foreigners Out!*

'Do you believe me now? See? They're not even bothering to hide anymore. They're not afraid of anyone. They say they are going to run us out of the city and get rid of us all.'

He tried to get up but he felt dizzy and was about to fall when Yıldız caught him by the arm and eased him back onto the stool.

'You had better take it easy for a while.'

Hüseyin gestured to his rear.

'There should be some water back there. Could you get me some, please?'

She went over and found a plastic bottle of water.

'Small sips only,' she said. When Hüseyin reached out to take the bottle, Yıldız noticed the red liquid oozing from of his hands.

'Hold on, your hand looks injured.'

Hüseyin ignored it and took the bottle from her.

'It's my head, not my hand. The bastard hit me over the head with an iron bar.'

In all the excitement, Yıldız had almost forgotten that he was injured. She hurriedly took out her phone.

'It might be serious. I'm calling an ambulance.'

'There's no need, Yıldız Hanım,' he said, taking a sip of water. 'It's nothing. We all have thick skulls in our family.'

He took the cigarette out of his mouth with his left hand and began taking huge gulps of water. Paying no heed to his comment, Yıldız called for backup and an ambulance, requesting Kurt and his team in particular, telling them it was an urgent case. When she switched the phone off, Hüseyin had emptied the bottle of water and was busy smoking his cigarette.

'How do you feel?' she asked. 'Any nausea or dizziness?'

On the contrary, he looked quite revived.

'Don't worry about me, I'm fine. A nice cup of tea and I'll be as right as rain... But that bastard caught me off guard. That's what pisses me off more than anything.'

He really did look okay and so Yıldız felt no qualms about asking him a few questions.

'What happened? Didn't you see him enter the house?'

'It was an ambush,' Hüseyin said, clearly embarrassed. 'Otherwise I would have torn that piece of shit a new...' He stopped, remembering he was talking to a woman. 'Otherwise I would have cut out his throat and ripped his other eye out.' For some reason, he tried to get up again. This time he succeeded and pointed to a place outside with extreme self-assurance. 'Just over there, that's where he set the trap for me. I was coming back from the shops. I had gone to pick up some food and drink. By the time I got home, it was getting dark. Everything seemed normal. Nothing unusual was going on. But when I got out of the car to open the front gate, he suddenly jumped out. Before I knew what was going on, he brought an iron bar smashing down on my head. I didn't pass out completely, but the rest is all hazy. He dragged me by the shoulders, sat me down on this stool and tied my hands and feet. But he wasn't happy with my position and so he tried dragging me, still on the stool, closer to the workstation. Don't ask me why. I don't know what he was going to do there. Anyway, that is when you turned up.' He looked at her with gratitude. 'I don't know how to thank you. You saved my life.' He fell silent, and then, as though it had just occurred to him, he asked, 'What were you looking for here?'

'For you,' she snapped. 'To stop you doing something stupid. Apparently, you were gathering up your hunter friends and had told them to bring their guns. Tell me, were you planning an attack of some sort?'

Caught red-handed, Hüseyin blushed. He dropped his cigarette on the floor and put it out angrily with his boot.

'Bullshit! Whoever told you that is lying. We do not interfere with the state's business. Yes, my friends were going to come here for a meeting. We have a group, a Hunter's Association… I called the other members of the governing committee so we could discuss certain issues. That is why I went to the shops, you see. To pick up food and drink for our meetings tonight and tomorrow. I wanted to put on a good spread for them.'

It was clear from his tone of voice and body language that he was lying.

'Now look here, Mister Ölmez. There have been two deaths in your family. Two murders. Your parents are besides themselves with grief, and you have a wife and children of your own. You have had enough tragedy for one family. Please, don't do something you will regret. I know you do not trust the police and I understand. You have your reasons, and they may even be considered justified too. But you can trust me. Believe me, I am going to find the people that killed your brother and your grandfather.'

His eyes flashed with anger.

'You don't have to look very far. It was Rudolf. All you have to do is arrest him, that's all.'

'Very well, if it is Rudolf Winkelmann behind these attacks, then I will arrest him and his gang.'

'And how are you going to do that?' he asked bitterly. 'He has the full support of the state authorities. They have been with him throughout. For all we know, it was Nazi groups within the police that organized these attacks. So, tell me, how are you going to do it?'

'You have to trust me.'

He wanted to believe her but he couldn't.

'Fine, let's say I trust you. What about your chiefs and your bosses? The further up you go and the more filth you expose, the more dangerous it will become for you.'

'Nothing will happen to me,' she said with a determined shake of the head. 'Don't worry, nobody will dare have me removed from office. They need me. They want me to solve this case and to stop these killings. This case is starting to hurt their public image. Yes, there are plenty of xenophobic elements in this country but the vast majority of the country abhors racism. But if you act rashly, you'll only be playing into the neo-Nazis' hands by making the attackers the victiMs So please, leave this to us. I am going to start proceedings to have Rudolf Winkelmann arrested. Now. Immediately. I won't be going home after this. After this, I am going to find him and question him. But you have to give me your word that you will not turn this into a personal feud. If you do, you risk making a complete mess of things.'

Although he looked to be coming round to her way of thinking, she could see that he was still not fully convinced and that she needed to break his last strand of resistance.

'Believe me, Hüseyin Bey,' she said, this time in Turkish. 'Your family's grief will not go unavenged. I will not allow it.'

10
Zeus, father to all creatures!

The paths upon which heroes walk is steeper, narrower and more dangerous than the paths walked by the Gods. No matter how brave, how selfless and how fearless a hero is, he can never have the power, wisdom or foresight of a God. This includes Perseus, Heracles and my own children. Heroism is limited by the event. It is fleeting. An attempt to restore good and defeat evil in that particular adventure. The hero demonstrates his strength, his courage and his abilities for that particular goal and to achieve that task. His mental and physical worlds are restricted to that mission and when the mission has been accomplished, his work is over. He has done his duty, he has been challenged, he has suffered and he has rescued his people from woe, risking captivity and death.

Heroes do only what they have been told to do. They obey the commands of a God, a king or a commander, or they answer a woman's distressed call for help. But none can command or instruct the Gods. I am the Lord of the Titans, the Giants, the Gods, Men and all the creatures because I know what must be done. The goal of such a lord is not merely to overcome evil, for good and evil, truth and falsehood, beauty and ugliness, mercy and ruthlessness, selflessness and selfishness are all required in order for the balance and order of the world to be maintained. The miracle that is known as life arises from the invisible threads that bind those forces together, and it is my duty to ensure that those threads remain taut and do not snap or become tangled. Heracles' sacred task would also be accomplished at the end of a series of events bound expertly together by such unseen threads. I needed to both create those threads and to ponder long and hard the tasks before setting them in place. Nor could I tell Hera or Heracles about this plan of mine, for it was too mighty, too cruel and too wicked for them to bear. Yet, in order for us to save the world form the barbarians, it had to be done. The queen of the Goddesses and the mightiest of the Mortals' heroes could only be performers in this savage plan I had formulated.

Yes, I admit that I, Zeus, used my queen, Hera of Argos, and Heracles, mightiest of all men, in my preparations for our final battle against the primitive beings that were being incited to revolt by Gaia, and I did it with great patience, stern silence, utmost secrecy and subtle dexterity. I did not hesitate in drawing up and implementing a bloody scheme that could spell death for my own grandchildren. I did not feel pride in this, nor did I feel sorrow, for I had no choice. Apart from the pain that sometimes stabbed at my heart or the guilt I felt whenever I gazed upon Heracles, creating this plan and implementing it were not arduous for me.

In my divine mission to save the earth and the sky from the dominion of the Giants, my greatest helper would be my wife's jealousy. Hera was no fool but when she was overcome with jealousy, her mind could only entertain revenge and evil. Her jealousy so blinded her that she could think of nothing else. Even before Heracles was born, she had become the sworn enemy of his mother, Alcmene, and she did all she could do keep us apart, just as she had done with my other lovers. Of course, her efforts would be in vain for I needed a strong, beautiful and wise woman who would give me a son that would aid me in my divine quest, and there was no woman worthier than Alcmene. Neither my wife's proscriptions nor Amphitryon, Alcmene's noble husband, could stand in my way. I seized my opportunity when King Amphitryon went to war. The only way to win the heart of an honourable woman like Alcmene was to take the guise of her husband and so I appeared before her as a triumphant Amphitryon returning victorious from the battlefield. Innocent Alcmene, suspecting nothing, invited me to her bed. So exhilarating was our lovemaking and such was the ecstasy I felt, I asked the Sun God Helios to extend the day.

Naturally, Hera, who always watched my every move, learnt about this amorous liaison. Unfortunately, the noble Amphitryon also learnt of our illicit liaison. Moreover, because he made love to his wife the day after me, Alcmene became pregnant with two children. Thinking his wife had cheated on him, Amphitryon set out to kill her but I reached him just in time and said:

'Do not, noble Amphitryon, your honourable wife is without blame. She did not even know that the man lying with her was me. She thought the man in her bed was you. If you seek the guilty one, then it is I. But let me say this, I made love to your wife for a sacred purpose. I cannot tell you now what it is but when the time comes, you will understand why I took this deviant path. I just ask you to trust me.'

Amphitryon was a pious man and he replied:

'I trust you, Exalted Zeus. If you did what you say you did, then surely you have your reasons. Henceforth, your son shall be my son. I shall care for him as my own and I shall raise him alongside the son Alcmene gives me.'

Yet, while the deceived husband behaved with such magnanimity, Hera would not accept this son of mine born of a Mortal mother and she spat abuse at Amphitryon, calling him the 'vilest of all cuckolded men.' But all her scorn and her spite were for nought for my plan had already begun to work.

Alcmene gave birth to my son Heracles first, and the following day gave birth to Amphitryon's son Iphicles. Upon hearing of the birth of my son, Hera lost her mind, which is exactly what I wanted. But to enrage her even further, with the help of my wily son Hermes, I had my newly born son placed in her lap as she slept, and while he was there, my ravenous son lapped up the Goddess' milk. And so, Hera became wet nurse to a child she detested and the boy took his name from her: *Heracles*, or 'the glory of Hera.' Yet still my wife's only aim was to harm the child. She sent two serpents into Heracles and Iphicles' room. Iphicles carried on sleeping, unaware of the danger, but my strong son captured the two poisonous snakes and strangled them to death with his bare hands. And so Hera's rage reached new heights, while I sat calmly on my throne on Olympus and watched events past and events-to-be transpire.

Heracles grew by the day. King Amphitryon kept his word and treated him as his own son. Heracles, though, was so strong that no one could best him and this superiority went to the boy's head. He began to rebel before his training and education were complete. Not even his teachers could control him. One day, when his teacher Linos attempted to reprimand him for a mistake, Heracles struck the poor man over the head with his own lyre and killed him. An act prompted by neither Hera nor myself, it was purely the result of Heracles unbridled rage, something neither I nor Hera could ignore. Heracles had learnt how to ride a chariot from none other than Amphitryon, archery from the master Eurytus himself, swordsmanship from the great swordsman Castor and how to wrestle from the invincible Autolycus.

Like me, Hera watched Heracles from day to day and received updates from her loyal informers as she waited for the right time to lay a trap for him. For Heracles to suffer, his loved ones needed to multiply in number. A young single man's only tie to life is his mother, but if he marries and has children and those he loves increase in number, so will his suffering increase. And so I waited, pretending not to know about my evil wife's macabre designs, waiting for the moment I could execute my own plan. I did not need to wait long. In a short time, my son, whose fame grew with his daily heroics, found himself a wife.

There was a dispute between Erginus, King of Orchomenus and Creon, King of Thebes, two rulers who were always clashing, fighting and arguing anyway. In this dispute, Heracles took the side of Creon and inflicted a crushing blow upon greedy Erginus' men. The people of Thebes began to view him as a God. As a reward, King Creon gave his daughter, Megara, to Heracles in marriage, and the marriage led to the birth of three children. Of course, it was not long before the news that my son was leading a blissful life reached Hera's ear. Ruthless as ever, she saw her opportunity and came down from Olympus to earth, where she learnt from the greatest sorcerers how to concoct the most potent elixirs, the most accursed recipes and the vilest hexes. And when a crimson moon rose in the sky, she performed her most powerful magic, directed straight at Heracles. The effect was felt immediately. First, he had a splitting headache, and then he became blind, after which he began to hallucinate, thinking cursed creatures had entered his house. Utterly overcome, he thought his own children were monsters and killed them all, one by one, by throwing them with his own hands into the fire.

Naturally, I saw everything. I knew before she did it what she was going to do. Had I wished, I could have intervened but I chose not to. Instead, I let her do as she wished, so she could expunge all her vindictiveness and all her destruction and take out all her rage on my son. I needed her evil for my own aims. It was imperative that Heracles become more than an ordinary hero, for I needed him in my war against the Giants. He had to pass the sternest of tests, but for him to partake of these tests, he needed to be crushed and feel the most profound guilt and remorse. And that is exactly what happened. When Hera's witchcraft wore off, he realized, too late, what he had done. He blamed himself for the calamity and went mad with grief. He would not eat or drink, he retreated into himself, and, like a wounded lion, roamed the mountains alone, howling in pain. It was a terrible sight to behold, one that grieved me too, but it was exactly what I wanted.

Some may say, 'What difference is there between you, Zeus, and Kronos, the father you deposed for his cruelty towards his own children? Kronos swallowed his children whole, while you, Zeus, King of the Gods, watched your own son fall into grief and despair. You are as evil as your father.' But no; I am not evil. There is a difference between Kronos and I. My father swallowed his children because he did not wish to share his power; his aim was to protect his throne, whereas I was prepared to let my own son suffer in order to protect the balance of the world. For I am not just the father of Heracles; I am the father of all creatures. I am responsible for their protection and ensuring they lead happy, just lives, and if I did nothing to counter the imminent attack by the Giants, there could be no justice or bliss in any life in the sky or on earth, for the Giants would create a world with lives like their own, lives without virtue or beauty. I had no choice but to vanquish them, and to do this I needed my

Mortal son Heracles to join the war, as per the command of the other Gods and the divine law. But he was not yet ready for such a conflict and so I needed to be utterly ruthless and single-minded. I needed to silence my conscience, disregard mercy and set aside my love. Because the divine law was clear: to defeat the Giants, I had to have a Mortal fighting in my ranks, and that Mortal could be no other than my own son. Therefore, I needed to prepare him for the war, whatever the cost. For at the end of the war, the barbarians would be wiped off the face of the Earth and all living things would thereby be saved. And so, I, Zeus, father to all, to the Titans, the Gods, the Giants, and all mankind, had to permit the ruination of my own son so that life would flourish. I knew Heracles was a man in all senses. I was sure he would pass any test placed before him and that he would be ready for the greatest war ever fought.

And so, while he writhed and howled in agony, I entered his mind and told him to go to the sacred house of Delphi. He obeyed and there, he approached the Oracle Pythia, who listened to him in utmost serenity. When his tears and words had ended, she rose and said:

'This is not a tragedy in which I can decide, noble Heracles. I must consult the Gods. They shall decide your fate.'

And she left Heracles alone in the sacred house and was not seen for seven days and seven nights. At dawn on the seventh day, she returned and said:

'Noble Heracles, I have consulted the Gods. The killing of one's own children is an unforgivable crime, even more so when the children are without blame. Yours is a terrible transgression. Were it not for the many good deeds you have done, even your father Zeus would not have been able to save you. So be grateful for your good deeds, for it is through them that the Gods have allowed a path to redemption to be cleared for you. If you successfully complete the penances, you shall be rescued from the torments of your conscience and your guilt.'

My broken boy bowed his head in reverence and said:

'I shall do whatever the Gods command. All I ask is for this torment to end. I shall do whatever is demanded, so long as I do not hear my children's screams ringing in my ears.'

The penance prepared for Heracles was shameful. He was to obey the commands of the most foolish, the most cowardly and the most reckless king of all time, King Eurystheus, a rascal made king by the efforts of none other than Hera. The rule that was rightfully my son's she had given to this fool Eurystheus and now the mightiest and noblest man on earth, the heroic son of Zeus, would have to do the bidding of this foolish and impudent king. As a father, it was truly an indignity but I had to endure this ignominy in order to defeat the terrible Giants.

To be a God is to know how to be utterly single-minded when necessary.

Chapter Ten

There was an annoying buzzing sound in the interrogation room. The room was bare, except for a table, four stools, a huge mirror to the right and a medium size screen on the wall to the left. One of the lamps behind the papier-mâche screen was, in its own particular idiom, informing those present that it was running out of life, and the buzzing noise it was making as it spluttered in and out of life was making the already tense atmosphere even more unpleasant. Having been hurriedly brought to the station, Rudolf Winkelmann now fidgeted on his stool and looked to his lawyer, sitting next to him, pleadingly for help. His lawyer, however, did not seem to realize his client was looking at him. He sat with his head leaning forward, exhausted, his expensive suit crumpled and his tie askew, trying hard to keep his eyes open. The poor fellow had to cut short an enjoyable evening to come to the station and by all accounts, he seemed quite drunk.

'Couldn't this have waited?' Rudolf growled. 'What is the meaning of this? Dragging a man out of his home in the middle of the night!' Even while he was talking, he was looking at his lawyer as though to ask him why he wasn't the one doing the talking but the usually alert and nimble lawyer was barely conscious. If he could, he would have put his head on the table there and then and dozed off.

'No, it cannot wait,' Yıldız answered assuredly. 'There is a killer wandering this city's streets as we speak. Three people have been brutally killed this week already. We cannot allow any more murders to take place.'

Rudolf's face went red. His thick neck tensed up and its purple veins throbbed. He placed his hands angrily on the table.

'What, are you trying to say I am behind those murders? Why don't you just come out with it — are you accusing me of murder or not?'

His voice came out so high that even his intoxicated lawyer seemed to jolt up. He covered his yawning mouth with his hand and reached out for the plastic cup of coffee on the table in front him. He downed the drink in one go.

'Please calm down,' Tobias warned him. 'Nobody is accusing you of anything. We are simply investigating three murders. More people may yet be killed.'

Tobias was not in the best of moods, either. He was still upset at his boss going off to deal with Hüseyin by herself without telling him. When he found out what had happened to Yıldız, he was shocked. He wanted to know what was going on but he had not had the chance to ask yet, which is why he was in such a foul mood when he entered the interrogation room.

'And what does any of that have to do with me?' Rudolf yelled, his right eye flashing with rage, whilst his left eye kept its usual blank look, a combination that gave the man an unusual countenance. 'Why did you bring me here then? What am I doing here?'

Although Yıldız was smiling, she was tired as she had been on the streets since last night. Moreover, every breath she took was causing her discomfort. The kick she had received from the killer must have caused serious injury to her ribs. She had disregarded the Chief's advice to go to hospital because she wanted to make sure Rudolf was brought in for questioning and she had successfully done so but now her discomfort was growing by the second. She could have taken a painkiller but it would have slowed her down mentally and she needed to be alert. She had no choice but to grin and bear the pain.

'Don't, Mister Winkelmann,' she said. 'You wanted this.'

'Me? How?' Rudolf was so angry, he could not think straight.

'You don't remember? This morning at the Germania Sports Club? You said, and I quote, "Don't come here again. If you are going to accuse me, then you can come back and arrest me."' She looked at her assistant. 'Am I wrong, Toby? Is that not what Mister Winkelmann said?'

'Fine, fine, I remember,' Rudolf said hurriedly. 'But did you have to do it in the middle of the night? What's wrong with the morning? Holed up in a room like this at this ungodly hour…'

Yıldız looked at him with a sombre expression.

'Mister Winkelmann, somebody else was almost killed this evening. If I had not arrived in time, the murderers would have had another victim in Rudow. Moreover, had I not taken adequate measures to protect myself, then I would now be dead too. That is why we have brought you in here, despite the time. Three o'clock, five o'clock, it doesn't matter. And we will keep you here as long as we need to.'

'That's terrible,' the lawyer managed to say, slowly awakening from his stupor. 'Really. I'm very sorry for you.' He licked his dry lips before continuing. 'However, I don't… I don't see what… This has to do with my client.'

He was having trouble getting the words out but at least he was talking. Rudolf Winkelmann looked at him in exasperation.

'Yes, what does it have to do with me?'

'Because the man who was attacked today was Hüseyin Ölmez. A man who has had a running feud with your client for twenty-three years.'

The lawyer was about to object but Yıldız held up a hand and pointed to the screen, where a photo of Hüseyin Ölmez appeared.

'Two of the three murder victims were relatives of Hüseyin Ölmez. Orhan Ölmez was his grandfather and Cemal Ölmez was his brother.' As she said the names, their photos appeared on the screen. 'Orhan Ölmez was an old man, but his grandson Cemal Ölmez was young and full of life. More importantly, however, your client once had a fight with Cemal Ölmez. A bloody fight during which a pane of glass was shattered…'

'Bloody?' Rudolf snorted. 'We didn't even have any weapons. It wasn't planned. It just happened.' He pointed to the screen. 'I saw this dude while I was walking past his shop. The man is a staunch enemy of Germany. And believe me, when I say a staunch enemy, I am not exaggerating. A terrorist Turk who set up a gang to kick native Germans out of Kreuzberg and who plans attacks on the indigenous people of this land.' Seeing the two officers in front of him stare at him disbelievingly, he went on. 'Fine, don't believe me. You've already made up your minds anyway. But let me tell you what happened. Yes, the fight you mentioned did take place. Like I said, I was walking past the shop when I saw that asshole. He saw me too and started calling me a "dirty Nazi". He came out of the shop and started walking towards me, saying things like "Spawn of Hitler, get lost!" We started arguing and then, when his insults got worse, it turned physical. But we didn't have any knives.'

'Thank you, Mister Winkelmann,' his lawyer said, clearing his throat. 'You do not need to talk about this.'

His client, however, did not seem to hear him and carried on with even greater passion.

'In addition, Hüseyin threw the first punch. Naturally, we retaliated. It turns out, however, that his brother was hiding inside and he attacked us from behind. The coward.' He looked Yıldız dead in the eye and with open loathing added, 'The kind of underhand move one would expect from a Turk.'

The veneer of civility Rudolf had adopted during their first encounter at the Germania Sports Club was gone entirely. He was seething with anger now and willing to lash out. Yıldız was reminded of the killer she had seen five or six hours earlier and who, she was certain, despite not having been able to fully see his face, had been staring at her with the same intense hatred behind his dark glasses. She suddenly felt the rush of air from the movement of the crowbar when the killer had tried to bring it down on her face. She wondered if Rudolf was being this aggressive because he had not been able to strike her in the garage. She maintained her composure, however, and ignored his last comment.

'Mister Winkelmann, please,' the lawyer said, tapping his client on his hand. 'There is no point in talking about events from the distant past. You are describing a fight that took place years ago. It's over and done with. A distant memory.'

Rudolf looked down in Conzempt at Helmut's effeminate pink fingers on his hand.

'I apologize, Mister Berger,' he murmured with an effort to sound respectful. 'I have been confronted with such distasteful lies and such unjust treatment that I momentarily lost my temper.' He quickly drew his hand back. 'You are right. Events of decades ago have no bearing on what is being discussed now.'

An annoying look of triumph appeared on Yıldız's face.

'Well, it seems they do, Mister Winkelmann,' she said, goading him further. 'If it had not been so important to you,

you would not have become so irate. Moreover, during our conversation this morning, you told us you did not remember Hüseyin Ölmez or your fight with him. So, in fact, you are the one that told us this lie that you have just described as distasteful. So, let me now ask you: are you going to carry on with these blatant untruths or are you going to cooperate with us?'

Worried that his client would again erupt in anger, the lawyer touched his hand again to warn him.

'You are under no obligation to speak. As your lawyer, I can answer any questions on your behalf.'

Rudolf pulled his hand away again.

'Thank you, Mister Berger, but I would prefer to answer the questions myself because I have nothing to hide. They are trying to ruin my reputation with these ludicrous charges but I will not allow it.' He turned to look at the mirror covering the facing wall. 'A tragedy. The police service of the great state of Germany has become the plaything of a bunch of dirty foreigners.'

He knew he was being watched by other officers behind the glass, and Markus was indeed watching the interview with great interest, having also been dragged away from his warm bed to the station in the middle of the night.

'Watch your step, Mister Winkelmann!' Tobias' ice-cold voice rang out. 'You will not insult the German state or its police officers here. You talk about your love of Germany and Germans and yet here you are hurling abuse and accusations at the state you proclaim to revere.'

Rudolf was taken aback and did not know what to say. He then turned to Yıldız with a burning look of hatred in his eyes.

'But this woman is setting up a trap for me and the state is allowing it. She has no evidence and no witnesses. I have been arrested on charges of murder and brought here in the middle of the night but as a citizen of Germany, I have rights too.'

'You have indeed,' Yıldız agreed and pointed to Helmut Berger. 'And you have with you a fine lawyer who will protect your rights to the fullest extent of the law. All you need to do is answer our questions. I do not know why you are behaving so belligerently. If you have nothing to fear, then you have no need for anger. Just tell us what you know, and without any lies. The truth, that's all. Mister Berger will know better than any of us how detrimental it may be to you if the atmosphere here were to turn sour.'

This was the final straw for Rudolf.

'What? How dare you! Detrimental, you say? Are you threatening me in my own country?'

Not even Yıldız was expecting him to become this enraged. It meant they were on the right track. If he was getting this angry, clearly he had something to hide.

'It is not your country, Mister Winkelmann. It is our country. I was born here too, and in this city. I have spent all my life here. Allow me to inform you that discriminating between German citizens is a crime as per the constitution, as is insulting a civil servant. So please, I would kindly ask you to compose yourself.'

Rudolf was so tensed up, he looked as though he could leap up from his seat and throttle Yıldız there and then. Tobias also sensed the danger and was waiting, hand on his holster, ready to intervene if necessary. Nothing, however, happened. Helmut Berger grabbed his client by the hand.

'Mister Winkelmann! Mister Winkelmann! I implore you! Please calm down. Look, I am on your side. Nobody is conspiring against you. You cannot be charged with something you did not do. The law does not allow it. Please compose yourself. We cannot proceed like this.' All signs of the lawyer's drowsiness had gone now. 'Please believe me when I tell you have nothing to worry about. We have not even heard the questions yet. Let them go ahead and ask their questions.' He paused and looked at his client. 'If you like, we can take a short break, so you can get some fresh air and some coffee.'

Rudolf's face was almost green, like an epileptic's after a fit. His fury had subsided and his working eye stared dead ahead, just like his false eye. Sucking in his lower lip, he leant back on his stool.

'I apologize. To all of you. You are right, Mister Berger. I overreacted. But it was only because of the unfairness of what is being done to me.' His lawyer was clearly expecting another outburst but Rudolf reassured him. 'No, don't worry, I've learnt my lesson. I understand. I'm calm now. I realize there is no need for me to behave in such a manner. I was wrong, I admit it.' He tried to smile and looked at Yıldız. 'Please, go ahead. I am listening. How can I help you?'

Too late, I'm afraid, you little... Yıldız thought to herself, the pain in her ribs getting worse by the second. She smiled courteously in response.

'Thank you, Mister Winkelmann. We are glad that you have started to see sense. Your cooperation will be a great help to all of us. This interview is being recorded and anything you say may be used in a court of law. Now, seeing as you have regained your composure, we can get down to business.' She glanced at the sheets of paper in front of her. She lifted the topmost sheet and looked at the one underneath. 'This morning you told us that you did not know Mister Otto Fischer. You said this despite being arrested together at a demonstration against foreigners held in Berlin last year and despite giving him a lift in your vehicle when you were both released.'

While Yıldız spoke, photographs of the demonstration appeared on the screen. In some photos, Rudolf and Otto were standing together, their faces contorted in fury as they crossed police barricades and marched in protest. In the next few photos, they were seen exiting the police station and getting into the Germania Sports Club van and driving off.

'Despite these images, you claim not to know Otto Fischer. But yesterday evening, Otto Fischer, who is the prime suspect in the murder of Cemal Ölmez, said he knew you.' She lifted her head and stared at Rudolf icily. No, he was not going to continue lying. He was not going to make any more mistakes. Yıldız turned to her assistant. 'Inspector Becker, would you be so kind as to tell us what Mister Fischer said during his questioning?'

Before Tobias started, a photo of Otto appeared on the screen, standing in front of a Nazi flag and flexing his muscles. A man with no skills or talents and who had achieved little of note in his life and whose only source of pride was his ideology. A lost man trying, along with his equally lost and useless friends, to give some meaning to his life by using the flag, trying to create some meaning — wild, destructive and hate-filled meaning — for himself with concepts like race and nation. The half-pint Nazi was standing in front of those accursed swastikas in the photo and staring defiantly at the camera, seemingly challenging the world.

'So that's how it is, Mister Winkelmann,' Tobias said, not needing to look at his notes. 'Otto Fischer, the man you see on the screen here, stated during his questioning yesterday evening that he has known you for a long time and that you have been friends since your youth. And what a coincidence — you were on the "Germanise Kreuzberg Project" together! You know, your fight against that street gang known as the 36 Boys. You fought side by side against them.' He looked down at his notes. 'Yes, this is what he said in his statement, which, by the way, we shall also make available to you. He also added that you were a loyal man and that you were not one to turn your back on your friends.' He smiled and looked at the lawyer. 'Indeed, he also told us that you were kind enough to send Mister Berger here to his assistance when he needed him.' He paused and leaned back. 'Now, when your own comrade-in-arms feels no need to hide your friendship, why would you deny knowing him, I wonder?'

A nervous Helmut Berger leaned over and whispered in his client's ear, 'You do not have to answer.'

In contrast to his visibly nervous lawyer, Rudolf was now free of any high-running emotion. Without even feeling the need to respond to Helmut, he crossed his arms over his chest, like Otto in the picture, and said, 'Because I thought you were conspiring against me. Because I did not trust you. Otto is not the sharpest tool in the box. He is prone to outbursts. People like him are always capable of harming others. I do not know if he is involved in these murders or not, and I hope he has not done something as stupid as that. But when you asked about Otto, I thought you were trying to entrap me. You have my files, you know my past. I know you won't find a better patsy to offer the press than me so I acted the way I did both because of the prejudices you have about me and because I know your aim is to pin these murders on me to somehow prove I am the killer. I worked that out the moment you set foot in the Germania Sports Club. That is why I denied my acquaintance with Otto. I admit now that it was a mistake. But know this; I am no longer the Rudolf Winkelmann of old. I am a respectable businessman now. As I said this morning, a lot of water has flowed under the bridge since then. I no longer believe we can realize our aims through violence. While our views are being heard and defended in parliament and our parties are growing stronger by the day, violence will only harm our cause. And bloody murders like this would serve only to alienate the people from us. It would be stupidity on our part to attempt such a thing.'

'Stupidity only people like Otto Fischer are capable of…' Yıldız offered. Rudolf unfolded his arms.

'I do not want to accuse my friend of anything, especially when there is no evidence. However, and unfortunately, yes, we do have such fools in our ranks.'

Yıldız wanted to lean back but she was in too much pain. She grimaced but carried on with the questioning.

'The problem, Mister Winkelmann, is that your comrade, Otto Fischer, because of this same stupidity you describe, is not capable of organising a series of murders on this scale. Moreover, even after he was arrested, the murders did not stop. Alexander Werner, who was an acquaintance of Cemal Ölmez, has been killed and this evening, Hüseyin Ölmez was attacked. So, even if Otto and his friends did kill Cemal and Cemal's grandfather, somebody else is behind this spate of killings. Other people. Smarter, stronger, shrewder people…'

Rudolf nodded his head in agreement.

'Possibly, but why do you insist on thinking that these people must necessarily be German patriots? Look, I'll say it again. These murders cannot benefit us. They can only harm us. What's not to say that the murderers and the person or people that attacked you this evening are not the enemies of German patriots? Why do you insist on choosing the easy path? Why do you insist upon arresting the suspects you have already formed in your minds?'

Rudolf was back to his own self but Yıldız was having none of it. She glanced at her papers and then looked the suspect in the eye.

'Because Cemal Ölmez and his family were being threatened by neo-Nazis. Because Otto Fischer's fingerprints were found on abusive and threatening letters sent to Cemal Ölmez. Because Otto Fischer was in Cemal Ölmez's house on the night of the murder. Because Otto Fischer's knife was used in at least two of the murders. Because you denied your acquaintance with Otto Fischer. Because, despite saying you believe your cause should be fought via political parties, you have not cut your ties with a man with a criminal background, a man like Otto Fischer. Would you like me to go on?'

Yıldız had started gently but by the time she had finished, she was almost shouting. The lawyer was quick to step in.

'You do not need to raise your voice like this, Ms Karasu. Everything you have just said is conjecture. Otto Fischer's connection to the murders you describe has yet to be proven and your accusations regarding Mister Winkelmann are nothing more than assumptions. It is clear now that Mister Winkelmann is worrying quite unnecessarily. In denying his association with Otto Fischer, he made a mistake but that does not make him a killer.'

'He didn't just deny knowing Otto Fischer,' Yıldız said. 'He also denied knowing the victim and the victim's family. He also concealed the feud he has had for twenty-three years with the man who was attacked in his home in Rudow this evening, Mister Hüseyin Ölmez. '

'Now hold on a minute,' Rudolf said, raising his arms. Everyone fell silent and stared at him. 'Are you now claiming that I went to this Hüseyin Ölmez character's house this evening? Are you claiming I went there and that I attacked him and then you?'

Yıldız sensed a trap but she could not step back.

'Yes, that is one of the possibilities. It is possible that the attack was carried out by you and your associates.'

'And what time did this attack take place, Ms Karasu?' he asked, his working eye now twinkling mischievously.

Yıldız paused to think.

'Let me see. When I called for help after the attack, that is when it was all over, the time was 21.35. The attacker, or attackers, fled around ten minutes earlier. So the incident took place between 20.30 and 21.35.'

'Wonderful,' Rudolf beamed, taking a mobile phone out of his pocket. 'I was at a cocktail party at that time. Between 20.00 and 22.00, to be precise. A cocktail party on the terrace of the Adler Civil Aviation company building in Kudamm. The owner of the company, Adler Geschwinder, is a good friend of mine. You can call him to confirm.' He pressed a few buttons on his phone and then gave the phone to the officers present. 'Even better, I have photos. Photos taken at the event. They are all here on my phone, with the time on each photograph too. Go on, take a look. Please. Go ahead. See for yourselves.'

Yıldız took the phone. There he was, holding a glass of champagne with a group of people, men and women, all smiling at the camera. In total, there were seven photographs taken at the cocktail at different times.

'So, as you can see, at the time you stated, I was not in Rudow, as you claim, but in Kudamm. I attacked neither you nor Hüseyin Ölmez. If the photos are not enough, I can find you a dozen people who will gladly testify to my being there at that time, including Adler Geschwinder, the president of the company.'

Yıldız now realized her mistake. Rudolf had not been directly involved in the attacks. He was organising them, choosing his best men to carry them out while he made sure he was tucked away somewhere safe, somewhere far from the violence, with plenty of eyewitnesses. She looked him in his eye, which was twinkling in triumph.

'Were your two bodyguards also with you at the cocktail? Those two blond man mountains I saw earlier with the identical uniforms and haircuts?'

Rudolf shrugged off the comment.

'One does not attend cocktail parties with bodyguards, Ms Karasu. There is such a thing as propriety.'

Dawn was breaking when they left the station. When she stepped outside after hours in that locked windowless room, Yıldız stopped at the head of the staircase and breathed in the fresh air, staring at the changing colours of the sky as the sun began its ascent. She blinked a few times and savoured the freshness of the morning. The pain in her ribs seemed to be subsiding. The painkiller Markus had given her after Rudolf Winkelmann had been hurried out of the room was starting to take effect. She had not been expecting the one-eyed Nazi to wiggle out so easily, but then again, life does not always conform to our hopes and desires. Rudolf Winkelmann had an irrefutable alibi, as well as witnesses. They no longer had reasonable grounds for detaining him. Even if they had charged and arrested him based on their assumptions, it would have been only a matter of time before he was released, and that in turn would have caused a whole new set of probleMs She could almost see the headlines in the right-wing press: *Turkish Chief Inspector Detains Respectable Businessman for Hours Simply for Being German!* That is why she did not object when Markus said they had to let him go. That did not mean she now believed he was innocent or that he was no longer the prime suspect and that Yıldız would forget about him and let him get on with his life. But she had to accept that Rudolf had won this round. As such, as she made her way down the staircase, she felt defeated, although having been on her feet for twenty-four hours also had a part to play in her dejection.

The Passat's bonnet was covered in tiny dewdrops. With some difficulty, she threw the keys to Tobias.

'You drive. The painkiller has kicked in and will only slow me down.'

'Sure thing, boss,' Tobias said, catching the keys in mid-air. He said no more. He was still feeling down too, not just because of Winkelmann's release but also because of Yıldız's solo visit to Hüseyin Ölmez's house. Why had she not called him? She had lied to him. She had told him she was going home when she had gone to see Hüseyin instead. Something fishy was going on.

They both got in. Yıldız seemed to jump up when she sat down. The car was cooler on the inside. Tobias started the engine and moved the car into first gear, while Yıldız lifted up her jacket collar and curled up in her seat. She kept her eyes open, though, and stared out at the desolate road ahead and at the light as it began to dispel the road's otherwise menacing countenance. They did not talk for some time but when she saw the red towers of the Oberbaum Bridge, under which she had sailed so many times with Franz, she seemed to perk up. She was staring out of the window to get a better look at the reddish waters of the River Spree when Toby finally spoke.

'What's going on, boss?'

At first, she did not understand and thought he was referring to something unusual on the river so she peered down to get a better look but apart from a couple of small boats and a barge that was carrying such a heavy load that the waters of the river were almost on the deck, she saw nothing of note. She turned around and when she saw his dark grey eyes, she realized what he meant.

'What's going on, boss?' Toby asked again. 'Why are you acting like this?'

There was no way out for Yıldız, nor was there much point in dodging the issue much longer. She braced herself and replied.

'You tell me, Tobias.'

'Tell you what, boss?' Toby asked, bewildered. 'You're the one hiding information from me! You're the one that went on an operation alone, without telling me!'

Yıldız sighed uneasily. She stared at the empty road ahead and at the river, and then pointed to a café up ahead.

'Park the car up there.'

The East Side Bakery located next to the bridge that linked East and West Berlin was about to open for business and a young lady was busy setting the tables outside. She stared at them with her big green eyes, wondering what they were doing there so early in the morning, but when she saw that they were not going to order anything, she relaxed and went back to her work. By now, Yıldız's painkiller-induced wooziness was beginning to fade away. She placed her hands on the table.

'Yes, Tobias, tell me, why did you hide that information from me?' Her light-brown eyes were locked on her assistant. 'Why didn't you tell me that your grandfather was a Nazi? Why did you tell me he was a communist who was killed fighting the fascists? What are you hiding?'

Tobias' face went white.

'What? What have I hidden?' He was not admitting to it yet his voice was so lacking in conviction that Yıldız simply cast him a disparaging look. A smart man, Tobias realized he was cornered and that there was little point in prolonging the charade.

'Oh, that,' he said, but that was all. He looked away, took out his packet of cigarettes and lit one. The breeze coming over the river carried the smoke away. He smiled painfully.

'Nobody likes to say their grandfather was a Nazi, boss. It's not an easy thing to admit to openly. Not something to be proud of. But if you're in a socialist country, it's downright dangerous and can get you into serious trouble. It wasn't me but my father that concealed my grandfather's past. Ernst Becker is the black sheep of our family. He was a Nazi with blood on his hands.' He looked and sounded sincere, free of trickery, and his body language was open and calm. 'I'm not lying, boss, when I tell you that I have never liked Nazis. I still despise them and so did my father.'

Yıldız was ready with her next question.

'You told me your father was not a believing communist.'

Tobias' shoulders slumped, helpless at being misunderstood.

'He wasn't. He was never a dyed-in-the-wool communist, but he was a stubborn and committed anti-fascist. Indeed, he hated all forms of totalitarianism and he was ashamed of what Ernst Becker had done. I never heard him refer to my grandfather as "father". He used to call him Ernst Becker, and speak of him as though recalling a curse. Anyway, my father was still very young when Ernst Becker died.' He tried to smile. 'If he had been older, who knows, perhaps he may have punished his father like this Kronos or try to remove him from power like Zeus but he was too young. He did not have any clear memories of his father. He was not even able to describe what he looked like; his eyes, nose, height, hair or what have you. For good or for bad, my father did not have a single memory of his own father.'

'If only he had. Memories are important. Memories are there to remind us of what has been experienced, of the good and the evil that have been committed, of pain and happiness. If we lose our memories, we lose our grip on the past and what was experienced, and if we lose our grip on the past, we risk repeating it.' She was talking sternly, as if giving a sermon. 'Do you know which part of this city has the most meaning for me, Tobias?' She stopped and waited. 'It is not that beautiful house with the garden by the canal in which I was born or our beautiful lakes or the fabulous Tea Garden or even our wonderful museuMs For me, the place with the greatest meaning in this city is the Holocaust Memorial. And do you know why? Because that monument represents the soul of Berlin. That memorial is proof that the city has the character and strength to come to terms with itself. It symbolizes the strength of a nation. The memorial, which is not far from the bunker in which Hitler killed himself, does not stand for a group of cowardly and selfish people desperately trying to cover up their tragic mistakes but a brave people that have accepted the role they had in a massive historical crime and are doing their utmost to make sure it does not happen again. It is that memorial to the victims of the genocide that I am most proud of in this city. Even living in the same city as the people that fought to have that memorial built fills me with pride.'

She took a deep breath. She felt a sting in her ribs but ignored the pain.

'Voluntary amnesia is a terrible thing, Tobias. Today, everyone is banking on it. Voluntary amnesia today has become the unannounced official ideology. It comforts, it lightens the load of the massive mistakes of the past, it makes one forget savagery. It may stop national pride from being hurt but it also distances people from the truth and paves the way for mass delusion. It prevents us from facing up to reality. Yet, no matter how much we run away from the truth or try to dismiss it, it is still there. Whether we admit to it or not, the victims and the killers still exist. More pertinently, if we forget, then there will be new victims and new killers. People like Rudolf Winkelmann, but smarter, stronger and more vicious than him, will begin preparing for new historical tragedies, and without any resistance. In fact, they already have... If they could, they would have no qualms about loading the immigrants in this country onto trains and sending them to the gas chambers, the way their Nazi forebears did.

'So no, Tobias, you cannot hide the truth. Deception is a far greater sin than shame. Don't do it. If you are not a racist, then it doesn't matter if your grandfather was a Nazi. On the contrary, the grandson of an SS officer being anti-fascist takes on even greater significance and value, even more so today. There was a time when it was an open secret that most of the country supported the Nazis. What is worse than people having forefathers that were Nazis or supported the Nazis is those very same people themselves and their children becoming Nazis, and the problem is that this is happening now and getting worse by the day. What counts is opposing this danger and countering it. That is why you should not have hidden your past.' She paused and then, in a challenging rather than suspicious tone, asked, 'Unless, of course, you have another agenda?'

Tobias was shocked.

'What does that mean, boss? You're not seriously accusing me of being a neo-Nazi too, are you?'

Yıldız lifted her hands off the table, although she was still looking at her assistant long and hard.

'Are you, Tobias?'

Tobias was incensed.

'How can you even think of it? I have told you why I hid the fact my grandfather was a Nazi. Why do you still not believe me?'

'Why should I believe you? You didn't even tell me you had been to Turkey.' She was speaking Turkish now. 'And don't pretend you don't understand. I also know you speak Turkish. Why, Tobias? Why did you feel the need for these lies?'

He was almost trembling. He took a series of deep breaths, gulping the air in, before answering, in German.

'I was stupid. That's all.' He took an angry, rueful drag of his cigarette and held the smoke in for some time before letting it out. 'Remember that story I told you about that friend of mine? The one who had a thing for Turkish girls?'

'You mean that high school friend of yours that went to Kayseri?'

'I told you his name was Herbert Brigel,' Tobias said with a guilty smile. 'He was a friend of mine in high school, and he was a good lad, old Herbert. But he never went to Kayseri. Forget Turkish girls, he was so shy, he couldn't even speak to German girls. No, he was not the one that went to Kayseri...'

The penny dropped.

'So it was you that kept falling for Turkish girls?' she asked.

Tobias smiled again.

'It was. But I didn't give you the whole story because I thought you might misunderstand, or that you wouldn't understand. To tell you the truth, most of the time, I don't understand myself. It's just this weird fixation. And I don't know why. I didn't have a Turkish nanny or some sultry, scantily-clad Turkish girl as a neighbour when I was young. I just find Turkish women fascinating...' He saw the flicker of doubt in Yıldız's narrowed eyes and flicked the cigarette away. 'Oh God, no, don't get the wrong idea. I don't have any feelings for you, no! Never have. You... How can I say it? You're like a sister to me, an *abla*. I have never looked at you that way. I'm not lying. Not telling you about this weakness of mine was a big mistake, I know. Probably a bigger mistake than not telling you my grandfather was a Nazi. But like I said, I was scared you wouldn't understand and that you wouldn't want to work with me. You're a great person to work with, boss. Every cop on the Berlin Force worth his salt wants to be in your team and I didn't want to risk my place. The more I have got to know you, the fonder I've become of you. That's why I didn't tell you. I didn't want to lose you.'

Yıldız did not know what to say.

'I know you're angry with me, boss. I shouldn't have done it but believe me, I meant no harm. You may be furious at all the lies and half-truths but it's done now. Believe me, I'm not a Nazi or a perv of some kind. That's the honest truth. If you say I've told enough lies, you'd be right. I don't know what I would do in your situation but if you no longer wish to work with me, I'll understand. I won't cause any probleMs If you like, I can tell the Chief in person that I am resigning.'

Yıldız felt sorry seeing Toby like this. She wanted to believe him but it was not that easy. If someone can tell a lie once, they could easily lie again.

'You shouldn't have done it,' she said quietly. 'You have really let me down, Tobias. I trusted you completely. I used to feel safe knowing you had my back. I never had to worry about what was going on behind my back knowing you were there. But now...' She fell silent and looked around, not knowing what to do. She then turned and faced her assistant again. 'We are in the middle of an investigation so we will have to continue as normal. As though nothing has happened. This matter will have to be adjourned. We will talk about it once this investigation is closed, not now. We cannot change horses midstream.'

Tobias was relieved and smiled gratefully.

'I've heard that proverb before, boss. Songül's mother used to use it. She was the mother of that girl from Kayseri...'

Yıldız ignored the remark. She did not even smile.

'Let's go then, if there is nothing else to discuss,' she said, disconsolate. 'I'm so tired, I'm about to keel over. And my ribs are aching again.'

As soon as she opened the front door, she heard the song. '*What are you doing around here, my red crane / My wings are broken and I am stuck here / My love, my rose, my wings are broken / Hey cranes, my hands don't work...*' Yıldız knew the song well but she could not remember when she first heard it. It may have been in her mother's lap, as that song was her mother's favourite and she used to sing it to send Yıldız to sleep. She sang it with such feeling too, in a sweet, high voice. '*Red crane, if you reach us / How happy we will all be...*' For a fleeting moment, she forgot about her exhaustion, the painful conversation with Tobias, the pain in her ribs, the Nazis and the whole investigation. She rushed inside and within a few seconds she could smell the delicious aroma of fresh tea. Her hazel eyes lit up. Her father was preparing breakfast. She poked her head around the kitchen door. Yaman was there, taking the cheese and olives out of the refrigerator while singing along to the folk song being played on Metropol FM, a Berlin radio station that broadcast in Turkish: '*If anyone questions us / Pale and destitute friend tell them / My love, my rose, my arm is broken / My sweet cranes, my hand does not work...*'

'Morning, Dad!' she said but Yaman did not hear her. She tried again, louder. 'Morning, Dad!'

Yaman turned around.

'Morning, my girl. Welcome home.' The smile froze on his lips. 'Yıldız! What happened to you?' He quickly put the bowls of cheese and olives down on the table and rushed over to his daughter. 'You look awful.'

Yıldız welled up with emotion. She felt like letting herself go like a little girl and falling into her father's arms and crying her eyes out but she knew she couldn't. She had never done anything like that before as a grown woman and she was not going to start now. The strong, professional police woman had to stand firm.

'It's nothing, Dad. Just a long night, that's all.'

Yaman did not believe her and looked at her carefully.

'You don't look good. New cases?'

'Don't worry, Dad,' Yıldız said with a wry smile, not wanting to talk about it. 'The cases in this city never end, anyway.' She scanned the kitchen. 'Where's Deniz? Is he still asleep?'

'No, he's awake, he's inside getting changed. I was going to rustle up some eggs. I'll make you some too. You'll feel better with some good food inside you.'

She was in no mood to eat but she also knew that her father would worry if she refused.

'That would be great, Dad, thanks,' she said and went off to Deniz's room. With every step she took, the stinging pain in her ribs got worse. Her father was right; she needed to eat a sound breakfast, even if she didn't feel like it, and then take a painkiller and get some sleep.

'Mum! Mum!'

Deniz had heard her voice and was waiting for her in the doorway to his room. Before she had a chance to tell him to stop, he had run into her arms. Reeling from the pain, she still hugged him tight and breathed in his scent. Leaning against the wall for support, she planted a big kiss on his forehead.

'Good morning Deniz, my love. How are you today? Ready for school?'

His lower lip dropped and he looked up at her with innocent eyes.

'Can't I stay at home with you today? Do I have to go to school?'

She leant over and kissed him again on the forehead.

'You know you can't, Deniz. But I promise, as soon as I have the time, you and I are going to go out and have some fun.'

His black eyes lit up in delight.

'On Dad's boat?'

'No, no, this time it will be just the two of us. Mother and son together…' She quickly added, 'But if you want, we can all go on a boat trip up the Spree River.'

Deniz whooped in delight.

'Yes, yes! A boat trip!'

Deniz's grandfather had heard his shouts of joy and was watching on in the doorway. Seeing his daughter and grandson in each other's arms filled him with happiness.

'Breakfast is ready. I've put the tea on and the eggs will be ready in a tick.'

As always, it was a quick breakfast, as they only had time for long, indulgent breakfasts at the weekend if and when she was off duty. Nevertheless, the food was doing her a world of good. Although her ribs were still causing her serious discomfort, her headache was lessening in intensity.

'I left an envelope in your room,' Yaman said after he had finished his breakfast. 'Some notes on how the Pergamon Altar was brought to Berlin.' Noticing her surprise, he went on. 'That's right, I was in the City Library yesterday as well.' He chuckled. 'Look at me, working nine to five for my daughter. But on a more serious note, thanks to you, I have been learning about something that I should have learnt about years ago. The Altar of Pergamon and how it was brought to Berlin. I looked at a number of sources and it has an interesting story. However, I found one article that summarizes the story quite neatly. It was written by an archaeologist from Ege University. You really should read it.' He looked away sheepishly. 'I should have looked into it years ago as it really is an important topic. Still, better late than never, I suppose.'

He was stopped by his grandson running out of his bedroom with his schoolbag.

'Come on, Grandad, let's go. I'm ready.'

After seeing them off, Yıldız went to the bathroom and undressed. The area around her ribs where she had been hit was red and swollen and sensitive to the touch. She switched on the shower and stepped into the cabin. At first, the warm water felt nice but then it only made her realize how tired she was. After her shower, she went to the kitchen and took another painkiller, after which she went to her bedroom. Before lying down, she placed a glass next to the bottle of water on her bedside table.

Behind the bottle was an A4 envelope, the one her father had mentioned. She decided to read it later and, placing a pillow under her head, lay down. When she closed her eyes, she felt a ringing in her ears. She turned on her side but the ringing remained and the pain in her ribs increased as her weight was now on her side. She went back to lying on her back. Again, the ringing would not go away. She waited. Still the sound would not disappear. She straightened up and placed the pillow under her back. She poured herself a glass of water and downed it. While putting the glass back, she noticed the envelope. She took the sheets of paper out and began reading. The article was entitled '*Zeus' Journey to Berlin*' and was written by Professor Ümit Çeteci. 'Ege University Faculty of Arts, Department of Archaeology' was printed under his name. She quickly read the article's subheadings. The introduction described the explosion of interest in archaeology and the rush to build museums that overtook Europe in the eighteenth century, as well as the competition between England, France and Germany in this regard. She skipped that part and began reading the section entitled '*A Highway Engineer's Passion for Archaeology: Carl Wilhelm Humann*':

'At the heart of the story of the Altar of Zeus' long and complicated journey to Berlin is a disease, specifically, tuberculosis, popularly known at the time as consumption. The individual that brought this illness, which was widespread in the 19th century, to the story was a gentleman by the name of Carl Wilhelm Humann. Humann was born on 4 January 1839 in the town of Steele, the middle child of a large family. At the age of 22, Humann, an engineering student at the time, was diagnosed with tuberculosis. The doctors' recommendations were unequivocal: 'If you want a long and healthy life, you need to live in a country with a warm climate.' Carl was lucky in this respect because his older brother Franz Humann at the time was working in construction on the island of Samos, which was then a part of the Ottoman Empire. Franz asked his brother to join him on the island, an invitation Carl gladly accepted, and the two brothers began working together, directly under the auspices of the Ottoman government. As such, they enjoyed warm relations with high-ranking officials. As well as being a skilled engineer, Carl was also open to new cultures and he had a particular interest in archaeology. He learnt Greek and Turkish in no time and was soon receiving the praises of the Ottoman government and began working on construction projects in various provinces around the empire. The disease that had brought him to Ottoman lands in the first place also began to disappear. In 1864 and 1866, he came to Bergama to work on various highway projects. During his second visit, he saw the Acropolis of Pergamon and was mesmerized by what he saw. Below is an extract from his diary:

'"*And then we ascended the castle… I was stunned into sadness there. I saw Corinthian columns there almost the height of adult men and I stared at the plinths and their rich adornments covered in bush and vine and the other marble pieces there. Lime quarries burnt and smoked next to these relics; people were crushing these artefacts with sledgehammers into smaller pieces and throwing them into the lime pits. The smaller the pieces were broken into, the easier they would burn. The relics unearthed in some newly opened excavation sites are but a hint as to the wealth hidden beneath the soil of this seemingly empty land. I found myself muttering, 'So this what remains of the once proud and impregnable capital of the Attalids.*"

'Nevertheless, he still did not realize that hidden beneath the very ground upon which he was walking lay a temple that once had no equal in the world. He moved his construction headquarters to this region, possibly to be closer to Pergamon, and that is when the journey that would lead to the discovery of Pergamon truly began. While continuing with his perfectly legal highway construction, he also began a series of secret and illegal excavations in Pergamon. In the Bergama of the time, nobody thought to stop him and question him as to what exactly he was doing and Humann, whose interest in archaeology had begun during his student years in Berlin, carried on digging with great gusto. He was all but in love with Pergamon. However, he was unable to inform the authorities of his activities and so he began amassing a personal collection.

'In 1871, again illegally, he sent two reliefs he recovered from the Acropolis to Berlin. One of the reliefs was a part of the frieze that decorated the outer rim of the Altar of Zeus and depicted Zeus' son Heracles fighting a Giant. However, the experts in Germany still did not realize that these reliefs were part of the Altar of Pergamon, considered the eighth wonder of the world during ancient times, until Professor Alexander Conze was appointed Director of the Department of Classical Antiquities of Berlin Museum in 1877. Conze was the first person to realize that the reliefs being sent from Bergama were part of the frieze that depicted the battle between the Gods and the Giants. It was a stunning discovery. Professor Conze knew that the Altar of Pergamon was the as-yet-unearthed eighth wonder of the ancient world. If the pieces truly were from the Altar, an archaeology museum could finally be built in Berlin to rival those already established in London and Paris.

'Consequently, he made a number of efforts to initiate a comprehensive excavation of Pergamon and its various sites. Conze's efforts soon began to pay dividends, first in Germany, then in the Ottoman Empire. Despite certain legal obstacles, on 6 August 1878 permission for excavations to proceed was given by the ministry. Preparations for the excavations lasted until 9 September 1878, when Carl Humann, with four workers on his team, finally began work. Within three days, and with little effort, more than ten pieces were unearthed. As the statues and reliefs came out from under the ground one after the other, the question of how they would be transported to Germany remained unsolved, even though all the German experts and authorities, Alexander Conze at the Berlin Museum above all, that were aware of the significance of the issue knew that the Pergamon Altar had to be moved to Berlin if the city really was to have a museum that could rival the British Museum and the Louvre. There were, however, powerful forces at play in this matter.

'According to Ottoman law, one-third of all objects and artefacts unearthed during the excavations were to be given to the owner of the land, one-third to the Ottoman government and the remaining one-third to the country undertaking the excavations. Bergama Castle was state property and the excavations were taking place on Ottoman soil, which meant Germany, which was organising the excavations via the Berlin Museum, was entitled to only one-third of the finds, something that was unsatisfactory to the German authorities, as well as to Humann and Conze. For them, the Pergamon Altar in its entirety was to be brought to Germany, but how was this to be accomplished? This is the question that was plaguing Carl Humann. The digs were going so well that all the pieces that formed the Altar would soon be unearthed. Yet if only one-third of the pieces was theirs, it would impossible to create the world-class museum the Germans so desperately wanted. It was a combination of Ottoman ineptitude, German diplomacy and political pressure that came to his rescue. Mention must be made at this juncture of Ottoman ignorance in this matter.

'The Ottoman view of history at the time was Muslim and Turkish history, a thousand-year view of history, whereas the land itself had a human history that stretched back tens of thousands of years, something that great leaders such as Sultan Mehmed the Conqueror were able to grasp. That is why Mehmed modelled himself on Alexander the Great and did not hesitate in proclaiming himself the "Emperor of Rome". How ironic that his descendants four hundred years later would have a much weaker vision when they ruled over the land. To only recognize a thousand years of history in this land and to show interest in just one period of the country's past was, in its essence, ignorance, and it was this ignorance that worked in the favour of those Germans that wished to take the Pergamon Altar back to Germany. A personal request was made by the heir to the German throne, whereby not one but two-thirds of the recovered pieces would be given to the Berlin Museum as payment for the costs and labour of the excavations, a request that was personally accepted by the Ottoman state. It was illegal but when the matter is the personal decision of the sultan himself, who could dare invoke the law? A year later, along with a new request for excavation rights by Germany, 20,000 franks, the last of the one-third share of the finds, was paid to the Berlin Museum. During subsequent excavations, the Ottoman State ensured the Germans met few difficulties, resulting in the Altar of Pergamon, a wonder of the ancient world built two thousand years earlier to commemorate the victory of the brilliant Attalid leader Eumenes II over the barbarian Galatians, being lifted from the soil on which it was built and transported thousands of kilometres away. Instead of rising on the hill on which it was built and being illuminated by the sun and the moon there, the palace of Zeus would be displayed fifty years after being taken away in 1930 in an enclosed space under artificial lighting in a museum bearing its own name in a completely different land.

'As for Carl Humann, the man behind the Altar's transportation to Berlin; he was appointed a Member of the Institute of Archaeology for his efforts and subsequently awarded the Prussian Order of the Crown. Although he received the medal in Germany, he continued to live in Izmir. He had a strange affinity to the land, most probably to Anatolian civilizations. Before dying in Izmir aged fifty-seven, he asked to be buried not in Steele, the town of his birth, but in the soil of Pergamon, where only the dais of the Altar now remained. He was a lucky man, for his request was fulfilled years later.'

Yıldız's eyes began to sting. As she put the sheets of paper back on the bedside table, she did not know what to think. She was feeling a mixture of emotions. Had the Altar remained in Ottoman lands, would it, as Carl Humann had said, have been smashed into pieces with a sledgehammer and then thrown into a lime pit to be burnt or would subsequent generations have realized its value and preserved, protected and cherished it in the manner it deserved? She was not sure. She suddenly felt cold and huddled down under the duvet. The last question on her mind before she slid into deep sleep was what her father's thoughts on the topic might be.

She was fast asleep when the phone started ringing. At first, when she opened her eyes, she was so sleepy she could not get her bearings but the phone kept ringing, forcing her to sit up and look around. She was in her home. Her lips were dry. A glass of water is what she needed but the phone just kept on ringing. She reached out for it on the side table. When she saw Toby's name on the screen, she quickly pressed the answer button.

'Hello? Tobias? What is it?'

'Hello, boss? There's been an incident at the Germania Sports Club. A fight.'

'What? How? On Rudolf Winkelmann's premises?'

'Yep. Gunshots were heard,' he answered, calm as ever. 'I'm on my way there now. I just thought I should let you know.'

Yıldız jumped out of bed, now fully awake.

'I'm on my way, Toby. I'll be there soon…'

A crowd had gathered at the end of the street. It was made up mostly of men and women still in their tracksuits and gym clothes who had run out the building and were now talking excitedly, some hysterically, amongst themselves or staring at the building in wide-eyed shock. Uniformed officers had set up a barricade between the club and the crowd and two police cars were parked at an angle in front of the building, with three officers standing on guard by the cars. As Yıldız got out of her car, she looked for Tobias but could not find him. Had he not arrived? That was impossible. She looked for him again amongst the officers trying to keep the crowd back but again she could not see him. She approached the officers by the vehicles and showed them her badge.

'Chief Inspector Karasu. What's the situation?'

A pale, red-haired officer holding a pistol in his right hand stepped forward.

'Three armed men have entered the premises by force and began firing, Chief Inspector. But according to eye-witnesses, the guys inside were armed too and returned fire.'

It has to be Hüseyin Ölmez, Yıldız thought. *The reckless fool has only gone ahead and done it.* But she needed to be sure.

'You're saying the guys inside knew there was going to be an attack of some sort, is that it?'

The officer nodded.

'It's hard to say but we do know that they returned fire inside. It was a major incident, a serious skirmish. There are wounded inside, maybe casualties too. These people only just managed to get out.' With a jerk of the head, he gestured to the building. 'The guns have fallen silent now but it was mayhem here just a few minutes ago.'

'And what are you guys doing?' she asked impatiently.

'We have taken the necessary precautions and are waiting for the Special Forces boys to turn up, ma'am.'

He was doing the right thing and acting according to procedure but Yıldız did not like all this waiting around. She looked out at the front door and the windows of the sports club.

'Are there any of our people inside?'

'Erm, we were the first ones on the scene,' the officer replied, a little hesitantly. 'There was no one here from our side when we arrived. As soon as we got here, we cordoned off the place, informed the Special Response Unit and called for backup. We also evacuated the premises and got everyone out. While we were doing that, a plain-clothes officer like yourself turned up. His name was Inspector Becker. Tobias Becker. He seemed very tense, very agitated, and asked us for a situation report. He was actually going to wait for the Special Response Unit too but when he heard the gunshots, he rushed in. We told him not to and tried to stop him but he would not listen.'

This is exactly what Yıldız had been fearing.

'When are the Special Response Unit going to be here?'

The officer shrugged.

'They said they were on their way but they're a good twenty minutes away...'

More gunshots from within cut them off. A pistol going off three times and then a response from an automatic rifle. A ripple of fearful anxiety passed through the crowd outside. A woman's screams rose up into the air.

'Get these people away from here!' Yıldız shouted. 'Evacuate the street. I want nobody near the club. Those are automatic weapons being used inside. If the attackers get outside and start firing, there is going to be carnage. So get these people far away from here now.'

As the red-haired officer strode towards the crowd, Yıldız began walking towards the club.

'Chief Inspector!' an officer that had spotted her called out from behind. 'Chief Inspector, wait! What are you doing? Ma'am?'

She did not even turn around to look. When she reached the entrance, she stayed close to the wall and took out her gun. She loaded the barrel and with her left hand, gently pushed open the door. She slipped inside. Once inside, she took up position behind the nearest column and waited. With her back against the column, she peeled her ears and listened. A tense silence reigned. Poking her head out to the left from behind the column, she looked inside. The first thing she saw was a blond youngster lying on the ground, one of the two bodyguards she had seen on her previous visit. It was most probably him and his twin that had carried out the attack at Hüseyin Ölmez's house. He was either dead or wounded enough to have passed out. She noticed the long-barrelled Smith Wesson on the ground around five centimetres away from his right hand. Lying face-down on the ground around half a metre away was another dark, moustachioed man she had not seen before with a pump action shotgun between his white trainers. She also saw someone squirming by the jogging machine and pointed her gun in that direction. A young woman in grey tracksuit lay on the ground staring at her in terror. Yıldız gestured for her to stay still and to remain where she was. The first thing she needed to do was ascertain the threat level but it was hard to do so from where she was. She turned around and looked to the right of the column; yes, the other bodyguard was lying on the floor around ten metres up ahead, his body covered in blood and twitching in shock. Next to his left knee on the floor was a Thompson rifle. It was an old weapon, a remnant of the Second World War, not that she had the time to go into such details at the moment. She carried on scanning the surroundings. Not far from the other bodyguard was another prostrate figure. He was holding a pump action gun in his right hand but he was not moving. When she took a closer look, she realized the right side of his face was missing and the ground underneath and around him was covered in blood. She looked at his weapon again. It was the type used by hunters. So she had been right in her suspicion. 'Hüseyin, you fool. What have you done?' she said to herself. He had done exactly what Kerem had feared and attacked Rudolf Winkelmann, in his place of business too.

Clutching her gun, she slowly and tentatively stepped out from behind the column. She now had a more complete view of the hall. It had a boxing ring, a jogging machine and a weights section. Apart from the people on the ground, there was nobody else there. She turned around to face the girl lying on the ground next to the jogging machines.

'Get out, now! Quick!' she whispered. After a few moment's hesitation, the woman got up and ran to the door and was outside within a few seconds. Yıldız carried on scanning the interior of the sports club, looking for Tobias. She searched every corner but there was no sign of him. And where was Hüseyin Ölmez? If he was the one that had planned and carried out the attack, then surely he had to be here somewhere? Nor was Rudolf Winkelmann anywhere to be seen. Making sure she did not veer too far into the open and using the column and the various pieces of gym equipment as cover, she inched forward.

Perhaps all three were upstairs on the second floor in Rudolf's office, although she doubted the old Nazi was treating them to his own personal blend of coffee. If they were upstairs, then he had probably greeted his uninvited guests with an automatic rifle, like the ones in his bodyguards' hands down below. She raised her head and looked at the window to Rudolf's office. There was no sign of movement. That is when she heard the noise. A man talking. There was no threat or anger in his voice. Just hatred.

'You are the one that incited them into attacking us.'

Where was it coming from? Yıldız looked around again but she could not pinpoint the voice.

'If you hadn't charged me, then this dog would not have dared attacked me.' A dull thud was heard, followed by a cry of pain. No, the cry was not coming from Tobias. It had to be Hüseyin Ölmez, while the speaker was definitely Rudolf Winkelmann. She quickened her pace. When she passed the boxing ring, she saw a metal hatch on the ground and slowly approached it, almost tiptoeing.

'You have committed the ultimate act of treason against Germany. Yes, you. The traitors within the state. You fear this lot, these slithering hyenas.' Another blow was heard, followed by another groan. But the sounds were not coming from beneath the hatchway, of that Yıldız was sure. She finally realized. There was a door open ajar next to one of the staircases going up. A pump-action gun was lying on the ground in front of the door. It was probably Hüseyin Ölmez's gun. There were bloodstains on the ground. Somebody somewhere was injured. Rudolf's voice was heard again. 'You are only patriots and stand alongside us when it suits you. But the truth is there is no difference between you and them. You are also traitors. You're even worse than that scum as you do not hesitate in killing the true patriots of this country.'

Yıldız was certain now that the sounds were coming from the other side of the half-open door by the stairs. Quickening her stride, she headed in that direction.

'Yes, you are the ones that killed those two youngsters from the NSU,' Rudolf was saying, spewing his hatred. 'First you used them, making them your informants and making them do your dirty work, and then you got rid of them.'

He was talking about Uwe Böhnhardt and Uwe Mundlos, two members of the National Socialist Underground that had been found dead years ago in a caravan. Although Yıldız was about to open fire on Rudolf and possibly kill, she had to give him his due, for he was telling the truth. Certain figures within the state apparatus had protected those two terrorists at first and had then brushed the killing of ten people, including a female police officer, under the carpet. In fact, not only had they stayed silent over the killings, they had sanctioned them but then when things began to spin out of control, they eliminated those involved and then, as always, the state and its officers had wiped their hands clean, rolled up their sleeves and had gone back to their soft, comfy seats. Until now, though, the charges had not been conclusively disproven.

'We didn't use anybody,' Tobias could be heard saying. 'Let him go. Give yourself in.'

Yıldız felt a surge of delight because Tobias was at least alive and seemingly well. It was still too early for relief, though, for although she could not see what was taking place on the other side of the door, it was clear that some kind of hostage situation was in play, the hostage most probably being Hüseyin Ölmez, whose idiotic attack had resulted in his friends and Rudolf's two bodyguards getting shot. As for Hüseyin himself, he had probably been shot too and been taken hostage by his bitter enemy. 'Idiot,' Yıldız said to herself again. 'The fool has gone and made a mess of everything.'

She was close to the door now and could hear Rudolf speaking.

'Uwe Böhnhardt and Uwe Mundlos' murderers also said they did not use anybody. They claimed that the two men committed suicide when they realized they had been cornered but that is a lie. They were both killed by the state because the state was scared. Scared of these vile insects. Of *kanake* like these with impure blood.'

Yıldız was now so close to the door she could hear the despair in Rudolf's voice, the voice of a man who realized he was at the end of the road. Angry men were dangerous but desperate men were even more dangerous. She needed to act quickly. She peeped through the open door inside. She saw Tobias' broad back and shoulders first and then Rudolf standing in front of him, using a bruised and battered Hüseyin as a human shield. Rudolf had his black Beretta under Hüseyin's chin. The still bleeding wound on Hüseyin's left shoulder was so bad, it could be seen through his hunter's jacket. His right eye was shut and his breath was coming in wheezes. He did not look in good shape at all and it was just a matter of time before Rudolf and Tobias exchanged fire. Tobias would have the upper hand only if Yıldız entered the room but Rudolf was facing the door and would see Yıldız the moment she entered the room. Her only chance of cover was Tobias' bulky frame. If she could somehow use Toby's large body as a screen, she may be able to slip in unnoticed. But if Toby moved, Rudolf would see her and an already tense situation would become even more volatile. But she had no other choice. She grasped her gun with both hands, took a deep breath, waited a second and then tiptoed as quietly as she could through the gap in the door. The first steps were a success and she was able to sneak in without Rudolf seeing her. Tobias was unwittingly protecting his own Chief with his bulky frame.

'And now you're going to kill me!' Rudolf was shouting. 'Even if I surrender, you won't let me off. That's why you got this dirty black dog to attack me. So you could claim there was an exchange of fire between two parties and that I had been killed during the exchange. You're going to get rid of me like Uwe Böhnhardt and Uwe Mundlos because your bosses have decided on it. And why? Because they are afraid of what I know. They are afraid I will talk. And don't look at me like that. I know your plans. I know what you intend to do. You were never going to let me live, you people. But don't you worry, I won't go down alone. I'm going to take you and this piece of shit down with me.'

Having said that, he pressed the point of the gun ever more firmly into his hostage's chin. A cry escaped from Hüseyin's bloody lips and he tried to wriggle his way free.

'Don't move!' Rudolf shouted. 'Don't move, you filth. You think I've forgotten what you did to me? You'll pay for what you have done, you Turkish bastard! You come over here to *my* club and attack me here? I'll show what it means to have a go at me on my own turf!'

'Rudolf, don't!' Tobias cried out. 'There is no need for any more blood to be spilled. You can still save yourself. I'll testify on your behalf. I shall state, for the record, that your premises were attacked. And it was, I know. You can legitimately argue that you acted in self-defence. But if you kill him, no one will be able to save you. You still have a chance. Put the gun down, surrender and we can walk away from here.'

Rudolf listened without interrupting. Was he actually coming round? Tobias noticed it too and, in an amiable and approachable voice, went on.

'Look, I promise, I'll tell them exactly what happened. You are the wronged here, that much is obvious. If anyone is going to be punished, it's this guy with the gun under his chin. But if you let things go on like this and if the police open fire on you or return fire, then you won't have a leg to stand on. They'll come down on you like a tonne of bricks.'

The hesitation was writ all over Rudolf's face and he was about to agree when Tobias, who had no idea Yıldız was behind him, shifted his body to the right. Rudolf's face went dark red.

'You bastard!' he shrieked. 'So that bitch is here too, eh? You bastard, you tried to pull one on me!'

Tobias was confused and did precisely the opposite of what he should have done — he turned around to look at the spot Rudolf was staring at. That is when it all happened. Pushing Hüseyin away, Rudolf screamed, 'I'll kill you all!' and pulled the trigger. As his hostage fell to the floor, Yıldız saw the blood spurt out of her assistant's neck. She raised her gun at the same time and without taking proper aim began firing too. The room shook and thundered with the sound of gunfire. Yıldız kept firing until her clip was empty. The Nazi trembled like a leaf caught in a hurricane before falling face forward behind the already prostrate Hüseyin. Rudolf was dead before he hit the ground but Yıldız could not leave it to chance. She reloaded and, keeping her gun pointed at Rudolf, approached his body and kicked his gun away, which was lying on the ground. She watched the man lying in a pool of blood for some time. Seeing no movement or reaction from him, she finally put her gun back in its holster. Ignoring Hüseyin, who had raised a hand in the air and was pleading for help, she hurried over to her assistant. He was on the ground but he was conscious. He had let go off his gun and was pressing down on his wound with his right hand but the wound was so severe, the blood was spurting through his fingers. She knelt down beside him and took off her jacket, while speaking to him in a soothing tone.

'Don't you worry, Toby, you're going to be okay.'

'I'm no Nazi, boss,' he said, with a hurt expression. He gathered his strength and lifted his head. 'I'm no Nazi.'

As she pressed her jacket down on the wound in his neck, Yıldız felt ashamed.

'I know, Toby. I know. Please forgive me. Let it go now. Save your strength. You're going to be okay.'

Tobias smiled through his pain.

'Okay… Okay…,' was all he managed to say before his dark grey eyes closed and his hands fell by his side. Yıldız looked on anxiously, unable to hold back her own tears.

'You're not going to die, Toby,' she said, knowing he could not hear. 'You're not going to die. Hang on in there, I'm going to get you out of here.'

11
Heracles has atoned for the killing of your sons

Time was running out. Every day, Hermes brought new news concerning Mother Earth's cunning manoeuvres. Gaia was grooming her sons to go to battle against me, Mighty Zeus, and she was now eager to execute this plan, which had been in the making for years. She did not want to see me on the throne. She yearned to snatch the crown from my head. But I did not hurry. I did not rush. I could not wage war until Heracles was ready. If I did go to war without him, defeat would surely be inevitable, and were I to be defeated, then this would not only endanger me but all the Olympians and all the creatures of the earth. But for my valiant son to be ready, he needed to successfully complete twelve difficult tasks. Moreover, these twelve tasks were given to him by none other than Eurystheus, lowliest of the kings, a man despised by his own people, by other kings and by the Gods. In order to atone for his transgressions, my valiant son had to fulfil the demands of this vile king.

Seeing Heracles waiting obediently for his orders pleased Eurystheus greatly. There he was, the world's bravest man, standing to attention before him. It was a cause for pride for Eurystheus, for now the whole world would see his power and his controversial rule would be affirmed. But at the same time, Eurystheus was terrified, for the man now standing silently before him awaiting orders was unpredictable. If he were to lose his temper, he could, with a single blow, break Eurystheus' neck and send him to the land of the unliving. Eurystheus wavered, wondering if he was doing the right thing, until Hera intervened and allayed the cowardly king's fears. And so the twelve impossible tasks were set. Or rather, they thought they had set the tasks, for in truth, I was the one that decided them all, and of course, I would make sure that my son would be granted gifts that would help him succeed in his tasks: an enchanted cloak from Athena, a keen sword from Hermes, a bow and arrow from Apollo, armour and a helmet from Hephaestus and two stunning horses from Poseidon. However, Heracles, whose self-belief was near-infinite, usually preferred as a weapon a simple staff he fashioned with his own hands from an olive branch.

His first task was to slay the Nemean lion. None dared face this savage beast. To hunt him was folly; his roar alone was enough to send men running in fright. King Eurystheus commanded Heracles to kill and skin this beast. And so Heracles, unflinching, headed for the region of Nemea and found the lion's cave. He heard its roar and felt the vile stench of its breath. He dragged him out into the open and the beast, despite Heracles' imposing size, leapt onto his tormentor like the wind and attacked. My son, however, stepped to the side and brought his club down on the animal's head. He then jumped onto the back of the beast, which had lost its footing, and squeezed the life out of it with his bare hands. Yes, with his bare hands he ended the beast's life there and skinned it with its own claws, fashioning a suit of armour for himself from that tough hide.

And so, with this first task, my son learnt how to turn his enemy's superiority to his own advantage.

His second task was to destroy the Lernaean Hydra, an immense serpent that lived under a giant tree by the Spring of Amymone. This beast had nine heads and nine tongues and was so venomous that its breath alone could kill a man. With his nephew Iolaus, Heracles found the lake in which the beast dwelt. When it saw the two men arrive, it lifted its head out of the water. Its green skin twinkled in the sunlight and its forked tongue cracked the surface of the water like a whip as it cunningly stalked Heracles with its eighteen eyes. My son made the first move and with two swift blows, he cut off two of the snake's heads but two new heads emerged and replaced the ones that had been severed. realizing he was up against a mighty foe, Heracles told Iolaus to light a grand fire. Once that had been done, Heracles cut off the snake's heads and then scorched and cauterized the necks so no new head could emerge. My heroic son severed all nine heads of Hera's nine-headed monster and buried them all.

And so with this second task completed, my son learnt the subtle intricacies that must be taken into consideration when battling an enemy.

The third task was to capture the Ceryneian Hind, a female deer that was as large as a wild boar and which was raiding the fields and devouring the villagers' crops, leaving them nothing. However, none dared touch this animal, for it was sacred to Goddess Artemis and in harming the animal, they would have violated a sacred law and incurred Artemis' wrath. Heracles waited for the optimum moment. He chased the animal across the mountains for a full year but the sacred beast was too swift. realizing he could not capture the animal thus, my brilliant son lightly injured the Hind and then caught the weakened beast by its antlers and brought it to the king. Nor was Artemis angered, as the beast was not killed.

And thus, Heracles learnt not to summon greater woe when attempting to solve a problem.

The fourth task was to capture the Erymanthian Boar, a great beast that devoured the local villagers' crops, thereby consigning them to deprivation. For days, Heracles searched the mountains for the boar, following its trail until he eventually found its cave. Detecting Heracles' scent, the beast attacked. At first, Heracles was stunned, for the animal was the size of a small hill, but he soon regained his composure and began striking the animal, hoping to bring it down. However, the boar was too strong, and no matter what my son did, he knew he could not best the animal thus. Nevertheless, the boar was also intimidated and it ran down the mountain to escape but my son fell in after him and chased it until it was too tired to run and eventually collapsed. Heracles dragged the exhausted beast to King Eurystheus.

And so, with this fourth task, Heracles understood the value of patience when facing an enemy.

The fifth task was to clean the Augean Stables. King Augeas owned a herd consisting of thousands of heads of cattle and his stables were swimming in filth as a result of not having been cleaned in years. A foul stench hung over the area, flies swarmed everywhere and disease and epidemic loomed. Of course, King Eurystheus' intent was not to prevent the spread of disease but to break Heracles' spirit by forcing him to clean the stables as an act of debasement. But my son did not mind. There was also money to be made from the task, not a bad thing in itself, and so he struck a deal with King Augeas whereby in payment of one tenth of the herd, he would clean the stables in one day. In order to complete this seemingly impossible task, Heracles dug a massive trench and rerouted two rivers so they would flow all the way to the stables, thereby completing the task and cleaning the stables within a day as promised.

And so, in completing this fifth labour, Heracles learnt to use the power of nature to overcome obstacles in his path.

The sixth labour was to chase away the birds of Lake Stymphalia. These were not creatures of bright plumage and sweet song but wild beasts bred by my son Ares with bronze claws and beaks that glimmered in the sunlight that fed on human flesh. Such was the threat they posed, the shores of the lake had become unapproachable. Moreover, any that dared to confront the birds risked incurring the wrath of the ever-belligerent God Ares. As Heracles sat and pondered his grave dilemma, his elder sister Athena came to his aid and gave him a large bronze rattle that had been especially made for him by Hephaestus. When Heracles began shaking the rattle on the shores of the lake, it made such a terrible noise that the birds flew into the air and fled, never to return to the lake.

And so, in this sixth task, Heracles learnt that certain problems can be solved without the need to resort to force.

The seventh labour was to capture the Cretan Bull. King Minos had once said to my brother Poseidon that he would sacrifice to him the first creature to emerge from the sea but that creature was a spectacularly strong and beautiful bull and the greedy king, captivated by the bull's magnificence, slaughtered his own herd instead of the bull. Angered by Minos' trickery, Poseidon made the bull go mad and it became so wild, that it began to attack every being it saw, living and non-living. The beast was untameable, and none dared approach it. Heracles, however, went to Crete and found the bull. Seeing my son, the animal's nostrils flared in rage and it attacked him with all its might but my son moved out of its way and then caught the beast by its horns and held on until the beast was exhausted and fell to the ground. Heracles then bound the beast by its feet and brought it to King Eurystheus.

And so, with this seventh task, Heracles learnt that sometimes raw physical strength is the only way to overcome an obstacle.

The eighth task was to capture the Mares of Diomedes, four wild horses owned by Diomedes, King of Thrace, which fed on the flesh of those poor souls that the brutal king wished to punish. It was an unacceptable punishment but the king was a dangerous tyrant and none dared to confront him. Eurystheus ordered Heracles to capture these flesh-eating mares and to bring them to him. Heracles therefore killed King Diomedes and fed his body to the mares, even though he had not been ordered to do so. realizing their master was dead and that they had been fed his body, the mares recognized Heracles as their new master and submitted to him. Driving the mares before him, Heracles brought them to Eurystheus.

And so, in this eighth task, Heracles learnt that one must also be merciless when dealing with tyrants.

The ninth task was to steal the Belt of Hippolyta, Queen of the Amazons. The belt was actually a gift to Queen Hippolyta from our very own warmonger Ares, a gift the queen had truly earned with her various acts of heroism, but King Eurystheus' spoilt daughter Admete wanted the belt for herself and so, wishing to please his daughter and fulfil her wish, Eurystheus ordered Heracles to obtain the belt. After a long and arduous journey, Heracles gained an audience with Queen Hippolyta and explained the situation to her. The queen was an understanding woman and was ready to part with the belt of her own accord but while my son was in the palace, the ever-malicious Hera told the Amazon warriors that Heracles planned to kill their queen, rousing them to suspicion and anger. Seeing the Amazons attack, Heracles thought he had been caught in a trap and so killed Hippolyta and grabbed the Belt. When he found out the truth, he was truly remorseful but by then it was too late.

And so, with this ninth task, Heracles learnt the value of remaining vigilant at all times when faced with a challenge.

The tenth task was to obtain the Cattle of Geryon. Geryon was a three-headed Giant who owned a herd of red cattle and the herd was guarded by a fearsome double-headed dog named Orthus. When Eurystheus ordered Heracles to bring him the cattle, Heracles set off for Thrace. There, he saw Orthus, whom he slayed with a single blow from his club. He rounded up the cattle and was taking them away when Geryon suddenly appeared. Heracles killed him with arrows tipped with poison from an eel he had killed at the Spring of Amymone. But that was not the end of his trials, for as he was approaching the city, a gadfly sent by jealous Hera scattered the herd. Heracles gathered his strength and rounded up the herd once more and finally, and with great difficulty, completed the task.

And so, with this tenth task, Heracles learnt that one does not attain victory simply by winning one battle.

The eleventh task was to steal the fabled apples of Hera, a gift to my wife from Gaia herself. Hera had planted them in a garden at the foot of Mount Atlas and had placed three nymphs known as the Hesperides in the garden to guard the precious gifts, along with a hundred-headed dragon. On his quest to find and steal the apples, Heracles encountered Prometheus, the Titan who was a friend of mankind. Wanting to help Heracles for saving him from my eagle, Prometheus said, 'Salutations to you, dear friend Heracles. Let Atlas be the one that collects the apples, not you, for only he has the strength to overcome the three nymphs and the dragon with a hundred heads.'

When Heracles reached the garden, he approached Atlas and asked him to collect the apples. Atlas agreed but told Heracles that he would hold up the sky on his back while he was collecting the fruit.

Heracles immediately shouldered the massive weight of the sky, while Atlas went down into the garden, where he killed the nymphs and the dragon and took the apples. However, the Titan found his newfound freedom intoxicating and when he returned, he said, 'I am sorry, son of Zeus, but I shall take these apples to the king.'

That is when Heracles displayed his keen discernment. He replied:

'Very well. However, the weight of the sky is too much and I cannot hold it up much longer. It is going to fall. Help me for a moment while I find my footing so I can hold it up better.'

Atlas was a gullible Titan and agreed. He placed the apples on the ground and shouldered the weight of the sky, giving Heracles the chance to snatch the apples and flee.

And so, with this eleventh task, Heracles understood the value of being cunning in certain situations.

The twelfth task set for Heracles by King Eurystheus was to capture Cerberus, the three-headed serpent-tailed dog that guarded the gates to the Underworld, and bring him to the surface. Despite his courage, I knew Heracles could not journey to the Underworld on his own and so I sent Hermes, the messenger of the Gods, to accompany his Mortal brother on his journey and to protect him. When Heracles reached the Underworld, he told Hades, his uncle and lord of the land of the dead, why he had come. Hades listened and told him that he could take Cerberus to the land of the living if he, Heracles, could defeat Cerberus unarmed, a challenge accepted by my son. Man and dog fought, and Cerberus began sinking the dagger-like teeth in his three mouths into Heracles' arms and legs. My son was soon covered in blood and cuts but he did not waver. He grabbed Cerberus by the neck where the three heads joined. He began squeezing with all his might and the dog surrendered, unable to withstand the pain. And so Heracles was able to take Cerberus with him to King Eurystheus.

And so Heracles learnt, during this twelfth task, that honesty, sincerity and courage can sometimes open all doors.

Having succeeded in all the tasks using wisdom, knowledge, patience, courage, strength, skill and geniality, Heracles atoned for the killing of his sons. More importantly, he matured, physically and mentally, enough to be able to take his place in our ranks in our war against the Giants. Nor did any Olympian, including Hera, object. I could now, without hesitation, let my son ride in my chariot next to me and fight alongside me.

Chapter Eleven

The rain that had started in the morning had begun to ease off by noon and the shapeless grey clouds had disappeared from the sky, as though they had been dragged away by an invisible hand. When Yıldız left the hospital and arrived at the squat, a hot summer's day had taken hold of Berlin's old streets. Tobias was still under sedation. He had lost a lot of blood and had the ambulance not arrived when it had, it may well have been too late. The operation had been a success but the hours ahead were going to be critical. 'We do not want to wake him up too early and put his life in danger all over again,' the doctor had said. Their wish was for him to wake up of his own accord, when his body was good and ready. He could wake up in the next few hours, they said, or a few weeks later. 'But he will wake up, won't he?' Yıldız had asked. 'He has to wake up.' The doctor did not give an exact answer and had simply replied by saying, 'We are hoping he will.' It had been one of the worst nights of Yıldız's life. She had stayed in the hospital until morning, hoping wildly that she could make a difference by being there, but unfortunately, when morning came round, Tobias had still not woken up. All they could do was wait, and, upon the doctor's insistence, Yıldız had eventually gone home. Not that there was any respite to be found there, as mentally she was still at the hospital. The following morning, she paid Tobias an early visit on the way to the station but his situation had not changed. For three days, the first thing she did every morning and every evening on the way back home was visit his bedside but each time, his eyes remained firmly shut and every visit ended in Yıldız leaving the hospital disappointed, disconsolate, and racked with remorse and a troubled conscience.

On the other hand, Hüseyin Ölmez, who was on the ground floor of the same hospital, was making rapid progress. He had organized and taken part in an attack that had led to the death of five people, including two of his friends, and yet, apart from the vicious beating he had taken from Rudolf, it seemed the bloody clash would leave him with nothing more than a broken collarbone. Although she was furious with him for what he had done, Yıldız was also glad that he had survived. Not for him but for his father Kerem, who had already experienced two tragedies. Hüseyin would be going to prison for a long time but at least Kerem's elder son would still be alive. It had been three days since the attack on the Germania Sports Club and there had been no new cases. If the day Alex had been killed was also included, there had been no murders for four days, something that pleased Markus, who confidently stated that the case had been solved. 'Rudolf Winkelmann and his gang were responsible for the murders. I mean, just look; they had a whole arsenal stashed away in the Germania.'

And it was true. A cache of arms large enough to equip a mini-platoon had been found in a secret room under Rudolf's club. Oddly enough, the stockpile found was made up of Second World War remnants; weapons and explosives used by US military forces during that global conflict. The question of why they were there was answered soon enough. It was all bound up with an operation that had taken place during the Cold War. The US had wanted to establish anti-communist civilian units behind enemy lines that would fight for them in the event of open hostilities between the US and the Soviets. The Americans had used ex-Nazis in this operation, known as Stay-Behind, and the weapons found in Rudolf's secret room were leftovers from those days. The long-since defunct Thompson rifle Yıldız had seen during the attack was one of them. Seeing as Rudolf was not that long in the tooth, the arsenal must have been passed on to him by an older comrade. More importantly, a list consisting of 500 names and home and workplace addresses, including those of Hüseyin Ölmez and Cemal Ölmez, had also been found. The list did not just include immigrants and foreigners but also a number of leftists, Green Party members and German anti-racist activists, such as a young Turk by the name of Burak who had been killed in an anonymous murder in Neukölln in April 2011 and a district governor for the Green Party whose car had been set alight. Their names, as well as those of Cemal and Hüseyin, had been underlined and in the light of this and other new evidence, Markus, who was now certain that the neo-Nazis had committed the murders, had held a press conference and informed the public that the case had been solved.

'It is very possible that the racist group headed by Winkelmann was planning further actions that would have been just as grisly. These murders, adorned with mythological motifs, would have garnered the attention of the media and would have then been followed up with mass killings that would have shocked and outraged the general public. That is what the cache of weapons that we found was to be used for: to terrify German citizens of foreign descent and to apply pressure on the government, whilst also emboldening the racism that is sadly on the rise in our country.'

Nobody thought to question this eminently reasonable statement. The Nazis had done such things before and they were quite capable of doing it again. But from the start, Yıldız had questioned this scenario and had been against charging the Nazis, which is why she also objected stringently to the staging of a press conference. Markus, however, was eager to announce their victory and had waved away her concerns. Yıldız did not attend the press conference. She knew her boss could be making a terrible mistake and that a few days later they could be forced to recant. Of course, she wanted the neo-Nazis brought to account but something in the case did not add up. She could not put her finger on it but she sensed something amiss. Mentally, she kept going over each murder, again and again. She examined each member of the Ölmez family, one by one, and went over Otto Fischer, his two cronies, Rudolf Winkelmann and all the events, people and acquaintances from their pasts up to the present day. She soon found out that Otto Fischer and Rudolf Winkelmann went back a long way and that they had connections to the National Socialist Underground. As such, blaming the neo-Nazi gang for the murders was reasonable and convenient. Yet, every time she went over the chain of murders, from Orhan Ölmez's abduction to Cemal's heart being removed and the skin on Alex's face being torn away, there was something not right, something unsettling about the neo-Nazis' presence in all of them. When his main target, his bitter enemy Hüseyin Ölmez, was there for the picking, why would Rudolf Winkelmann kill an old man like Orhan Ölmez? And not just kill him but go to the trouble of abducting him and castrating him? Rudolf's hatred for Cemal was understandable but what did killing Alex and peeling the skin off his face gain him? These were some of the gaping holes that emerged when she looked at the bigger picture, and the cache of weapons and the list obtained after the deadly clash at the Germania Sports Club were not enough to fill those gaps.

This was why she had come to the memorial service at the squat. To find answers, real, meaningful answers that could fill those gaps. Rafael had told her about the service when he had called her for an update. Noticing her interest, he had said, 'If you would like to come, you are more than welcome. The door is always open for the person that captured Alex and Cemal's killers. You would be our guest of honour.'

Yıldız did not particularly want to go, and she also knew that a police officer would not be received warmly at a squat, and had therefore asked Rafael if it was possible that her identity be kept secret. Rafael understood her concerns and offered to meet her at a nearby café and then accompany her to the service.

She was on her way to the café now. While she was parking the Passat in a carpark near the squat, she noticed an old dark-blue BMW convertible go past, driven by a woman whose blonde hair fluttered in the wind. The lady parked the car a little further up from Yıldız. Yıldız could feel the same stinging pain in her ribs but she ignored it. There was something about the BMW and its driver, a beautiful woman, but she also looked familiar. Where had Yıldız seen her before? The blonde lady got out of car. Dressed in black from top to toe, she stopped to adjust her sunglasses on her head. That is when Yıldız recognized her. It was Kitty. Peter's ex, the sculptor she had seen in the video Cemal had taken in Pergamon... She casually waited for Kitty to walk past. When she was close enough, she called out. 'Excuse me, Ms Kitty?' she said. She then sheepishly added, 'I'm sorry, I don't know your surname.'

Kitty did not seem to mind.

'Have we met?' she asked, a sweetness in her voice. Yıldız smiled.

'No, we haven't. But I know you. You are a close friend of Cemal's, aren't you?'

Kitty took off her sunglasses. Yıldız saw the sorrow in her eyes.

'Ah, poor Cemal... He was such a lovely guy. So sweet, and so talented too. It's all so sad. And what they did to Alex...' She sighed. 'You're here for the memorial, I suppose?'

They began walking together. Yıldız was glad to have bumped into her like this. After all, hadn't Haluk the archaeologist told her to speak to Kitty? But what she was supposed to ask her? How she was supposed to start the conversation?

'Is Peter coming too?' she suddenly asked, and as soon as the words had left her lips, she regretted such a crass intrusion into her personal life. 'I mean, does he know about the memorial?' She tried to make amends but Kitty didn't seem to care.

'I don't know. Most probably he is coming. He adored Cemal.'

'He was a good boss,' Yıldız murmured, relieved. 'And a good friend.'

'And a good mentor too,' Kitty added, putting her glasses back on. Seeing Yıldız's confusion, she went on. 'It wasn't just work. Peter also guided Cemal in his artistic endeavours. I'm sure you know about Cemal's big project, the one about the Altar of Pergamon. The one in which he was going to replace the faces on the figures in the friezes with the faces of his family members and basically make the figures his relatives.'

'Yes, I know about it,' Yıldız replied, still pretending to be a friend of Cemal's. 'Such an amazing idea. But a bit weird.'

Kitty stopped and looked at Yıldız over her sunglasses again.

'That's what I said. I said it was weird. Frightening, even. But neither of them listened. Peter was extremely defensive of the project.'

'You mean Cemal,' Yıldız said, correcting what she assumed was an innocent mistake. 'The project was his idea.'

'No, it wasn't,' Kitty said, shaking her head. 'The idea was Peter's. Don't look so shocked. Peter may not be a painter but his sister Angela was an unbelievable artist. She was a genius. Peter grew up with her, and Peter was the one that got Cemal into mythology. I remember him saying, "Your family has been involved in the Pergamon excavations since their inception. This is a rare and precious privilege, an amazing story. I don't know why you don't use it in your art." I heard it with my own ears because I was there when he said it. Cemal was not keen on the idea at first because he was angry with his family but Peter would not let up and went and found books about the Pergamon Altar for Cemal. He talked to him about Greek mythology for hours on end.'

'He talked about it for hours?' Yıldız asked in amazement. 'He knew it that well?'

'Of course, he did. He grew up with the Altar of Pergamon. His mother worked for the Pergamon Museum when it was in East Berlin. You know those sour-faced officials you see in museums sitting glumly in the corner on their little stools? She was one of them. Who the Gods, Goddesses, Giants and Titans were in those statues, why Heracles was amongst them in the friezes; she knew it all off by heart. Better than most archaeologists.'

Yıldız remembered her conversation with Peter. When she had asked him if he was interested in archaeology, he had said, 'Only as much as the next man.' And yet here was Kitty saying something completely different. She glanced at her out of the corner of her eye. There was nothing abnormal about her. Moreover, she had no reason to lie. So why, then, had Peter claimed not have any interest in archaeology? Why had he hidden the fact that he knew so much about the Altar of Zeus? Trying hard to stifle her excitement, Yıldız asked, 'What did Peter's father do? Did he also work for the museum?'

'No,' Kitty said in a detached tone. 'He actually had two fathers. His biological father was a Russian who worked for the KGB, so he obviously had links with the Stasi too. When the Wall came down, he abandoned his wife and two kids and fled. He was probably afraid of being arrested and being tried. You know how it is in that world, the world of counter-espionage. All cloak and daggers. All very secretive, sinister stuff. For all we know, he may have had another wife and other children in Moscow. Peter does not like talking about it but the topic came up once when we were talking about his sister. I remember what he told me: "It was my sister that suffered the most. Our mother married again, to a heart surgeon. Actually, he wasn't a bad guy. We used to play football together. But when our real father left us, it hit my sister hard. Luckily, she had her art. That is what kept her together."'

Yıldız could barely believe what she was hearing.

'What about Peter himself? How did it affect him?' she asked breathlessly. Kitty suddenly stopped and stared at Yıldız.

'Why are you so interested in all this? Do you know Peter?'

'I do,' Yıldız said. She realized there was no way out now. 'We met after the murders. I am the police officer heading the investigation.' She extended a hand. 'My name is Yıldız. Yıldız Karasu.'

Although her eyes were hidden by her glasses, Yıldız could still feel Kitty's annoyance.

'You should have said so. This is nothing but entrapment, what you have just done. Approaching me and pretending to be Peter's friend is inappropriate and utterly unacceptable.'

And with that, Kitty began walking off, too angry to listen to Yıldız's apologies. Yıldız was upset too, not at having offended Kitty but because the conversation had been so abruptly ended. But there was little she could do now and she too began walking away, heading for the café where she was to meet Rafael. *He grew up with the Altar of Pergamon. His mother worked for the Pergamon Museum when it was in East Berlin.* Why had Peter lied to her? Was it because he had been afraid of being charged? But he had not looked anxious or scared when they had last spoken. She needed to talk to him to understand. He would most probably be at the ceremony too.

'Ms Karasu? Ms Karasu?'

She turned around and saw Rafael waving at her from the corner of the street.

'Hello, Mister Moreno. How are you?'

'As good as can be,' he said, smiling sadly and then extending a hand. 'I would like to thank you for catching those villains.'

Yıldız felt like telling him that the investigation was still ongoing but she decided not to. Telling him would not help him. Thinking the killers had been detained made him happy and she did not want to snuff out that happiness.

'Peter is coming too, isn't he?' she asked, shaking his outstretched hand. 'To the ceremony, that is…'

'I'm afraid he can't as he is attending a conference in London on renewable energy. He is going to be a speaker there. It was planned months ago. In fact, he's already there. He was very upset at not being able to cancel his plans and come today because he loved Cemal like a brother.'

Peter had mentioned the conference during their last conversation as the reason why he would not be able to attend Cemal's funeral in Bergama. But Rafael's last sentence caught Yıldız's attention. *He loved him like a brother.* There was a tangled mass of ideas in her mind but a clear and complete picture would not emerge.

'Was Peter also interested in archaeology?'

The question seemed to fall from her lips by itself.

'A little, but his real area of expertise was energy. But you already know that… I was not as close to him as Cemal was so I don't really know.'

'Was it Peter that gave Cemal the idea of a project about the Altar of Pergamon?'

Rafael's dark features formed a frown.

'Probably. I don't remember that clearly but Cemal may have mentioned something on those lines to me once when he was praising Peter for having such a grand vision. Yes, I think it was Peter that suggested personalizing his picture of the Pergamon Altar. In fact, I think that may even be the reason behind some of his arguments with Alex. Alex was terribly jealous of Peter, but that's hardly a surprise. Alex was a madman. I won't lie, I was not too keen on Alex.' He paused. 'That doesn't mean he deserved to die like that, though. I think I may have been the last person to see him. The night he died, he came here, to the squat.'

At first, Yıldız did not know what he was talking about but when he mentioned the squat, she began to understand. She still wanted to be sure, however.

'Alex was here that night? The night he was killed…?'

Rafael nodded in sorrow.

'Yes. I was making some changes to the painting of the "Pacifist Christ" in the hall and I saw him come in looking very flustered. I was on the scaffold and called out to him. He just waved at me and went straight into the room he shared with Cemal. He seemed to be in a great rush. He didn't stay inside long, only around ten minutes or so. Then he came out and left. Walked under the scaffold and walked away, without even saying bye. I read in the papers the next day that he had been killed that night. The poor guy didn't even know he was rushing towards his own death.'

Yıldız looked back to that evening. How Alex had called her from the station in Leipzig to tell her Cemal had left a message on his answering machine but that the machine was playing up and he could not listen to the message. 'I'll listen to the message and call you when I get home,' he had said. He had not called, however. Instead, it seems he had gone to the room he shared with Cemal.

'The room Alex went into that night... What's in that room?' Rafael hesitated. 'This is critical information, Mister Moreno,' she added gravely. 'Please do not withhold information from me.'

Rafael looked at her sheepishly, like a naughty child that was being scolded.

'It's where they kept their stash. Weed and other stuff.'

Would Alex, coming home from Leipzig in the middle of the night, rush into their room just to pick up a handful of weed though? Perhaps. If he had a substance abuse problem, some kind of dependency, and Yıldız would have been more than happy to accept this explanation were it not for the message on the answering machine. That message, and the fact that Alex had called her and told her he would call her again and had then failed to do so, meant there were other possibilities at play.

'Can I take a look at this room?' she asked. Rafael tensed up.

'You mean Cemal and Alex's room? Why?'

'As part of the investigation. In fact, it is no longer a request.' Rafael's face fell.

'It's not that easy, Ms Karasu,' he whispered, frightened that he may be overheard. 'I cannot let a police officer into the squat to look at a room used by two of my murdered friends. The people here have absolute trust in me. I cannot abuse that trust.'

'Please, Rafael,' she said, dropping the formal language, her hazel eyes pleading with him. 'I am not looking for weed or cocaine in there. I have no intention of harming anyone here or causing any discomfort. I promise you now that no matter what substances may be found in there, it will not be used to the detriment of anyone here in the squat. I just want to find the people that killed Cemal. Nothing else.'

'You mean you haven't caught the killers yet?' Rafael asked, clearly disappointed. 'Aren't the neo-Nazis behind all this?'

'We think we have apprehended the perpetrators but we have other leads we are following up, other hypotheses,' Yıldız said with a sigh. 'We need to be sure. What I see in that room will help me confirm or disconfirm some of those hypotheses. So please, Rafael, for Cemal's sake. I need to see that room.'

The painter was still not sure and looked around indecisively.

'Okay,' he eventually said. 'I'll let you in but I'm coming in with you.'

Alex's and Cemal's giant paintings hung on the walls of the squat. Speakers played melancholy music and the crowd gathered in the garden was growing by the minute. Actually, Yıldız was not that much of a stranger to such places. Years earlier, when her father reacted angrily when told that she wanted to join the police, she had spent some time in a squat in Kreuzberg. It was a strange situation. She was rebelling against her family but the rebellion was because her parents did not want her to join the police force. As such, she did not tell anyone in the squat why she was there and what had caused the rift with her parents as she knew they would have taken their parents' side. Within a month, she was out of the commune anyway. Walking through the garden of the squat now, she recalled those days in her youth.

As they made their way through the crowd, Yıldız kept her eye out for Kitty, the only person she knew there besides Rafael. Eventually, she managed to pick her out, glowing like a sun amongst the gathered throng of people. She was trying so hard to remain unseen by Kitty that she was not aware of what was going on around her and someone bumped into her. Without looking up, she muttered an apology.

'No problem, Ms Karasu,' came the response. The voice was familiar. She turned around and saw the smiling face of Özcan Mutlu, ex-Green Party MP. 'Congratulations, you managed to track down and apprehend the culprits.'

She did not have time. She could not lose sight of Rafael, who was moving ahead through the crowd.

'Thank you, Mister Mutlu… But I really need to be going. Let's talk another time.'

Rafael, expertly snaking through the crowd, had already reached the apartment building's main entrance. Yıldız quickened her pace. Rafael was talking to a tall, long-haired man with tattoos covering his arms leaning against the front door. Opting for caution, Yıldız held back a few metres. After a brief exchange, the man handed something over to Rafael, who looked relieved and gestured with a jerk of his head for Yıldız to come forward. The two of them slipped into the building through the front door. Inside, she picked up that familiar smell of paint and glue. A few steps later, they were facing a large painting of a black Jesus. His skin was a beautiful brown tone, like rich chocolate, yet he also had bright blue eyes that reminded her of a clear, cloudless sky. A bright yellow sun that looked like a sunflower shone behind his head, which was leaning to the right. There was a delicate sorrow in his face and a profound compassion shining in his huge eyes, while his dark hands held bouquets of flowers bursting with colour against his chest.

'This is a wonderful picture,' Yıldız muttered. 'If only everyone's Jesus was so full of love.'

Rafael's face lit up.

'The real Christ was. He was the Christ of the poor. He owned nothing, had no wealth. All he had was love.'

They walked past the hem of Christ's gown until they reached a wooden door a little further ahead. Rafael took the key he had obtained from the man on the door with the tattoos, put it in the lock and turned it twice. The door opened easily into the interior of a room that was better lit than the hall outside. It was a large room which had double windows with a wooden frame, a table, a bed, two armchairs, a little bookcase and a guitar hanging on a bare brick wall. While Yıldız stood there wondering where to look, Rafael said, 'The stash is usually over here,' and walked towards the window, where he lifted the dirty green curtains and began feeling the wall. 'There is a little cubby hole behind one of these bricks. One of these bricks should come lose, but which one?'

He sounded unsure of himself. Meanwhile, there was something about the guitar that had caught Yıldız's eye. She walked towards it, picked it up and shook it gently. A rattling sound came from within. She was right; there was something inside. She turned it upside down over the bed. There was a voice recorder wedged between the strings in the main body of the guitar which she managed to fish out. Rafael had stopped feeling the wall for the loose brick and was staring at the machine in amazement. She wasted no time and pressed its button.

'I'm sorry I'm calling you so late at night. I know you're angry with me but I don't know who else to call. You are the first person I thought of. My grandfather, Orhan, went missing two days ago. My mother phoned me this morning to tell me. He often goes missing but something odd happened today. Peter gave me a lift home because my bike broke down. When I got into the car, I could smell my grandfather's aftershave in it. It has a distinctive smell because it's made from tobacco that comes from Bergama. He has the aftershave

sent over especially. I'm telling you, there is no way any other person in Berlin has that cologne. When I asked Peter about it, he told me the smell probably came from the valet who had parked the car the previous evening at the reception he had attended but something didn't feel right. He did not sound very convincing. What's more, there is still no news about my grandfather. Please call me when you get home.'

It was the fourth time Yıldız was listening to the recording. She had been stunned on the first listen but Rafael had been with her and she did not want to discuss the recording in detail with him so when he did ask questions, she gave him a few bland and perfunctory answers and then left the premises and went to her car, where she listened to the recording again. While listening to Cemal's anxious message, the missing pieces began to emerge. A generous businessman, a friendly boss and a handsome and courteous gentleman. There were still question marks and she needed to be sure but was he the one behind all this carnage? She listened to the recording again, which she had all but memorized by now, and on her way back to the station, she pondered each word, each turn of phrase, each inflection and each intonation carefully. She was now listening to the recording again, this time with Markus, but he showed no signs of excitement at all. He listened until the end, staring at the device, and then looked up, eyes like a dead fish.

'And? So?'

He was so convinced the neo-Nazis were behind the murders that he was all but warning her not to kick up a fuss over nothing.

'What do you mean "so"? Didn't you hear him? Cemal has just revealed the killer.' She paused. 'If I'm not mistaken, that is.'

'If you're not mistaken?' Markus sniggered. 'And how are we to prove that then?'

'Easy. We get a warrant to search Peter Schimmel's residence and his offices,' she said, ignoring his condescending manner and pushing a piece of paper on the table towards him. 'Here's the address. If we get a search warrant now, we can find out if I'm mistaken or not by this evening.'

Her Chief did not even look at the piece of paper.

'And have you called Mister Schimmel and spoken to him? He may have a perfectly sound explanation as to why that smell was in his car?'

She realized Markus wanted to stall but she was determined to see this through.

'I did call him but he didn't answer. And that's what frightens me. He may well be out there already on the trail of his fourth victim.'

'His fourth victim?' he asked with a sardonic expression that infuriated Yıldız

'Kerem Ölmez. Cemal's father… It has to be him.'

'Has to be?'

There was no trace of seriousness in Markus' voice but Yıldız kept on.

'Yes, it has to be him. Listen Markus, this is a tough case. Until just a few hours ago, I was having trouble getting my head around it. The neo-Nazis dragged the investigation into a dead end and Hüseyin Ölmez's idiotic attack muddied the waters even further. Worse than that, they led us to false conclusions. No, wait. Just hear me out. You know I can't stand neo-Nazis. Decades ago, they plunged this country into a nightmare and if measures are not taken, they may well cause further mayhem again, and not in the distant future either. Nevertheless, I do not believe they are the guilty party here. No, it makes no sense for Rudolf to plan and carry out these murders. These killings have something to do with the Ölmez family. Something within the family. Just think about it. The first person to be killed is Orhan Ölmez, the grandfather. His mythological equivalent is Uranus, and like Uranus, the poor old man was also castrated. Then a second murder was to follow, Kronos, according to the mythological orders. In other words, Kerem Ölmez, who, due to his disorder, actually thought he was Kronos.'

Markus was tapping the table nervously.

'But that is not what happened. It was not the father that was killed but Cemal. The son who painted himself as Zeus. And after Zeus, Alex was killed, all of which means the killer was not bound by the myths. What that tells us is, the Nazi thugs used the mythological rituals and motifs to lead us astray.'

'No, Markus, you're wrong. The mythological motif is of the utmost significance for the killer. The murders *were* carried out according to the myths. That is how they started. By killing grandpa Orhan, who represents Uranus. But something went wrong. Something the killer had not foreseen. Orhan Ölmez used a specific cologne that is made only in Bergama. I know the smell because a bottle of that cologne shattered on the floor during that encounter in Hüseyin Ölmez's garage. The whole garage reeked of it. It has a very heavy smell, that cologne. But the killer did not know that Orhan Ölmez used that cologne. Most probably, when Orhan started to deteriorate physically and mentally, his son began spraying it on his father's clothing so it would mask any unpleasant smells coming from his father's sick and frail body. The killer did not know this, of course. When he abducted Orhan Ölmez, took him to his secret location, castrated him and killed him and then left his body on Teufelsberg, Orhan Ölmez's cologne, a scent that is very hard to remove, was left all over the killer's car seats. The killer did not even register this fact as he had no way of knowing that this may be what gives him away. But things had already started to go wrong. Cemal's bike broke down and he made the mistake of offering Cemal a lift home, not realizing Cemal would notice the aftershave's lingering scent in the car, which he did the moment he got into the vehicle. He asked Peter about it, who came out with the first lie he could think off. You just heard it. He says he was at a reception and that he had given the car to the valet to park and so the smell must have been his. Cemal, however, did not fall for it, which is why he called Alex as soon as he got home. But Alex was not at home so he left a message on his answerphone. The killer, however, knew Cemal well. He knew how smart he was, and when Orhan Ölmez's body was found, he knew Cemal would work out who the killer was. And that is why that night, instead of killing Kerem Ölmez, as per the order of the mythology, he chose to kill Kerem's son instead. But he made sure he still employed the mythological rituals and symbols. Like you said, to lead us astray.'

With his right middle finger, Markus pushed his glasses up towards his eyebrows.

'So why did he kill Alex then?'

'Don't you see, Markus?' Yıldız said, the exasperation beginning to show in her voice. 'Alex heard the message on the answerphone and he wanted to tell me about it. He even tried calling me but then changed his mind. He was hard up, whereas Peter is a wealthy businessman. Cemal is dead. He called the killer, mentioned the recording on the answerphone and asked for money. The killer pretended to agree to pay up and then wasted no time in killing Alex, making sure he included a mythological element to the killing.'

Markus' face was like ice.

'This is all conjecture, Yıldız. You do not have any evidence or witnesses. Nothing with which we can charge Peter Schimmel. We have in custody now members of a gang who were caught in possessions of a cache of arms and a damn hitlist. Moreover, Cemal Ölmez and Alexander Werner were killed with a knife that belonged to a member of this gang. So why do you keep insisting on this denial? We've caught some of the men, some have been killed. Case closed. Why do you refuse to accept it?'

'The case is not closed,' Yıldız said, shaking her head. 'It won't be closed until Kerem dies. Kronos has to be defeated for Zeus to assume power and Kronos has not been beaten yet.'

Markus could not take any more and got to his feet.

'I'm sorry, Yıldız, but I cannot waste any more of the public prosecutor's time with these wild scenarios. As far as I am concerned, this investigation is over and the case is closed. We cannot just go around disturbing prominent businessmen on flimsy pretexts. I know this has been a difficult period for you. You're tired and your partner is still in critical condition. It's affected you, I'm sure.'

Incensed, Yıldız pushed her chair away and rose to her feet.

'Yes, it has been difficult, yes, I am tired, and yes, it has affected me but none of that has anything to do with what I am saying! We have not caught the killer, Markus. This is going to come back and bite us hard. The killer is not going to stop until he has killed Kerem Ölmez, and even then, I don't know if he is going to stop. The man is a maniac. Off the rails. He thinks he's Zeus. Please, for the love of God, please have a search warrant made out. Otherwise it's on you.'

Markus' green eyes flashed in fury.

'What the hell do you mean it's on me? What the hell is that supposed to mean? Pull yourself together, Yıldız! I'm in charge here. I do not have to take part in your delusions! The way you've been acting and the things you've been saying have been nothing short of scandalous! First, you accuse the force of protecting neo-Nazis but that didn't stick because the Nazis got collared and hauled in, didn't they? Now you're saying the Nazis are innocent. What are you playing at? What's your game?'

They were both on edge. Tensions were flying dangerously high.

'Nothing. I don't have a game. You just carry on.' Yıldız reached out and picked up the sheet of paper with Peter's work and home addresses on it. 'I'm off. That's all from me today.'

Her boss stood rooted to the spot, not knowing what to say, but he knew her well enough to speak up and warn her.

'Yıldız, look, I'm warning you. Don't do anything stupid!'

Yıldız pretended not to hear and walked out of the room.

When she finally reached the Passat and slumped down in the passenger seat, even she did not know what she was going to do. What if Markus was right and her suspicions about Peter Schimmel were baseless? What if Cemal had imagined the smell in the car? Or the valet really had used a similar cologne? She was at a loss as to what to think or do. She reached out and opened the glove compartment and saw Tobias' packet of cigarettes. Just one perhaps... Then she saw the mobile siren next to it. She took a deep breath. She reached out, not for the cigarettes but the siren. There were far too many coincidences at play and they could not be ignored. She had to follow them up, see them through to the end. If she were wrong, she would gladly pay the price, whatever it was, but one way or another, she had to find out the truth. She opened the window, placed the siren on the roof of the car, put the car into gear and hit the gas.

Yıldız parked the car around fifty metres away from Peter Schimmel's house, a beautiful two-storey stone villa with a magnificent view on the edge of a lake. She loaded and locked her gun in the car, got out and began walking. The villa's well-kept front garden stood in the shade of two giant pine trees just like the ones that stood in front of the Der

Blitz offices. She breathed in the trees' scent, drifting on the damp breeze. She soon reached the front garden's iron gates but the gates were locked. She rang the bell but there was no answer. She rang again, keeping her finger pressed down on the buzzer longer this time, and waited, but again, there was no movement from within. It was impossible for a house such as this not to have a maid or housekeeper. She looked through the iron gates into the garden. Apart from a family of bees buzzing around the flowers, there was little other activity. She pressed the buzzer one more time. No, it was as quiet as a graveyard inside. She looked around and once she was sure she was not being watched, she swiftly and expertly climbed over the gates. When she hit the earthy ground on the other side, she stumbled and almost fell to her right but she stuck her right hand out to stop the fall. Her hand sank into the rough soil and the skin was slightly torn in one place but she did not mind. She wiped her hand clean on her trousers and straightened up. The pain in her ribs was still there but she did not have the time or inclination to deal with that. She scanned the garden and the stone building fifty metres up ahead. No sound, no movement. She hurried towards the building.

Passing through an open pathway lined with columns on both sides, she reached the white mahogany front door of the villa. The door was shut. She rang the bell. Again, there was no answer. She called out.

'Is anybody home? Hello? Is anybody there?'

No answer. Her gaze slid over to the security camera pointing at her. She knew Markus would have a field day with her if she did not find what she was looking for but she was beyond caring now. She gave the door a shove but it did not dodge, nor was it likely to. She walked around the building to the rear and saw a large garage, the door of which was ajar. She also noticed a grey Audi coupé and behind that a large vehicle under a beige cloth cover. Walking over, she lifted the corner of the cloth and saw a white minibus underneath. She lifted more of the cover away, bent over and looked under the vehicle. At the front of the vehicle, where the hood edged down, she saw some black marks on the ground. She walked over to the side and saw the same black lines there. She touched them with a finger. It had to be the minibus Peyman had described. If it was, it meant Peter had had it painted white. She tried to open the minibus' doors but they were locked. She looked around for some keys but found nothing. That was when she noticed the door that led into the house. With a thrill, as though she had found the hidden treasure, she rushed to the door and tried to open it but it too was locked. She stayed in the garage for some time and examined the surroundings but there was little of use or significance.

She left the garage and carried on to the rear of the house. When she reached the shade of a pine tree whose thick trunk was leaning towards the lake, she noticed a door with glass panels. She walked straight over to it, took out her gun and struck the pane of glass above the lock with the grip. The pane shattered and the glass fell to the floor on the inside of the house. After clearing away the last shards of glass sticking out of the empty square in the door, she reached in and unlocked the door. She made sure she looked around one more time. No, there was nobody there. She slipped inside.

She found herself in a narrow hallway. She silently walked through until she came to a large kitchen but there were few signs of activity there. There were no fruits or vegetables on the table, no plates anywhere, no draining tray for dishes. When she checked the coffee machine, it was clean, untouched. Clearly, nobody had been at home for days. Walking through the door that led from the kitchen further into the house, she found herself in a dark passageway. There was a wooden staircase a little further ahead that led upstairs and next to the staircase, another set of steps that led down to the basement. She began walking down the steps to the basement. When she reached the final step, she found herself facing a mahogany door that had been painted white. She turned the knob, fashioned into the head of a lion, and pushed but the door was locked. She turned around and climbed back up the wooden staircase, past the ground floor and up to the first floor. There were two bedrooms there and a large lounge with two broad windows looking out onto the lake. The interior of the house was dominated by cream and brown tones and was minimally decorated, with only strictly necessary furniture and items present. Hanging over the fireplace in the lounge was what looked like a large family portrait of an attractive woman in her thirties standing between a girl with skinny legs and a blond boy. They were smiling at the camera but there was a sadness in their eyes, a sorrow writ deep in their faces. It had to be Peter Schimmel, his sister Angela and their mother. But where was their father? Aside from some abstract paintings on the walls, as well as a handful of statuettes and other decorative ornaments on the tables, there were no other photographs to be seen. There was another staircase leading upstairs. Yıldız climbed the stairs. The upper floor was a little smaller and its ceiling lower. There was another bedroom at the rear of this floor and a huge study in front of it, its windows also looking out onto the lake. On the wooden desk in the middle of the study were a computer and numerous sheets of paper, with stacks of files, folders, binders and boxes on the wooden shelves that lined the walls. Yıldız rifled through the sheets. They were all work-related. She walked over to the window and looked out. The lake in all its entirety was at her feet. People were swimming and sunbathing in and around it, making the most of the short-lived Berlin summer. She went back to the study and looked around the room again. No, it did not have what she was looking for. She hurried down the stairs back to the basement.

She was standing in front of the white mahogany door again. She pushed against it with all her strength. It shook but did not open. She tried again but the door stood firm. This was not going to work. She rushed back up the staircase, went to the kitchen and began rummaging through the drawers. Saucepans, plates, glasses... None of them were of any use so she opened a cupboard on the other side of the kitchen. Bottles of olive oil, jars of sauces, sacks of grains and pulses... Just as she was about to give up, she saw a bag on the bottom shelf. She reached out and picked it up, hoping to find what she had in mind. It was heavy, which was a promising sign. When she opened the bag, she realized her instincts had served her well — the bag was full of hardware tools. She hauled the bag down to the basement and stood in front of the door, holding a cutter in her left hand and a hammer in her right. She could hear Markus' voice in her head: *Listen carefully, Yıldız! I'm warning you! Don't do anything stupid!* Ignoring the voice, she thrust the end of the cutter into the gap next to the lock and brought the hammer down. The first blow was a little too restrained, so she struck it again and again, harder each time, until she lost count of the number of blows. The tip of the cutter eventually found metal. She put the hammer down and with both hands began twisting the cutter. The mahogany began to splinter but still the door would not open. She picked up the hammer again and forced open a new hole in the door. Her palms were now aching. She thrust the sharp tip of the cutter into the new gap and then bent down and took a thick screwdriver out of the bag, which she then used as a support for the cutter as she began twisting them both. Finally, a gap appeared between the door and the frame. She downed the tools, stepped back and then, putting all her weight behind the shoulders, shoved the door. A creaking sound was heard. The door gave way.

She took a deep breath and waited a little before stepping inside. As soon as she did, movement-sensitive lamps lit up a huge room. On the wall hung a familiar picture: a long-haired, bearded Zeus with a crown on his head bathed in red light staring sternly at Yıldız. The Goddess Nike was perched on his right hand and in his left was his staff with an eagle on one end, staring, like Zeus, menacingly ahead. It was a near-replica of the picture in Cemal's flat, except for one difference: in this painting, Zeus did not look like Cemal but like Peter Schimmel. 'I knew it,' Yıldız muttered excitedly. 'I knew it.'

She approached the painting and examined it more closely. No, these were not Cemal's strokes. She was not that well versed in art but it was clear that this was the work of a far more accomplished artist. 'Angel,' she whispered. 'It must have been Peter's sister Angel who painted this.' She took a few steps back and examined the painting again. Why had Angel painted it? Did she also see her brother as Zeus? Confused, Yıldız looked around. There were no windows in this room. Huge paintings hung on all four walls. In the painting to the right was a depiction of Olympus in which the seven Gods and five Goddesses could be seen sitting on golden thrones in the largest chamber of a palace in the shade of vast trees, festooned with flowers and studded with stupendous marbles and wonderful crystal clear pools. In the centre was Zeus, with Peter Schimmel's face, with the other deities lined up on either side of him.

Yıldız stared at the painting in amazement before moving on to the others. In another tableau, two muscular-looking men were fighting to the death under a dark red sky, with streaks of lightning flashing in ashen clouds above giving the image a dark, hellish feel. When she moved closer, she saw Peter Schimmel's face on one of the figures. It had to be Zeus, which also meant the other figure had to be Kronos. Yıldız peered at the figure of Kronos, intrigued. The artist had painted the face of the Titan, howling in pain, with great clarity. It was just as she had expected: the person struggling to hang on to life as Zeus held him tight in his powerful arms and choked him into submission was none other than Kerem Ölmez. But what did Peter's sister Angel have to do with Kerem?

She turned to the other paintings on the wall. Once again, a picture of the Altar of Pergamon stood out, in all its splendour. On the steps were three people — a man, a girl of around ten and a boy around five years of age. They were the children she had just seen in the family photograph above the fireplace only this time the mother was absent and it was the father with his children. Her blood running cold, Yıldız approached the painting and looked at the father first. A young Kerem Ölmez stood smiling on the steps of the Altar, looking smart, strong and dashing, while the blue-eyed girl lovingly pressed her father's hand against her face. The blond lad, who had black eyes just like his father, was also clinging on to Kerem Ölmez's hand, as though imploring him not to leave. Yıldız could barely breathe. She recalled Peter Schimmel's eyes, and the deep sorrow within them, despite the sense of confidence and gravitas they expressed at first. And she also remembered Kerem Ölmez's words: '*I used to hold his hand and show him every part of that monument, every nook and cranny, every minute detail, and tell him the stories about the Gods and Goddesses and the Titans and the Giants carved into the friezes. He was so smart, he memorized all the stories straightaway. The Altar of Pergamon for him was like a magic park. He loved the story of Zeus most of all. I remember the way he used to proudly say, 'When I grow up, I am going to be Zeus. I shall ride my golden chariot driven by my flying horses towards my enemies and rain thunderbolts down upon them.' But after that day, for years, he could not go to the museum with his father. My eagle... My poor unlucky eagle...'*

The picture that had been so murky for days suddenly emerged in all clarity. Although he seemed to have been talking about Cemal that day, Kerem had actually been talking about Peter. Yıldız felt her chest constrict. 'Oh my God, Kerem, what have you done...' she said, standing in shock in front of the painting. Looking around, she saw a little table in the corner of the room. It was a child's desk... She walked towards it. On the desk were various notebooks with bright, colourful covers, textbooks published by the government of the former West Germany, the remaining two thirds of a blue rubber and a half-used pencil. She picked up a notebook with a blue cover. It had a label on the front with its owner's name: *Kartal Brückner*. So Peter's first name had been Kartal. That is what his father used to call him. She then looked at the name on another notebook with a pink cover. *Melek. Melek Brückner*. Once more, she cried out in horror. 'Kerem, what have you done...'

In the corner by the wall with the painting of Zeus and Kronos was a large refrigerator. Next to that was a treatment area similar to the ones seen in hospitals all over the world, complete with a light green drape that acted as a curtain that sectioned off the area. Yıldız walked over to the corner and pulled the drape to one side. Inside was a bed, an IV stand and rows of syringes, bandages and other medical equipment on a small table. On a nightstand to the right, she saw a saw and a scalpel. He must have killed Cemal with the knife first and then cut his sternum open with the saw. She walked over to the refrigerator and opened its door. Inside, were two blood bags, one half-empty. On the shelves were numerous bottles and vials of medicine: ketamin, heparin and rohypnol were the first to stand out. She went back to the blood bags. What were they for? Had he administered blood to Orhan Ölmez? It was highly doubtful as the old man seemed to have had all the blood drained out of him. It suddenly dawned on her. She hurried back to the table. There was a large inkstand next to the notebook and at the end of the stand, a long, white quill pen, with what looked like a swan feather. She picked up the quill, dipped it into the ink and pressed it down on a sheet of paper. Sure enough, a dark red blot appeared on the white paper. She threw the quill away, as though it had burnt her fingers, and took a succession of deep breaths. Once again, she scanned the room and the paintings on the four walls of the room. Her eyes came to rest on the painting of the two children and their father on the steps of the Pergamon Altar. There was no point in holding it off any longer. She took out her phone, found Markus' number and called him. He answered almost immediately.

'Hello? Yıldız? What is it?' he asked nervously. She knew what she was about to tell him was not going to go down well.

'Hi Markus,' she said calmly and surely, getting straight to the point. 'Please listen carefully. I'm calling you from Peter Schimmel's house. From a secret chamber he has under his house, to be precise.'

'What?! What the hell do you think you're doing?'

'Anger is not going to solve anything, Markus,' she replied firmly. 'Please just listen without interrupting. Afterwards, you can say whatever you like. If you want, you can start official proceedings against me. You can even fire me. But first you need to listen. The neo-Nazis have nothing to do with the murders. When you get here, you'll see what I mean.'

'See what?' he growled. 'What the hell are you on about?'

'You'll see that Peter Schimmel is the perpetrator. All the hows, whys and wherefores are here, in this chamber. You'll understand when you see it. But we do not have time to lose. If we do not act fast and stop him, he is going to kill Kerem too. You need to contact the Turkish Police immediately, and Interpol. And I need to get to Turkey too. Now. Right away.'

The Koca Seyit Airport was right on the edge of the Gulf of Edremit. When her connecting flight from Istanbul began its descent, it was well past noon. Yıldız stared out of the window. The sea below looked like a huge cloak of shimmering silver, with its foaming white waves clinging to the shoreline like embroidery. *Zeus' sea and Zeus' land*, she thought to herself. *An entire mythology taking place right here, by these waters*. She looked for Pergamon in the hills in the distance but could not find it. Looking out at the land that was her parents' motherland, she had mixed feelings. It was the same whenever she came to Turkey: a sudden rush of elation, followed by a strange melancholy, the anguish of an incomplete story. She felt deep within her those fragmented memories, memories of grandfathers, grandmothers and relatives long since gone, their final resting places now possibly unknown and lost for good. They were the stories and memories her mother had passed on to her. In all honesty, she did not feel she belonged to Turkey, although that did not mean she felt completely severed from it. Most of the passengers on the plane were Turks and she had been listening to them in wonder. Hearing Turkish spoken with such a variety of accents amazed her once more. She had observed the people on the plane. Studied them and analysed their behaviour. They struck her as decent, honest, genuine people. Many of them had struck up conversations with her and it had not been long before formalities were shelved and they began filling her in on their entire life stories. Whether this was a good thing or not, she could not decide. They were different from Germans, that much was clear, but they were not like the Turks of Berlin either. Or, to put it another way, the Turks that had moved to Germany were no longer like the people that lived here, in this country. They may have spoken the same language and followed the same religion but the differences now were too pronounced. The Anatolians that had moved to Germany all those years ago were like branches that had been cut off from a vast tree. Although the tree had been wounded by the separation, it had not been weakened by it. As for the branches that had been cut away, they had begun to bloom in their new environment too, and the water, earth and air of their new surroundings had transformed them into something new, into a new species of tree, neither Turkish nor German. Yıldız was not sure whether this was a bad thing or not. Indeed, if both cultures were understood and appreciated, it could be an advantage but staying in between and being neither German nor Turkish would be something unbearable and, unfortunately, many if not most of the Turkish immigrants in Germany fell into this category. Many of the Turks in Germany said they missed Turkey but the country they missed no longer existed. The country their grandparents and parents had described and for which they say they yearned had undergone a massive transformation. Not just that but the Turks in Germany were no longer those helpless, shivering migrant workers that had left their homeland decades earlier to look for work abroad. They had managed, by scrimping and saving and toiling, to create new lives for themselves, and seeing as they had not come back to Turkey, these new lives had to be good ones.

These were the thoughts going through her mind when the plane finally touched down on the runway. It felt very warm in Edremit, especially after Berlin. She walked down the boarding stairs and onto the open tarmac, which they had to walk across to get to the terminal. She got out her mobile phone, pressed the power button and waited for it to power up as she walked to the terminal building. After around fifty metres or so, she was inside. She looked at her mobile. Markus had called twice during her flight. She called him back immediately.

'Hello, Markus? You called? Any news from Peter? Has he left London?'

'No, the British have yet to get back to me. Have you managed to speak to Kerem Ölmez?'

'No, I've only just got off the plane. I haven't reached Bergama yet.'

Yıldız could hear Markus exhale heavily on the other end of the phone.

'I hope we're not too late,' he said and paused before going on. 'And I hope you're not wrong about the killer. Otherwise we're both in deep shit.' Despite the gravity of his words, he sounded cheerful. 'Well, we'll soon find out, that's for sure. Here, I'm handing the phone over to a friend of yours. Hold on.'

There was a short silence and then a tired male voice spoke.

'Hello! Boss? How's it going?'

'Toby!' Yıldız cried in delight. 'Toby, is it really you? So, you've finally come round?'

'I sure have, boss. But I've got to say, this will not do. Locking me up in this dingy little hospital while you saunter off to sunny Turkey? That's not cool. Not cool at all.'

Yıldız laughed.

'Don't you worry, my lad. Once all this is over, we'll come back here for a holiday. And we'll do it Turkish style.'

'Wow! Is that an invitation?'

'At the very least. After what I did. I wronged you, Toby.'

Clearly moved, Toby did not answer at first.

'You didn't wrong me, boss,' he said, choking up. 'Had it not been for you, I would have been toast. Gone for good. And anyway, I would have done the same in your position. I shouldn't have concealed that information.' His voice took a sudden serious tone. 'But now surely you must realize I'm not a Nazi.'

'No, I reckon you're the secret head of the National Socialist Underground…,' Yıldız joked. 'Of course, you're not, Toby. I see that now, anyone can see it. The matter is closed. The end. No more. But I'm serious about the invitation to Turkey. I'd be delighted if you accept.'

Tobias let out a weak but still hearty guffaw.

'Ha! I've finally found a Turkish woman that loves me!'

'Like a brother.'

'Naturally, boss. I wouldn't have it any other way.'

'Good. Now, enough of all that. You concentrate on getting back on your feet because I'm going to be needing you soon.'

After ending the conversation with Toby, she called Kerem Ölmez once again but with the same results — a female German voice informing her that the number she had dialled could not be reached. She put her phone away, hoisted her backpack over her shoulders and walked out of the baggage reclaim section. As soon as she stepped outside, she saw a handsome young man with messy hair and a tough but impish look holding up a piece of cardboard with her name on it. He had to be one of the local police officers that had been assigned to accompany her. She raised her hand and began walking towards him. He had also seen her. The frown on his face disappeared and his face softened.

'Hello, I think you may be looking for me. Chief Inspector Yıldız Karasu from the Berlin Homicide Division.'

The young man stepped aside and made way for another gentleman with greying hair and a warm, bright face.

'Welcome, Yıldız Hanım,' he said, extending a hand. 'My name is Nevzat. Chief Inspector Nevzat.'

'Thank you for coming all this way,' Yıldız said, after her initial surprise. She looked at the younger man again, who was standing respectfully to one side. It was a genuine respect she felt in him, not a show.

'Oh, my apologies,' Nevzat said. 'This is our very own Inspector Ali. We are on the same team.'

Whether it was the warmth and the sense of trust between the two men she could not tell but Yıldız felt good in their presence. On her way over, one of her concerns had been the prospect of having to work with officers with whom she did not get on but seeing these two men, even after only a few seconds she realized they were consummate professionals.

'It's a pleasure to meet you both.'

'I can carry that for you,' Ali said, reaching for her backpack.

'Thank you, but I'm fine. I can manage,' she replied, her eyes lighting up with appreciation of the offer.

'Are you hungry, Yıldız Hanım?' Nevzat asked before they began walking. 'Would you like something to eat?'

It felt reassuring to know that these two men whom she had only just met had the best interests in mind but she wanted to track down Kerem Ölmez as soon as possible.

'Thank you, I'm full. If it's okay with you, I'd like to set off immediately.'

They began walking towards the exit.

'Your Turkish is excellent,' the Chief Inspector remarked. 'Genuine Istanbul Turkish. You must have moved to Germany later on in life.'

'Actually, I was born there,' she answered, readjusting her backpack. 'My parents were born and bred in Istanbul and they moved from there to Berlin. They both had a profound love of literature so I grew up reading Turkish novels.' She stopped before asking, 'And you? Are you from Istanbul?'

'We are indeed,' Nevzat nodded. 'From the Istanbul Homicide Desk. We were told to come out here for an urgent mission, for an investigation taking place in Germany. But I'm afraid we do not have much information about the case. It's a one-and-a-half-hour drive from here to Bergama so perhaps you could fill us in on the way. From what I gather, some of the victims in this killing spree are Turks.'

'Yes, two of them were from Bergama and one was German. It's quite a complex case with a number of strands but I'll be happy to get you up to speed.' She stopped and, suddenly remembering something, put her hand in her pocket. 'But I need to make an urgent call first. I've tried so many times but can't seem to get through.' She took out her phone and began pressing some buttons. 'He may well be the fourth victim…' She keyed in the number and waited with the phone held to her ear. 'No, still no answer. I don't even know if he is in danger or not.'

Nevzat could tell the situation was critical by the tension in her voice and demeanour.

'We should call the local police here in Bergama.' He got out his phone. 'What's the person's name?'

'Kerem Ölmez. But I do not have the address, I'm afraid. Maybe the guys at the station can find the address for us.'

They were out of the building now and Yıldız was struck by a wave of heat. While Nevzat made his call, Ali escorted her to the waiting Megane, where she placed her backpack in the boot next to some small suitcases.

'I need to make another call,' Yıldız said, politely moving a few steps away from Ali. 'My son.'

'By all means. I'll be in the car.'

Yaman answered on the second ring.

'Hello? Yıldız? Have you landed, love?'

'Have you been waiting by the phone all this time, Dad?'

'God no, I just happened to be walking past the phone when it rang,' said Yaman, who was never one for sentimentality. 'How was the flight?'

'It was fine. Smooth as you like. No hiccups. How's Deniz?'

The mention of Deniz's name was enough to make Yaman's voice light up with joy.

'He's doing just fine. We're doing a dragon jigsaw together. Hold on, let me give it to him…'

'Hi, Mum! How are you?'

'Hi, Deniz! How's my handsome boy?'

'I'm fine. We're doing a huge jigsaw puzzle. We've almost finished. I'm on the dragon's wings. How are you, Mummy? Are you okay?'

'I'm doing just fine, sweetheart. I've come all the way to Turkey but as soon as I've finished my work here, I'll be on the first flight back home. And do you want to know why? Because I miss you so much.'

It seemed the jigsaw dragon, however, was more captivating.

'That's great, Mum. I'm giving it back to Grandad.'

Before she could stop him or call him back, Yaman was on the other end of the line.

'Hi, Yıldız? Don't you worry about us. We're fine. But you be careful. Call me if anything goes wrong. I can find people out there that can help you.'

Ah, dear Dad, you don't know anybody like that in Turkey anymore.

'Don't worry, Dad. I will. I've got to go now. I'll call again this evening. Speak to you later.'

When she lifted her head, she saw Nevzat standing by the back of the car waiting for her, mobile phone in hand.

'I've just been on the phone to Nazmi, the chief of the local police here. He's a good friend of mine. He says they don't know Kerem Ölmez's address now but that they will soon have it and once they have, they'll go to the address and look around to see what's there. They'll call back soon.' He opened the back door. 'Please. I'll sit with you and you can tell us about the case. Ali will listen while driving.'

'Thank you so much, Nevzat Bey. You've gone to so much trouble.'

'And please, let's ditch the *Bey*. We're on the same team so we're family now,' Nevzat said, a fatherly expression in his eyes. Yıldız's face lit up.

'Then you must call me Yıldız. Both of you.'

They got into the car and fastened their seatbelts. Ali started up the car.

'So the perpetrators have yet to be caught, as far as I can tell. Is that right?' Nevzat asked.

'Well, I believe he has yet to be apprehended. We have yet to correctly identify the perpetrators and corroborate the evidence. However, there is one person I have in mind, someone I strongly suspect of being behind the murders. I am waiting for the results of a blood analysis. Once the results come through, I will know for sure.'

'You say you strongly suspect this person but you must be pretty certain otherwise you would not have come all the way here from Berlin. I guess you just need conclusive evidence to sew things up. Am I right?'

'Exactly,' Yıldız said, glad that someone finally understood. 'And that is why I believe Kerem Ölmez is in grave danger. His father and son were killed by the same person. And that person is probably Kerem Ölmez's son from another woman.'

Rather than appear confused, both men were intrigued.

'Some kind of inheritance squabble?' Ali asked.

'In a manner of speaking, but the killer is not after property or money. He is angry at his father for not being fair in his affections. I suppose you could say it is jealousy of a sort, although it is a little more nuanced than that. The man is psychologically imbalanced. Obsessive-compulsive, in a way, I suppose. He is under the illusion that he is Zeus.'

'Zeus as in the Greek God Zeus?' Nevzat asked in astonishment.

'The very same. In fact, he is carrying out the killings because he wants to cement his identity as Zeus. That is why he murdered his grandfather. Because he saw him as Uranus, and his father as Kronos.'

At the wheel, Ali frowned, finding parts of the story hard to follow, in contrast to his boss, who asked, 'So he castrated his grandfather?'

'You know your mythology, Chief Inspector,' Yıldız said admiringly, brushing the hair from her face. 'That is exactly what he did. He was going to kill Kronos too but he couldn't because other people got in the way.'

'And the Kronos here would be the person you are trying to call, this Kerem Ölmez, I assume? In other words, the killer's father.'

'If you like, I can start from the beginning. That way it will be easier.'

'You're right. My apologies. That would be much better, rather than us diving into the deep end straight off. Please.'

As the Megane made its way along the highway to Izmir, Yıldız began.

'The events that are behind the murders go all the way back to the days when the Berlin Wall was still standing. The Ölmez family were amongst the first guest workers to arrive in Germany. But the family has an interesting past. The great-grandfather was one of the workers that began work on the excavations for the Altar of Pergamon.'

'You mean the Altar that was taken to Berlin? The one that is considered the eighth wonder of the world?'

'I'm impressed, Chief Inspector. You seem to have a sound grasp of archaeology too.'

Nevzat smiled modestly.

'I visited Bergama as a child. You see, my mother loved history and everything connected to it. Anyway, I came back a number of times afterwards as an adult. It really is a fabulous place.'

'I visited it too. As you say, it is an amazing place. And the Altar — well, that is also incredible.'

Nevzat's face darkened for a moment.

'More the pity that it is not on display in the place in which it was built.'

'Sadly, yes,' Yıldız said, although she did not want to get dragged into that particular discussion. 'Anyway, as I was saying, Pehlivan Efendi, the grand patriarch of the Ölmez family, worked with Carl Humann on the first Pergamon excavations and this then became a family tradition, with men from subsequent generations of the Ölmez also working on later excavations in the area. Such was the family's involvement in the digs that they began to see themselves as part of the ancient city. And I do not mean that figuratively. Pehlivan Efendi became so obsessed with Pergamon he ended up telling his wife that he was Poseidon.'

'What? He didn't really believe he was Poseidon, did he?' Nevzat asked in amazement.

'It wasn't so much believing it, Chief Inspector, as feeling it. You see, it's an illness of some kind, a psychological disorder known as Paranoid Grandiosity. It's an advanced stage of megalomania, apparently. It may also have a genetic component. For instance, around a century later, Pehlivan Efendi's grandson's grandson Kerem Ölmez began to think he was Kronos. Yes, I'm afraid so. He is taking medication for this condition too.'

'Then it's perfectly normal for the killer to think he is Zeus,' Ali, who had remained silent up to now, muttered. 'The whole family is afflicted.'

Nevzat was also moved by the story.

'How strange that an ancient city can affect an entire family so profoundly...'

'It is strange,' Yıldız went on. 'But Pehlivan Efendi's condition did not stop the other men in the family from joining the digs because it paid well. Naturally, they were affected by the country's economic conditions and when the Germans began accepting Turkish guest workers in the 1960s, two brothers from the Ölmez family, the recently murdered Orhan and his brother Recep, went to Berlin with their wives and children. Kerem is the son of that same Orhan Ölmez who came to Germany from Turkey. Orhan had also worked on the Pergamon excavations at one point, and Kerem, despite his tender age, used to accompany his father to work. Orhan had wanted to become an archaeologist, and Kerem nurtured the same ambitions. But whether it was immigrant children in Germany not being given the same opportunities as native kids or just bad luck I do not know but things did not work out for Kerem. He could fulfil his dream of becoming an archaeologist and he ended up working as a security guard at the Museum of Egyptian Civilization in Berlin. But he was still obsessed with Pergamon, and so he would cross the Wall into East Berlin frequently just to see the Altar of Zeus in the Pergamon Museum in the East of the city. While he was there in the museum, he used to feel at home, as though he were back in Turkey and in Bergama. Anyway, by this time he had gotten married too, to a lady by the name of Munise Hanım, and had had a son, Hüseyin. But his obsession with the Altar remained. During one of his visits to the museum, he met a lady by the name of Nina Brückner there, a museum official like Kerem, and when Kerem told her that he was originally from Bergama and that his family had worked for years on the digs, she could not fail to be impressed. Their friendship soon turned into something else and they became lovers. Kerem did not tell her he was married as he thought it was just a casual fling and that his visits to East Berlin would soon stop. However, it turned out he could not let go of the Altar or of Nina. Worse still, Nina became pregnant and gave birth to a girl. They named her Melek. Kerem now had two children from two different women but the situation did not seem to have overly disturbed him as he carried on with this double life and with his two partners. A few years later, in 1981, he became father to two more children. Two boys, one from each woman. The child born of Munise he named Cemal, after his grandfather, while the child to whom Nina gave birth he named Kartal, taking his inspiration from Zeus' eagle.[1] Nina did not mind the name. In fact, she liked the name because, like her lover, she had spent a large part of her life around the Altar of Pergamon and was in awe of character of Zeus and the myths surrounding him and the Altar. Had Kerem continued seeing Kartal and his mother, then there wouldn't have been a problem but that, unfortunately, is not what happened. Suspicious of this man that came to East Berlin every weekend, the East German

---

[1] *kartal*: eagle

Secret Service took him aside for questioning. It did not take them long to realize he was not a spy but they did not leave it at that. "You can visit the Pergamon Museum whenever you like but we want you to help us. That is our condition. If you do not agree, then you will not be allowed here again." Kerem was too frightened to openly refuse so he told them he would think it over and inform them of his decision on his next visit. He rushed back to West Berlin, but now it was the turn of the West German Police to suspect something was up. They took him aside and grilled him, asking him what the East German Police had wanted with him and what he had been offered. He told them everything and they believed him but they also told him to accept the Stasi's offer but to actually work as an informant for them, the West Germans. Finding himself in the middle of an espionage tug-of-war, Kerem panicked and never went back to East Berlin. That's right, he forgot all about his beloved Nina, his two children and the Altar…'

'What a lowlife,' Ali muttered. 'How can a man just forget about his own children like that?'

Yıldız smiled. Her father also liked to spit out the term *lowlife* when he was angry, and as a mother she definitely agreed with Ali. Nevzat's mind, however, was on something else.

'And this is what Kerem told you?'

'Partially. Of course, he did not tell me he had had a wife and children in East Berlin. I filled in the gaps. If only he'd told me. Had he done so, then he would not be in the danger he is in now. We would have had the investigation done and dusted a long time ago had he told me.'

'Then what happened?' asked Ali, listening intently whilst staring ahead at the road that ran alongside the coast.

'After that, Kerem carried on with his life with his family in Berlin. He eventually retired and opened up two baklava shops with his son Hüseyin, while his younger son Cemal got into IT and became a programmer. Basically, Kerem chose to forget about his partner and two children in East Berlin, while Nina Brückner ended up marrying another, a surgeon by the name of Doctor Schimmel. By all accounts, he was a good man who was happy to adopt Nina's two children. All they did was change the children's names: Melek became Angela and Kartal became Peter. Angela was extremely talented and became an avant-garde artist, while Peter was educated in and went on to work in the energy sector. Angela led a somewhat bohemian lifestyle that tragically led to her death at a young age. After she died, her paintings began to increase substantially in value and when Nina and her doctor husband also passed away, Peter inherited everything and he went on to set up a company called Der Blitz. At the time, it seems the son Kerem had abandoned when he was just five years old had no plans for revenge or murder.'

Yıldız fell silent and stared out of the window, distracted momentarily by the scenery.

'How wonderful it is out there. Just look at those trees. And the colour of the sea.'

Nevzat also looked out, at the olive tree-covered hills in the distance sloping gently down towards the sea.

'It is beautiful indeed. Summers here have a beauty of their own, as do winters. Autumns also have their own charm. I won't even start on how wonderful springs are here.' He was saying it simply for the sake of it, for the story set in Germany was fascinating him. 'So when did Peter start killing? There must have been a tipping point.'

'It's hard to say for sure. I can only guess. I suppose we should start with the collapse of the Wall, because when the Wall came down, Peter's life took another drastic turn. Unlike many East Germans, he ended up becoming extremely wealthy.

This wealth, along with the confidence that comes with being a man who has achieved his aims, made him feel magnanimous enough to privately forgive the man that had abandoned him and his mother and sister all those years before. Or so he believed. He was so confident and sure of himself that he even found out where Kerem Ölmez lived and picked up information about him. He did not actually introduce himself to Kerem but chose, rather, to watch him from afar. Had it stayed like that, it would have been fine but he ended up giving Kerem's son Cemal, in other words, his own stepbrother, a job at his firm, which brought him yet closer to his biological father. Peter began to grow fond of Cemal because Cemal, for various other reasons, was also a child that had been cast out by his own family. The Ölmez family disowned Cemal because he was gay.' She turned and faced Nevzat. 'Cemal was also a talented artist and he wanted to paint the statues that used to line the walls of the Altar of Pergamon. The weird thing is, Peter, who encouraged him in this idea, suggested replacing the faces of the Gods, Titans and Giants on the statues around the Altar with those of his relatives and family members. Cemal took to the idea. He painted himself as Zeus and I think this may have been the tipping point. As a child, Peter had grown to love the figure of Zeus thanks to Kerem, his father, so much so that even when he was still just a boy, the young Kartal had begun to envision himself as that particular deity. So when he saw Cemal's face there on the figure of the deity with whom he identified, old wounds were reopened and the old trauma was revived. Or, at least, that is my theory. If you ask me, the trauma of being abandoned had rocked him to his core, and that may have been what caused the same psychological disorder that had afflicted his ancestor Pehlivan Efendi and his father Kerem Ölmez to be triggered in him.

'Only a psychiatrist will be able to tell you of his mental state after the onset of the disorder. I can only describe what he has done. He castrated and killed his grandfather Orhan, whom he saw as Uranus. However, something went badly wrong — Cemal worked out what had happened and Peter, sensing the threat, had to change the order of the killings and so instead of killing Kerem Ölmez, or Kronos, next, he killed Cemal. However, another problem then arose. Cemal had worked out what was going on and had disclosed the identity of the killer to his friend Alex and so Peter had to get rid of Alex too. The person Peter actually wants to kill, his father Kerem Ölmez, is still alive, and it is impossible for Zeus to ascend the throne without defeating his father. That is why he needed to come here, to Bergama. To kill Kerem…' The last sentence she uttered hesitantly. 'I say he needed to come here because I do not have anything to back any of this up. But this is what I believe is happening. Peter has to come here. To complete the circle.'

'An interesting fellow,' Nevzat remarked. 'Usually, fatherless children find refuge in God. He, on the other hand, chose to become a God.'

Yıldız nodded in agreement.

'He was so wounded that even if the father was sacred, he still rejected him. He wanted to be so strong that he would not feel the need to have a father. That is why he chose to be Zeus. Because the Gods do not need a father.'

Nevzat's mobile phone rang.

'It's Nazmi, from the Bergama Police… Hello? Nazmi? Yes, I'm listening. I see. Really? He lost it at Izmir Airport? Yes, possibly, they may have called him… Kerem Ölmez is at the wake, you say? You're sure? What's that? Your own men saw him? Very well. In that case, do me a favour, will you, and send me the location of the house in which the wake is being held?

Thanks, old friend. What's that? Of course. Sounds good. You get those coffees ready and I'll be there soon…'

'Is Kerem okay?' Yıldız asked breathlessly.

'He's fine, he's currently at the wake,' Nevzat said distantly. 'Apparently, he lost his telephone in Izmir. He may have misplaced it. He is here for a funeral after all. Two, in fact. It can't be easy, having to bury two bodies. Someone may well have swiped his phone by now. Anyway, there's nothing amiss, thankfully. We'll be there in around an hour.'

It was good news but Yıldız was still not entirely at ease.

'I'm glad nothing has happened to Kerem Ölmez,' she said in a muted voice. She then shook her head from side to side. 'Maybe I was wrong. Maybe Peter isn't the killer. But it seems there are no other explanations. I'm at a loss, really.' She tried to smile but failed. 'I hope I haven't dragged you all out here for nothing.'

Nevzat looked at Yıldız, slumped dejectedly in her seat.

'I have this good friend, a doctor. Doctor Seher. Anyway, she once said to me, "When attempting to diagnose a patient, tests, analyses, x-rays, tomographies and MRG scans are of course important but the first thing I do is look at the clinical reports. The thoughts and intuitions of the doctors that have seen, spoken to and treated the patient are crucial." What Doctor Seher said about medicine is also valid for our profession. The most important thing in this investigation are *your* thoughts and feelings and *your* intuition. You were out in the field, you were at the crime scenes, you saw the victims, spoke to the suspects, collected evidence and followed up leads, and throughout all this, you formed hypotheses and set out possible explanations. Yes, you may be mistaken and you may make further mistakes and miss certain details. These things happen, they are part and parcel of the job, but we will eventually learn the truth. But your thoughts on this matter will always be of crucial importance.'

'I hope you're right, Chief Inspector, otherwise my boss won't let me set foot in Berlin again.' She gave a wry smile. 'Not that I mind. If he's going to fire me, he's going to fire me. Who knows? Perhaps I'll get a job working alongside you guys in the Istanbul Homicide Division.'

'Why not?' Nevzat said warmly, patting her on the shoulder. 'But I don't think you're wrong. As for us, thanks to you, we'll get to see the beauty of ancient Pergamon again. And while we're there, we'll make sure we eat their speciality dish, *patlıcan çığırtma*. The way it's made in Bergama is out of this world.'

When they left the highway and turned off onto a dirt road, it was already well past mid-afternoon but it was still scorching hot. The dirt path was so rocky that Ali had to slow the Megane down. The windows were slightly open and the car was filled not just with the dry heat but also with the wonderful scent of thyme. Leaning forward, Nevzat pointed to a three-storey building in the middle of a fenced-off garden bursting with trees.

'That must be it over there.' He looked at his phone. 'Yep, the location I've been sent says this is the place. On the left of Kozak Path. There are no other buildings here anyway so this must be it.'

'Yes, this is it, Chief Inspector,' Ali said, gripping the wheel tightly as the car lurched along the bumpy road. 'Look at all those cars lined up outside. People have arrived to offer their condolences.'

Yıldız was already stirring with excitement, even before they passed through the green metal gates and into the garden and its numerous plum, apricot, walnut and olive trees. Heaven only knew how Kerem was going to react when he saw her but his real shock would come when he found out that it was the son he had abandoned decades earlier that had killed his father and Cemal. For a moment, she wondered whether she would be doing the right thing in telling him as it had yet to be conclusively proven that Peter was behind the murders. If Peter were the killer, then he had to be here. Hadn't he? What if he had decided to wait for Kerem in Berlin? No, if the killer really was Peter Schimmel and if he really was killing in order to become Zeus, then he had to come here. This was where he needed to defeat and destroy Kronos. Although it was now behind them, she thought about the ancient city staring regally down at them and the marble columns of the Temple of Trajan she had seen glimmering in the amber sunlight when they had driven into Pergamon. Indeed, if Peter Schimmel was to become the king of the Gods, it could happen nowhere else but here, in Pergamon, where the Altar of Zeus was originally located. But where was he? This was the question she was pondering when the Megane finally came to a stop under a huge apricot tree. When they stepped out of the car, they could hear the murmur of whispered voices coming through the trees. At first, Yıldız could not work it out but then, after few steps, she heard some Arabic phrases and realized it was prayers for the departed being recited. For some reason, she slowed down. The closer she got to the house, the louder the sound became. The words made no sense to her but they could now be heard loud and clear.

A young lady wearing an embroidered black headscarf over her streaming hennaed locks stood in the doorway at the entrance to the house, watching them approach.

'This way, please. The ladies are in the room on the right, the men are in the living room.'

Ali stepped forward.

'Our condolences,' he said and showed her his badge. 'Police business. We would like to speak to Kerem Bey, please. Kerem Ölmez. Could you call him out please, if possible?'

The grief on the girl's face turned to concern when she heard the word *police*.

'Brother Kerem is not here at the moment.'

'Where is he?' Ali asked. 'Is he somewhere nearby?'

'I... I don't know,' the girl said, her chestnut-coloured eyes widening in fear. 'He left about an hour ago.'

'Did he go alone?' Nevzat asked. 'Was anybody with him?'

The girl began stammering.

'He... He... He was alone. Or at least, that is what I saw. He got into the car by himself.'

A voice came out from inside.

'What's going on, Gamze? Why don't you show our guests in? Why are you keeping them standing outside?'

She turned around. A man in his fifties was making his way down the stairs inside the house.

'My apologies for keeping you on your feet like this,' he said with genuine remorse. 'She is still young, she doesn't know how things are done.' He gestured to a door within. 'Please, do come in.'

'Please, Gamze has done nothing wrong,' Nevzat said. 'Bless her, she did invite us in.' He showed the man his ID. 'We are police officers. We would like to speak to Kerem Bey but he does not seem to be here.'

The man's face tightened and he narrowed his copper-coloured eyes.

'Have they found the killers then? Is it Uncle Recep's grandsons? Is it Davut's son?' Seeing the blank looks on the officers' faces, he bowed his head. 'They live in Berlin. I thought it might be them.'

'No, it is not Haluk,' Yıldız said, genuinely saddened by the man's grief. 'Very little is clear, at least for the moment. Do you know where Kerem Bey is?'

Although the man was startled at the confidence with which she spoke, as well as the fact that she knew Kerem, he did not hesitate in answering.

'Brother Kerem has a guest from Germany. He was our late Cemal's boss at work, apparently. By sheer chance, the person he asked at the hotel about the Ölmez family, Lütfü, is a relative of ours. When Lütfü questioned him, the gentleman mentioned Cemal and told Lütfü that he had come for the funeral so Lütfü called me to tell me. That's how the gentleman got in touch us. He told us his name too but it was a foreign name so I am afraid I cannot wrap my tongue around it.'

'Was it Peter?' Yıldız asked excitedly. 'Peter Schimmel?'

'That's it,' the elderly gentleman said, his eyes lighting up in recognition. 'Kerem told me to look after the guests as he was going to pick up this other gentleman. He doesn't know Turkish, you see. Kerem went to pick him up in my blue pickup. It's a Toyota.'

'So he is here,' Yıldız muttered. 'I was right. Peter is here.' Her excitement did not last long, however, and she turned to face the brother-in-law again. 'Do you know where they are going to meet?'

'He called from Bergama, He is staying at the Hotel La Bella,' he replied, somewhat taken aback by Yıldız's excitement. He paused for a moment before going on. 'Actually, they should have been here by now. The hotel is not far from here, fifteen minutes at the most. Kerem may have taken his guest out to lunch but we have plenty of food here.' He looked out onto the road. 'They'll be here any minute now. Please, come in, have something to drink, an *ayran* perhaps to cool you down. We have plenty of food too, so please, if you are hungry.'

'No, thank you,' Yıldız said anxiously. She was thinking about what Kerem had told her about the inheritance squabble he had had with his brother involving a house and an olive orchard. She remembered him telling her the argument had gone all the way to court and that, in the end, he had been awarded the orchard. Haluk had also mentioned the orchard and had told her about a dried-up old cistern there that was more like a well which Cemal was going to use as a model for his painting of Tartarus. 'Tartarus,' Yıldız muttered. 'Of course. Tartarus is where Zeus imprisoned Kronos.' The others around her were staring at her as she muttered to herself but she ignored their confused looks. 'The olive orchard,' she said turning to the brother-in-law. 'Kerem Bey had an olive orchard by the Selinos River. Is it near here?'

The brother-in-law looked out to the road again and pointed to the right.

'It's not far. You passed it on your way here. Once you hit the asphalt road, drive for five minutes, back in the direction from which you came, towards Bergama. You'll see an old disused mill on the right. The orchard is there by the mill. There is an old cistern there. You'll see the gate when you get there. There is also an entrance to the cistern under the slope but don't use it, it's not safe, it can collapse at any time.' He cast Yıldız a quizzical glance. 'Why are you going there? Is there something amiss at the orchard?'

'Oh no, nothing at all. Seeing as we have come all the way out here, we thought we may as well see it,' Yıldız replied, not wanting to cause any unnecessary worry. She turned to Nevzat. 'Shall we go, Chief Inspector?'

He nodded and they began walking towards the Megane. Once they were out of earshot, Nevzat asked if the killer would be at the orchard.

'I think so,' Yıldız replied, her eyes full of questions. 'If what I know about the killer is correct, he will perform his last murder in the cistern at the olive orchard.'

When they got into the car, Nevzat got into the front seat next to Ali. While they waited for Yıldız to settle in on the back seat, he took out a matt black Cz 75 from the glove compartment.

'Here, take this. Obviously, we don't want you to use it but at least have it with you. Just in case.'

Yıldız took the gun without a second thought and loaded and cocked it while Ali put the car in gear and set off. She placed the gun in the belt of her jeans.

They were out on the main road again. None of them spoke. Their eyes were fixed on the right of the road, gleaming under the hot golden sun, looking for the ruins of the old mill. Nevzat was the first to see it. It was just as the brother-in-law had described; a five-minute drive away, at the head of a ramp on a sharp bend in the road.

'There it is, over there. See? Swing to the right, Ali.'

'Okay, boss,' Ali said, taking his foot of the gas. 'Hold on. It's going to get bumpy.'

The car turned onto an incline. Olive trees with dusty leaves stubbornly clung onto the soil on the sharp slope.

'Stop the car, Ali. It's too steep. We may as well leave the car here and walk.'

Ali drove over to a layby and stopped.

'Not another car in sight,' Yıldız muttered in wonder. 'If they were here, then the Toyota pickup should be here too. I wonder if they're still on their way?' She looked at Pergamon on top of a hill in the distance. 'Or has he taken his father to the ancient city?'

Nevzat had already opened the door.

'Let's check out this cistern first. If we don't find it, we'll go up to Pergamon.'

He was right. They got out of the car. The scent of thyme was even stronger now, enough to make Yıldız's head spin. She closed her eyes and took a deep breath.

'It has to be around here.' Nevzat's voice brought her back round. 'See? You can even see the entrance from here.'

Yıldız looked at a ramshackle structure a little further ahead. 'It doesn't look much like a cistern.'

Nevzat pointed to the mound next to the structure.

'That's not it. There, right next to it.'

This time, Yıldız saw it.

'Now I see it.' She turned and looked at the road, which curved sharply downwards. 'The other entrance must be at the bottom of the hill. That's what the man said. He said there were two entrances.'

Nevzat nodded and turned to his assistant.

'Ali, check out the lower entrance. We'll try up here.'

'Yes, sir,' Ali said without hesitation. 'I'll see you inside.'

With assured steps, Ali made his way down the dirt path by the side of the road while Nevzat and Yıldız headed for the olive orchard. The wind was picking up now, making Yıldız's hair and cream-coloured blouse billow out as they walked across the soft earth towards the ruins. When they reached the first trees, a family of sparrows hurriedly fluttered away. Approaching the old building, they saw that the roof had long since been blown off and that only the walls remained. Yıldız and Nevzat poked their heads inside. Aside from a couple of lizards, who looked up and then quickly disappeared between the stones, and an old fig tree leaning against the walls of the mill whose scent filled their nostrils, there was little of interest there. Stepping over the drying grass, they headed for the cistern, large grasshoppers flying up from the grass with every step they took. A few steps later, they were standing in front of the cistern.

'Doesn't look too sound,' Nevzat said, looking at the rickety keystone in the arch over the entrance.

'You're right but we have no choice. We have to go in,' Yıldız said, smiling helplessly. Nevzat smiled warmly in return and said, 'In that case, in we go.'

They stepped inside, into what felt like a small tunnel but it was too dark to tell. Light was coming in through the ceiling that had collapsed around ten metres ahead. They walked towards the light. The scorching heat had given way to a damp coolness and they could hear the gurgling of water. However, within that cool silence, they also heard a faint moaning. At first, Yıldız thought it was the wind but then the sound grew clearer. No, it was not the wind; it was somebody talking. Was it Ali? Was he calling out to them? But he could not have it made it down so quickly. Nevzat and Yıldız peeled back their ears and listened. When they heard it, only Yıldız understood as it was German being spoken, by a male voice filled with rage, sorrow and denunciation. Yıldız raised her hand to hold Nevzat back.

'It's Peter,' she whispered. 'We've found them.'

Both officers got out their guns and carried on walking, more cautiously. A few metres later, Peter's voice came through much clearer.

'So here I am, Father.' He was wailing, clearly in some anguish. 'Even if you do not want me, here I am. Here, on your lands, in your homeland. You would have never brought me here. It would not have even crossed your mind. Because you never loved me. You rejected me. Because you feared me, Father.'

'What on earth are you talking about, Mister Schimmel?' Kerem's frightened and confused voice could be heard saying. 'Father? What father? What are you saying?'

'Don't feign ignorance!' Peter shouted. 'You know everything! Because you did it all knowingly. Your own father was heartless but you turned out to be even worse. Even more heartless. You became a tyrant. Instead of holding us tight to your breast, you turned your back on us. Instead of raising your children with love and care and compassion, you abandoned them and you fled. Why? Because you were afraid of losing power, Father.'

Kerem was now panicking.

'Believe me when I say I don't know what you're talking about! What are you saying, Mister Schimmel? Why did you hit me across the head? Why are my hands tied like this? Please untie me. Please. I don't understand. Why are you doing this?'

'It's not Mister Schimmel, it's Zeus!' Peter replied in the same anguished tone. 'Don't you remember, Father? You are Kronos, and I am your son, Zeus.'

Although the situation was grave, they sounded so utterly absurd that it was almost funny.

'Are you mocking my condition, Mister Schimmel? What has happened to you? Why are you acting like this?'

'Stop calling me Mister Schimmel! I am not Schimmel! I am your son. The son you used to call Kartal.'

There was a silence. The only sound that could be heard was that of water dripping.

'Kartal?' Kerem said. 'Are… Are you Kartal? My son? My son, Kartal?'

'Yes, I am,' came the reply, choked but full of rage. 'Your son, Kartal. Your child from your grand love, Nina. The son you once held to your chest. Yes, I am Kronos' son. But I am no longer that helpless child you abandoned when he was five. I am now another Kartal. Another eagle. I am now the eagle that is the King of the Gods. Don't look at me like that. I am Zeus, king of all the creatures of the sky and the earth. I am no longer that snivelling child crying over his absent father. I am Zeus, the King of the Gods. Zeus, who shall defeat the mightiest of the Titans and send his cruel and heartless father into the depths of Tartarus.'

'My son, what are you saying?' Kerem cried, his voice echoing around the empty water tank. 'My poor lad, have you also been afflicted? Has the curse sunk its claws into you too? Oh my God, my poor child!'

'I am not a poor child!' came the furious reply. 'You are the one to be pitied. Unlike you, I did not try to hide my true identity. Nothing and nobody can sink their claws into me. None would dare. Nor am I afflicted, for the Gods cannot be afflicted by anything. All I have done is become aware of my true power. I have discovered my true self and realize now what I am supposed to do. I shall start again. I shall start again, from the place where people forgot me. Even Uranus lost his power, and now it is your turn. You know as well as I do that children cannot live in their father's shadow and so I have no choice but to bring your rule to an end, Father. Mankind has lost its way. The creatures of the world have all lost their minds. The divine order has been upset, and I am needed to restore that order. Outside, the Titans' sun is about to set and the Dawn of the Gods shall soon break. The winds of freedom and not fear shall blow across the earth. Fathers shall not fear their sons, sons shall not be compelled to kill their fathers and siblings shall not become embroiled with hatred for each other. That is why I have come, Father. That is why I have come to Pergamon. Because you stopped the flow of life, and so I shall stop you. That is why I have come to Pergamon. So that I can dethrone you. I shall send you into the dark dungeon of the Giants. I shall send you into the depths of Tartarus.'

Yıldız was not surprised at her theory being proven right but she was shocked at seeing someone as calm and composed as Peter become so unhinged and turn into someone capable of committing such gruesome atrocities. But this was the absurdity of the creature known as man; so fragile and yet so utterly cruel.

Yet, this was neither the time nor the place to ponder such grand philosophical ideas. If she did not act quickly, there would soon be another dead body. Just as she was preparing to make her move, she felt a stone shift beneath her foot. No, it wasn't just that stone—the ground was giving way beneath her. She hurriedly took a step back and saved herself from falling just in time. The sound boomed across the walls of the cistern.

'Help me! Somebody help, please!' came Kerem's voice.

'Nobody can help you now!' Peter bellowed. 'It's too late!'

'Stop! Wait, don't!' a voice shouted before the sound of a heavy object striking bone was heard. Kerem cried out in pain. Another blow was heard, and another cry of pain, followed by yet another blow.

'He's killing him!' Yıldız cried out. She jumped over the hole in the ground and began running. Nevzat ran after her. A few seconds later, they were at the entrance to the underground cistern. Peter was around seven or eight metres below them. He was wearing dark trousers and a brown linen shirt with a round collar and yellow stripes and was standing over his father, who was lying inert in a pool of blood, his skull smashed open. Peter was so sure his father was dead that he no longer felt the need to strike him. Yet he had not let go of the murder weapon. He held on to it like a mace.

'Stop!' Yıldız shouted. 'Stop or I'll shoot!'

Peter turned and looked up. His face was streaked red with his father's blood. He glared at Yıldız with a wild look in his black eyes. Without stopping, he let out a terrible cry and raised the iron bar in his hand. Yıldız could have shot him but she did not and Peter, sensing his opportunity, slipped through the walls to the side. The iron bar fell with a clatter from his hands onto the staircase leading down into the cistern and tumbled down onto Kerem's lifeless body. As the two officers watched on in amazement, there was a scuffle in the doorway through which the killer had fled. Peter had run into Ali on his way out and Ali, unsure as to what was happening, had lost his balance and had only stopped himself from falling by reaching out with his hands and holding onto the wall. Peter saw this split-second of opportunity and swiftly turned on Ali. The first punch grazed Ali's chin, whilst the second one Ali fended off with his right arm. The wall, however, on which Ali was leaning could not take the weight and a section began to give way, covering the two men in grime and dust. Ali was the first to recover and he grabbed his adversary, who was temporarily blinded by the billowing dust, by the shoulders and threw him into the remains of the wall. Peter crashed into the wall but it did not take him long to gather his wits and he rushed outside, wanting to get away before the other two officers arrived. Ali was having none of it, however. He jumped up and caught Peter by the right shoulder but Peter was no pushover and shook himself free. Ali's fingers caught hold of the leather strap of Peter's messenger bag. He held on for dear life, the strap his last chance of keeping the suspect within reach, but it was in vain as Peter ran ahead with all his strength, leaving the bag behind and Ali clutching its strap. Now free of his any restraints, Peter raced outside and Ali was about to give chase when another section of the wall caved in over him, leaving him covered in rubble. Peter did not even bother looking back and ran on ahead to the Toyota pickup he had arrived in with Kerem. Meanwhile, Yıldız and Nevzat had reached the bottom of the stairs and were now with Ali.

'Ali, my lad, are you okay?'

'I'm fine, sir,' Ali spluttered, staggering to his feet in the dusty rubble. 'But he's getting away!'

Yıldız had already started running but by the time she got outside, it was too late; the Toyota was already moving off in the direction of Bergama, leaving Yıldız behind to stare at it as it disappeared into the distance. A cough was heard. Nevzat and Ali had stepped out of the cistern.

'Has he got away?' Ali asked angrily, clearing his throat. 'Why didn't you stop him?'

'I couldn't. But I know where we will find him.'

Nevzat also looked angry. She had had the chance to shoot him just now but hadn't and now she didn't seem to care that he had managed to escape.

'And what if we're not able to capture him and he gets way and goes on to kill more people?' he asked.

'He won't, Chief Inspector,' Yıldız said with the conviction of someone that has read the future. 'He is going to Pergamon. Don't worry, he will not harm anybody now. He can only harm himself now but he will not do it until he sees us because he wants an audience for his swan song.'

'Is that why you didn't fire?' Nevzat asked. 'Because you had the chance.'

'I did, yes, but it wouldn't have accomplished anything. He had already killed Kerem. Didn't you see it? He caved the poor man's skull in.'

Nevzat still did not understand how Yıldız could remain so calm.

'You look like you've given up on him. Don't we need to catch this man? Bring him in?'

'We will. You'll see, Chief Inspector. He'll be waiting for us in Pergamon. Most probably on the empty dais of the Altar. The circle is now complete. Peter is no longer someone of this world. He has merged with the ancient Gods of mythology. But we can catch him before he kills himself.' She noticed the bag in Ali's hand. 'What's that?'

Ali shrugged his shoulders.

'No idea. Just a bag. It was left in my hands during our altercation. It slide off his shoulder when he made a run for it.'

'May I have a look?' It was a dark green, handmade leather bag. When she opened it, she saw various parchments inside, probably the parchments Peter had bought in Pergamon during his visit the previous year. Just as she had predicted, there was writing scrawled over them. She began reading aloud.

'*I shall start where you have forgotten. In the last city where my name was erased, in the last temple where my last statue was destroyed, from the last words of my last prophet's final prophecy, in the smoking flesh of the last animal sacrificed on my Altar, from my last subject's last pleading invocation, uttering my name with love, veneration and terror…*'

Her phone rang. It was Markus.

'Hello, Chief? It seems I was right. Peter is here.'

Markus was not surprised.

'I know. The results of the analyses on the blood in those bags you found in his house have come through. It is Grandpa Orhan's blood. That psycho used his grandfather's blood as ink! I wonder what he wrote?'

Yıldız looked at the parchment in her hand.

'Stuff about mythology. I have his notebook here. He wrote mythological stuff in the guise of Zeus on the parchments he bought in Pergamon last year. And yes, with his grandfather's blood'.

'Nutter. He wants everyone to know how serious he is.'

Yıldız nodded her head and looked into the distance, as though she would see Markus appear at any moment.

'I doubt it, Markus. He didn't write it for anyone. He wrote it for himself. To convince himself that he is Zeus. To prove he is as ruthless and as unforgiving as him. But it's of little significance now. He has already killed his father. Sadly, we could not save Kerem Ölmez.'

'But did you get him? Tell me you caught him!'

'We haven't yet but we will. I have to go now, Markus.'

'Be careful, Yıldız,' Markus said, actually sounding concerned. 'Please. Be very careful.'

'I will, Markus, don't worry.'

She switched the phone off. She could feel Nevzat's puzzled gaze on her. All she could do was smile weakly in return.

'Please do not look at me like that, Chief Inspector. Shooting him would have meant nothing. Believe me, nothing. Had I shot him, all we would have acquired was another corpse. But we can still save him.'

12
They are coming, Zeus, Mother Earth's wild children are coming for you

I was walking in a hallowed forest, amongst knee-high grass and under trees whose canopies reached for the sky. A fine mist arose from the ground and a fragrant breeze was blowing through the trees while the forest nymphs hummed a sacred song. I had defeated all my enemies. I was free of all woe. Peace reigned. The Gods were happy, the Goddesses were smiling, mankind was in a state of joy and all the creatures of the world were Conzent. My body was strong, my mind clear, my soul at peace. That is when I heard the sound.

'They are coming, Zeus. Mother Earth's wild children are coming for you.'

It was Hera's voice.

'Wake up, Zeus. Open your eyes. They are coming. The Giants are coming... Wake up, Zeus, Gaia's brutes are coming. They are leaping from the volcanoes, clambering over the mountains and tying the hills together to get to Olympus. Wake up, Zeus. The terrible children of the earth are coming for us.'

When I opened my eyes, I saw the Queen of the Goddesses shaking me awake. She said:

'Gaia's Giants are rising up, Zeus... War is upon us...' I could hear the sound of boulders striking the walls of our palace. 'Hurry, Zeus. Hurry. They have almost reached Olympus.'

I shot out of my bed. The dome of the sky was reverberating ominously with the war cries of the Giants. Smoke was rising up from the earth, the seas were in a fury, the plains were on fire and the valleys were opening up into deep chasMs Gaia had moved earlier than I had expected. The Giants had launched a surprise attack, which meant it now fell to us to fight. As I began to put on my armour, I cried out to all the Olympians, to all the comrades that were to fight alongside me shoulder-to-shoulder:

'Hey, you Gods! Brothers and sisters! Sons and daughters! Prepare for battle! The day of which I foretold is upon us. The barbarians are coming to destroy our palace, to burn down our houses and to trample our freedom underfoot. Brothers and sisters, war is upon us. Now is the time for courage, valour and sacrifice. They are coming. To make their darkness reign supreme again, to spread their evil, to destroy all that is good and beautiful. But they will not succeed. We shall give Gaia and her terrible children the lesson they deserve. We shall send them so far into the depths of Tartarus that their dull eyes will never see the light of day and their foul bodies shall never contaminate life again. We shall give Gaia, our mother, our blood, our love, such a lesson that she will never dare stand against us again.

'Come, my sons, come my siblings, come, comrades! Come, warriors of the light, of nobility, of all that is good. We shall not let the soldiers of the darkness, of brutality and of evil pass. Fight! Death to the emissaries of death!'

The defenders of earth and sky heard my call to arms and took up their fighting mantle, all of them heroic defenders of liberty. And of course, Heracles, the son I had been grooming for this very day, was with me, brought to my side by my flying horses. With my son my side in my war chariot, I gathered my eagle and my thunderbolts. And thus began the war that would end the Giants forever. I saw Athena, with her deadly spear and shield, immediately dive into battle and engage with Alcyoneus, the mad Giant. Apollo, too, did not falter and began raining winged arrows down upon the vile creature known as Ephialtes, who was causing the mountains to tremble. My brother Poseidon took up his trident, leapt into his chariot and fell in after one of the Giants' leaders, Polybotes. My intrepid son took up his staff and faced down the young Giant, Eurytos. Our blacksmith Hephaestus, he of the calloused hands, began hurling vast cannonballs at the head of the brutish Mimas. Hermes, wearing Hades' helmet, fell upon the neck of the arrogant Hippolytus, Artemis the hunter cornered the huge-headed Gration and Hecate, the worldly-wise, raked her nails over the face of the abominable Clytius. Atop his warhorse, my son Ares, master of the art of war, attacked with all the strength he could muster an allegedly invincible winged Giant, while the usually sensual and playful Aphrodite no longer smiled with sweet seduction but instead, with her son Eros, prowled menacingly like a tigress before the Giants.

As I watched the theatre of war with my son Heracles, we felt a blow, as though we had been hit by a mountain, that sent the two of us tumbling over the clouds. When we looked up, we saw Porphyrion, the leader of the Giants. He had fallen upon us with his massive body. One cannot lie; Porphyrion was a fierce warrior, and he was now bringing his deadly fists down upon us with utmost strength. With great difficulty, Heracles and I warded off the blows. We regained our footing and were about to retaliate when Porphyrion leapt up with unexpected agility towards our palace in Olympus, to the most hallowed spot on our sacred mountain. And there, when he saw Hera in all her wondrous beauty, he forgot about the battle and became like a wild beast in heat. Even while I was riding my flying horses on towards Olympus, the foul creature had already put his vile hands on my wife. The blood rushed to my head and I hurled every thunderbolt there was in the sky towards that abominable being. My spears of light struck his foul body, creating deep gashes, but still that enemy of honour would not perish. And that is because the sacred law had stated that the Giants could only be defeated by an Immortal in alliance with a Mortal. And so my valiant son stepped forward, stretched his bow and sent an arrow into Porphyrion's black heart. And so began the tragic tale of the fall of the Giants.

Athena continued to battle Alcyoneus on the earth. It was no simple task and so Heracles ran to his Immortal sister's aid and struck the Giant across his head with his staff over and over again until his lifeless body fell to the ground. But it did not stay there long. He soon rose to his feet, for whenever he fell, Mother Earth revived him. I warned my son:

'We must cut off his feet, Heracles, for Gaia is aiding Alcyoneus. Whenever he touches the earth, she gives him new life.'

And so we took Alcyoneus far from the earth and there my brave son grabbed the miserable Gigas by his neck and throttled him. This time, wise Gaia could not save her son and Alcyoneus was sent to the land of the dead.

And so we rushed to the aid of Apollo, who was battling the prince of darkness, Ephialtes. No matter how many arrows my son fired, the beast would not die. And so I said:

'Apollo, my wise, brilliant son, aim for his left eye and Heracles shall aim for his right. But be sure to stretch your bows and fire at the same time.'

They did as I instructed, firing an arrow each simultaneously into the eyes of the hideous ogre. Ephialtes rocked on his feet, the way mountains tremble in an earthquake, and he too was sent into the darkness of Hades' domain.

And no matter how many times blue-maned Poseidon stabbed Polybotes, the most fearsome of the Gigantes, with his trident, the monster would just laugh it off. Heracles and I set off to help but Poseidon signalled for us to stay where we were for he wanted to defeat the demon by himself. It was, however, impossible. If not me, he needed to at least let Heracles join him in the fight. And so my valiant son leapt into his uncle's war chariot, pulled by his flying horses, and they carried him into the middle of the sea to face the vilest of Gaia's progeny. There, Poseidon and Heracles tore the island of Kos in half and buried Polybotes underneath it, in the dark depths of the sea.

And Dionysus, using his vine staff as a weapon, overcame and bested the young Giant, Eurytos. Such is the wrath of wine, Gaia's beloved son was bloodied and bruised, but like the other demons, he refused to die. Heracles came to his drunken brother's aid in a hundred steps and sunk his arrows into Eurytos' neck, ending his life there and sending him into the waiting arms of Hades.

But although Mimas was staggering under Hephaestus' assault and his missiles, neither fire nor keen steel could cut Mimas down. Such was his strength, any other being would have succumbed to Hephaestus' attack and willingly made their peace with death. But Mimas was the most stubborn of the Gigantes. When approaching death, he was reborn; when dying, he found new life. It was only when Heracles entered the battle and with his sword removed his gnarled head from his lumbering body that his battle was over.

Hippolytus, too, after being brought low by Hermes' blows, would rise again and smirk at us, showing us rows of massive rock-like teeth. Hermes' skills and efforts would have come to nought had Heracles not come to the aid of his brother and brought his staff down upon Hippolytus' head, stunning him, and my Mortal and Immortal son then beat the life out of the Giant forever with their fists. And thus, another brute was dispatched to the world of the unliving.

And although Artemis was beating foul Gration's stinking body to a pulp, his flowing blood making the battlefield resemble a slaughterhouse, still the Giant stood strong and unbowed, retaliating each time, almost overpowering my beautiful chapleted daughter until Heracles' arms of steels came to her aid. First, he threw the vile Gration off his sister, and then he and his sister drew their bows simultaneously and fired enchanted arrows into the Giant's misshapen throat, consigning him to the same fate as the others and sending him into the darkness.

And Ares; who knows how many times he cut open the pink body of the winged Giant with whom he was fighting yet the monster still fluttered and soared around my son, trying to sink its claws into my son's face. Ares must have tired for he welcomed Heracles' entrance into the battle. After my half-mortal son drew his sword and cut off the Giant's wings, Ares ended the Conzest with his spear and stamped out the last glimmer of light in his opponent's eyes.

And Aphrodite, she fought as though the greatest warriors are also the most beautiful, hacking and slashing away at her enemy's deformed body. While Eros' arrows flew not into the Giant's heart but his back, the Goddess of love clawed at his chest but of course, like the others, the brute would not succumb and would not die. But his resistance was in vain; like the others, he could not run from fate and Heracles took the Giant's life, planting his sister Athena's spear into his neck.

When the battle was over, none of Gaia's foul children remained on the earth. The Giants had been vanquished. The barbarians had been routed and the Gods were victorious. But one task remained. Before celebrating victory, before raising my golden goblet filled with nectar with my fellow warriors, before toasting our triumph and making my victory speech, I descended to the earth again and approached Gaia. She was distraught, our grandmother. The lines on her face had deepened, her cheeks were sunken, her head bowed. Her eyes, which once shone with compassion for me, now glared at me with hatred. I, however, did not look at her with hatred, but I no longer revered her as before. The love between us had flickered and faded away.

I said: 'Salutation to you, Gaia, insatiable Goddess, queen of intrigues, most alluring and captivating of females. Know this; your era is at an end. You gave us life and for this we thank you, but it is now over. We all came from you but to you we shall not return. It cannot be denied that life began with you but it shall not continue with you. You are no longer a Goddess, so renounce your claims. You shall not rule the earth again, so desist from your provocations and your incitements of your sons. The world is mine now, and the age is mine. This is my kingdom now and my word shall rule, for I am the strongest, wisest, bravest and most able of all the Gods. The Titans revolted, and I defeated them. The Giants mutinied, and I crushed them too. Now none shall stand before me. For I am invincible.'

Mother Earth simply stood there, the hatred in her eyes growing ever keener. With great dignity, she lifted her head and stared at me with fury and loathing. And she said:

'And greetings to you, Zeus. Pitiful Zeus who considers himself invincible. Weak Zeus who thinks he is the greatest and strongest of the Gods. I am Mother to you all, Creator of you all, Giver of Life to you all. I have but one wish: that you live as brothers and sisters, that you love and honour one another equally. What I desired was equality amongst my children and for none to be treated unjustly, for those of my body and my flesh to live in peace. But first your grandfather Uranus, your father Kronos and now you; you have destroyed brotherhood, love and equality. You have embraced oppression, greed and avarice. You were afraid, which is why you wished to establish an empire of fear. I could not turn a blind eye to this. Naturally, I had to stand up to you, you cruel, stupid males, and I did. I dethroned Uranus and I snatched Kronos' crown from him. But sadly, I could not defeat you. I never would have imagined it would come to this, for I never imagined that you would be so callous as to risk your own children's lives in your pursuit of victory. But you have become a master in the arts of bloody intrigue, of guile and cunning, and of cold-hearted ruthlessness. Do not deny it, Zeus. You have surpassed all other kings in villainy.

'I concede defeat, Mighty Zeus. Yes, you have won. But your triumph shall be fleeting. You are right; my age is over. You have ended it, but such was the will and the wish of time. Now your age is truly beginning, so enjoy your reign while it lasts. For time shall eventually defeat you too. Nothing shall survive. Olympus, your palace, the sky, the earth; none shall remain. Fame, glory, eminence, temples and Altars, the friezes you shall have made to adorn the walls of your Altars; they shall all fall into nothingness. Time will take them all from you, just as it took them from me. Your reign shall end and your word shall fall meaninglessly onto silent ground.

'Zeus! Most valiant of my grandchildren, tyrant who reveres my own power, foolish child who mistakes tyranny for justice. Mark my words; new Gods shall emerge, wiser, braver and more powerful than all of us. Mankind will adore them, revere them and worship them. You, Zeus, shall be forgotten. This is inevitable. Your name shall be mocked by mankind. Your grand loves, your miracles, your heroic deeds; they shall be ridiculed and scorned. Believe me, this is what shall transpire. Only your cruelties and excesses shall remain, the wars, pestilences and catastrophes inflicted upon the world and the pain you caused all living things. The blood on your hands…

'Yes, Zeus, my powerful grandson, dispeller of clouds, lord of the thunderbolt; Zeus who roars with the storMs You have defeated me. I am no longer a Goddess. I am Mother Earth now. But watch me, for I shall continue to embrace Titans, Gods, Giants, Men and all the creatures of the world. They shall live with me and I with them. Yes, I concede, I shall not be a Goddess, but I shall live on, whereas you, Zeus, shall not. Like an unfulfilled prophecy, like a false idol, like a bad dream, you shall be forgotten. There is no escaping me. Now, go back to Olympus. Go, rise up to the clouds, and, while you still can, enjoy your rule. Celebrate your triumph with those that believe in you. For your downfall is imminent.'

This is what she said. She then began to shrink and turn brown and then red with the blood of her sons, before slowly turning to dust and vanishing in front of my very eyes. I was neither angry nor affronted. I did not care for her words, as I knew why she had uttered those words. She spoke thus because she had been defeated, because I had slain her sons and because I had ended her reign forever. I mounted my war chariot and rode up to Olympus, where my comrades had gathered. The feasting began. Music filled hearts with joy, plates overflowed with ambrosia and nectar filled golden chalices. I praised my comrades and I handed out precious gifts to the Gods and Goddesses. I granted Heracles a seat in Olympus too. And once more, I roared:

'Here I stand. Zeus. King of the Gods, Overlord of all the creatures of the earth and sky. Zeus, who vanquished the mightiest of the Titans, who sent his callous and hard-hearted father into the depths of Tartarus, who crushed the barbarian Giants without mercy. The storms are my rage, the rumbling sky my roar and the thunderbolts my spears. I am Zeus; Lord and Ruler of all Gods, of all Titans, of all Giants and of all Men.

'I am Zeus; the strongest and wisest of them all, the most brilliant and most audacious of all the Gods that have ever existed. I am Zeus, and my reign shall last forever.'

Chapter Twelve

The tree-lined road that encircled the hill of Kale Tepesi in Pergamon spiralled upwards until it reached the Acropolis at the summit. The Toyota was there, at the entrance to the ruins of the ancient city. Ali parked the Megane next to the blue pickup. When they got out of the car, they were greeted by a stiff wind but even at that height, the heat had not abated. All three officers walked over to the pickup. As expected, it was empty.

'The way you are able to work out what he is going to do next is quite remarkable. Your hypotheses have all turned out to be correct,' Nevzat said. He was no longer crossed with Yıldız but was looking at her with admiration. 'How long have you known this Peter Schimmel?'

'I don't really know him. I didn't know him at all at first. I only got to know him over the course of this investigation. I initially viewed him as a suspect but then he began assisting us with our enquiries. I met him three times before today. Today was our fourth encounter.'

They were walking hurriedly towards the turnstiles at the entrance to the site of the old city.

'Well, I must congratulate you on your analysis of a suspect, and in such a short span of time too. Outstanding police work, I must say.'

'Outstanding?' Yıldız asked in shock, as though she had been insulted. 'This is anything but outstanding. I have not been able to stop any of the murders. I have not saved a single life. If anything, it is the killer who is outstanding. You saw it for yourselves just now. The man killed his own father in front of our very eyes and all we could do was watch. There may have been some bumps along the way but the killer has executed his plan almost to the tee. We may catch him soon but he may still have a surprise in store for us. He has won, I am afraid, Chief Inspector. He is the outstanding one.'

She said it with such genuine feeling that Nevzat felt a need to console her.

'I am afraid I do not agree. At the end of the day, you solved the case. You worked out why the perpetrator was carrying out the killings and you correctly analysed his personality. That itself is enough. One cannot control all aspects of an investigation. We are not Gods, after all.'

Yıldız smiled bitterly.

'That is true. We are not Gods. But Peter is. I am just a police officer who keeps falling flat on her face in this particular investigation. You say I correctly analysed the killer's personality. But which personality? Kartal, Peter or Zeus? The boy who was abandoned by his father when he was just five, the suave, successful businessman and conscientious environmentalist, or the King of Olympus and ruler of the earth? Which one did I "correctly analyse"?' She shook her head firmly. 'You may be saying this to cheer me up, in which case, I appreciate your efforts, but I am afraid that I have lost this particular case, Chief Inspector. The killer thwarted me, and that is the simple truth.'

'Who are all these people?' Ali said, stopping Yıldız in her flow. 'Where did they pop up from?'

They turned their heads and saw a large group of people of all nationalities — Germans, Japanese, English, Arabs and Turks — streaming out through the turnstiles.

'They are exiting the complex because the museum is closing,' Nevzat informed him.

'Good,' Yıldız whispered, quickening her stride. 'I hope the area is completely vacated. We need things to be as calm as can be up there on the hill.'

She was right. Throngs of tourists milling about would have only made things more difficult for them. They hurried towards the turnstiles. A uniformed museum official appeared in front of them. The name *Mirkelam Batmaz* was printed on the name tag on his chest.

'We're closing in fifteen minutes,' he said but as soon as Ali showed him his badge, he stepped aside. 'I'm sorry, officer. Please. Go right through. If you need any help, I'll be happy to…'

'Has anybody come through recently? A tall, blond man, perhaps? He would have been wearing a brown shirt with a round collar and dark trousers.'

'Yes,' Mirkelam said. 'A German tourist. I let him go back in because he told me he had forgotten his bag and that he was going back inside to pick it up.' He stopped, scared that he may have blundered. 'Why? Should I have not let him in?'

Ali slapped him affably on the shoulder.

'Don't worry about it, Mirkelam. It's not a problem. But don't let anybody else in now, got it?'

'Understood, sir,' Mirkelam said, standing to attention. 'Don't you worry. Nobody will be allowed in.'

Leaving a rather anxious-looking Mirkelam at the gate, they walked through the turnstiles and navigated their way through another group of tourists towards the steps that led up to the ruins of the ancient city. They began climbing. When they reached the top, the whole of the Bakırçay Plain stretched out before them down below. Yıldız saw something shimmering kilometres away in the distance. She had a feeling as to what it might be and looked more carefully. She was right. Turning red under the glimmering sunlight, was the rolling sea.

'Which path do we take from here?' Nevzat asked, pointing to a fork in the road. Yıldız thought it about for a little before pointing to the path on the left.

'This way, Chief Inspector. The Altar is this way. Peter must have taken this path.'

'Well, if the guy is Zeus and the Altar is that way, where else is he going to go?' Ali laughed.

Neither Yıldız nor Nevzat responded. They hurried down the dirt path, almost running, until they reached the now bare dais of the once sacred monument. All that remained now, though, were a few stones on the ground. A large pine tree grew in the spot in which sacrifices and offerings used to be made to the Gods. The sunlight was striking the spot and giving the ruins a poignant appearance. There was nobody around, not by the pine tree nor in the area surrounding the ancient site.

'Have we made a mistake?' Nevzat asked. 'He's not here it seems.'

The three of them looked around but Peter Schimmel was nowhere to be seen. Yıldız looked down and saw a cemetery under a cypress tree. Another German whose life had been irrevocably transformed by the Altar, Carl Humann, was buried there but there was no sign of Schimmel. Her gaze returned to the side of the Altar that faced the sea and where the steps would have been. With the Altar behind her, she looked to the right. The theatre was up ahead. No, she did not believe he would be there. She turned around, lifted her head and stared at the walls where the Temple of Athena was located. No, Zeus had no business in grounds that were consecrated to his daughter.

'The Acropolis,' she muttered excitedly. 'He must have gone up the hill, to the Acropolis.'

Ali was about to turn around and go back when Yıldız showed him the scarp.

'This way, Ali. There is a short cut to the theatre. I remember the tour guide taking us that way.'

When they reached the narrow path snaking through piles of rocky rubble, the wind had picked up and they were having trouble traversing the path. Luckily, however, they did not have long to walk and the path soon took them into the middle of the old amphitheatre.

'What kind of theatre is this?' Ali asked, looking up in amazement at the stone steps that once made up the audience's seats. 'It's so steep!'

'It is. Right now, we are standing in the steepest theatre of the ancient world. Be patient, we're almost there.' She pointed to a spot above. 'That gate up ahead on the hill is the way out.'

They climbed up the sheer stone steps until they reached dark cloisters above and a passageway around three to five metres in height that would lead them to Athena's Sacred Grounds. All three were scanning the area carefully but, just as Yıldız had guessed, there was no sign of Peter. She looked at the marble columns of the Temple of Trajan.

'We need to go up, to the Acropolis. To the highest point.'

They walked for some time along the derelict streets of what was once the Attalid's great capital, built by the eunuch Philetaerus with the fortune gathered and abandoned by Alexander's fearless commander Lysimachus. When they reached the ruins of the grand temple that had been built for the Roman Emperor Trajan, all three were wheezing. Of course,

Peter was not there either, as it was not the highest point in Pergamon. To reach that point, they needed to go to the walls that surrounded the palace to their rear. After stopping to regain their breath, they set off again hurriedly and after passing the large water reservoir in the forum, they reached the remnants of what would, once upon a time, have been a stunning palace.

'There he is! Over there!'

Ali was the first to see him. Peter was standing in the open atop the walls, staring at the sun as though in a trance, eyes shut, arms held aloft. The blustery wind filled the loose sleeves of his linen shirt, making them look like wings and giving him the appearance of a huge eagle preparing for flight, a look further enhanced by his hair, which the light seemed to have painted gold, and by his superb physique, already that of a Greek God. Standing there on the tired and crumbling city walls, he seemed to be a part of the ruined palace, of the old abandoned city, of a sun that had lost its ferocity and was now beginning to set.

'Yes, that's him,' Yıldız whispered.

Even though he was not looking at them, Peter realized they were approaching but he did not care. He stayed where he was, standing in the wind, eyes shut, arms stretched out as wide as they could go. Yıldız called out to him softly.

'Mister Schimmel…. Mister Schimmel.'

He heard her but he did not turn around.

'Mister Schimmel,' she said again in an even softer, almost defeated voice. 'Okay, you have won. You have taken your revenge. You have done what you set out to do. But that's it. It's over now. It's time to surrender.'

His lips curved into a momentary sneer, then he narrowed his eyes and lowered his arms. He turned to face the three officers. The manic look in his dark eyes was gone. In its place was that familiar soft, sad melancholy look.

'I'm afraid not, Ms Karasu,' he replied, with his usual graciousness. 'Unfortunately, I cannot surrender. Not now. I killed my grandfather, I ripped my own brother's heart out of his chest, I tore the skin off another man's face and I have murdered my own father. I cannot go back.' He paused and looked around, as though he was seeing the earth in all its entirety. 'I hate your world. It's better up here. More beautiful. More meaningful. Apart from my childhood, I have never liked this life. The life that I led. Not one single moment of it. If I go back, that is the life and the world to which I would be returning. Indeed, it will be even worse. An uglier, harder life. No, Ms Karasu, I won't go back. It's better to stay in the realm of the Gods. I have to take this adventure to the very end, otherwise all the pain that was suffered will be rendered meaningless and the blood I shed will have been shed in vain. If I go back, I will be seen as just another ordinary madman.' He smiled a wry smile. 'No, Ms Karasu, I am not insane, nor have I lost my mind. But I cannot live in such a harsh, cruel and loveless world. I cannot ignore the cruelty and pain of the world. I cannot just turn a blind eye to it all.' He stopped and looked at the sky, which was turning deep red. 'Anyway, they are calling me. My beloved wife Hera, my wise daughter Athena, my son Apollo, the God of light, my brother, the great Poseidon; they are calling out to me. They are telling me that enough is enough. They are summoning me...' He fell silent. All that could be heard in the ancient ruins of the Acropolis was the howling wind. Yıldız looked on helplessly.

'Don't!' she shouted. 'Don't!'

Peter Schimmel smiled bitterly.

'There is no other way. Life has left me no other choice.'

He then turned around, opened his arms out like an eagle, and gently stepped off the wall, falling into the void below.

The flapping of an eagle's wings seemed to ring through the sky, and a savage cry seemed to pierce the clouds. The three police stood frozen at the foot of the walls. The sun, oblivious to what had happened, began to vanish behind the hills surrounding the ancient city, as it had done for thousands of years.